NEPHIL'S DESTRUCTION

Book Six of the Chosen Chronicles

Sirena Robinson

Supposed Crimes LLC • Matthews, North Carolina

Published in the United States.

ISBN: 978-1-938108-67-9

www.supposedcrimes.com

This book is typeset in Goudy Old Style, licensed by Ascender Corporation.

Nephil's Destruction

PROLOGUE

AMAYA WOKE when the door slammed downstairs. She blinked in the dark, reaching for the pink lamp on her bedside stand to cast a dim glow over the room. Glancing around for Gabriel, she felt a sharp bolt of relief when she didn't see her Angelic uncle. Father. Whatever he was. Shaking her head, she slipped from bed and pulled on her robe, tying it tightly around herself before exiting the room.

Her brother and sister were sound asleep in the next room, both oblivious to whatever was going on. Finley, in the third room, and older than Amaya by nearly two years, rolled over and adjusted her pillow under her head, clearly ignoring whatever was happening on the floor below.

Amaya descended the stairs carefully, poking her head around the corner into the kitchen. Her parents were at the table with two adults she didn't know and two teenagers she had never before seen. Alaria turned and sighed when she heard Amaya step off the stairs.

"Come on in, Amaya. We know you're there."

Slightly defensive, Amaya entered the room. "I wasn't sneaking. I heard the door and then voices."

The strange woman, a redhead with a kind smile, spoke. "We didn't mean to wake you up, Amaya." She rose and crossed to the girl. "I can't even believe how you've grown. I haven't seen you in nearly ten years."

"I don't know you."

Braxton glared at his daughter. "Be polite, Amaya. Aradia and Gage are two of the six. You know who they are, even if you haven't met. This is their daughter, Lux, and another Nephil, Zane."

Amaya looked at the teenage girl and offered a smile. "It's the middle of the night. If you don't want to sit here and listen to whatever they're going to talk about, you can come up to my room and sleep."

Lux immediately pushed out from the table. "Anything is better than this." She looked at her parents. "Is it okay?"

Gage nodded. "Go get some sleep. We'll be here for a little while."

Alaria waited until the girls had gone back up the stairs before turning to the other three. "I always knew they'd get along. If only Damon and Greer could be here with Zeke."

Aradia lowered herself back into the chair. "They'll arrive in a day or two. It's time they all started training together as well as separately. Damon and Greer have been training Ezekiel since she was a toddler, and we've been working with Lux since she was ten. I know you've tried to give Amaya a childhood. I know you've been keeping her shielded. Gabriel told us she only recently found out about who you are and who she is. I respect the decision to keep her sheltered, but it is time that they came together."

Alaria poured cups of coffee. "That's a discussion for another day. Right now we need to figure out what to do with Zane. How did you find him?"

The teenage boy, sullen and quiet up until then, looked up. "I can talk for myself."

Braxton held up his hands. "Then talk. All I know is that you were apparently found fighting off nearly a dozen Cambion by yourself and winning."

Zane stared at his leather-clad hands. "It's pretty easy to win when you can kill someone just by touching them."

Alaria blinked and sank into a chair. "Your father is the Angel of Death."

The boy jerked a shoulder. "I dunno. Never met him."

She looked to Aradia and Gage. "What happened to his mother?"

"We don't know. He hasn't told us." Aradia reached out and laid her hand on Zane's shoulder. "Other than the fight he was in when we found him, all we know is that he looks to be about fifteen."

Alaria blinked rapidly. "That's older than Amaya. I thought she was the first, other than Deacon."

"Apparently God allowed a few Angels to use the essence transfer trick before Gabriel and Michael found out about it to make sure it would result in a Nephilim. Michael has another boy and a girl, his twin, he's training. They were born to a female Angel, so they obviously tested that out before filling us in on it, too. I think we should send Zane to Michael to be with them." Gage drank his coffee and leaned back in the chair. "What do you think, Zane? Are you done being on your own?"

Zane looked between the adults. "My mother is dead because I killed her." He stared down at his hands. "It wasn't always like this. I didn't know about what I am until three or four years ago. I don't remember exactly. I think I was eleven, but maybe I was twelve. It was her birthday. I hugged her and she went stiff. Started jerking and fell over. She was dead. I thought she'd had a heart attack. Then, the next person I touched did the same thing. Just dropped over. I figured out pretty quick that I was the common denominator."

Aradia's grip tightened. "Oh, honey. You must have been so scared." She ran her knuckles over his cheek. "You're safe now. We'll figure out how to teach you to control it. Was your mother human?"

Zane nodded. "She was a witch. That's how she kept me safe for so long. After she died, I found a couple other Nephilim." He blinked back tears. "We were together until a few months ago. There was a girl, a Nephil, who joined with us. She and I, we, uh, we kissed." He angrily wiped his eyes with his hands. "She died, too."

Aradia forced herself not to snatch back her hand. "Did you touch her with your hands at the time? Or does the ability come from touching any of your skin?"

"I don't know. I haven't wanted to test it out. I'd touched the guys before, in battle or whatever. Sometimes it doesn't work, sometimes it does. I never know when it's going to happen. It's not as often if someone touches me. I think I have to make contact. Except with my hands. If you touch my hand, you die. That's why I wear gloves."

"Have any of the other Nephilim touched your hands?"

Zane nodded. "I don't know how it works. It seems to be more powerful in my hands, but some of the guys could touch me. I thought I was safe with other Nephilim until Tracy died. The others got scared, and they kicked me out. I've been on my own ever since."

Alaria leaned forward onto her elbows. "You're not alone anymore. We'll get you the training you need and figure out how you can control the power you have. But it's up to you. We won't force you to go train with Michael. We won't make you do anything. You're old enough to make the decision."

Zane raked his hands through his hair. "You think I could get to the point where I could touch people without being afraid of killing them?"

Aradia looked sad. "I don't know, sweetie. I hope so, but we'll certainly try."

"Then I want to go. I want to be able to touch people. I don't like not being able to. This sucks."

Gage laughed softly, his expression sympathetic as he looked at Zane steadily. "Yes, son, it does at that." Pausing, he turned to the others before continuing. "Okay, Aradia, can you take Zane to Michael? I'll stay here to settle Lux in and wait for Damon and Greer before I come and join you." He looked at Braxton and Alaria. "You're sure you can manage six of them?"

Alaria laughed. "We manage four just fine. Two more isn't going to be a problem, and you guys are just a flash away if I need something. It's time the girls got to know one another. They're going to need to work together on this. It's going to be their time soon, and they need to be prepared for it. We'll keep them safe, just as you will when it's your turn to train with them. Besides, Michael is going to be working with Amaya, too, and it'll feel good to have the other girls here when I don't have her. Amaya needs to know Deacon. They all do, really."

"I think they've all met Deacon when Michael checks in on them. He goes with Michael often." Aradia stood as she prepared to leave. "You'll forgive me if I check in on Lux frequently." She hugged Alaria and Braxton swiftly before brushing her lips over Gage's. "Give her a hug for me when she wakes." She held out her hand for Zane. "Ready to go?"

The boy shrugged. "Sure. What the hell?"

CHAPTER ONE

August 25th, 2060 – Kennebunkport, Maine

LUX WINDSOR lay on the beach, watching the waves roll over the sand and enjoying the feel of the cool water on her legs. Dark sunglasses adorned her face, and her hair tumbled down her back in a red curtain. Behind the lenses, grass green eyes were half closed as she enjoyed the combination of sun, water, and sand.

It wasn't often she got the opportunity to forget about Cambion and Devils and Lucifer, but when she did, she intended to take advantage of it. Of Beelzebub's eight children—five men and three women—there were six left to locate and kill. Gage Windsor, Lux's father—and the most connected man in existence—had informed her two days before that a third of the offspring would be visiting a small colony of Lucifer's worshippers in Maine the last week in June.

So she had gone to Maine, and she would wait, just out of range of detection, until the Cambion made an appearance. In the meantime, she saw no reason not to enjoy an opportunity for tanning on the beach.

"What are you doing?"

Lux lowered her sunglasses and peered over them, looking up at Zane with a small smile. "I'm tanning."

"What are you wearing?"

She looked down at the royal blue bikini. "A bathing suit." She grinned at him. "I could conjure you some trunks if you'd like to join me."

Zane glared down at her. "You're out of your fucking mind. What if someone sees you out here? What if you get attacked? What if the Cambion come?"

Amused but not yet mad, Lux lifted her eyebrows and settled her sunglasses back onto her nose. "And what if an asteroid crashes into the house while we're sleeping? Being alive is a risk right now, Zane." She waved a hand. "I put up a shield. That's the joy of being a witch and a Nephil, darling. I can protect myself very well. As can you, seeing as you have the same heritage I do."

Zane snorted. "Last time I checked, I don't have a drop of vampire blood in me."

Lux smiled and flashed fangs she hadn't had seconds before. "Lucky for you, I don't need blood to survive." She patted the sand next to her. "Sit down, enjoy the sun. When's the last time you got to lay on the beach and just enjoy?"

"Never."

"Exactly. Take advantage of it. Relax and live a little. Think about it. Zeke and Dev are happy, healthy, and nesting. Two of Beelzebub's Hell-spawn are dead, and we're less than forty-eight hours away from taking out a third. That'll mean we're a third of the way done. After that, it's our turn to relax and lay around Michael's while Amaya and Deacon take us in for the home run."

"You're overly optimistic and reckless." Zane shoved his hands into the pockets of his jeans. "You need to put on some clothes and come into the house." He glanced down at her. "Did it occur to you that you might get sunburned?"

Lux snapped her fingers and a bottle of sun screen appeared in her palm. She extended it to Zane. "Wanna do my back?" When he didn't laugh, she pushed herself into a sitting position and angled her face upward to study him. "I'm teasing you."

"As you're constantly reminding me, you're a witch. You can coat yourself in that crap with absolutely zero effort."

"It was a joke. Lighten up a bit."

"There's nothing light about this, Lux. We should by lying low and staying out of sight until this Cambion gets here. If we don't, then we're going to end up getting ourselves killed."

Starting to get annoyed, she waved a hand, gesturing to the beach. "It's not like the place is teeming with tourists. We're miles from the settlement, and I used a shield. I could run around out here naked with my hair on fire and no one would see me!"

Zane actively fought off that mental image. "Did you put up traps and protections?"

"I'm not going to spray paint the sand." She huffed. "If you're just going to stand there and lecture me, go back inside and hide. I'm not coming in until I'm done tanning."

He snapped his fingers and watched with a hint of humor as clouds formed and thunder clapped. Lux ripped her sunglasses off her face and climbed to her feet, eyes flashing with annoyance.

"That's petty and immature. Just because I'm doing something you don't like doesn't mean you get to use your pansy-ass magic to make me fall in line."

Zane chuckled. "You're just mad because you can't control the weather, and I can."

Her voice regal, and just a touch defensive, Lux spoke. "All witches have limits to their powers." She shoved her feet into sandals and stalked toward the house. "You win this round."

"When it comes to the beach, I'll win them all. I can make it rain. You can't make it stop."

"I could cast a spell."

"Which would attract attention, and you know it." He caught himself reaching to support her as they climbed the slope back to the house and made himself shove his hands back into his pockets. "Like I said, we're supposed to be lying low and not tanning on the beach."

Lux grinned at him over her shoulder. "Don't even try to convince me you don't like watching my ass in this bikini. Or the rest of me, for that matter."

"That goes without saying, of course." He glanced at the ass in question and admired the curve of it in blue bikini bottoms. Just because he couldn't touch didn't mean he couldn't look. "There's nothing better than a woman in a bikini. Except, of course, for a woman in lingerie."

Lux snorted. "Have you ever even seen lingerie except in old magazines? There aren't exactly stores where you can buy it anymore." She opened the door to the house they were staying in and kicked off her sandals. "I wasn't in any danger down there. There's no harm in enjoying a little downtime."

"Then enjoy it on the deck, where you're still protected by all of the herbs and traps."

She stooped next to her backpack and pulled out a pair of well-worn jeans, sliding them up her legs and over her hips. She drew on a white camisole over the bikini top and turned back to Zane. "Have you ever been able to figure out where your witch powers end and Nephil ones begin?"

"Well, for starters, I'm not a witch. But no, I don't know what's magic and what's Nephil. I think that was the point of Angels mating with other supernatural creatures. More power, stronger, faster, harder to find. Conjuring is Angelic and magical. The abilities of one magnify the other. For some things, it's obvious. My father can't control the weather. But I can, so that's magic. Throwing out fire and power is both."

"I kind of wish I knew which were which. I can't make a nonplace like Michael can, but I can conjure almost anything on Earth that you would want. I can't heal people, even though most Angels can, because my mother's magic doesn't run to healing. I can flash like a Nephil and cast spells like a witch. I can't have psychic conversations. Sometimes it feels like there aren't limits to what I can do, but then I train with Amaya and I'm reminded that most of what I have is parlor tricks compared to her."

Zane moved into the kitchen and withdrew two cans of ravioli from the pantry. "I've seen you take out Cambion. I've seen you fight. You've got way more than parlor tricks."

Lux slid onto a stool and folded her hands on the island. "Is there anything other than ravioli in that cabinet?"

"Three cans of pickled beets, five cans of creamed corn, two jars of pasta sauce—but no pasta—and a whopping seventeen cans of baked beans."

"Someone really liked baked beans."

"Or really didn't like them, depending on how you read into that."

She tapped her fingers on the marble. "I could just snap my fingers and conjure us a steak dinner. Seriously, I could."

"I know you could. So could I. We're supposed to avoid using magic when we don't have to. It's like a homing beacon. You know it's a risk whenever we do anything."

"Says the man who conjured a storm to keep me from getting a tan."

A smile quirked the corners of Zane's mouth. "I'll give that to you. I shouldn't have done it, but you pissed me off." He dumped the contents into a pan and turned on the stove. "It's enough that we're using magic to maintain electricity wherever we go."

"No need to live in the stone-age when we don't have to. Unless we do something big, no Cambion is going to pay attention to the tiny bit we use to turn on some lights." Her nails clicked on the counter. "It's just a teensy bit more magic than that to have good food."

"Didn't your mother ever teach you not to use magic for personal gain?"

"My mother is smart enough to know sometimes personal gain is necessary."

"I've met Aradia. She's way more disciplined than you with her magic. You like to show yours off." He stirred the ravioli and poured it into bowls. "Your face is red."

"I won't burn. If I do, I'll fix it."

His expression and tone turning serious, Zane handed her a fork. "Is that your solution to everything? Magic?"

Lux took a bite, chewed thoughtfully, and swallowed. "No. It's my solution to unimportant things. Right now, the only thing that matters is being able to kill Beelzebub and his crew. My powers are limited on Cambion and Devils, so we both know we're going to be playing almost exclusively with whatever we have that is truly magic. That's why it's us for this one. We can take on Cambion hand to hand. Even some lower Devils, since our fathers are both Archangels. I'm not ashamed of what I am, and I don't see any reason not to use it to make life easier. When push comes to shove, it's magic that either ensures we live or fails us so that we die." She looked at his leather clad hands. "We need to practice with me funneling your powers. It worked on Zeke to be able to heal her when she was dying. If we could perfect that, it might make it more controllable for you."

"No." The refusal was immediate and left no room for argument. "It destroyed your prism. Without that, or a few seconds longer, and you'd have been dead on the ground."

"You don't know that." Lux took another bite. "You can touch Deacon."

"Who is way more powerful than I am. If anyone has less than I do, I kill them."

"But not every time. I believe we can figure out how to control it." She reached out and laid her hand on his, annoyed at the feel of the leather. "You haven't killed anyone accidentally since you were twenty-one. That was ten years ago."

"I haven't put my bare hands on anyone I didn't intend to kill since then, either."

"Except for Deacon, Michael, and Dev."

He nodded. "Except for. And you the one time." Zane pulled his hand out from under hers. "Drop it, Lux. You're not talking me into it."

Lux stared at him, her eyes filled with sadness. "Don't you ever want to know what it's like to hold someone's hand? To feel a woman under your fingers?"

"There are plenty of women who don't care about me touching them."

"Yeah, the type you have to pay."

"Sex is sex, Lux. Doesn't matter if it's free or not." Zane rose and rinsed his bowl. "I'm going down to the gym."

CHAPTER TWO

ZANE VIEWED his body as a tool—a weapon to be used against enemies, and a vessel for the power that flowed through him. It was his job to practice with that weapon, to make sure that it was prepared and well-honed to ensure his continued survival and be able to do what he needed. That required regular training and exercise.

Lux thought differently, and that annoyed him. She moaned and complained when he dragged her for a run, whining about the early hour, or the heat, or cold, or whatever it was about it that annoyed her on that particular day. She was willing enough to spar, enjoying being able to kick and punch. That was exercise worth doing, she claimed constantly.

Annoyed that she was on his mind even when not in the room, Zane punched the bag hanging from the ceiling and watched it swing. Whoever had owned the house before the world had ended had valued physical health and strength. There was a treadmill, stationary bike, rowing station, free weights, a punching bag, a bench press station, sparring mat and two yoga mats. Zane intended to take advantage of all of it while he had the opportunity.

Exercising was one of the only times he allowed himself to take his gloves off. His hands were strong and broad, with short nails and wide palms. From looking at them, they appeared to be hands that had seen work. They didn't look like hands that killed. Zane knew from experience that appearances were deceiving. His hands were more deadly than a gun.

Frustrated with his train of thought, he raked his hands through his hair and tugged in frustration. He could hear Lux on the main floor and went to the treadmill to try and tune her out. Since he'd discovered his powers two decades earlier, he had learned to prefer his own company to that of anyone else. Deacon and Dev were the two exceptions he had learned to like, but being with Lux, being subjected to all of her opinions and female moods and eccentricities, was enough to make him long for loneliness.

However, as much as she annoyed him, and as much as he longed for a break, Zane was smart enough to know that having her with him made the job easier. Lux was an incredibly powerful witch. She was talented in a fight, a hell of a sparring partner, and easy on the eyes.

Lux was an interesting combination of Aradia and Gage. Her mother's hair—that cascade of red and gold that looked more like a sunset than it did a head of hair—and Gage's striking bone structure. She had a bold sweep of cheekbones, a slim nose, thick eyelashes, and a full mouth that was just a touch too wide. Unlike Zeke, who was tall and strong, or Amaya, who dripped with sexuality, Lux was bright and beautiful. She lit up a room when she walked into it, and her smile illuminated her whole face.

Zane cursed her as he pummeled the punching bag. He cursed her smile and the careless way she used her magic. He cursed that perfect curve of ass, her creamy skin, her slender curves, and the way her breasts looked in a tiny bathing suit. He cursed himself for reaching for her without thinking in a move so natural for so many but so deadly for him. Most of all, he cursed them both for being stuck alone when he hadn't bedded a woman in more than two years.

Thirty-one-year-old men were not meant to be celibate, and they certainly weren't meant to have to live with beautiful witches they couldn't touch. He punched the bag so hard the chain broke and the sand-filled bag flew across the room, striking the wall hard enough to split the leather, spilling sand all over the thick rubber mat.

Lux appeared at the top of the stairs. "What's wrong?"

Zane glared at the wall sullenly. "I broke the chain. Hit it too hard." He glanced toward the weights. "There are other things I can work on."

"Do you want me to change and come spar with you?"

"I need a break from the gloves. I have to put them back on if I spar with you."

Lux rocked back and forth, bouncing from her heels to the balls of her feet. "You don't if you don't try to pin me." She narrowed her eyes. "Y'know, when I was little, my dad brought me a bunch of old comic books. There was this one—"

"Rogue from the X-men. I know. Deacon called me Rogue for about three years after your mom took me to Michael. I read them, too." He grinned and went to the weights. "Unfortunately, I can't fly, I don't have super strength, I can't absorb Cambion powers if I hold onto them long enough, and people die within a second of my getting my hands on them."

"It would be cool if you could fly." She sank her teeth into her bottom lip as she watched muscles ripple as Zane hefted the weights. "Dev and Deacon can both fly."

"And I can't." Zane grunted at the weight as he hefted it. "Have you heard from your dad lately on when this Cambion will be arriving?"

"Tomorrow, the last I heard. Unless something changes, they won't take the chance of contacting us right now. It's too risky. Do you want to go over the plan again?"

He glanced over at her. "Do we actually have one of those? Or is it like normal and we just charge in, guns blazing, and hope for the best?"

Lux chuckled and sat down on one of the weight benches, swinging her legs. "That is a plan. We always have a plan, even if it is just charging in with our guns blazing. However, in this particular case, there are three hundred humans in the settlement where the Cambion are going to be. From the intel we have, Beelzebub's daughter Ingrid is going to be coming in tomorrow morning with a small squad to collect volunteers for possession. There will be fewer than ten of them, and it should be easily dealt with."

"Nothing is ever easy. We need to minimize human casualties. Even if they worship Lucifer, they're still human, and we still don't kill them unless we have to."

"I know. That's why I'm thinking that I'll hang out outside the building where they're going to hold their church service or whatever the fuck they call it. I'll work a nice spell to freeze the people, and you go straight for Ingrid. I can dampen the ability to flash for a few seconds, so you'll have to be fast, and you'll have to be good, but we can do it without endangering the idiots."

"Don't call them idiots."

Genuinely confused, Lux turned her head to the side. "Why the hell not? That's what they are. They're making a decision to go to Hell. They know the stakes, and they've made the call. I don't understand why we're still bothering to protect them in the first place. If you want my opinion on the whole matter, we should be helping them get to where they're going."

Both whirled when a third voice sounded in the room. "That is not your decision to make, and disregarding the edicts made by God in regard to His creations would be a grave mistake."

Lux sighed deeply and turned to look at Gabriel. "Do you know how to knock?"

"Yes, why do you ask?"

Zane laughed and dropped the barbell onto the mat. "I'll be the less polite one. She means that you shouldn't just pop in on people. It's rude."

"I don't understand your need to object to my presence when you should be well aware that I only come here in order to offer information and assistance."

Lux crossed her arms. "Then offer your information and assistance and go. We have everything under control without your help."

Gabriel adjusted the cuffs on his suit. "The Cambion have already arrived in the settlement. There are eleven of them, not including Beelzebub's daughter. She is the only female Cambion present at this time. I do not believe that the two of you can effectively take on twelve Cambion without helo. I am willing to be available for assistance if you believe that it is necessary."

Zane grabbed a towel and dragged it across his forehead to sop up sweat. "How powerful are they?"

"All Cambion are powerful. They are the children of Devils and demons. You should never underestimate their abilities and the danger they possess."

Lux sighed and tipped her head back to stare at the ceiling, taking a deep breath. "He's asking you whether or not his power will work on them. If all he has to do is lay one bare finger on them, then there's no risk of sending us in alone. I can hold them for long enough for him to touch them."

Gabriel pondered the question as he paced. "I believe the

majority of Cambion are susceptible to your ability, Zane. The Angel of Death is one of the most powerful Angels in Heaven, and as his child, with your mother having been a witch of not inconsiderable power, it is my theory that your abilities are effective on all Cambion except those with a high ranking Devil as a parent. Even then, you may get some efficacy dependent upon the abilities—or lack thereof—of the mother of the Cambion, or father, as the case may be."

"I know that. What I want to know is about the parentage of these particular Cambion."

"Oh. Well, I'm not entirely sure on that. Several of them will be parented by demons, of course. Ingrid, who is Beelzebub's daughter, was born of a werewolf, so I suspect your powers will be ineffective on her, unfortunately."

"I'll contact Michael and ask him to send Carys and Elisa down to help. With four of us, there's no reason why we couldn't handle them all." Zane glanced at Gabriel. "It's got nothing to do with you. Angelic help is welcome if you want to stay, but if you show up, they'll know exactly why we're there, and Ingrid will take off. I don't want to risk having to take another shot at her if we can avoid it. I'd be grateful if you'd hang close to make sure we don't need help, but I'd prefer you out of sight unless necessary."

Gabriel's mouth quirked in a ghost of a smile. "I approve of the reasoning, and of the plan. I will notify Carys and Elisa myself in order to limit the chance of your communication being intercepted. Their church service will start at nine in the evening tomorrow. I will have them to you by six in order for you to have time to go over the plan."

Lux was silent until Gabriel was gone. "Why do you like that guy?"

Zane's brows drew together. "What do you mean?"

"That was Gabriel."

Confused, he pulled his shirt on over his head and stared at her, wondering where he had gone wrong and what he didn't understand. "Yeah. So?"

"Gabriel as in Amaya's father." Lux spoke slowly, as if she was speaking to a small child.

Zane tugged at the collar on his shirt nervously. Lux's tone told him that he had made a horrible mistake, but he had no idea what he had done or why it was wrong. "I know he's Amaya's biological father." He ran one hand over his hair. "Look, I can see I've done something wrong here, but I don't know what it is. I'm hoping you're not going to pull the 'if you don't know, I'm not going to tell you' thing, because I'm kinda curious what I did."

Lux fought off a laugh, replacing it with a long suffering sigh. "Gabriel tricked Amaya's mother into sleeping with him in order to get her pregnant. Then, when she got together with Braxton, he ran her through with his sword. While she was pregnant with Amaya. Add to that the fact that he was the one to tell Amaya he's her father instead of letting Braxton and Alaria do it."

Zane struggled to make sense of that. "Okay." He took a deep breath, fully understanding that anything he said could and would be used against him. "What does that have to do with you? Or me? Am I supposed to be mad at him on Amaya's behalf because of something he did thirty years ago?"

"Yes."

Sighing, he stared at her. "You understand that's crazy, right?"

"Amaya hates him, so I do, too."

"Amaya doesn't hate him. From what I saw, she thinks being around him is somehow a betrayal to Braxton, which is absolutely fucking insane." He twisted the top off a bottle of water and drank deeply. "It's obvious Gabriel cares for her in whatever way he can. I don't understand why I'm supposed to care about their dysfunctional relationship to the extent that I turn my back on an ally just to make sure I don't piss off a woman I've met a handful of times."

"If you don't care about that, then what about the fact that he tried to get my parents and Amaya and Zeke's parents to stop trying to fight Lucifer and pulled all of the Angels from Earth in order to allow them to fail. You've heard the story. God stopped believing they could do it, so it stopped being possible."

Zane was much more comfortable with that topic. "Well yeah, I think it was a stupid move. I don't agree with what was done, and I wish it would've gone differently, but I don't think Gabriel deserves all the blame for it. At the end of the day, he's an Angel. Angels were created to do nothing other than take orders. We can't blame him for doing what he was created to do. Other than the Fallen, Michael is the only one I've ever known of who has resisted what God says. My own father has never acknowledged my existence. Carys and Elisa don't even know who their fathers are. I know it's different for you because you have two parents, and Michael just added in a bit of DNA. The rest of us have had to get used to the idea of Angels being Angels. They can't control what they are any more than you and I can ignore what's going on." He started up the stairs. "I think we need to keep our noses out of it."

Lux followed Zane to the main floor. "You were there when he told us all what he did to Zeke's parents. He let them die. More than just let, he actively arranged for it."

Zane frowned. "If you'd started with that, we wouldn't even be having a debate. That was wrong, there's no two ways about it. If he'd have told us, or Zeke and Dev, or anyone, we could've figured it out. As it was, they had to leave and get the sword a different way. There's no defending the choice he made, and I'm not trying to. I think it was a dick move, and it really calls into question whether or not we trust him when he tells us something is necessary, but I don't believe he would plot to get us killed. He gave Damon and Greer a choice. It was a shit choice, but they had one."

"I think he'd do the same to us. He would let us believe dying was the only choice even if it wasn't."

"I don't disagree with you. But the advantage we have is we know that, and we can question whether or not he's telling us the truth or whether or not he really has our best interest at heart at that point."

She waved her hand and went to the kitchen window to look out at the darkening sky. "Are you going to call up a hurricane if I go for a walk?"

Zane chuckled and stood next to her, surveying the empty, rundown houses and the abandoned expanse of beach. "I don't think I could call up a hurricane. A few clouds and some thunder are about the extent of my talent with the weather." He looked at her pointedly. "The worst I could do is a rain cloud over your head until you come back in."

"Like the donkey in that old cartoon?"

He looked at her blankly. "Is that some sort of code or something?"

Lux laughed. "Never mind. I'll stay close and yell if I get into trouble, but I want a break from being inside for a while, and it's so nice out there at night."

"Be careful."

She smiled and slipped out the door. "I always am."

CHAPTER THREE

LUX DRESSED for battle. She tied her hair into a thick braid and wore black leather leggings, tall boots, and a black jacket zipped to her throat. There was a pistol sitting on one hip, a sword strapped to her back, and a knife in her boot. Attached to each thigh was a strap with extra ammunition. On her utility belt, she carried a bottle of Holy water, a stake, a pouch of salt, a bottle filled with blood, and a bag of an herb mixture she favored for spell casting.

Zane was almost exactly the opposite. He wore dark jeans and a t-shirt, leaving his hands and arms exposed. He carried only a gun and ammo across his chest, and a knife in his belt. His hair, pitch black and too long, was tucked behind his ears and shoved back from his face. A two-day stubble darkened his jaw, and his eyes showed his intensity in their dark blue depths.

"Somehow I always picture a witch with a long skirt and her hair loose with wind blowing it all around."

Lux snorted and strapped a watch to her wrist. "Long skirts are easy to trip in and loose hair is perfect for pulling. Neither of those things will get us anything other than killed." She bent to check the laces on her boots. "Have you ever fought with Amaya? Like against other people."

Zane shook his head. "No, why?"

"She has Alaria's ability to conjure weapons out of thin air.

When she does, she transforms into tight leather pants and this corset thing. The first time she did it, Braxton's eyes nearly bugged out of his head. I don't think it occurred to them that the wardrobe was genetic." She shook her head slowly. "That corset thing gives better cleavage than any bra does. I swear it pushes her boobs up almost to her chin."

Zane lifted one eyebrow. "I'm sure Deacon quite enjoys the view."

"Wouldn't you?" Curious, Lux opened the door and started down the steps toward the road.

"Any man would. Just because I can't touch doesn't mean I don't look."

"You could touch Amaya. She's more powerful than you." She crossed the street and strode between cars, winding her way amongst the burned out and rusted bodies. "We could practice in the dreamplane. It's a more neutral place, and I definitely have more power there than you do. Graciela is there, too, and she could help us harness it."

Zane rolled that around in his mind for several moments. "That isn't a half bad idea. If it'll get you to leave me alone about it, I'll work with you on the dreamplane."

"Good enough." She held up a hand to stop him and ducked behind an old pickup truck. Zane joined her, pressing his back against the metal and using the rear tire to hide his feet and legs.

"What do you see?"

"Patrol. Demons. Looks like three of them. I don't think they've seen us yet. If they manage to call in that we're here, the Cambion, and especially Ingrid, will take off."

Zane's lips peeled back in a grin. "Don't worry. Carys and Elisa are up on the roof across the street. I'm sure they see the demons. Let's just hang back here for a minute and see if they handle it. If not, I'll go out and sneak up on them if I can and just kill them."

Lux pressed her back against the truck and lifted herself slightly with her knees in order to see over the bed of the truck. "I can get them. If I incinerate them, then they go back to Hell and it'll take a little while for them to get out, find a new host, and get back here. It would give us enough time to get in and get done, and I can handle them all at once."

Zane peered over the roof of the truck and swore. "I don't see Carys and Elisa. They were just up there, and now they're gone. If they aren't down here in thirty seconds, I'll flash up to check on them, and you take care of the demon patrol."

"We're too close for you to flash. The Cambion will know within a second that we're out here." She smacked the back of her head against the truck. "Dammit to fucking hell. I knew we should have just taken care of things on our own. Bringing Carys and Elisa into this are two more unknowns that we have to figure out." She squeezed her eyes shut and gave herself a moment to think. "Okay, here's what we do. Either Carys and Elisa ran into trouble on the roof, or they flashed out. The only way to know that is to get up there. Our mission is to kill Ingrid. You go look for her, and I'll clean up things here. Whatever you do, don't let her get away. I'll try to catch up with you if I can, but if worst comes to worst, we'll rendezvous back at the house."

Zane sneaked one more look and didn't see the other two Nephilim. "Okay." He looked at her out of the corner of his eye. "Be careful and don't do anything stupid."

"I won't." Lux stood up and walked out from behind the truck, her eyes fading from green to gray and finally to white as she whipped up her magic around her. "Go find the Cambion bitch. I've got this."

The three demons sensed her within seconds and came running, armed with rifles and knives. Their red eyes glowed in the night, a beacon showing her exactly where they were. Lux bared her teeth in a vicious snarl and held out her hands, reaching out with her magic and wrapping it around all of them.

"Tonight seems like a good night to die." She yanked on the cord that she had wound around the demons and brought them close. "Where are the two Nephilim that were up on the roof?"

One of the demons growled at her. "Why the fuck would we tell you that, witch? What do you even care? Witches serve Lucifer."

"Not this one." Lux clenched one of her fists, and the demon gasped as his air supply was cut off. He tried to expel his essence from the host, but she whispered an exorcism backward, forcing the demon back into the body. "I can do that all night. We both know you can't. You're demons—cannon fodder. You're nothing other than watch dogs and expendable assets."

"Fuck you, bitch."

Lux turned her hand to the side and popped the head off of the demon that swore at her. The other two paled and trembled as they saw what she had done. One held up its hands, palms up, and took a gulping breath.

"The two Nephilim were captured. They got taken to the church by the Cambion to be sacrificed as part of tonight's services. It was very last minute. They only took them five minutes ago. They might still be alive if you hurry."

Lux made a considering noise in the back of her throat. "Hmm. Is Ingrid still there?"

"Ingrid is at a safe-house four or five blocks from here. She isn't going to be at the church service. Once we detected the Nephilim, it seemed safer for her to stay out of sight." The demon brightened as he stumbled across a thought. "Hey, I could take you. If you'll not kill me, I'll take you right to her."

Lux stared into the demon's eyes, using her power to slip past the pitiful barriers and into his mind. She read his memories, getting a good view at the safe-house and the security around it. She shook her head.

"Thanks, but no thanks. You're not needed." She drew her knife and slashed upward with it, burying it to the hilt in the demon's chin, extending up through the softer roof of its mouth and into its brain.

Dead, the body slumped to the ground, a puddle of red blood seeping out. The other demon shrieked and threw itself against Lux's power, trying to escape. She clucked her tongue and tipped her head to the side.

"Not so fast." She snapped her fingers and watched in satisfaction as its head snapped to the side fast enough to break its neck. Allowing her curtain of magic to fall, she strode purposefully away from the building and toward the safe-house. Knowing Zane had gone in to find Ingrid, she knew he would be able to handle rescuing Carys and Elisa. Cursing herself for suggesting they separate in the first place, leaving him without the knowledge she had gained, she picked up her pace to a jog, wishing she was sure she had the time to go and get Zane before leaving to take on Ingrid.

Zane slipped through the cars in the parking lot of the church, sneering at the well-dressed humans who entered the double doors to what had once been a synagogue. After Lucifer had escaped, one of his first missions had been to either overtake or destroy all of the churches erected to God.

For the first few years, most people had fought back. Many had learned how to battle vampires, Hellhounds, and demons, and humanity had done all right. Cambion and Nephilim had been born at astounding rates. Angels and Devils both searched for the offspring of the other, trying to kill them before they achieved maturity and were ready to fight.

The six had failed in 2031. By 2040, there were only a handful of countries still with any sort of government. Zane remembered clearly when the United States had fallen, on September 30th, 2042. In the eighteen years since, the entire world had changed. Some humans made attempts at starting colonies, others stayed on the road, traveling from place to place and scavenging and stealing what they could to stay alive.

Others had continued to join with the Warriors and the Nephilim, taking up arms and fighting for Earth. Then there were the Luciferians. There had only been a few at first, mostly those who had already worshipped Lucifer before he had escaped. As time passed and the world got worse, more and more flocked to Lucifer.

With Lucifer, there were luxuries and amenities. Wealthy men and women lounged in pools and lived in resorts. They had expensive parties and ate the best food. The price for living there was simple. When Cambion came and asked for volunteers, no one said no. They raised their children to believe it was an honor to be chosen to host a demon or to be chosen to carry a Cambion child. They produced weapons, helped capture Nephilim and Warriors, even lured in stragglers with promises of a life worth living before handing them over to the demons.

One of the rituals Zane hated the most was the mockery they made of religion. They gathered at least once a month and made a sacrifice to Lucifer. Since Lucifer's power ran through blood and fear, each time they slit a throat, he got a jolt of power. Of the eight billion people on the Earth when Lucifer had shaken free, over three-quarters were dead. Some had been turned into Familiars, some into vampires, still others into hosts for demons. Michael estimated that there were fewer than a billion free, unpossessed humans living.

Of course there were Cambion and Nephilim, which numbered close to three million combined. Some areas had highly concentrated population centers. Los Angeles and New Orleans belonged to Lucifer, with hundreds of thousands of creatures between the two. There were dozens of places just like those all across the world. For the Nephilim, fighting without God at their back, their existence was much less organized.

Zane shook his head to clear the thoughts and concentrated on the task in front of him, which was finding Ingrid and killing her. He crept through the parking lot as quickly as possible, keeping his head down to minimize the chances of being seen.

He dashed from between the cars to the side of the building, taking care to make sure that his powers were dampened. If there were any powerful Cambion or Devils inside they would be able to tell he was there if they tried, but he was banking on the only strong Cambion being Ingrid, and she would likely be too distracted with the pomp and circumstance to be paying attention to him.

There were two guards at the back door, both demons. He snuck up on them silently, reaching out and clamping one hand on each of them. He felt a hard jolt, and within ten seconds, the demons were dead and laying on the ground, their eyes glassy and blind and blood trickling from their ears and nose.

Killing someone was never comfortable. It hurt to use his powers. Even when he touched Deacon or Dev, it still caused him pain. Regardless of the reason for the contact, touching anyone skin to skin caused him pain.

His hands were the worst of it. If he kept them covered, all but the weakest demons and humans were safe from him. If he covered his arms, he wasn't lethal, and the most someone got from touching anything else was a low hum. That sort of contact wasn't bad. It didn't deter him from enjoying sex, and he could wear shorts without fretting about everyone who walked by.

Zane caught himself reaching for his gloves as he entered the synagogue and deliberately placed them back in his pockets. He needed to be at full lethality if he was going to kill Ingrid and figure out what had happened to Carys and Elisa.

He glanced at his watch and looked back at the door in concern. Lux should have been done with the demons and caught up to him. Worried about her, and about the other two women, Zane debated briefly between going back to check on Lux and continuing forward.

Scolding himself for even harboring the thought, he pressed forward. Lux was a damned powerful witch and would be just fine. If she wasn't, well, he likely wouldn't be for long either because if something was powerful enough to take Lux out, it was powerful enough to do the same to him.

Zane looked around the back of the building and swore under his breath. There were at least ten demons and three Cambion that he could see. They were gathered around two chairs, where Carys and Elisa were tied up, their backs to one another.

One of the demons addressed the Cambion. "We found them on the roof a couple blocks over during our normal patrol. We don't know where they were headed, but there's no sign of more that we could sense."

Zane dampened his powers to the best of his ability to make sure they didn't sense him. With Carys and Elisa in such close proximity, the odds of most demons or Cambion being able to tell him apart from them were low, but Ingrid certainly would be able to. Edging closer to them, he shifted his priority from Ingrid to rescuing his friends.

One of the Cambion spoke. "Idiot. You know we can't tell how many there are. All we can do is tell whether or not they're there. For all you know, there could've been another ten. Did you send a patrol to the area to look for more?"

"Three were left behind to finish the sweep, sir. We're being careful."

"That's better than nothing, then." The Cambion looked at the two Nephilim. "These two will make a nice sacrifice tonight during the service. We'll do the normal rituals, then bring these two out to be killed, and finally we'll send for Ingrid. When we got word of the Nephilim, she was shuttered back to the safe-house, and she'll stay there until we're ready for her to come out and get people excited. Beelzebub said that a couple of his kids have been slaughtered lately, and the last thing we want is for this one to get killed on our watch. Ingrid isn't all that important to the boss man, but she is his kid, and if we lose her, he's going to be pissed."

Zane closed his eyes and gritted his teeth. Ingrid wasn't there. He was going to have to rescue Carys and Elisa, find Lux, and then find whatever safe-house it was that they had stashed Ingrid in. All before she sensed their presence.

Forcing himself to focus solely on the task at hand, Zane nearly got to his feet when the other Cambion spoke.

"One of the patrols further out is reporting that they found a house that looks like it's been inhabited. There are some weapons, some food, and there was water still in the sink, so it hasn't been empty long. He said there are embers in the fireplace, so we're talking about a matter of hours."

One of the demons shrugged. "It might be where these two were staying, or it might be something more. Call for a Cambion squad to be waiting there until morning. We'll see if someone comes back to it. It could be some humans, could be these two, or could be more like them. There's no way to know until and unless someone shows up there."

Zane swore under his breath. They'd found the house he and Lux were using. If they got there before he found her, then she'd be in a lot of trouble. Clenching his hands into fists so that his nails dug into his hands, he took a deep breath and watched as two of the demons left the others and moved into the office a Rabbi had once used.

Moving stealthily, he followed the two demons. Unlike Lux, who had inherited Michael's ability to be invisible for short periods of time, he had to simply be sneaky. Heart pounding in his chest, he stood and rapped on the door.

One of the demons opened the door. "What is it? The ceremony doesn't start for..."

He never got to finish the sentence. Zane pressed both hands to the demon's head, sucking out the life within five seconds. The other one swiveled in his chair.

"Who is it?"

Zane dropped the body and closed the door. "Death."

The demon didn't have time to scream.

Zane tucked both bodies into a closet and peered out a crack in the door, checking to see where the other demon and two Cambion were. One of the Cambion was standing guard over Carys and Elisa, and he didn't see the other two. Deciding to take his chances, he slipped out the door and crept toward the Cambion.

He knew the moment it sensed him. The Cambion stiffened and whirled, striking out with a whip made of fire that hadn't been in his hand even a moment before. Zane dodged most of the strike, emerging with an angry burn over one side of his face. Carys, who faced the Cambion, kicked out with her legs and managed to strike it in the back of the knee. As it stumbled, Zane reached out and grabbed it, pressing his hands to the Cambion's throat.

He worked quickly to break the lines of the Angel traps holding Carys and Elisa from flashing out and severed the ropes that held them. Carys stood and helped her girlfriend to her feet.

"Thank God you got here when you did. Another thirty minutes and we'd have been done for. There are two demons on the back door and another demon and one Cambion in here somewhere. I'm sure they're on their way with that little display."

Zane pulled on his gloves to minimize the risk to his friends. "I took care of the ones on the door. You two need to get out of here. Get back to Michael's. I need to find Lux and get to this safe-house they've put Ingrid in before she figures out what's going on."

Elisa hugged him swiftly. "No, you get out of here. If we're both still here, they'll figure we escaped. We can handle one demon and one Cambion. Go find Lux and get to the safe-house. We'll be fine."

Zane turned and fled the building, heading back for where he had left Lux. When he got to the truck, he saw three dead demons, and no sign of her. Fear rising in his gut, he reached out with his magic, trying to find her.

He caught her trail several blocks West of where he was. His mouth set into a grim line, he turned that direction and took off at a run.

CHAPTER FOUR

LUX STRODE across the lawn of the safe-house, her arms up and a magic bubble covering the house. She focused on drawing traps on every available surface, knowing that she couldn't keep the Cambion contained in them but that they would stop her from flashing.

She heard panicked voices in the house and smiled grimly. They knew she was there. She let magic rise within her, opening the hatch and allowing black magic to be funneled through the prism of her citrine to purify it into magic she could use. Her mother had taught her how to use black magic from the time she had been a child, knowing that there was no way to do the things they needed to do without it.

Demons ran from the house, some armed, others not, and Lux cocked her head to the side, studying them. Instead of running to confront her, they tried to flee, running straight into her barrier and incinerating as they crashed into the wall of magic.

A woman exited the house, naked and with her hair flowing down her back in long blonde waves. She placed her hands on her hips and studied Lux, taking in the magic.

"You're a very powerful witch. I'm going to give you ten seconds to leave here because I'm assuming you don't know who I am. I am Ingrid, daughter of Beelzebub. Leave here now and I'll let you live."

Lux lifted one eyebrow and chuckled. "I'm here for you." She gestured to Ingrid's naked body. "I'm happy to wait to do this until you're dressed if you don't want to die bare-assed."

Ingrid bared her teeth. "My mother is a Lycan. I need to be bare in order to change my form more readily. Just because you're uncomfortable with nudity doesn't mean I am."

Lux shrugged. "Have it your way, then." She struck out with her magic, whipping fire around the Cambion.

Ingrid leaped and rolled, landing on her haunches and rolling to her feet with a sword in her hand. She charged Lux, her body moving smoothly, rotating and twirling as she avoided Lux's strike.

"You stupid witch. A demonstration of power this size is going to have every Cambion within ten miles rushing to help me."

"And they'll burn themselves trying to get in. There are very few Cambion that stand a chance against me. Aside from being a witch, I'm also a Nephil. You may have heard of Michael."

For the first time, fear registered in Ingrid's eyes. "You lie. Michael sired only one son, and that bastard was born to Lilith."

"He also sired two daughters. With a Healer and with a witch. One guess at which one I am."

Clarity dawned on the Cambion. "You're not truly a Nephil. Your father is the vampire, one of the six." She laughed. "Oh, honey, you have no idea what you've gotten yourself into, do you?"

Lux lifted one shoulder in a graceful shrug. "I suppose we'll see which one of us is out of their depth."

Ingrid held out her hand and conjured a sword, using her power to light it on fire. She charged Lux with a warrior's yell. Lux threw out a stream of magic and drove the woman back, blasting her with power over and over again until the woman lay on the ground, trembling and nearly unconscious.

Lux stood over the Cambion, lowering her arms to dull her magic temporarily.

"Your mistake is in thinking your father's blood makes you invincible. It makes you strong, strong enough that my Nephil powers won't work on you, but not so much that my magic won't. Remember, my mother was the one to capture your father, and I am even more powerful than she is. I'd say to remember this lesson for next time, but there isn't going to be one."

Lux bent and dragged the Cambion to her feet by her hair.

"Let me make this clear. You're the third of eight. Five more and we'll go after your father. After that, we're going to kill Lucifer, and all of your kind will die out. You're a plague, Ingrid, you and all the Cambion. You weren't ever meant to exist, and it is my great joy to make sure that I remedy this particular mistake." She drew a knife from her belt. "Any last words?"

Ingrid looked up at Lux, her face bloody and bruised. She made an attempt to shift into her wolf form but was too weak to do so. She sagged piteously. "Fuck you, bitch."

"Succinct. Heart felt. I like it." Lux drew the knife back and slashed, slitting Ingrid's throat with one swipe of the blade.

She cast the body aside, watching as the gray essence of Cambion floated out. Satisfied, she turned and dropped the wall of magic, extinguishing the flames and starting down the road back to the safe-house.

Zane found the safe-house within minutes after Lux had left it. He knew she hadn't been gone long from the freshness of the blood beneath Ingrid and the heaviness of the magic hanging in the air. Not even bothering to check inside the house or stay to see if Lux was still around, he headed in the direction of their house.

He felt demons and Cambion coming in response to the magic she had used and swore under his breath. If she made it to their house before he caught her, they were both going to be in trouble. There hadn't been anyone around that the two of them couldn't handle, but the more creatures that came, the greater the danger became.

He stayed to the shadows, choosing to hug close to houses and cars instead of being out on the street where he increased the chance of being seen. Within ten minutes, he caught sight of Lux and dashed onto the road, sprinting toward her.

"Lux!"

Lux whirled and grinned when she saw him. The smile faded as she saw the angry red burn on his face, and she reached up, trailing her fingers over his skin.

"What happened?"

"I got hit with a whip. It's fine." He made sure his gloves were on and took her by the elbow. "They found our house. We have to get out of here now. There are demons and Cambion flooding in and the longer we stay, the more danger we're in."

"Did you find Carys and Elisa?"

"They're fine. They're safe. They finished things up at the church for me, and now we need to get out of here so we don't end up with more trouble than we can handle."

Lux didn't object when he pulled her in the direction away from both the church and their house. "Where are we going to go for the night? If we get too far outside of the city here, we'll have vampires to deal with."

"Then we'll just have to deal with vampires." He looked down at her boots. "How far can you walk in those things?"

"As far as I need to. They're not high heels." She looked at the side of his face. "Does that hurt?"

"It doesn't feel good, that's for sure."

"I could fix it for you."

"When we stop. Not now. We don't have time, and neither of us needs to use our abilities for a few miles, anyway. I would flash us out, but I don't want them to be able to track the flash signature."

"We could steal a car. There's bound to be one in some of these garages. I know how to drive if you don't." She wiggled her eyebrows at him. "I mean, I know you like to flash everywhere, so if you never learned, I can drive."

"I know how to drive." He turned up a driveway and stooped to pick the lock on the door.

Together, they moved directly into the garage. Inside was an SUV covered in dust. Lux, in deference to the danger they were in, slammed her shoulder against the door into the house three times before the lock gave way and the door swung open. Moving quickly, she cast a glance on the hall table, the kitchen counters, and struck gold in the entry hall. Snatching the keys from the hook on the wall, she rushed back into the garage and slipped into the driver's seat while Zane opened the garage door.

The first time she turned the key, nothing happened. Annoyed, she pushed a tiny bit of magic into the engine and cleared out the clog stopping the pistons from firing. Satisfied, she turned the key again, and the engine roared to life. She eased it into gear and guided it out of the garage, waiting until Zane lowered the door behind it and hopped into the front seat before taking off.

"Where to?"

Zane leaned his head against the window, enjoying the feeling of cool glass on his burning face. "Well, West."

She stuck her tongue out. "Okay, smartass."

"You asked." He leaned the seat back to give his long legs enough room. "In all seriousness, I would like to put a hundred miles or so between us and here before we stop. If you can, stick to the back roads and keep off of highways. Keep the headlights off, and let's try to avoid towns for the moment."

She pressed three fingers to her forehead. "Aye, aye Captain."

Lux pulled into the driveway of what had, at one time, been a bed and breakfast. A sign forty minutes earlier had informed her that New Hampshire welcomed them with an eerily applicable sign proclaiming 'live free of die'. Too tired to appropriately appreciate the literality of the sign and her eyes burning from a lack of sleep, she cut the engine and looked over at Zane, who was sleeping next to her.

They'd stopped once to scrounge for fuel for the car and then had continued on. Zane had offered to drive, but Lux, at that time, hadn't been tired, whereas he was exhausted and in pain. He'd fallen asleep soon after refueling and she'd been forced to endure three hours of no conversation, which had made her so tired that she could barely keep her eyes open.

She reached over and touched his arm, smiling when he jumped and sat up. Her fingers tingled from making contact with his bare skin. "Wake up, sleepy head. We're in New Hampshire. I figure this is as good a place as any for the night. We'll get some rest, find something to eat, make contact with Michael or my dad, and figure out our next move from there."

He blinked rapidly and looked around. "Where are we?"

"Some old B&B about twenty miles from the nearest town far as I can tell. Most of the windows look intact, so I think it's as good a place as any. I don't sense anything inside or in the nearby vicinity."

"Neither do I." He opened the car door and slid out, stretching his arms over his head. "Let's check it out then."

Lux used magic to unlock the front door, and they both went inside, closing it behind them. She used her power to flip on lights, illuminating the first floor. Everything was covered in dust, but it looked untouched.

"I'll look around down here, you check upstairs."

Zane started for the stairs. "Pay special attention to the kitchen. I'm starving."

Lux shook her head and left the foyer. "I know."

The house was empty, as expected. The kitchen yielded a case of canned green beans, two bags of chips, several boxes of pasta, three dry cake mixes, vegetable oil, and four cases of soda. A pantry in the mudroom also produced an industrial sized can of applesauce, some condiments, spaghetti sauce, and nine cans of beef stew.

"If the water works we can have some pasta."

Zane shivered in delight as he came back down the steps. "Sounds good to me. Places like this are almost always on well water, so our odds are pretty good. If not, there's a creek out back that we can haul water in from."

"That won't be happening tonight." She turned the knob on the faucet hopefully and squealed when the pipes coughed and water leaked out. "What time is it?"

"Almost dawn. If you want to go upstairs and look for some clothes that are comfortable to sleep in, I can start this."

"Works for me."

Lux dug through the dressers in each of the rooms. She found children's clothing, some lingerie and a menagerie of sex toys that told her someone had had a fun weekend, clothes that looked suited for a ninety-year-old woman, and a drawer full of men's briefs. Cursing her luck, she moved into the last room and jerked open the armoire, swearing when the hangers were empty.

She opened each of the dresser drawers and took stock of the contents. Jeans that might fit Zane, a black t-shirt she could make use of, and two boxes of condoms. She shook her head and smiled at the boxes.

"Someone was optimistic."

Zane laughed from the doorway. "Water's on, so about fifteen minutes until food. Who's optimistic?"

She pointed to the condoms. "There's a whip, some handcuffs, four types of lube, and some nipple clamps in one of the other rooms."

"Did we come to a B&B or a sex shop?"

Lux giggled and opened the last drawer. "Hard to tell." She pawed through the contents. "I found a couple pairs of jeans that might work for you, and one shirt that probably would, but that I'm stealing for myself." She shook out the garments in the drawer. "I could maybe get one leg in here." She cast the jeans aside. "Well, we struck out on clothes, that's for damn sure."

"Don't even think about conjuring them, Lux. We need to not use powers unless it's necessary while we're in between. The last thing we need is to draw attention."

"I'm not an idiot. I know that."

Lux stripped off her jacket and the thin camisole beneath. Zane turned and headed for the door, intending to give her privacy while she changed.

"I don't mind you looking at me."

He turned and looked over his shoulder. "What?"

She strode to him, looking up. "I don't mind you looking at me." She jutted her chin up. "We both know you do. I watch you, too." She reached out and ran her hands over his chest, gripping his t-shirt in her hands. "You haven't made a move in the six months we've been training together, Zane."

"To be fair, three of those months were spent living with your parents." He reached out and moved her hands. "You're tired and hungry. I'll be downstairs when you're ready to eat." He walked out into the hall and looked back over his shoulder. "I'm not noble, Lux. If you make another move, I'll give you what you're asking for, but that'll be all I give. You need to be sure you can handle just sex before you ask."

Lux screeched in frustration and slammed the door shut behind him. Damn that man.

"They're all terribly frustrating."

Lux whirled, her eyes going white as she faced what she assumed to be a threat. When she saw a blonde woman in a white suit, she lowered her guard slightly. "Who are you?"

"I am Griffin. Gabriel asked me to come and give you some instructions."

"You're getting out of Heaven pretty regularly these days."

Griffin shrugged. "Believe me, I know. A girl can't even be left in peace when she's dead." She looked down. "Gabriel loves the color white. Drives me crazy. If I was still human, I'd ruin this in an hour. Tops."

Lux pulled on the t-shirt she'd found. "What do you want?"

"One of the Cambion you have to kill is going to be in New York with a Cambion squad in four days. His mother was a human with no known supernatural powers. From all that we know, he is a very weak Cambion and should be easy to kill. However, you should also know that the remaining four have all gone into hiding. The news of Ingrid's death has reached Beelzebub and he has ordered for his progeny to go to ground. I would not be surprised to find that he is hunting you himself."

"Good to know. Do you know where in New York?"

"White Plains. There is a group of Cambion that have

colonized there. They raid nearby towns and kill any human who come through. It should be relatively simple to get to him." Griffin looked at Lux pointedly. "You need to be more careful with your magic. You are powerful, yes, and you can do much damage, but each time you use your magic, you are sending up a signal to anything seeking to kill you and giving them your exact location. One of the horrid things about this war is that the things you need to hunt can oftentimes sense you coming."

"We'll take care of it."

"No. You will take care of it. For this, I am afraid you will do it on your own."

Lux stared at the woman blankly. "What do you mean I'm going to do it by myself? I have Zane to help me."

Griffin folded her hands in her lap as she sat. "Lux, Zane is a threat to your cause. He can kill other Nephilim. We suspect that he can kill Beelzebub, and he may be able to kill Angels. His father is by far the most powerful Angel in existence. Michael has tried for years to teach him how to use his abilities appropriately, and we had hoped that being paired with you would allow the two of you to work together on a solution."

"We are. We're going to go to the dreamplane and ask my grandmother to help us. We'll figure it out." Lux glared at the blonde woman. "You're beginning to sound an awful lot like Gabriel."

"My time in Heaven has removed me from human emotions and has made me much more like an Angel than a human. I don't feel things like you do. I didn't come here to fight with you about this. It's not my decision whether or not it's necessary. I'm just sent as a messenger to you. Gabriel feels that seeing me makes it easier for people than seeing him, especially given how your last encounter with him went. Zane is being taken by his father to Heaven where he will be trained in how to use his abilities. When he is returned to Earth, he will no longer be a danger."

"What if he truly can't be trained? What if they can't teach him to control his abilities?"

Griffin looked sad for a moment. "I don't agree with this decision, and if I had any power over anyone, I would try to talk them out of it. Gabriel fears that Zane could use his abilities to kill Angels, and if he can't learn to control those powers, then Gabriel has issued the order to have him killed."

CHAPTER FIVE

July 3rd, 2060

LUX STORMED into Michael's nonplace, her hair streaming behind her, and slammed the door. Amaya looked up from her position on the couch and offered a smile.

"Well, you always have liked to make an entrance. What's going on?"

"Call for your father."

Amaya sat up and placed her coffee cup on the table. "Dad's with Eden and Donovan. They're training some Warriors right now. What's going on?"

"No, Amaya. Not Braxton. Call for Gabriel. Now."

"I don't take orders from you." Starting to get annoyed, Amaya stood and walked toward her friend. "Tell me what's going on."

"Gabriel ordered that Zane be captured and taken up to Heaven. They took him from the house where we were staying and had Griffin come down to tell me about it. They just took him, Amaya! Snatched him from the kitchen where he was making pasta."

Amaya looked over her shoulder to where Deacon was stirring something on the stove. "Go get your Dad."

Michael spoke from the office. "I'm here. Come in, Lux. Tell me what's happened."

Lux yanked on her hair. "I just did! That's all I know. Griffin came to tell me about one of Beelzebub's offspring. Then she slipped in the fact that Gabriel had ordered her to tell me that they were taking Zane so he could be trained in how to use his powers appropriately. And she said if he can't learn, or it's not possible to control them, they'll kill him! Gabriel is going to have him killed!"

Michael's eyes flashed with anger before he managed to calm himself. "No one is going to kill Zane. I'll go up to Heaven at once and figure out what is going on. If it is merely to train him in how to use his abilities, then that is not something that I am opposed to. However, I will not allow anyone to terminate him. Don't worry about that at all."

"That's only half my point. They left me alone and told me I have to continue to go after the Cambion without him. I killed Ingrid just fine, and the one in New York was a joke, but we still have all the most powerful Cambion coming up. There are a few that will be able to match my power. I'll need Zane if we're going to tip the scales in our favor."

Michael did look angry then. "Why did you not call for help? Was he taken before you went for Ingrid?"

"No, after. We'd already killed her when they did this."

"And Gabriel decreed that you be sent after another of Beelzebub's offspring without Zane and without informing me?"

"Yes."

There was a shimmer and Gabriel appeared in the room. He immediately took a step toward Amaya. "How are you, Amaya, my darling girl?"

Amaya huffed and flopped down on the couch. "I am not in the mood to deal with you today. What are you even doing here? Come to kidnap someone else?"

"Zane has not been kidnapped. He is being retrained."

Fear knotted in Lux's stomach. "Retrained? What does that mean?"

Gabriel gave a long-suffering sigh. "Zane was never properly instructed in how to control his abilities. Now that he is an adult, he is unable to learn to do so. We are removing his emotional tendencies and allowing him to learn what he must do. He will be returned to you within the next week completely in control of his abilities. We are confident that he will be able to kill Beelzebub at that point."

Lux nearly gagged. "You're taking his emotions?" She lashed out with a bolt of power before she could stop herself, striking

Gabriel and driving him back. "How dare you? You want to turn him into a machine like you!" She struck out again.

Gabriel flicked the wave away with one swipe of his hand and looked to Michael. "I suggest you control her before I have to."

Michael crossed his arms. "It would be an interesting fight. Lux, calm down for a moment and let's hear him out. Brother, have you removed the boy's emotions?"

"Not all of them. His abilities are tied to his emotions. When he is angry or exceedingly happy—any periods of strong emotion, really—he is most apt to kill someone. By disentangling his powers from his emotions, he will be able to control things most effectively."

"Yes, I understand all of that. I know what you have done to him. What I am asking you is whether or not he will be able to experience human feelings when you are done."

"I do not know the answer to that question." Gabriel brushed his shirt cuff absent mindedly. "I do not know why the answer matters. It is of no consequence whether or not the Nephil feels things as a human does. In fact, it may make his job easier if he does not."

Lux shrieked in frustration and looked at Amaya. "I'm going to kill him! I'm going to rip his fucking head right off of his shoulders!"

Amaya took a deep breath and stood, placing herself deliberately between Lux and Gabriel. "You had to know when you did this that we would be upset. Zane is Deacon's best friend. They're like brothers. We're all a team. You knew this would make us mad. Why did you do it?"

"Because it had to be done."

Amaya held up one finger. "That's where you don't get it. It *didn't* have to be done. You decided it had to be done, so you did it. You didn't ask Zane whether or not he wanted it—so much for free will—you didn't consult with any of us on the possible consequences, and you didn't take anyone's feelings into consideration. Just because you don't have them doesn't mean they don't exist and that they shouldn't be thought about." She met her father's gaze for the first time. "You keep saying that you want a relationship with me. That you love me and want to protect me. That you want me to be happy. Kidnapping my friends and reprogramming them does not make me happy." When Gabriel started to speak, Amaya shushed him. "No, for once you shut up and listen to me. Having two people who were family to me killed does not make me happy. Making two of my friends do the killing does not make me happy. We aren't Angels, Gabriel! We aren't meant to blindly obey. We have choices because we are human!"

"You're not human. None of you are."

"I bleed and die the same as they do. That makes me human. I grew in a womb and was born to my mother. That makes me human." She jutted her chin up at him. "My heart beats and I age. That makes me human. Just because an Angel sired me doesn't take away what I am. What Zane is. What we all are."

Gabriel looked down at Amaya, his expression flickering in what might have been regret or remorse. Clearing his throat, his expression settled into neutral disregard and he continued. "You are my one and only priority, Amaya. Whether or not you see it, I do everything I do to ensure that you are safe. If doing that means that you're angry with me, then so be it. I can handle your anger. I could not handle your death." He reached out and cupped her cheek in his hand, his gaze showing when she allowed the contact. "I do love you. I want to see you happy, but your happiness is secondary to your safety."

Amaya closed her eyes. "I loved you, Uncle Gabe. Your stories and the nights you came to watch me were some of my favorite nights growing up. What you did to Mom is between you and her. She's forgiven you, so I have, too. I'm not mad at you because of anything in the past. I'm angry that you defied my parents to tell me on your terms instead of theirs. I'm angry that you seem to think you have a right to still parent me when I am a grown ass woman. I'm angry that you continually make decisions that affect everyone here without even notifying them of what is going on. I'm angry that you gamble with life and death. But I am fucking pissed off that you claim to love me and want to protect me but then set out to destroy everyone around me that I love! My friends—my family—are what gives me the strength to do what I need to do. They are what will get me through this, and God willing, they're why I will survive." She stepped back and out of his reach. "If you want any sort of a relationship with me at any point in my life, you will go back to Heaven and bring Zane home again. You will bring him home in one piece, and you will bring him home with all of his memories and emotions intact. If you don't, so help me God, I will never speak to you again."

Gabriel looked past Amaya to Michael. "Even though we have

had our differences, I have trusted you with my child. You know, more than anyone else, that I could shutter her away to Heaven and keep her safe there while the rest of you fight and die."

Before Amaya could say a word, Michael answered. "Brother, if you were to do that, I fear Heaven would not survive her wrath." A wry smile quirked the side of his mouth. "Don't make threats, Gabriel. Tt does no good for either of us."

"I'm not threatening. You know I could do that, and yet I have not out of respect for Alaria and for your teachings." He turned to Amaya, who was obviously seething. "You all need to remember that you don't have the power. I do. I took Zane because it is for the best, and I do not care whether or not you can see that. If you are truly human, Amaya, then you are as short-sighted and pathetic as the rest."

Amaya clenched her hands into fists until her fingernails broke through the skin on her palms. "You're a bastard. Nothing but a rat bastard. My mother swears there was a time when you were gentle and kind, but I don't see it now. You've changed, Gabriel. You're bitter and petty, and you've become something God should be ashamed of." She glared up at him. "It is my biggest wish that there is no part of you in me. I want nothing to do with you."

Gabriel didn't speak as Amaya stormed up the stairs and slammed the door. Deacon uncrossed his legs and spoke for the first time.

"Well, you royally fucked that up."

Gabriel's head swiveled to the blonde man. "Your input is completely unnecessary." He glanced at Lux. "Your friend will be returned when he is done, and not a moment earlier. I suggest that you continue looking for the other Cambion without him."

As soon as Gabriel disappeared, Michael held up a hand to stop Lux from speaking. "Don't. I'm not going to let it go, and no, we're not going to sit here on our asses and do nothing. Is that what you were going to screech at me?"

Slightly embarrassed, she nodded. "Something like that."

Michael smiled. "I do know you all very well by now. Deacon, you're in charge. I'm going to go up to Heaven and attempt to reason with Father. There is a possibility, and in fact a likelihood, that he may not be aware of what Gabriel is attempting to do with Zane. I imagine there will be quite a debate, and I may not succeed, given that I am not going to be a welcome sight behind the gates, but I will do my best to bring him home. Regardless of what Gabriel has said, I would prefer that you remain here until I return. That may be several days, and I do not wish for you to be out on your own without me on Earth to assist you."

Lux rushed to Michael and threw her arms around the Angel, pressing her face to his chest. "Thank you."

"No need to thank me. Zane is like a son to me and a brother to my son. I'll do everything I can to bring him back as he was."

Lux sat cross legged on Zeke's bed and stared at her friend, who was studying herself in the mirror. "You're getting huge."

Zeke laid her hands on the curve of her stomach. "I'm five months pregnant. I'm supposed to start getting huge right about now."

"Do you know if it's a girl or a boy yet?"

Zeke whirled around and bounced excitedly. "A boy! We found out last week."

Lux's brows drew together. "I don't exactly think there are gynecologists around anymore. How did you find out?"

"If you didn't think I could find out, then why did you ask?"

"Habit." She shook her head and grinned. "Seriously though. How do you know?"

"Your dad."

Lux laughed and flopped back on the bed. "Of course. He can get anything from anyone at any time." She curled against Zeke when the blonde laid down next to her. "Where's Dev?"

"He's off with Carys and Elisa after some Cambion terrorizing a colony somewhere in Idaho. Supernatural strike force and all." Zeke yanked the blanket up over them. "He's really happy. I thought I wanted a girl because, well, I'm a girl, and I know what to do with a girl, but when the tech your dad brought told me it was a boy, I was genuinely excited. But Dev, he's on a whole other level."

"I can deal with a nephew." Lux reached out and laid her hand on Zeke's stomach. "He feels strong."

"He kicks me to death, that's for sure." Zeke rolled onto her side. "Do you think we should go see Amaya?"

The door opened and Amaya crept in, holding a pillow. "I'm here." She crawled into the bed with the other two. "I can't let you two have a sleep over without me." She wiggled her way into the middle, smiling when Lux laid her head on her shoulder. "I miss this when we're not all together."

Lux giggled. "I bet Dev loves the thought of the three of us in bed together."

Amaya snorted. "I'm sure they all do." She looked at Zeke. "I'm sure by now Lux has filled you in on what happened."

Zeke made a noncommittal noise in her throat. "I got the basics of it."

"Care to impart some wisdom?"

"It's no secret that I hate Gabe. I'd be happy to never be in the same room with him for as long as I live. My parents will never meet their grandson. I don't even have pictures to show him, so he'll never know them at all. Gabriel did that. He made a conscious decision to take them away from me because it was whatever he uses as the definition of necessary." Zeke took a deep, trembling breath. "That being said, I don't doubt that he loves you, and your mom, in whatever way he can. Angels are different than us, guys. They don't feel things like we do. It's like trying to give a guy a blowjob with his pants still on. It might feel good, but it's not like it should be."

Lux giggled. "You would use a perverted example."

Zeke shrugged. "I'm perverted. That's no secret." She looked at Amaya. "I'm not defending him, sweetheart. I think what he did is a shit move, but I don't think he understands why we think that. Unfortunately, with him, if you want any sort of a relationship, you're going to have to go off of the intention instead of the action because he just truly does not get it."

Amaya snuggled in close to Zeke. "I love the idiot, that's the thing. I used to wish more than anything that I could have three parents. I wouldn't trade my dad for anything, and if I had to choose, there's never been any comparison between the two. Braxton is my dad. He has been there for everything. But I used to be excited when Gabriel came to visit. I loved his visits. I loved seeing him and hearing the stories. Once I found out he was my real father, I was really bitter for a long time. I felt betrayed and stupid and like he was trying to take me away from Dad. Things just got worse and worse until I stopped talking to him at all. I think the worse I felt, the harder he tried, which made me hate him even more."

Lux flopped onto her back. "I don't like him. I don't care what he used to be or why he does things. I don't like him. He snatched Zane from the middle of the kitchen after we'd both just risked our lives—again—to do what he told us to do. Zane isn't dangerous."

Zeke made a noise in her throat. "Honey, yes, he is. Not to us so much, but he is dangerous to humans."

"Which would be an issue if he were homicidal, but he's not!" Lux sat up and stared down at her friends. "I've been with him for more than six months. In that whole amount of time, I've never seen him touch anyone out of anger. He touched me once, when it was that or let you die, Zeke." She crossed her arms. "And I've tried my best to get him to make a move. If I can't inspire a man to put his hands on me, no human woman is going to be able to."

"It's too risky for him to." Amaya propped herself up on one elbow and looked at Lux. "Michael will get him back. Hopefully with full use of his hands so he can give you what you want." She winked at Zeke. "But if he can't, I know a couple places where you could find a very nice male escort. Rhad runs quite the business down in New Orleans."

Lux tried not to laugh, but the urge got bigger and bigger until she was laying on her side with tears running down her cheeks from the giggling. "For Christ's sake, I can get myself laid if I want to. Besides, New Orleans is baddie central. I'm certainly not going there."

Zeke looked at Lux seriously. "Is wanting sex all that it is? Or is there more?"

Lux jerked a shoulder dismissively. "I like him. He's a nice guy. Honorable, which is not a word I throw around very much, but no, there's nothing more to it. I want him. He's an incredibly attractive man, he challenges me, and I want him. It's as simple as that." She tugged the blanket up higher. "I don't want anything more. I don't have some previous love that I'm mourning. I don't have Deacon. I don't want what my parents have, or what any of our parents have. Maybe Alaria and Braxton. They're so pragmatic that I could see myself there."

Amaya's eyes darkened slightly. "My parents love each other. They have two other children together and they've been with one another for almost thirty years. It may have started off as nothing but a practical arrangement, but they love each other."

Zeke patted Amaya's arm. "I don't think Lux meant to say she thinks they don't. I understand what she means. Lux doesn't think she's suited for love in all caps."

Amaya snorted. "Of course you are, but I don't see it being with Zane. If you want my advice, which you do, or should, anyway, bang him, get it out of your system by the time this is over, and find someone that you can see a future with. We all know there's no future with Zane. He doesn't want it."

"Neither do I."

Zeke giggled. "Sure you do. You just don't want to admit it." She rubbed her hands over her stomach. "I think we want ice cream. Do you guys want ice cream?"

Amaya rolled out of the bed, going over Lux and hopping up onto her feet. "I always want ice cream."

Lux groaned and let Amaya pull her out of the bed. "Sure. Why not? It's not like I'm getting lucky, so there's no reason not to binge on sundaes."

CHAPTER SIX

September 1, 2060 – Wilmington, North Carolina

LUX FELT a storm brewing. She could feel electricity in the air and reveled in it. She loved a good storm unlike almost anything else. There was something amazing about nature—the way it raged and roared with no regard for anyone other than itself. Gazing through the window, she enjoyed the raw power hanging heavy in the air and how it affected every particle within reach of the storm. The ocean was gray and choppy, and black clouds gathered over the water. It was going to be bad.

"Feels almost like a hurricane."

She looked over her shoulder and smiled at Zane. "Can you predict the weather as well as control it?"

He lifted one shoulder and walked over to join her. "It doesn't matter, because this isn't real."

Lux looked at him and wrinkled her nose. "What are you talking about? We're not in the dreamplane. This is as real as anything else."

He shook his head. "How did you get here, Lux? Do you remember driving here or flashing?"

She thought back, wracking her brain for any memory of how she'd gotten there. Finding she had none, she turned to him, confused and worried. "What is this place?"

"The place is real enough, it's me that's the issue. Gabriel and my father have been digging around in my brain trying to figure out how to fix my powers. What they've done is manage to form a break between my consciousness and my body. Instead of making me better, they made it worse."

Lux's hand flew to her mouth. "Where are you? Still in Heaven? Or somewhere else?"

"I'm showing you where Gabriel has my body. This is where they have me now. This house, this place. I'm here. You're not. I don't know if you can help me, but if anyone can, it's going to be you. Michael is pleading his case with God, and God has ordered that I be put back to Earth, but He is not willing to get involved with what he thinks is a spat between siblings. Gabriel can't figure out how to fix what he did. It's not like when Aradia got locked out of herself during the tasks. This is different. It's like my soul has been pulled out of my body. I can see and hear and am aware of what's going on, I just can't wake myself up."

"I'll come there right away. I can fix it. I'll figure it out. Somehow or another, I will fix it." She reached out and wrapped her fingers around his wrist. "Is Gabe there with you?"

"He is. He's still trying to figure out what he's done so he can undo it."

"Don't go anywhere. Like, no following the white light and don't go into any tunnels." She looked almost panicked as she gripped his arm. "Promise me that you won't leave. I am coming to you, and I will fix this. No lights. No tunnels."

Zane laughed. "I'm not going anywhere. Wasting away as some stupid fucking Angel tries to figure out what he did to me is not the way I want to die. I'm fine. Just get here when you can."

Lux was tossed from the dream and woke up in the bed she shared with Amaya. Quietly, she rolled off of the mattress and reached for her jeans and shirt, padding into the bathroom to get dressed. Five minutes later, taking care not to wake anyone, she slipped outside the house and flashed out.

Gabriel paced. He looked down at Zane's body, his brows drawn together and worry in his eyes. Zane lay in the bed, pale and unconscious, his chest barely rising and falling. Gabriel raked his hands through his hair and muttered under his breath.

"I don't know what happened. It should have been simple. It was supposed to be a matter of rewiring him. Nothing complicated about it." He jumped and turned when a crack filled the room and

Lux appeared. "Why are you here? How did you know I'm here?"

"Zane found me in a dream." She stared at the prone body. "What the fuck have you done?"

"Zane came to you? So his consciousness is still functioning?"

She narrowed his eyes. "What do you think you did?"

"I can't sense his soul. I feared that he had lapsed into a vegetative state."

Lux leaned against the wall and stared at the Angel. "What did the two of you do?"

"Death and I conferred, and we agreed that there was likely a problem in his brain. Something that blocked his ability to control his powers. It's not a problem with the powers. They're fine. Death has no issue with controlling who he kills, and we determined that there was no reason the boy should be having the problems that he is. We initially suspected the issues were a lie and he enjoyed killing, in which case he had to be neutralized. After some time, we realized his powers are directly tied to his emotions, so we decided to remove those. It didn't work, and that is what has caused my current predicament."

Lux closed her eyes. "Do you even hear yourself when you talk? Like, does that sound even the slightest bit reasonable when you say it out loud?"

Gabriel sighed deeply and looked at her, his gaze only slightly hysterical. "You don't understand, Lux. I don't hate the boy. I don't hate you. I care for all of you. My priority is Amaya, but that does not mean I am blind or deaf to what the rest of you do. I am not." His blue eyes bored into her. "During the tasks, the six asked that I no longer be their guide. I made stupid decisions with Alaria, and I pay for them still. I know you weren't born, but it seems as if I continue to make poor decisions. I just don't understand why you don't understand why I do the things I do!"

Lux bit the inside of her cheek to stop the giggle from bursting out. She had never seen Gabriel harried before. "I think I understand what you just said. Maybe." She took the Angel's arm and led him from the room. "I don't hate you. Not really. I don't think Amaya does either, if you want the total truth. I don't like you, and I think you're a jerk most of the time, but I know that you believe you're doing the right thing." She sat down on the dusty couch and patted the cushion next to her. "Sit down for a minute. I can fix Zane."

"How?"

"With magic. You probably don't want to know. Just leave him here with me, and I'll make sure he's fixed." She crossed her legs and folded her hands on top of her knees. "Let's talk for a few minutes, you and I. We haven't ever done that before."

Gabriel smoothed his hands over his hair to fix the displaced strands. "Okay. Of what would you like to speak?"

"I'm going to give you some advice, Gabriel. Unsolicited, I know, and likely unwelcome, but advice nonetheless. I want things to be better. We're all fighting a war." She paused. "Well, not you so much since you're in Heaven, but the rest of us are fighting a war, and when you're fighting a war, you need all the help you can get. Michael is stretched thin. He's the only Angel down here trying to help the Nephilim. There are more dying every day and more achieving puberty. It's too much for one Angel to handle. Have you gone and just looked at Earth recently?"

Gabriel shook his head. "I avoid Earth."

"That's the problem. There are battles being fought. Hundreds of people die every day. Humans, Nephilim, Cambion. We're all dying. Every big city is a battleground day in and day out. People are scared to go out at night. We know from Damon and Greer's future that if the timeline is similar, within the next fifteen years, unless we manage to kill Lucifer, that the Cambion win. Humanity is nothing more than groups of people living underground or moving from place to place, terrified to make a sound. The Nephilim need to be better trained. They need to be better protected—they need to have access to Angels, and to God. He needs to send the Host back to Earth. It's been thirty years since He ordered them to Heaven, and humanity is still fighting. We're still trying to survive. How much longer are we to be punished for the actions of a few?"

Gabriel pursed his lips as he mulled over her words. "You make a persuasive argument. However, my fear is that if Heaven is left unprotected, then Lucifer will order a siege upon it."

She looked at him drolly. "Seriously. How long does it take you to get back there when you flash out? A millisecond?"

He nearly smiled. "Duly noted."

"If Amaya is the most important thing to you, and you really want a relationship with her, then you have to take an interest in her life. That doesn't mean just telling her what to do and expecting her to listen."

Gabriel scoffed. "I'm her father. I know what's best for her."

Lux smiled patiently. "No, you're not, and no, you don't.

Braxton is her father. He's the one who rocked her to sleep and held her hand while she learned to walk. He pulled her first tooth and baked her birthday cakes. He's her dad. And she's a grown woman. She's a Nephilim. She's the most powerful Nephilim out there, and she is going to kill Lucifer, Gabriel. Not just hurt him, kill him. She needs to be self-assured and confident to be able to do that. She needs to trust herself, and she needs to be able to trust those around her. If you want to help her, you need to be trustworthy. You aren't."

Gabriel looked affronted. "I am an Angel of the Lord. How dare you suggest that I am anything other than trustworthy?"

Lux took a deep breath, held it until her lungs burned, and expelled the air slowly. "Gabe, listen to me, and please try to understand how it looks to someone else. You did what you did with Alaria, which, while we know you had your reasons, was a shit thing to do, and you know it. Then, you told Amaya about her paternity before Alaria and Braxton could, which further degraded the situation, which was anything but perfect. Follow that up with fifteen years of sporadic contact during which you very rarely do anything other than tell her what to do or try to convince her not to do something. She hasn't ever felt supported by you. Then, look at her best friends, me and Zeke. You go to Zeke's parents, tell them of this danger, convince them to sacrifice themselves without even giving us a chance to save them, and then get mad when their daughter, who just had to shoot her father in the head, refuses to fuck the Cambion who made her do the shooting. Can you see where I'm going with this?"

"You're obviously leading to the situation that we currently have found ourselves in."

"Well, you're not stupid, I'll give you that. Yes, you kidnapped one of Amaya's friends and managed to screw around in his brain so much that you thought you killed him! And yet you wonder why she isn't calling you Daddy and asking for advice on her life." Lux took another deep breath. "You need a different approach, dude. If you want to fix things, and don't get me wrong, I don't know if they can be totally fixed, but if you want to try, you need to go to Zeke and apologize for Damon and Greer. You need to mean it. Even if you don't think what you did was wrong, she lost her parents, and you handled the situation badly. Tell her you're sorry for her loss and wish you'd have handled things differently. Then, you apologize to Michael and Deacon for running off with Zane. Ask Michael if you can help. Offer to help train recruits. Get your hands dirty. Be involved. Be there for her. Don't be pushy. Just be available. Let her come to you. She can't come to you if you're always up in Heaven and only come down to tell her she's wrong. She dreads seeing you because that's what you always do. You don't want her to dread seeing you, Gabriel."

Gabriel tapped one index finger against his chin as he considered what Lux had said. "You believe this strategy would work?"

"I think it would give you the best chance you're going to get, yes."

"Are you going to tell Amaya that we had this discussion?"

Lux snorted. "Hell, no. I don't want her to know any more than you do. I just want you to either stay out of our hair or be useful, and we both know you aren't going to stay away. So this is my compromise. God help me, but I'm trying to help you."

"The advice is appreciated, if not solicited." Gabriel stood. "I will take it under advisement. Are you sure that you can correct what is wrong with the boy?"

"I'm sure. Just leave us alone." She looked out the window and gestured to the gathering clouds. "I think a storm is coming."

"I believe that is a hurricane."

Lux rolled her eyes. "Go on, get outta here. I've got work to do."

CHAPTER SEVEN

LUX TOOK her time preparing Zane before she tried to do anything. One of the biggest mistakes was in being unready or poorly prepared. She placed citrine at each of the points of Zane's body—his feet, hands, and his head—to channel power and energy through. Rain lashed the windows, and the sky rolled with thunder. Lux smiled and glanced out at the black clouds. The storm was charged with electricity and energy. It would give her a boost.

Very carefully, she lit a bundle of sage and whisked any negative energy out the door. Even though she had her doubts about the efficacy of burning herbs and cleansing negativity, it was better to be safe than sorry.

She placed candles around the bed in a wide circle, lighting them all with a careless flick of her wrist. The chunk of citrine around her neck glowed soft yellow as she worked, and she touched her finger to it, enjoying the warmth of the stone on her skin. Humming under her breath, she picked up an athame and scored the palm of her hand.

"Blood of life, blood of death, heart slow beating in his chest. Soul without, body within, free of doubt, clean of sin. Nephil warrior fighting for light, bring him back, do what's right. Nephil rise, Nephil seek. Find the sight, find your way, hear my voice, heed my cry. Outside your body to roam no more, finish this fight, open the door."

Lux reached out with her magic, feeling for Zane's soul. She felt whispers of it, far away and weak, and focused on pulling it nearer as she chanted the incantation under her breath. She tugged gently on the essence of Zane, trying to direct him back into his body as she whispered. Her citrine glowed and warmed on her chest, and the stones surrounding him lit up.

She didn't know how long she tugged on that string, trying to lead Zane back. Each time she thought she made progress, she was jerked back as the soul ripped itself out of her grasp and she was forced to start over again.

Frustrated and confused, Lux wracked her brain for a solution, keeping a firm grip on Zane's soul while she considered her options. Remembering how Javal had had to separate Damon and Greer before going after Greer on the dreamplane, she mulled over the possibility of constructing a temporary link tying Zane to herself.

Deciding that idea was better than the alternative, she retreated deep within her own mind and concentrated on weaving a cord. She formed several strands, braiding them together until she had a thick, solid rope that shimmered green and extended up through her consciousness. Working quickly in order to preserve her energy, she detached her consciousness from her body and worked her way toward Zane's soul, wrapping the cord around the silver mist until she had it secured to herself.

Then, slowly and carefully, she dragged the soul back to the body, sinking deep within him in order to plant the soul back where it belonged. Blood dripped from her nose as she forced herself to stretch for more and more power whilst refusing to let black magic in to tamper with the white she needed for her current task.

Lux anchored Zane's soul to his body with the rope, then followed that same cord back into her own body, opening her eyes and blinking rapidly as her vision cleared. She could feel an itch at the back of her brain and shook her head in a feeble attempt to dislodge it. When she still itched, she rubbed the heels of her hands over her eyes and wiped the blood from her lip. Zane's chest rose and fell rhythmically as he slept on the bed, and she thought his face held slightly more color than it had even moments before.

Looking down at Zane, she reached out and squeezed his hand, her whispered words more for herself than for his benefit. "All I can do now is wait and see if it worked."

Lux rubbed her head to fight off the oncoming headache and stared at Zane for several more seconds, assuring herself that he was improving. She could feel him in the back of her mind, strong and steady, and tried to ignore the sensation of having another person in her head.

Thinking of Damon and Greer and the psychic link that had connected them even through to the moment of death, she shook her head in disbelief and spoke out loud, desperate to fill the deafening silence of the house as it waited for the storm to strike. "How the fuck did you people get used to this?"

Muttering out loud, she wound her way down to the kitchen to scrounge for food. In what she assumed was a parting gift from Gabriel, there was a bunch of bananas on the counter, a half dozen apples, and a basket of strawberries. Curious, Lux began opening cabinets, humming in delight when she found coffee, tea bags, dried fruit, oatmeal, pasta, jarred sauce, some soup and a myriad of other canned and dried goods.

"Either I hit the jackpot or Gabriel was feeling generous."

She took a chance and opened the fridge, her face splitting into a wide grin when she saw a whole chicken, eight eggs, a chunk of cheese, some bread, and what appeared to be some sort of beef. Blessing Gabriel's name, she grabbed an apple and sank her teeth into it, enjoying the sweet gush of juice that swept over her tongue. More than almost anything she wanted to cook some of the fresh food, but she was determined to wait until Zane woke up for that. She would make do with some of the fruit and a can of soup in the meantime.

Gabriel wasn't a fan of being nervous. He hesitated half a dozen times as he paced his room, debating on whether to go down and speak with Zeke or not. The advice from Lux rolled its way through his mind, bouncing off everything and ricocheting back and forth, allowing him to think of nothing else. Amaya was the most important thing in his life. More than he had ever wanted anything—including Alaria—he wanted a relationship with his daughter. The distance between them tugged at his heart and pained him, and he wanted desperately to close that gap.

Closing his eyes and throwing caution to the wind, he disappeared and reappeared in Zeke's bedroom. The woman in question was standing at her dresser, clad in a baggy shirt and flannel pants, with her arms above her head plaiting her hair into a braid. Dev, her husband, sat at the foot of the bed, tugging off his boots. Gabriel immediately realized it was late in a human day and that he had likely chosen the wrong time to come. Cursing himself, he looked between the two and spoke, cringing at how pompous and stiff his voice sounded.

"I would like to speak with Ezekiel privately."

Dev lifted his eyebrows. "That's not likely to happen. What do you want, Gabriel? In case you haven't noticed, she's pregnant. She can't exactly run out on any missions for you for the next few months."

"I am not here to argue or to order. I wish to speak with you, Ezekiel, for no more than ten minutes. We can talk here if you do not wish to leave this place, or you could accompany me to my room. It is your choice."

Zeke exchanged a look with Dev, who sighed and stood. "I'll go hang out with Deacon downstairs for a little while. If you need anything, just yell." He stooped to kiss her head and rubbed his hand over the protrusion of her belly. "I won't be far."

"I'll be fine. Gabe's not here to hurt me. Are you, Gabe?"

Gabriel scoffed. "Certainly not. I would not ever even contemplate such a thing." He waited until Dev had closed the door and his footsteps descended the steps. "I've come here to apologize to you, Ezekiel."

Zeke's brow creased and she sat down on the bed, folding her legs beneath her. "You've come to apologize? Have you ever done that before?"

Gabriel glared at her. "Is it too much to ask of you that you do not mock me as I do this?"

"Yes."

He huffed. "Very well. I'll say this quickly then, and I hope you take this as sincere, because it is. I am truly very sorry for the loss of your parents. Damon and Greer were good people. They were good warriors, and they were good parents to you. Their greatest testament is you. I do not doubt that they were incredibly proud of you when they died, and they would be proud of you still. I am sorry for how things turned out. I never contemplated that Rafael would do as he did, and for that I am very sorry. Had I known, I would have considered other options. I have made mistakes, Ezekiel. To my own chagrin, I am not perfect, try as I might. In any case, it is my desire that you know I regret how things turned out with your parents, and if I could take it back, I would, but as you know, the time line must remain intact to preserve the present."

Zeke goggled at Gabriel, visibly struggling to make sense of what had just happened. Tears welled in her eyes and she wiped her hand across them angrily. "Thank you for saying that." She offered a half-smile. "I'm angry with you over it, and probably always will be, but I think it'll help knowing you're angry with yourself, too. It really sucked thinking you still believed you'd done the right thing." She stood and crossed the room to stand in front of him. "I accept your apology, Gabriel. I don't forgive you, but now I'll work on it."

"When I went to them and told them of the problems that you faced, they did not hesitate. They did not question." He smiled sadly at the memory. "For what it's worth, I would not have asked you to whore yourself. That was a petty response to a barb from my brother. I should not have said it, and for that I am also sorry. I hope you know how much they loved you and how important you were to them. I also hope you take comfort in the fact that in some way, they are still alive now. Greer is currently carried in the belly of her mother, much as you carry your son. Your father is a small child, still holding his father's hand to walk."

Zeke reached out and squeezed Gabriel's hand. "Thank you for coming here tonight. I appreciate it. I know you did what you thought you had to. I disagree with you, obviously, but it makes it better knowing you feel bad about it."

Gabriel looked uncomfortable. "You are welcome. That is all I had to say. Unless you wish to continue to converse, I have business with Michael. Shall I send Dev back up to you?"

Zeke shook her head. "Nah. Let him enjoy playing poker with Deacon."

"Only Gabriel could sound like a complete pretentious prick while apologizing." Zeke stared up at the ceiling as she spoke. "I think he seemed honest enough about it, and I'm glad he did it, but damn can that Angel sound like a dick no matter what the occasion."

Amaya giggled. "Yes, he can." She folded her arms under her head. "Deacon said that after he left you, he went down and told Michael he'd had a change of heart and would like to start working with some of the Nephilim. He's going to start training some of them and commanding some of the squads. He didn't even try to talk to me. It's like there's an alien living in his body or something."

Zeke groaned. "Don't even mention aliens. That would be the last fucking thing we need right now. God, what are those old shows people used to watch in the middle of the afternoon when they weren't working?"

Amaya wrinkled her nose. "Soap operas?"

"Yeah! That's the one! Can't you just see that as the plot to a soap opera? The world is at war, demons and Angels battle for dominance when out of the sky comes...dun dun dun...the Kardashians!"

Amaya snorted and rolled onto her side to laugh. "Oh my God, Zeke, you are awful at pop culture! The Kardashians used to be a family. It's the Cardassians that were the aliens!"

Zeke waved her hand dismissively. "Close enough." She yawned. "Dev's going to be coming up to bed soon, and he won't want to sleep with you."

"Then his taste is questionable."

"I think he has good taste, personally." She propped herself up on her elbow. "Seriously, though, I wish I knew what was going on with Gabriel. He's not acting like himself."

Amaya shrugged carelessly. "Good. Who he is hasn't been working for a while. Maybe he's making a change. God knows he needs to. I hope he is. Whatever the reason, he's apologized to you, which is a plus. He's taking an interest in the war, which is an even bigger plus, and he didn't even try to talk to me, which means, for the moment anyway, he's respecting me enough to keep his distance from me. All of those are bonuses as far as I'm concerned."

"I hope he's changing, for your sake. If he comes down here, gets involved, and starts being who your mother has always claimed he could be, you might get to have a relationship with your father worth having."

Amaya made a noncommittal noise in the back of her throat. "I don't know if I want one at all, but I certainly don't want one with the way he's been acting for the past few years. He was different when I was a kid. Then when we got old enough to fight, he changed and got to be like he is now."

"I believe him when he says he wants to protect you." Zeke sat up and flipped on the lamp. "Though for whatever reason, he's trying now, and I think you should at least wait and see if he fucks it up. I'm certainly not a Gabriel fan, but I'm curious to see how this goes." She looked over her shoulder at her friend. "I'm going back to my room."

Amaya yawned. "Okay. I'll see you in the morning. Do we know what's going on with Lux yet? Did Gabe say anything about

Zane?"

"No, he didn't. If I'd have thought about it, I'd have asked him. Maybe he said something to Michael. We'll check on it in the morning. Right now, I want sex with Dev, and then I want sleep."

Amaya laughed and jerked the blankets up to her chin. "Have fun."

"Oh, don't worry. I will."

Amaya lay in bed for another fifteen minutes, unable to relax and sleep. She rolled to her feet and left the room, padding down the stairs to where Michael sat at his desk, working on something.

"Hey."

The Angel looked up and smiled. "You should be sleeping. This is well into your sleep cycle."

"I know, but I couldn't fall asleep. Zeke told me about Gabriel's visit. Did he say anything about Zane or Lux?"

"Lux is with Zane and is correcting the damage Gabriel and the Angel of Death did with their little experiment. She has assured him that Zane will be fine. He made sure the house they are in is stocked with food and is well protected before he left. There was some mention of a hurricane, so I imagine they will be there for a few days."

Amaya dropped into one of the chairs. "Do you believe him?"

"I do. Gabriel is many things, Amaya, but he is not a liar. Angels do not lie. They can omit, but they do not lie. I trust him when he tells me Zane is fine. Lux is with him, and they're both safe. I anticipate that they will continue their search for the offspring of Beelzebub once Zane is ready to continue. For what it's worth, Gabriel reports that Lux is very confident she can reinstate Zane to his previous state. Unless I hear otherwise from Lux, I see no reason not to believe them."

"Do you know where the other four Cambion are?"

"Gage is working on that as well. We have a preliminary location on two and nothing on two. We're also beginning to keep tabs on Beelzebub in order to insure that we can get to him when we need to as well. The problem there is that it appears he is with Lilith and Azazel. The three of them seem to be keeping close these days. I suspect it is to avoid what happened thirty years ago from happening again."

"They don't have any more wings to carve out." Deacon spoke from the doorway as he entered the room. He looked down at Amaya as he sat in the other chair. "Couldn't you sleep, either?"

She shook her head. "Too much going on for sleep."

Michael smiled at his son. "Regardless of the state of their wings, they are sticking together because they know when we come for Beelzebub, that is but one step away from coming for Lucifer."

"Lilith wouldn't die for him. She'd run screaming and trying to protect her own ass." Deacon ran his hands through his hair and scowled. "I hate that fucking bitch."

Michael's eyes flashed. "That's a very common emotion when it comes to your mother."

Amaya giggled. "It gets me every time. I always forget she's your mother until someone says it and then it hits me all over again. Jesus, Deacon, your mom is worse than my dad."

"There isn't even a comparison to be made there." Deacon leaned back in the chair and extended his legs out in front of him. "Lucifer has to know we're getting close. He's going to make a move sooner rather than later. Lux and Zane need to be careful. I think we took them off guard with the sword because we did it differently than we normally do things, but with this we're just using plain old force, which is what they're expecting. They know we're coming and they're going to come for us, too."

Amaya bared her teeth in a savage grin. "Let them come." She reached out and gripped Deacon's hand in hers. "This is what we were born for, Deacon. They'll come, and we'll kill them."

CHAPTER EIGHT

September 2nd, 2060 – Wilmington, North Carolina

LUX RAN her fingers over the dusty top of the piano that sat in the corner of what had once been a formal living room. It was amazing how well preserved some places were. In some homes, there was dried blood and debris. Others were burned to the ground. In the cities, almost everything had been raided until there was very little left. Further out, in the rural areas, houses could be found that looked as if the inhabitants had simply gone out to dinner and would be back later.

Clothing still hung in closets and was folded in drawers. Televisions sat on mantles, and wood was stacked for the fireplace. Lux had found enough clothing to fit her to last a lifetime. There were a few things she thought would work for Zane, though most of the men's clothing had consisted of suits.

She pushed one key on the piano and shivered as the sound filled the room. She lifted the seat of the bench and pulled out a sheaf of sheet music, rifling through until she found something that looked appropriate for the stormy weather.

Testing the keys, she adjusted the pedals and positioned her fingers over the ivory, depressing them as her eyes scanned the page for the notes. Haunting music filled the house, rising up to the second floor.

Lux let the notes surround her, closing her eyes as she

remembered the music and smiling as her fingers flitted over the keys from muscle memory. She felt Zane before she heard him, and she whirled, her elbows striking the piano with a sour note as she saw him at the foot of the stairs.

His black hair was mussed and hanging around his face while a thick scruff covered his jaw. He was shirtless, the muscles in his chest rippling as he walked. His eyes burned dark blue as Lux stared at him.

"Are you normal?"

Zane looked at her in confusion. "What are you talking about? Where are we? How did we get here?"

Overcome with relief and emotion, Lux leapt from the bench and raced across the room, throwing herself into Zane's arms and clamping her mouth on his. She grabbed his hair with both hands and wrapped her legs around his waist, crushing herself against him.

Taken aback, Zane stumbled several steps trying to get his balance and tripped on the three stairs leading into the recessed living room. They tumbled down them in a tangle of limbs and landed in a heap at the bottom of the steps. Lux grunted as she came to a stop resting against the couch and giggled.

"I suppose that's what I get for attacking a man who's been unconscious for what could have been the best part of a week."

Zane looked at her blankly. "I have no idea what you're talking about. The last thing I remember is stirring noodles."

"Gabriel Nephil-napped you and took you up to Heaven for him and your father to scramble your brains trying to figure out why you can't touch people without killing them. They tried to remove your emotions but ended up removing your soul. Somehow you managed to find me in a dream, and I came here and fixed you." She looked at him sheepishly. "I may have been slightly excited to see you awake and cognitively aware. You're also not drooling and soiling yourself, which are both giant pluses."

Zane laughed and turned his head to look at her. "Thank you for putting me back, even if I don't remember being gone in the first place." He glanced down at his hands and paled when he realized he wasn't wearing his gloves. "Did I touch you when you attacked me?"

Lux followed his gaze. "I don't know. I don't remember. I was too busy kissing you senseless." She sat up. "Full disclosure. To put you back, I had to create a link—think like Damon and Greer had—between us to anchor your soul to something. It had been out too long and didn't want to go back in, so I had to force the issue. You can probably feel it. It feels like your brain itches."

Zane grimaced. "Now that you mention it."

"Sorry. Had to be done. You'd be dead otherwise." She lifted one shoulder in a shrug, scowling when her night shirt slipped off, baring the top part of her arm. "Everything here fits almost right. Anyway, I don't know if I'll be able to take it out. We can try in a few weeks once you're stronger, but it may have to stay put."

"What will it do?"

"We should be able to figure out how to talk to each other psychically now. Other than that, as far as I know, not a whole hell of a lot. I'm not a Healer, so I won't be needing to borrow your energy for that. Neither of us can die on the dreamplane without severing the link, which is a plus, so I don't think there's a downside other than the fact that we'll have to learn how to not be in each other's heads when we don't want to be." Lux looked sheepish. "See, right now I know that you're wishing you could finish what I started, and while I'm perfectly on board with the sentiment, I don't think you want me knowing what's in your head."

Zane ran his hands through his hair. "No, I don't, and I don't want to know what's in yours, either. We'll figure it out." He stared down at his hands. "Fucking hell I wish I could remember if I had put my hands on you or not."

Quick as lightning, Lux reached out and grabbed one of his hands in both of hers, holding it tightly. Zane tried to yank away, then relaxed when she didn't immediately keel over.

"I'm not dead."

"Am I hurting you?"

She shook her head. "No. It feels a little tingly, but that could just be excitement. This could also be because of the link. Our brains are connected now. It would hurt you to kill me, so your power might not work on me at all now. Or maybe they fixed you and now you only can kill the bad guys. Or maybe they installed an off switch so that you have to actually try to use your power. I think that would be best."

Zane studied their hands—her bare skin on his—and smiled. "I hope it's not just this link you installed. It would be a miracle to not have to worry about bumping into someone on the street and killing them." He rubbed his thumb over the back of her hand. "You have really soft skin."

Lux made a noise in her throat and glanced around, trying to allay the nerves in her gut. Her heart pounded in her chest, and an uncomfortable heat formed in her gut. "I should let everyone else know you're okay and make you some food. I'm sure you have to be hungry."

He laughed. "I could probably use a shower and a shave, too. My whole face itches along with my brain." He climbed to his feet and pulled her up, tugging her close. "Lux."

"Zane."

"I'm seriously considering propositioning you."

Lux grinned and tipped her head back. "Funny, I was just sitting there wondering how in the world I was going to convince you to take me to bed later. Even if this is temporary, we've both wanted this for a while, and I'm not going to waste an opportunity to jump into bed with you."

"Are there condoms anywhere in this house?"

"I don't know."

Zane glanced at the window and the rain striking the panes viciously. "Well, let's hope whoever lived here way back when believed in safe sex. Otherwise, we're either being uncomfortable until the storm breaks, or we're getting wet running from house to house on a search for rubbers so we can both get laid."

Lux pressed a hand to her stomach. "I'll make dinner. You shower, shave, and search."

He slid one hand around the back of her neck and drew her close, savoring the feel of her skin beneath his fingers. "I can touch you."

She leaned her head on his chest for a moment. "I know."

"I don't know how long it'll last. We have to assume that it'll go away when you sever the link. If my soul is only anchored to my body through this link to your mind, then it makes sense for me to be able to touch you now. This will probably not last forever."

Lux rubbed her cheek over his skin and closed her eyes, enjoying the feel of his fingers on her neck and the heat from his body next to hers. "I'm not a planner. I like to live in the moment. If you had been able to touch me and had known that you could when we left Michael's and started this, would we have been in bed together already?"

"Yes."

It was said simply, without inflection, and without hesitation. Lux felt a sharp tug of something around her abdomen at the statement and took a half step back to look up at him, her eyes serious.

"I'm an honest person. I don't see the point in games, and I've never been the type to wait on what I want. I want to go to bed with you. I'm not particularly interested in marriage and babies and the proverbial white picket fence. I like fighting and hot sex and never being bored. I like being challenged. You challenge me, you turn me on, and I want to get into bed with you. If we fuck one time and it doesn't work, well, no harm no foul. If it's awesome and we do it a hundred times before the link severs and you can't put your hands on me, well, we can be creative, and I don't mind a little kink." She chuckled when he glared at her. "My point is that I'm a live in the moment girl. Here, in this moment, I can feel your hands on my body, and you don't have to be scared to put them there. So take advantage of it, and worry about everything else when it comes. Because it will come. It always does, and we will meet it head on just like we always do."

Zane rubbed a lock of her hair between his fingers. "I feel like I'm doing this wrong. God, Lux, I want this, but I want to do it right. I don't want you to think you're just the first willing female I found now that my hands aren't more deadly than bullets."

"We don't know that. It might just be me that you can touch. And I am the first willing woman you found, but I've been willing for months, so that's okay." She slid her hands down to his belt and toyed with the leather strip. "Let's be honest here. We're not Amaya and Deacon. They're so in love with each other they can't see straight, and neither of them will admit it or act on it. Okay. That's their business. Dev wanted Zeke from the second he saw her, but he wanted all of her, forever. He set out to convince her that his way was the right way, and he's just so damned sweet and persistent and such a nice guy that he did it.

"I'm not looking for anything long term. I'm not after a husband. I'm not after a future. I accept that we might die, and I accept that as soon as we sever that link, we might go back to how things were before you got Angel-napped. I'm okay with that. I'm sorry, but for me, this is physical. I've been attracted to you for months, and I want to have sex with you. No strings, no apologies. If it's good, I'd like to continue having sex with you until such a time that one of us decides that we don't want to any longer. If that's okay with you, can we stop talking about the what ifs and the hypotheticals and get on with the condom search?"

Zane studied her, his eyes serious. For a long moment, Lux

feared he was going to say no. His gaze said more than she understood, and her eyes flitted back and forth between his, trying to make sense of what she saw there. After a long moment, he nodded.

"I'll check upstairs after I take a shower. If you want to wait until I'm done, I'll help you with dinner."

She took a step back and continued to study him. "Gabriel left some steaks. I think I'll toss them in a skillet and pop some of the potatoes in the microwave. I can make it work with not very much magic at all. It won't take long."

Zane headed toward the stairs, paused, and turned back. "Lux?"

She looked over her shoulder at him, her hair flowing down her back, escaping the braid that she had contained it in. "Yeah?"

"It's not scratching an itch for me. I want you. Not a woman in general. You, in particular. I hope you feel the same way about this."

The corners of her mouth turned up, and she pulled the wrap she wore over her nightshirt tighter around her body. "If it was just a penis I wanted, there are any number of truly excellent vibrators available, and no shortage of attractive Nephilim I could fuck. I haven't."

He stared at her intently for several more seconds. "Okay then. I'm going to go wash off and find some rubbers."

CHAPTER NINE

LUX HUMMED under her breath as she flipped chunks of meat. She picked up her glass and sipped the wine she'd found in the pantry, approving of the rich flavor. At least alcohol preserved well.

The tiles under her feet were cold, and she glanced toward the fireplace, making a mental note to make a fire before they went to bed. Shivering, she decided to light the damn thing and warm the house. Continuing to hum, she descended the three steps into the living room and walked right into an invisible wall.

She was flung back ten feet, crashing into the island and slamming her head against the wood of the cabinets. Confused and disoriented, she rubbed her head and climbed to her feet, the hair on the back of her neck rising as she looked around the room. Sensing nothing, she walked back to the spot and extended her hand, searching for anything to explain the jolt of energy she'd received.

The moment she touched it, she knew what it was. Swearing under her breath, Lux followed the trap around, finding the edges to determine how much room she had to work with. Reaching out, she tried to follow the link up to Zane, but found it blocked off by the trap.

"Fucking hell, I'm human! I can't get caught in traps!" She paced the length of the kitchen. "Zane! Zane, there's a trap! Get down here if you can!"

Zane appeared at the top of the stairs, wearing jeans and a black tank with his hair wet and curling around his face. He looked confused. "What the fuck are you talking about?"

"Don't come over here. There's a trap. Get out of the house and figure out who's after us. They're using some sort of magic or power that I've never seen before. You need to find the trap and break it so I can get out. I've never seen one we can get stuck in before. This is fucking new, and fucking annoying."

"I don't sense anything."

"Neither do I, but I got tossed across this kitchen. Now get out of here before they get you sealed in, too."

Zane disappeared with a crack and Lux was left to pace, and to fret. She heard a second crack and whirled to scold Zane for coming back, stopping when she saw a tall blonde woman. The woman wore a lace sundress and had curly blonde hair and blue eyes. Her fingers were tipped with inch long, blood red nails.

"Good evening, Lux. How are you?"

Lux crossed her arms. "Who the fuck are you?"

The woman sighed. "Why is it that I have to keep introducing myself to you people? Why is my reputation not preceding me? You should know who I am, you stupid twit. I birthed one of your very good friends." She smiled. "Tell me, how is my darling Deacon? Doing well with his father?"

For the first time, a ball of fear formed deep within Lux's stomach. "Hello, Lilith."

"Ah, see now, you do know who I am. I'm glad to see that Zane ran off to try and deal with your cage. He's going to have more than he can handle on the roof, I suspect, dealing with Isaiah."

Lux cocked her head. "There's a Cambion with a Biblical name?"

Lilith giggled and tapped her fingers on her chest. "Isn't it just hilarious? I thought I'd rub it in God's face just a bit when I named that one. I did the same thing with Deacon. It means 'pastor'. Did you know that? Of course, I intended for him to be fighting on my side, but then Michael got ahold of him and that dream was dashed. This time it's been much different."

Warning bells went off in Lux's head. "Isaiah is your son?"

"Yes, of course. And I have a daughter as well. Serafina. She's beautiful. Just like her mother. And her father."

"Who is their father?"

Lilith smiled demurely. "All of my children have different

fathers. Michael of course is Deacon's father. That pregnancy was accidental. Isaiah is Beelzebub's. He was not very good in bed. I refused to continue to reproduce with him after the once. He couldn't give me an orgasm for anything, and I insist upon orgasms when I have sex. Come to think of it, Michael didn't give me an orgasm when I conceived Deacon, either, but he was trying to piss me off after I betrayed him and had Braxton's whole family killed. But that's neither here nor there. You were asking me about Serafina's father, weren't you?"

Lux swallowed. "Yes. Who is her father?"

"Why Lucifer, of course. Who else would it be? You couldn't have possibly thought that it was going to be Azazel's, did you? That Devil has, at last count, three thousand Cambion with his blood. I certainly wasn't going to let him impregnate me. I do have standards, you know."

The whole room did a sick spin as Lux struggled to make sense of what Lilith had said. She took a deep breath and closed her eyes for a heartbeat. "Why are you here? We didn't even know about Isaiah and Serafina until you just told me."

"Well, no one else is going to find out since I'm going to kill you." Lilith twirled in a circle, girlish and full of energy. Lux wondered, not for the first time, whether or not the she-Devil was all there in the head.

"Did Beelzebub send you? He sent you and his son into danger so that he could go somewhere and hide where he's safe? What kind of father does that?"

Lilith blinked several times as if trying to make sense of what Lux had said. She smiled brightly. "You aren't going to fool me, little witch. I volunteered to come and take care of you. We've had to lie low for way too long. I am sick to God-damn-death of sitting in Hell and twiddling my fucking thumbs while all the Cambion and Nephilim get to have all the fun. I wanted to have some fun, so when we sensed the power signature off that spell you did earlier—powerful little bit of magic, by the way—we decided to take advantage of it. I thought it would be good for Isaiah to come and kill some Nephilim. He needs to learn sometime."

Lux listened for some sign of a fight but couldn't hear anything over the sound of the hurricane raging outside. "How old is he?"

Lilith waved her hand dismissively. "Oh, I don't know. Twenty, twenty-five. Something like that. He was born several years after Deacon. How old is Deacon?"

"Almost thirty."

"Then closer to twenty-five." She closed her fist and smiled when a whip appeared in her hand. "I never got to fight your mother much. They tricked me when they came for my wings. I so desperately wanted to kill that redheaded bitch that I could taste it, but she's stayed just out of my reach all these years. I'll have to settle for gutting her child like a fish."

Lux's citrine glowed bright yellow on her chest, and she let her power whip up within her. "Don't think I'm going to be so easy to kill, Lilith. I'm just as strong as my mother. Plus, there's a touch of Michael in me."

Lilith giggled. "Honey, I've had more than a touch of Michael in me." She crossed over the boundary of the trap. "It took my witches the best part of ten years to figure out how to trap Nephilim, but we've got it now. You can't get out, and we can walk through like there's nothing there at all." She grinned, baring her teeth. "It'll be so much easier to kill you when you can't run away."

"I wouldn't run away even if I could." Lux's eyes turned white as she allowed her power to course through her. "Drop the trap, Lilith. Let's do this on equal footing. Unless you're scared of me."

Lilith scoffed. "I'm not scared of anyone. I can't have you running away. If we don't keep you from killing Lucifer, you'll keep trying to put us all back, and we don't want that. We've only been out three decades. That's not nearly long enough. The easiest way to keep that from happening is to kill you all. That's exactly what I intend to do." She reached out with her hand and very deliberately closed her fingers, wrapping an invisible vise around Lux's neck. "Your power doesn't come close to mine, child."

Lux reached within herself and let black magic flow through her. She forced Lilith back, driving the Devil back several steps. "Don't bet on it. My mother wrapped you up in witch rope once, and I can do it, too."

"They got me in a goddamn trap and had six other people. It wasn't a fair fight. I wasn't ready for her, and I had just given birth. I was at the weakest I have ever been in my existence. Delivering the whelps took me years to recover from. It took so much of my power to bring them to term that I had to hide out for close to five years after each of them. I'm not nearly so weak now." She lowered her voice to a conspiratorial whisper. "Those rumors that I'm stronger than Lucifer? They're true, darling girl. There's a reason Michael couldn't chain me to a rock."

Lux chuckled. "I'm sure it had nothing to do with the fact that he was fucking you." She lashed out with her magic, knocking Lilith back several feet.

She drove the Devil back with a stream of magic, keeping her within the confines of the trap. She formed fire with her mind, circling them both with it, spreading her arms, and wrapping Lilith in her power.

"Silly little girl, you'll blow yourself up before you take in enough of the black to destroy me."

"You know I could do it. I could let enough in that you would die."

Lilith looked scared for the first time. "You could. Possibly. I'll give you that. I don't think you're willing to give up your life for it, though. Not with so much left to do."

"If I'm going to die anyway, I'm going to take you out with me, you Devil bitch."

Lux opened the door further, flooding herself with black until the citrine around her throat cracked and broke open. Magic poured out of it, fractured, and a myriad of colors poured out. Her eyes darkened until they were black. She struggled to control the flow of magic, to direct it, engulfing Lilith in a tidal wave of power. The Devil screeched in outrage as she was enveloped and flailed to get through the haze at Lux.

Lilith was stronger. Lux had no doubt about that. Her only trump card was making Lilith believe that she was willing to die in order to defeat the Devil. The amount of magic that she could produce and control with her death would maybe be enough. Maybe. If she was lucky. But Lilith didn't need to know that.

Lux felt the give in the trap and Zane flood into her mind, his panic palpable just as her vision went black. Lilith disappeared with a scream and a loud crack. The fire that Lux had been using flared out of control, engulfing the kitchen and spreading through the lower level in a matter of seconds.

She struggled to close the door. Blood dripped off her chin as it leaked from her eyes and nose. Her eyes flickered between white, red, and black, and her knees wavered. Pain speared through her body and she toppled over, striking her head on the tile and sinking into cool blackness.

"There's a girl. Come on out of it."

Lux groaned and shifted away from the voice, her head

throbbing as she gained consciousness slowly. Zane's voice was persistent.

"Come on, Lux. I know you're awake. I can feel your annoyance in my head. Open those pretty green eyes and give me a good glare."

Obliging him, Lux peeled open one eyelid and directed what she hoped was a death stare at him. "Just leave me alone and let me die."

"If I'd been willing to do that, I wouldn't have run into a burning house to save your ass."

The events flooded back and Lux sat up quickly, grabbing her head as pain speared through it. "Lilith has two more kids! She has a fucking kid with Satan! That Cambion you were fighting is Beelzebub's kid. It isn't really a Cambion. Can't be."

Zane laid his hand on her shoulder. "Devils can't be born. If it was born, it's Cambion. That's how Deacon's human. Only humans are born. The kid was fucking powerful as hell, but not trained very well. I can tell it's his mother who's been in charge. I almost fucking had him when the house went up in flames. He flashed out before I had a chance to grab him. He'll be hard to catch, but from the little I saw, he's as mentally unstable as she is. I'm just glad that we found out about him before we went after Lucifer."

"Zane. Lucifer has a daughter. Spawn of Satan, literally. We're going to have to kill her, too, before Amaya and Deacon can go after Lucifer."

"Calm down. I doubt we could kill her. You were about to blow yourself up from the black magic trying to take out Lilith. We can't take out Lucifer. That's for the others."

"I wasn't going to blow up." Pouting, she crossed her arms. "I just wanted to make Lilith think that I was willing to do it. I didn't actually intend to go through with it, but I had to make her believe I would."

"You made me believe you would." He stroked his hand over her hair gently. "You scared me."

"I scared me, too." She looked around. "Where are we?"

Zane followed her gaze, taking in the bare mattress on the floor where she was lying, the one bare light bulb on the ceiling, and the toilet in the corner. "Best I can tell, it's some sort of a studio apartment. I grabbed you and just started flashing as far as I could, trying to put as much distance between us and that house as I could. Once I had flashed a dozen times, I was drained and needed to rest.

I hotwired a car and drove for three hours before I got too tired to even keep my eyes open, and this is the first place that I found. You've been unconscious for almost twenty-four hours. I slept for damn near twelve myself."

"I'm going to need to go see Mom. My citrine fractured and I'm completely drained. I'm going to be useless to you for a couple days. We need to let them know about Serafina—Lucifer's daughter—and we need to start hunting down these damn Cambion again. They're coming for us, Zane. We're being hunted. There's no safe place to go. We have to get this going, and fast."

"I agree with you. Do you know where your parents are? Because I can't do much of anything right now. So if we can drive there, great, but I'm not up to flashing far for another day or two."

Lux leaned her head on his shoulder. "Aren't we a fucking pair? I nearly blow myself up going after the Devil bitch, and then you run yourself into the ground saving my ass after I did it."

Zane expelled a long-suffering sigh and laid his hand on hers. "All that and I never got sex. Never even found the damn condoms." He looked around woefully. "Even if I could overlook the fact that we're both covered in soot and smelly, I seriously doubt we're going to find any in here."

Lux giggled despite herself. "I think our plans of getting laid are temporarily suspended, darlin'. We'll have to pick up once we find some running water, clean clothes, and a bed that won't give us an STD." She grimaced at the state of the mattress on which she lay. "Is there food?"

"Not a fucking thing. I checked the other units in the building and got nada. I didn't want to go too far in case you woke up and I was out of range or something." He stretched and winced when he smelled himself. "Lux, I stink. I do not enjoy smelling bad."

She heaved herself to her feet. "Well, let's find a car with some gas in it and get out of here. We'll find some food, some clothes, some water, and a bed, in that order."

Chapter Ten

September 8th, 2060 – Indiana

Aradia opened the door and bit the inside of her cheek to keep from laughing when she saw Lux and Zane. Both wore ill-fitting clothes, Lux's hair was ratty and greasy, and Zane desperately needed to shave.

"Gage, Lux is here! Zane, too!"

Gage loped down the stairs, still spry after having aged thirty years, though his hair was graying and lines had started their determined march across his face. "Is everything okay?" He drew to a stop and let out a low whistle. "What the fuck happened to the two of you?"

Lux pushed her way into the kitchen. "Lilith."

Aradia's eyes darkened. "Say no more. Come in, Zane, won't you, and close the door. It's still so hot out there today."

Zane stepped into the kitchen and closed the door behind him. "I'm sorry to just pop in this way."

"Nonsense. We told you before that our home is your home. That hasn't changed in the last few months. Won't ever change as far as we're concerned." Aradia went to the stove. "I'll start some dinner. You both look like you're starving. There's one bathroom down here and one upstairs, so you can both shower. Gage, while I'm cooking, see if you can't find Zane some clothes to wear in one of the neighbor's houses. There's some stuff in the second bedroom upstairs that should fit Lux, but nothing here for Zane, I'm afraid."

Gage hugged Lux and clapped Zane on the back. "I was glad when you called. We hadn't heard from you in a while. Your mother worries when you go too long without calling."

Aradia smiled softly and didn't say a word until the door was securely shut behind her husband. "We both worry. Go, wash. You'll both feel better clean than you do now. I guarantee it. There were the remnants of a pretty impressive garden behind the house that I managed to finesse, so there are some fresh vegetables with dinner, though not much in the way of fresh meat, I'm afraid."

Lux laid her hands on her mother's shoulders. "It's okay, Mom. At this point, we've been eating whatever we can find straight out of the can. Something hot is going to be a vast improvement." She headed to the stairs. "I'll shower upstairs since that's where the clothes that will reportedly fit me are located."

Zane looked at Aradia's back, not sure what to do or say. She turned to study him, her stormy blue eyes lit up with curiosity.

"Is something wrong, Zane?"

He thought about lying to her. He thought about saying nothing was wrong or avoiding the question. Aradia and Alaria had mothered him when he hadn't wanted to be mothered. Aradia had taken him to Michael and stayed with him for months, leaving her own child to do so. She had been there when no one else had.

"I love you."

Aradia's eyes filled with tears and she hugged Zane tightly. "Oh, baby, I know you do. I love you, too. So does Gage." She framed his face with her hands. "I'm glad it's you helping Lux with this. I trust you with her."

"There's something I want to tell you, but I'm afraid she'll be mad at me for doing it."

"Don't you worry about her." Aradia lifted one eyebrow and glanced toward the stairs. "I made that temper, and I can handle it. What's going on?"

"I'm sure we'll tell you the whole story later, but Gabriel and my biological father kidnapped me to try to fix my powers so that I could touch people. We don't know if they're fixed, but I can touch Lux now. The problem is that when they were messing around in my head, they separated my soul from my body and to put it back, Lux had to link herself to me. So we're not sure if I can touch her because what Gabriel did worked or because of the link."

"Well, that's easy enough to figure out. Why is that a

problem?"

"That's not the problem." Zane yanked on his hair in frustration and paced the kitchen. "Dammit, I don't want to say this to you because you're her mother, but fucking hell, Aradia, you're the closest thing I've got to one, too!"

Aradia fought back a new wave of tears and very deliberately grabbed Zane's hands, cursing the leather that shielded his skin from hers. "Zane, my love, I've known you since you were a boy. I've helped train you, I worked with you. I am here for you the same way I am for Lux. She is my daughter, yes, but I love you, too, in much the same way. When you came to us and decided to stay, you became a part of this family. You're mine in the same way Deacon and Dev are mine, or Zeke and Amaya. Not by birth, but in my heart. The same way Lux belonged to Damon and Greer and does belong to Alaria and Braxton and Michael. Tell me what you need to say."

Zane dropped into one of the kitchen chairs and put his head in his hands. "I'm in love with her."

Aradia sat next to him. "With Lux?"

He nodded miserably. "Head over heels, totally gone, can't see straight in love with her. I didn't know it until I woke up and I came downstairs and she was playing a piano, with her hair in this braid. All I could think about was how she looked, sitting there on that piano bench, with this hurricane going outside, and it was like the whole world ground to a halt. I've had feelings for a while, but that was the first time I thought I loved her. After the attack, when I thought Lilith had killed her, well, that just cemented things."

"And Lux doesn't return the feelings?"

Zane grimaced. "This is the part that I didn't want to tell you."

"Zane, I have had sex. I'm not going to kick you out or string you up if you've deflowered my daughter."

"I haven't." He took a deep breath. "I don't think she feels the same way, Aradia. She wants me, but in a physical way, not for more. I want that, too, please don't hit me, but I want more than that."

"Of course you do, and I'm not going to hit you." Aradia laughed and patted his hand gently. "Here's my bit of sage wisdom. Do with it what you will. Lux is stubborn, and she is headstrong. If you want her for the long-term, then you need to let her come around to it on her own terms and in her own time. Be patient, be there for her, and give her only what she asks for. If you push, she'll get scared and run. If you give her only what she asks you to, she'll ask for more and more until you're both where you want to be." She laid her hand on his cheek and stood. "For what it's worth, son, my money's on you." Bending to kiss his cheek, she hugged him close. "Now, please go shower."

Aradia watched as Zane went into the bathroom. She heard the shower start and went back to the stove, preoccupied with thoughts of Lux and Zane. Gage slipped back in the kitchen door holding a stack of clothes.

"I think this should do it. Is he upstairs or down?"

"Down." Aradia stood on her tiptoes and kissed Gage gently. "Zane is in love with Lux."

Gage's eyebrows drew together. "Well fuck." He sighed deeply and looked at the closed bathroom door. "I like the boy. I like him a lot. He's a good man, and he's trustworthy and stable and strong. But I don't know if I see a future there. He can't touch anyone without gloves on, Aradia."

"We'll see about that. Gabriel may have fixed the problem. He can touch Lux now. Gabriel apparently took it upon himself to fix Zane and ended up separating his soul. Lux linked the two of them to save him."

"So they're like Damon and Greer were, which would explain why he can touch her now. The only way to know for sure is for him to touch someone else and see if he can control it. I'm not a fan of that idea."

"I know you're not, but I am. I'm going to talk him into trying it out on me after we feed them. Lux has lost weight. I don't like it."

"They look like they've been having it rough, that's for sure. It's unusual for them to drive in instead of flash, too."

"We'll find out what's going on after we get some food in the both of them. Take Zane those clothes, please."

Lux stepped out of the shower and wrapped a towel around herself. She wrapped her hair in a second one and walked to the mirror, wiping her hand across the steam on the glass to clear it so she could see herself.

The skin under her eyes was bruised from little sleep and food, and her cheeks had started to hollow as she'd lost several pounds she couldn't afford to lose. She rubbed her hands over her face and whispered a glamour, doing nothing more than erasing the dark circles.

Satisfied that she looked more alive than dead, she entered the bedroom and began opening and closing drawers, pleasantly surprised at the contents. She founds jeans that fit, a bra only slightly too large, and a tank that was the right size. Most of the clothing in the drawers would work for her, and she made a note to take a few changes with her when they left.

She descended the stairs quickly, grabbing the newel post at the bottom of the steps and swinging to the left and into the kitchen. Her mother had placed bowls of salad on the table. She stood at the stove, checking the temperature on a pan of something, and a larger pan with a lid boiled on the back burner.

"I found some rice, so I made that, and there were four cans of beef stew, so I threw them in a pot and warmed it all up. I know you guys have to be starving. There should be plenty, and there's an apple tree in the back yard. I had your father pick some, and there were some oats in the pantry. I managed to make a crisp. I hope it'll be edible. I didn't have butter, so I had to make due with shortening."

"I'm sure it'll be great." Lux pulled the towel off her head and ran her fingers through her hair absently. "Where're Dad and Zane?"

"Dad is in the office making some calls. Zane is in the backyard. You took much longer in the shower than he did."

"I took a bath. The tub was there, and it just looked amazing, and I couldn't resist. I shaved my legs. It was awesome."

Aradia smiled. "I imagine so. I've got about ten minutes on the rice. Will you go tell Zane dinner is almost ready?"

"Sure."

Lux opened the kitchen door and stepped out onto the back deck. A cool breeze had begun to rustle through the leaves on the trees, and the sun was just starting to sink below the horizon. Zane was fifty yards behind the house, sitting on a swing and idly pushing himself back and forth with one foot.

She slid onto the bench next to him. "Mom says dinner in ten."

Zane looked over and offered a slight smile. "She wants to try me touching her after dinner."

"I think that's a good idea. That way we'll know for sure what's going on with your abilities. Mom's very powerful. You know that. You're not going to hurt her. I'll be right there."

He looked down at the gloves covering his hands. "I don't

know whether to be hopeful or terrified. I think that after today, I might not need these anymore, and I get this knot in my gut. Then I warn myself not to get my hopes up because the odds are still good that I'm still deadly to other people and that you can only touch me because of the link. I don't want to hurt your mom."

"You won't."

She reached out and tugged the leather gloves from his hands, twining her fingers with his. They both stared at their hands for a long moment before Zane spoke.

"Not to change the subject, but I'm really kind of afraid that your dad is going to try and kill me in my sleep if he thinks there's something going on between us. I like Gage, and I want him to keep liking me."

Lux snorted. "For fuck's sake, Zane, he's not a monster. He's my dad. Besides, it's not like you've de-virginized me or anything." She looked up at the trees. "It's pretty here. When you're running all the time and bouncing around so much it's easy to forget how pretty the world is."

"The world is gorgeous. It's the people in it who can be ugly." He glanced back toward the house. "Can you see out here from the kitchen?"

"No, why?"

Zane shifted and gripped Lux by her elbows, lifting her and settling her in his lap, cradling her head on his chest and covering both her feet with one of his hands. "Because I didn't want one of your parents to see me do this just yet."

Lux laughed. "Why are you suddenly so shy?"

Serious, he looked down at her. "Regardless of what's between us and what we've talked about, no parent wants to see their daughter start something with someone who can't give her a future. Even if she doesn't want it." He ran his finger down her face. "We both know what we're doing, but they don't. I respect your parents. I don't want them to think that I'm trying to take advantage of you or that I'm doing anything to hurt you. I don't want to lose their trust and respect, and to me, part of that is not pawing at their baby girl in their house."

She stared up at him, taking in the strong line of his jaw, the curve of his mouth and the dark slash of eyebrows. "My father was a vampire when he met my mother. I think they know more about thinking there's no future than just about anyone else."

Zane leaned down and brushed his lips over hers. "I'd bet our ten minutes is up. Let's go eat and break the news to them that Lucifer has reproduced."

CHAPTER ELEVEN

ARADIA HELD her hand up. "There's no sense in continuing to talk about it. Lilith had two more children. That's a blow, yes, but it's not insurmountable, and taking on the child of Lucifer is certainly not going to fall to you. If anyone, it would fall to Amaya and Deacon or to the Angels. Your job is to kill Beelzebub's spawn. This will include Isaiah, so yes, we needed to know about him. Now we do. It changes nothing other than that it's one more Cambion we have to hunt down."

Gage deliberately placed his cup of coffee on the table. "I agree with Aradia. It's a wrench, but it doesn't change much. I've got locations on two of the remaining Cambion that you're after. One of them is in Alaska. It's a very remote settlement, very few people there, and this particular Cambion is living as a human. It's going to be tricky to get to him. Ever since the order went out for them to go to ground, it's been harder to keep track of them than what it's been before. I'm still working on the other two, now three, and I'm hoping to have something for you soon."

Zane wrapped his hands around his own cup and stared down into the black depths. "Have you given any thought to how we might manage to kill Beelzebub?"

"I have. There's only one way to do it." Gage leaned back and stared at them both intently. "Purgatory. That's the only place where we can really, truly kill another being. On Earth, only a Devil can kill an Angel, so that's great, Angels are safe. Yay for Angels. With the Devils, if we kill them, they go back to Hell, they find another body, they come back. Even with the blade that Griffin used, Lucifer was able to fish Beelzebub back out of the Lake to bring him back. I don't know about any of you, but this time, I want it to fucking count. No more do-overs."

Lux glanced to Zane. "Purgatory is jail. It was made before the Choosing was decided on as a place for demons and Devils to go if they got killed on Earth. After that meeting, Lucifer took most of them back to Hell, and Purgatory was left empty. Now, it just sits there, basically empty. The trick is that if you're killed in Purgatory, you cease to exist. No soul to go to Heaven, nothing goes to Hell, you're just gone. It's like you never existed. That's what happened to Abaddon. It's the one place where if we manage to destroy Beelzebub's body, he's going to die with it. If we can get him down there, we know that his powers will be muted. The problem is, so are Angelic powers, so we have to assume we'll be weaker, too."

Zane took a gulp of the coffee. "Sounds like we know what we have to do then. For better or worse, we're going to Purgatory once this is done. We have to assume that Beelzebub is going to know what we're doing with it. He'll be waiting for us to make a move for him."

"I have no doubt about that. I would be willing to bet that's why he's staying so close to Lilith and sending her out to do his dirty work. I wouldn't be surprised if we don't see appearances by Azazel and Abalam as well." Gage stood and poured himself a second cup. "You've just got to keep doing what you're doing. Four down, five to go. You're making good progress. Go get these two and I'll work on the rest. I've prepared files on them both. Everything I know about their parentage, what they look like, any weaknesses, so on and so forth. It should be enough to keep you occupied for a week or two. Getting to Alaska will take several days, and then you'll have to spend some time killing the bastard. After that, you're going to be heading to London for the other. We'll need to arrange for Carys to come and get you or for Angelic transport." He grimaced. "It used to be I could just call and have my jet waiting, but I'm afraid those days are over." He reached out and patted Aradia's hand. "Fond memories of my plane, aren't there darling?"

Aradia rolled her eyes. "Jumping out of it into the ocean as it crashed comes first to mind." She shuddered. "I, for one, was not sad to see that kind of transportation leave us."

Lux chuckled. "Are you going to tell us some old war stories next? Like about the time Mom ripped Garrick's heart out or when Dad took on thirty Familiars alone? Or maybe the one where Mom dressed up like a whore and groped Uncle Damon to get Azazel to proposition them and then tied him up with witch-rope?" Her eyes alight with good humor, she straightened. "My favorite was always the one where you all went to Atlantis. That was a great story."

Aradia pinched her daughter's ear gently. "We're not old and buried yet, young lady. We may be getting gray and slightly slower, but neither your father nor I are ready for retirement just yet."

Gage shrugged. "I don't know, Aradia. I've been going for fifteen hundred years. Maybe it's time to take a vacation for a decade or two. I think we've earned it." He grinned at Lux. "When this is all over and I can buy a plane again, we'll go somewhere warm and sandy and do nothing but relax for a month at least."

"Sounds like a plan to me." Lux yawned. "Okay, let's stop putting this off. We need to see if Zane's powers are fixed."

Aradia held out her hands. "Take off your gloves."

Zane looked at Gage, only slightly panicked. "You aren't really going to let them do this, are you?"

Gage sighed deeply. "Son, let me give you a little bit of advice about the Windsor women. They're beautiful, smart, and fucking stubborn as hell. You'd have more luck reasoning with the refrigerator. Once they get something in their head, that's it. Your best option is to take off those gloves and let her touch your skin. You aren't going to hurt her. If I thought for a second that she couldn't handle any jolt you might give her, I wouldn't be sitting here giving you advice and drinking coffee. I'd be hauling Aradia up off that chair and dragging her away from you, kicking and screaming if necessary. And to be clear, she'd be kicking. I'd be screaming."

Aradia smiled demurely. "Twenty-nine years and he's finally almost trained." She snapped her fingers. "Gloves off. We're all tired, and we'd all like to go to bed. The sooner you peel off the leather, the sooner we sleep."

Reluctantly, Zane pulled off his gloves and laid his hands on the table. His heart pounded in his chest, and he felt a bead of sweat run down the back of his neck and trail between his shoulder blades. Lux stood, rounding the table to lay her hands on her mother's shoulders, just in case.

Confidently, Aradia reached out and gripped Zane's hands. He squeezed his eyes shut and concentrated everything he had into not hurting her. His head throbbed as blood rushed into his ears, and for an embarrassing moment, he wondered if he might faint.

"Zane." Aradia's voice was gentle and insistent. "You're not hurting me. Relax."

Incrementally, his hands relaxed until they were laying under hers. He opened his eyes and stared at their joined hands. When he spoke, his voice shook.

"Are you sure I'm not hurting you?"

"I'm sure, sweetheart. You're not hurting me."

With a whoop and a cheer, Zane leaped from his chair and snatched Aradia into a bone crushing hug. Aradia wrapped her arms around him and hugged him tightly, squeezing just as hard. Lux watched the scene, her hands pressed to her mouth and her eyes shining with tears.

Gage extended a hand, and they both grinned when Zane shook it firmly and nothing happened. The older man clapped him on the back. "Congratulations. It would seem that you can now control your power."

Zane ran his hands through his hair. "I never thought a handshake would feel so good. I've dreamed of this day since I was twelve years old and this started happening." He turned and looked at Lux. "Thank you."

Their eyes met, and the shift was tangible. She moved forward, sliding her arms around his neck and pressing her mouth to his in an enthusiastic kiss. Zane hugged her to himself, breaking the kiss after a moment. He looked over his shoulder at Gage and blushed, stepping back from Lux and shoving his hands in his pockets.

"Um."

Gage chortled and shook his head. "You're a grown ass man. Don't make me like you less by acting like a pubescent boy over one kiss." He slid his arm around Aradia. "I'm going to bed. All the excitement is more than us old folks can take. We'll leave in the morning after breakfast to notify everyone else of what you've found out. It'll keep you, and them, safer if you have a little distance right now I think."

Lux beamed at her parents and hugged each of them quickly. "We'll see you in the morning."

Zane didn't speak until they had disappeared down the stairs into the basement. "Why do they sleep down there?"

"My dad likes it really dark. Plus, that's where he'll have his office, so it's multi-tasking." She grinned at him over her shoulder. "Another bonus is that it means there is absolutely no way in hell they could hear us if it's possible for me to convince you to come to bed with me."

He was shaking his head before she finished the sentence. "No. Absolutely not." He reached out and took her hands in his own. "I want to. More than you know. Believe me, I want to, but not in your parents' house. Especially not the first time. Maybe not ever, but especially not this time."

Lux shifted closer and looked up at him. "We'll be quiet. Come on, it'll be fun. I won't even ask you to stay afterward."

Zane bent and kissed the shell of her ear gently. "Lux, when I finally do get my hands and mouth on you, I don't want you to be able to be quiet. I'll make it my fucking mission to make you moan so loud you'd wake the whole damn house. And I'll be damned if it'll be a quick lay and then we'll both go back to our respective beds and sleep. When we do this, I want to have the time to do it right."

Frustrated, she wound her fingers into his hair and jerked. "Damn you, we've been circling this for fucking ever. I want you."

In a heartbeat, he spun her and slammed her back against the wall, pressing his body fully into hers. He caught her hands in one of his and lifted them above her head, pinning them there. Shifting forward with his hips, he slowly pushed into hers until there was no doubt as to his desire. Passion flared in Lux's eyes and she stared up at him through a fog.

"Do you think for a second that I don't want you, too?" He nibbled at her jaw, quick little bites that weakened her knees and sent bolts of electricity through her body. "I can touch you. I can put my hands on you and not hurt you. I worry that once I start I won't want to ever stop."

Frustrated, she tugged her hands loose, pressing them to his shoulders and using the leverage to hike herself up so that her legs were wrapped around his waist. "Why do you get to call the shots? Just because you're the one with the penis doesn't mean you get to be in charge."

Amused, Zane kissed her nose. "It's not about being in charge. It's about not wondering if every single noise is someone coming up the stairs about to walk in and shoot me. It's about being able to take the time to do this right." He slid his hands up her thighs and over the curve of her bottom. "I don't want a quick roll in the hay. I want to take my time with you. I want to bury myself in you and bring you more pleasure than you've ever had. And when we've caught our breath, I want to be able to do it over again. No worries about being loud or being in a hurry or being able to hold you after. Dammit Lux, we both deserve more than what we could have here tonight."

Touched, but still slightly annoyed, Lux leaned her head on his shoulder. "I don't think you understand how horny I am right now."

He laughed. "Do you not feel the hard-on I'm currently stabbing you with?" Trailing his mouth over the line of her jaw, he slowly drew his fingers across the tanned skin of her stomach. "I'm right there with ya, babe."

Lux moaned softly and jerked her hips into his. "We could go upstairs and fool around."

Zane shook his head. "Nope." His tongue darted out to taste the skin on her neck. "I'm not giving your dad any reason to shoot me. Not a single one." He scraped his teeth over one of the tendons and smiled when her head rolled to the side. "Besides, fooling around could lead to sex, and we're not doing that here."

"Then what do you call this?"

He kissed her, hard and fast, and stepped away from her before she really knew what was happening. "A goodnight kiss." He started up the stairs. "Goodnight, Lux."

Lux woke up feeling more rested than she had since leaving Maine. She showered, dressed, packed several changes of clothes, and was downstairs eating fruit cocktail from the can when her father came up from the basement, dressed and holding a duffel bag. He looked at hers sitting next to the door and smiled.

"Leaving?"

"We need to head out after the two Cambion you found."

Gage went to the coffee pot and started a pot. "We're going to go to Michael's and tell him what you've found out about Lilith. I imagine we'll be there for a few days at least while we gather some information on Serafina and Isaiah. Are you feeling like your powers are back up to full, or are you still recovering from the fight with Lilith?"

"I'm not completely there yet, but I will be before we get to Alaska. I'm not going to go into another fight without being able to handle it, Dad. I know better." She glanced toward the stairs. "I'm going to go wake up Zane and make sure he's ready to go. We need to get on the road as quickly as we can if we want to make some progress before night. It's going to take close to a week to make this drive."

"It might be better if you stayed here one more day and left tomorrow. We could stay, too. There are plenty of houses around. We could find a good vehicle, some gas cans, and get you as much fuel as possible so you have some to get you further before you have to stop. Supplies. Some canned food, bottles of water, weapons, that sort of thing. Between the four of us, we could canvas quite a bit of the area in one day."

Lux considered that as she chewed a bite of peach. "I thought you wanted to get to Michael's."

Gage ruffled her hair. "I do, but I also don't get to see my daughter enough, and I want to make sure that you're safe for this. I'd feel better if you waited another day to go and let your powers build back up after that fight. I know you well enough to know the only way you'll stay is if I stay to watch you. What do you think? One more day with your old man?"

She grinned up at her father and rose onto her tiptoes to kiss his cheek. "I love you, Daddy."

"I love you too. Aradia and I are very proud of you. You're a wonderful young woman. You're smart and brave and beautiful. Everything a parent could want in a daughter. We're lucky beyond words to have you, darling." He hugged her tightly, breathing in the familiar scent of his child. "I only wish I could have made this world better for you."

Lux laid her head on Gage's shoulder and relaxed against him. "If you had, I might not exist."

"Then I'm glad we failed."

Chapter Twelve

September 13th, 2060 – British Columbia

"WE'RE MAKING good time." Lux leaned her head against the passenger seat of the SUV Zane drove and looked at the side of his face as he maneuvered through several cars left to rot on the road.

"It hasn't been bad. Four days of driving. I figure it'll take two more days to get through this area, two days to get through the Yukon, and a day and a half in Alaska before we get to this settlement where the Cambion is at if your dad is right about where he is."

"My dad's always right about this stuff." She yawned and looked at the sun sinking below the horizon. "How much gas do we have left?"

"Not much. We got about fifty gallons before we left, plus a full tank. With what we've scavenged on the trip up to this point, at the last time I put fuel in the tank, I think there's about ten gallons left in the cans back there. We'll need to take some time tomorrow to scavenge for fuel and for some food. I'm going to stop at the next town that looks large enough to have what we need."

Lux stretched her arms over her head. "The good thing about being in these areas is that there hasn't been much looting going on. There weren't enough people here to be doing the looting." She rubbed her head. "Can you please not worry so loud? It's giving me a headache."

Zane glanced at her out of the corner of his eye. "If we can't find enough fuel, we're going to have to walk. Or flash a hundred times and be wiped out for days. That's a pretty big worry."

"Then stop the car and let's check these."

He looked at her drolly. "They've obviously been looted. The tires are gone, batteries stripped. There's nothing here but some metal. If I thought that there was a chance there'd be some fuel, I would stop."

She opened the glove compartment and pulled out the map Gage had given them, checking their position on it against a road sign lying on the ground. "Unless the sign has been brought from elsewhere, there should be a town about fifteen miles up ahead. We should be able to find something there, and we'll have a few minutes of light left. God knows I'm sick of sleeping in this car."

Zane made a noise in the back of his throat. "A bed will be nice, that's for damn sure. A shower will be even better. Hell, at this point, I'll take cold water and a bar of soap."

Lux snorted. "It's not fair, is it? Zeke and Dev get to live in LA where there's every luxury they could ever want, then they get to go to Scotland, where everything's comfortable, then the cabin, where it's the same, then to New Orleans. We're the ones who get stuck out on the road with no running water, no electricity, and no soap. We end up sleeping in the car, smelling bad, and eating cold soup from a can."

"That's the way the vast majority of humans live now. Aside from some of the colonies forming, people have been living like this for the last fifteen years. Longer, even, in some parts of the world. We've been lucky to be raised the way we have."

They rode in silence until buildings came into view. Lux sat up straight and reached into the backseat for a pistol, holding it in her lap as Zane parked the car outside what had once been a bar and grill.

Simultaneously, they exited the SUV and surveyed the small town. There was a tackle and bait store, a grocery store, a post office, doctor's office, two churches, one lawyer's office, a courthouse, two diners, an apartment building, several clothing and souvenir shops, and one hotel.

"Well, not much to look through, but I don't see a lot of broken windows, so that's a positive." Lux opened the back door and dragged out her utility belt, fastening it around her waist. "Do you want to go through together or split up?"

"I think we should stay at the hotel unless it's too bad. If it's gross, we'll look for a house a little further out. We don't have a lot of light left. Grab a couple of the flashlights and our packs so we can carry stuff out from these places. We won't take much out tonight, but if there's a lot, we'll spend tomorrow kind of going through things and gathering what we need before we leave."

"Well, then, let's address the most immediate need, which is food, followed by a bath. Both of those should be addressed by the grocery store." She looked at it suspiciously. "Even if they just abandoned it, the smell should be gone after this long, I'd think."

Zane chuckled. "Should be." He slung the empty backpack over his shoulder. "Let's see what we shall see."

Together, they moved toward the door at the grocery store. The doors were glass and covered in dust. Zane wiped them clear with his sleeve and peered in. When he saw nothing, he used the blade on his knife as a wedge to pry the doors open and they slipped through quietly.

Lux sniffed appraisingly. "At least it doesn't smell like rotten meat."

"Odds are that it sold out of most things before it got bad. Most stores were picked pretty clean early on, but this is a tiny town, hours outside of any city. We might get lucky."

She led the way into the store, turning right and passing by the empty produce section to head toward the canned goods. Most of the shelves were empty. They rifled through the debris on the floor, Lux turning up three cans of fried apples and Zane finding a jar of salsa and a can of Vienna sausages.

"Those are gross."

Zane chuckled and tucked them into his pack. "They're food. Hey, look!" He jogged down the next aisle and triumphantly held up a box of crackers. "We can dip the salsa!"

Lux made a face. "They're all yours." She shined her flashlight along the bottom and kicked at some metal on the floor. "I was hoping it would look like it did before everything happened. I wonder what these places looked like back then. Do you remember?"

Zane absentmindedly added a packet of rice to his bag. "Vaguely. I remember clinging to a cart my mom was pushing and everyone just slinging stuff into their carts. Up front, those machines were where you used to pay for what you wanted. The owners of the stores had people stand there with these handheld things, and every item in here has a code that they scanned so they knew how much it was."

"Weird. My parents never took me to the store or anything." She stooped to look under the shelves. "Hey, there's a couple cans under here. Look under those. I bet people dropped them and they rolled. There're quite a few."

Zane dropped to his knees and shined his own flashlight under the shelving units. "You're right. Can you reach them?"

"Yeah." Lux laid on her side to stretch. "Beef stew. That at least tastes good. My mom used to tell me stories about these places where you could literally buy anything. From furniture to food to medicine. All in one building."

"Convenience." He grinned when he came up with a can of baked beans and two cans of spam. "That's a decent meal. Find some mustard and spam is edible. Not good, but edible."

"We might get enough for a few days from in here after all. Ooohh." Lux squeaked. "Macaroni and cheese!" She climbed to her feet. "I'm going to check for soap and such in the personal aisle. You keep gathering this stuff up. Check out the soda and water, too. Grab a cart if you need it."

Zane glanced up. "I thought we weren't going to clear everything tonight."

"We're not, but we also want to take a full load out, and I think there's more than one cartful in here if we look hard enough. It's picked through but not empty."

Lux carefully made her way through the store to the aisles where there had once been bottles of shampoo, conditioner, hairspray and boxes of dye. She found a tube of gel that she discarded without a thought, a comb that she tucked in her pocket, and a pack of ponytail holders that went into her bag.

Frustrated, she crouched to dig through the debris and remnants of shelves. Turning up three boxes of tampons was a welcome surprise, which she took for herself. She dropped to her stomach and peered under the shelves. Against the wall, all the way in the back, was a bottle of what looked to be either body wash or shampoo.

Determined to get it, she shimmied back, feeling her fingers brush the lid. She scrambled to grab it, flailing with her fingers, jubilant when she grasped the lid in her hand. As she sat up and stuffed the bottle into her bag, she froze, the hair on the back of her neck rising.

Vampires. Lux's teeth lengthened and sharpened into the fangs that she normally kept hidden, and her eyes darkened from green to red. She felt for the link to Zane and traveled along it, finding her way into his head with little effort.

"There are vampires here."

His response was almost instant. *"I know. I feel them, too. What do you want to do?"*

"Well, killing them is a good start. I don't think this is anything other than a few vampires living in an abandoned town, but they likely think we're about to be their dinner."

"Agreed. Should we let them come to us?"

Lux considered that while shoving a three-pack of powder scented deodorant into her pack. *"Have you gotten everything we need for the night?"*

"Yeah. Water, some cans of soda, the food we already gathered, and a few other things I found."

"Let's head for the exit and let them hit us near the car. I've only got one stake on me, and I don't want to fire a weapon and draw the attention of anything else around. This may very well just be a pack staying here while they travel, or we may have stumbled into their territory."

"If it's a lair, there are going to be a lot of fucking vampires in this place, Lux. Could be hundreds."

"Only way to know is to go outside and find out. Most lairs in a place like this would be twenty to thirty. It couldn't support more than that. You don't get hundreds much outside of big cities. They need people to feed on."

Lux shouldered her pack and pulled her stake off her utility belt, heading for the exit. Zane was waiting for her at the door, and they both stood and looked out at the street where there were fifteen vampires waiting for them.

"I see another ten on the roofs across the street."

Lux followed Zane's gaze. *"There are a few demons in the mix, too. Mainly up there. If you look to the West, I see some Familiars."*

Zane turned his head and swore. "I fucking hate Familiars."

Demons and Devils had the ability to detach a human's soul from their body and take control of basic motor function, turning the person into a Familiar. They were completely at the bidding of the demon, unable to break free, unable to do anything other than what they were ordered to do. Familiars were mindless, unrelenting, empty shells.

Lux slipped into Zane's head. *"I don't think we want them to know what we are. Vampires can't tell Nephilim unless we use some powers, and most demons don't care. They'll know we're Nephilim but think we're weak if we just fight them hand to hand. It'll make it tougher for us, but I think it's worth the risk."*

"*I agree.*" Zane squeezed her fingers and shouldered his way through the door. "Can we help you?"

One of the vampires stepped forward. "You're in our town."

Zane looked around. "I didn't see any signs. We were just looking for some food and a place to pass the night. There's no intention for us to stay. We're happy to leave now, though, if we're encroaching on your area."

"It's too late for that, boy. This is not a place Nephilim are allowed to leave." One of the demons drew a knife and held it close to his side. "You made your last mistake coming here."

Lux held a stake in one hand and a buck knife in the other. "I was so hoping you'd say that."

With a practiced move, Lux struck out with the blade and planted it in the chest of one of the demons. He looked down in shock and gripped the handle of the knife for a long moment before falling to his knees. The vampires around him stared as he fell before charging Lux and Zane.

Zane braced himself for impact, holding his arm out and snapping one vampire to the ground, stomping his foot into its throat as he jabbed the stake into the chest of a second, watching with satisfaction as it burst into dust before stooping to end the one under his heel.

Lux dashed to the car and wrenched open the hatch, yanking out her broadsword. "Get up to the roof. I've got these fuckers." She tossed him a sword and turned to the twelve vampires and four demons left. "Eventually they'll learn not to come after beings higher up on the food chain than they are."

She twirled to avoid a demon before slashing down with her blade and severing its head from its shoulders. The vampires were significantly weaker than even the weakest Nephilim. She hacked through them with pathetically little effort, tearing into one with her teeth when her sword was knocked away.

Blood ran out of her mouth and dripped off her chin, bitter and black. She spat it out and snarled at the demon who charged her. He conjured his own sword and she stooped to grab hers, blood slickening her grip on the weapon as they faced off, two warriors ready to fight to the death.

Their blades struck one another, the sound echoing through

the abandoned town. Lux gritted her teeth and forced the demon back, her muscles screaming with effort. She blocked and parried, keeping the demon from striking her with the blade, rotating from side to side to avoid his blows.

The demon bared its teeth in a vicious grin when his sword dug deep into her shoulder, glancing off bone and tearing through muscle and cartilage. Lux gasped as pain rocketed through her body and blood gushed down her arm, dripping off her fingers and soaking into the cracked pavement beneath her feet. Tendrils of red hair had escaped from her braid and she blew them out of her eyes in annoyance as she tossed the sword to her other hand, testing the grip with her right hand, unfamiliar with fighting that way.

Surrounding her were the remaining vampires and the Familiars. She spared one look up to see Zane fighting vampires on the roof. The one drawback to his power was that a vampire was already dead, so he had to use stakes and swords the same way she did. He couldn't use his Nephil abilities to eradicate them the way he could on other creatures.

"You're very strong for someone with seemingly very few Nephil powers." The demon lowered his sword slightly to look at her. "Is one of your parents a Warrior?"

Lux sneered. "Wouldn't you like to know?" She ached to use her magic and just wipe out the whole group, but feared alerting any Devils in the area to her presence. Without using magic or her Nephil abilities, she was left with brute strength, and in that area, she was lacking.

"If I didn't want to know, I wouldn't have asked." He tapped the blade against the pavement. "Such a shame that you stumbled into this town tonight. Instead of fucking your lover, you're going to die next to him."

"Don't count us out just yet."

Lux charged, her blade flashing in the moonlight. She swiveled to avoid his block, ducked under his blade and slashed, burying the blade in his chest. The demon's eyes sparked, flashed, and went dead, his essence pouring out of his eyes and mouth as he died. She wrenched the sword from his chest with a wet ripping noise and watched as three of the Familiars fell as their master died. Four more still stood, controlled by the other demon who conjured a whip and faced her.

"Now that he's broken you in for me, let's finish this off, shall we?"

Lux laughed. "We shall."

She glanced to the roof line where Zane was effectively dispatching of the last vampires. She saw him anchor his rifle to his shoulder and knew that the fight was over. Shots rang out and the Familiars dropped, bleeding and dying on the hard blacktop. The demon turned to see where the shots had come from, having dismissed Zane as dead, and Lux slashed once, separating his head from his shoulders with a practiced swipe of her blade.

"Are you okay?"

Lux looked up. "It's not too bad. A few stitches and I'll be fine." She glanced around nervously. "I think we'd better move on from here. Let's load up the food we found, check these cars for some fuel and get down the road a little ways."

Zane flashed down to the street and reached out to examine her shoulder. "You're lucky he got you right there on the edge. Not a lot of muscle to cut through. That'll help it heal more quickly." He cast a glance around. "Those vampires were relatively young. I don't think a single one was more than fifteen or twenty years turned. The demons were lower level. That was all the Familiars they could have controlled. Any more and they would have been stretched too thin." He grinned at her. "One flick of magic and you could have incinerated all of them."

Lux smirked. "That's not entirely true, but I like being flattered, so I'll let you keep thinking that." She reached up and touched her fingers to a shallow cut on his cheek. "Are you hurt or just scratched?"

He looked at the smear of blood on her fingers. "Huh. I didn't think they even got me. Just scratched, I guess." He smoothed a lock of escaped hair back from her back and laid his palm against her cheek, reveling in the feel of her warm skin against his. "I know this might sound odd, but I love watching you in the middle of a fight like that. The way you move. I can see your brain working. You're thinking about everything your opponent is doing, but your body moves like music. It's fluid and graceful and beautiful to watch."

Lux's heart constricted and a puddle of heat formed in her belly. She offered a smile and swallowed nervously. "That might be the sexiest compliment anyone has ever given me in my whole life."

Zane stared down at her, his eyes burning into her. "I aim to please." He took a half-step back. "Let's see if we can't fill up the car and the gas cans and get out of here. I don't think there's any backup coming, but I don't want to take a chance."

CHAPTER THIRTEEN

September 16th, 2060 - The Yukon

"I DON'T think it gets more remote than this." Lux put her hands on her hips and stared at the cabin. "We might be the first people in thirty years to find this place."

"Good." Zane checked his pistol to make sure it was properly loaded and glanced over at her. "Let's do a quick sweep of the outside and look in the windows to see if we can see anything inside. There's a couple sheds in the back that we'll need to check as well."

Lux snapped a clip into her own weapon and rounded the side of the house, stopping to peer in each of the windows. "It doesn't look like anyone's been in there in a while. There's an inch of dust on everything. I don't see any blood. No signs of a struggle. Nothing is broken." She drew to a stop and grinned. "Hey."

"What?"

She pointed. "Generator. We might get power."

Zane shook his head. "They're too loud and you know it."

"We could do a dampening spell to make it not loud. That doesn't take much magic."

"But it does take some magic and any magic that we use is magic that the Cambion can track. It's a risk we don't have to take." He shouldered open the door to the first shed. "This, on the other hand, we can use."

"What is it?"

Zane poked his head out. "All the fuel for the generator." He handed her two full five-gallon gas cans. "Let's get the gas-tank full and as many of these in the car as we can before we go inside. That way they're already loaded in case we have to make a hasty retreat."

Lux nodded and holstered her weapon. "Let's get it done then."

It took thirty minutes to finagle all of the gas cans into the car. They stopped once, pulled them all out, poured the fuel into the largest of the containers, and had to put them all back in. Once they were loaded, they argued for another five minutes over whether or not to leave the windows down to combat the fumes from nearly two hundred gallons of gasoline in one vehicle. Finally, after realizing winning the argument would do very little for his chances of not sleeping on the couch, Zane had admitted defeat and lowered the windows, resigning himself to worrying about rain for the foreseeable future.

Once inside the house, sweeping it took very little time. The basement consisted of a cannery with shelves that had, at one time, been stocked with homemade canned goods but were long since bare. There was a kitchen, living room, half bath and office on the ground floor and a loft with a bathroom up the stairs.

The house yielded several gallons of drinking water and a variety of cans of soup. Zane found a pack of licorice in the back of a cabinet that they split while digging through the rest of the shelves.

"It looks like there's a big water tank in the back that catches rain water. I'll check to see if there's anything in it." Zane studied a stove in the back of the kitchen. "This is a wood-stove." His face lit up. "Okay, I get it. You put wood in this thing. It heats the house. The pipe takes the steam into a tank where water from the reservoir outside goes to heat it up. It's well water and rain water. We should have hot water. It's all wood heat."

Lux placed her gun on the counter and shrugged off her jacket. "Good. It's starting to get chilly at night, and we both could use a shower. Let's go see if there's any wood. If there isn't, I guess we're chopping." She slapped him on the back. "Please be better at it than Dev. Zeke told me that when he chopped wood, he ended up burying the ax blade in his thigh and nearly bleeding to death all over the kitchen floor."

Zane shook his head. "How the fuck did he even manage to do that?"

"I don't even pretend to know." She shouldered open the kitchen door leading to the backyard and tipped her head back to stare up at the darkening sky. "Thank you, Lord. Firewood."

"That should be enough for the night." He bent and filled the basket sitting on the porch with chunks of already cut wood. "It'll take a little while for the water to warm up. I'll get this going and bring stuff in from the car if you'll put up the wards and protections."

"Sure thing." She stepped to the side to let him back into the house. "I'll start upstairs."

Lux retrieved the bag of supplies from the SUV and carried it up the stairs, taking out a can of spray blood and painting traps on the walls and ceiling. She felt a pang for vandalizing what had been someone's home as she did it, and she thought about a simpler time when people had been able to just live in houses without defiling every inch of them to keep evil out.

She stitched herb bundles into the pillows to keep anything from dragging them onto the dreamplane and laid salt lines across the windows. A quick search of the bathroom yielded a first aid kit they'd take with them, clean towels they'd make use of, a razor she would use and then take, and an array of lotions and perfumes she planned to thoroughly examine after bathing.

The tub was an old claw-foot, big and deep. Lux shivered from the anticipation of sinking into water neck-deep and soaking away all the tension in her muscles. She wandered back into the bedroom and opened the door to the armoire, expecting to see the clothing of whomever had once lived in the house.

She did not find clothing.

"Zane!"

Zane loped up the stairs. "What's wrong?" He looked at where she pointed and stared. "Wow."

An array of paddles and leather whips hung where shirts and ties should have. Handcuffs dangled on the inside of the doors, vibrators and dildos were lined up from smallest to largest on the bottom, and videos were stacked neatly at the back.

"I'm afraid to open the drawers."

Zane chuckled. "I'm not." He reached out and opened the first drawer, finding a half dozen bottles of lubricant and several small baskets of items. "I don't know what those things are."

Lux couldn't help herself. She looked. "I don't know what it says about me that I do know what those things are. The first basket is filled with nipple clamps. They do exactly what you would think they do. The second basket is cock rings. They go on your penis to either keep you from going limp or turn your dick into a giant vibrator. The third, well, the third is a very impressive collection of anal beads. You can guess what they're used for."

Zane stared at her. "How the hell do you know all that?"

"When Zeke and I were eighteen, we were in Boston fighting some Cambion. We got pinned down with more than we could handle and had to run. We lost them, but it was night and we didn't want to flash for fear that they'd trace the flash signature. We ducked into the first place we found with an unlocked door to hide for the night. Lo and behold, it was a porn store. Apparently during the apocalypse, people don't really loot sex shops. We got quite the education in there."

Zane shook his head. "I'll bet you did." He closed the first drawer and opened the bottom one. "Hey, condoms!"

Lux stooped. "Enough for the next ten fucking years." She rifled through the contents. "We have flavored, ribbed, cooled, warming gel, ones with ticklers, magnum sized, glow in the dark, regular latex, lambskin, extra-thin, his-and-hers, vibrating ones, these ones have knobby things on them—my God, did we fall into the den of iniquity or something?"

"Some middle-aged man bringing his hot mistress here for a weekend away from the wife and kids."

"Or a cougar and her young, sexy pool boy." She glanced up. "Provided that you still want to have sex with me at some point in time, we should pack the ones that we could use without bursting into laughter so we have them."

"I veto the ticklers, knobby things, and the vibrating ones. And the cooling ones."

"Which would be the his-and-hers, too." She held up a box. "Magnum sized?"

Grinning, Zane lifted one eyebrow. "I think I can fill them out."

A rush of heat swept through Lux, and she cleared her throat as she tossed them up to him. "Noted."

He continued speaking as if they were discussing something as mundane as the weather. "I'll stick these in the car and check on the hot water heater. You should finish warding downstairs."

Zane refused to use magic to create electricity and insisted that the generator made too much noise, which meant they were limited to the light from the small fireplace upstairs, the woodstove downstairs, and candles as their only way to see. Luckily, there were plenty of large jarred candles to light.

Lux lit several and placed them around the loft, allowing her to see as she stripped off her clothes and stepped into the tub. The hot water engulfed her as she sat down, and she sighed in sheer pleasure as tension slipped from her muscles. A line of stitches was harsh black against the creamy paleness of her shoulder, and she winced when the water burned the still healing wound.

Unlike Zeke, Lux didn't much care for the look of scars on herself. She preferred fighting with a weapon that allowed her to keep some distance, and magic afforded her that. Her shoulder would scar, and the idea annoyed her. A demon had managed to mark her when even Lilith hadn't managed to leave a physical indication of injury.

Shaking off the annoyance, Lux held her breath and slipped beneath the surface, wetting her hair and face. Surfacing, she reached for the bottle of shampoo at the side of the tub and squeezed a dollop into her hand, rubbing it through her long locks until she formed a rich lather that smelled of apples and coconut.

"Hey, Lux! I'm going to go do a sweep of the outside one last time while you're in there. Yell if you need anything."

Lux smiled as Zane's voice trickled up the stairs and a feeling of warmth washed over her. "I will. Be careful."

Zane leaned against the bottom of the stairs and glanced longingly up them. "I will."

He turned and left the house, securing the door behind him. The beam from his flashlight illuminated the night, and he inspected every inch of the outside of the house for threats before going a hundred yards into the woods to do the same. Finding nothing other than some disturbed owls and squirrels, he trekked back to the cabin and dead-bolted the door behind him.

Lux was sitting on the couch, the light from the candles bouncing off the rich red and gold of her hair so that it glowed and moved. He was captivated by her—the way the light caressed the planes of her face, the pretty warm glow of her skin from her bath, the length of leg exposed from the end of the long t-shirt she wore as a nightgown. Her fingers, tipped with short, blunt nails, tapped idly on her knee.

"Did you find anything unusual?"

"Nothing." He unzipped his jacket and removed his utility belt. "This is a pretty remote area. We'll be safe, I think. I was giving it some thought, and we could both use a break from the road. Why don't we stay here tomorrow night, too, and leave the next morning to head for Alaska? We can rest, enjoy sleeping in a bed instead of a car. You can have tonight, I'll have tomorrow night. There should be enough wood, I think, and if not, I can chop some. We have hot water. There's enough food."

"There's no reason not to. We want to get there, yes, but we can't be exhausted and worn out when we do. Unfortunately, we aren't as powerful as Angels. We can't flash across the planet in an instant, at least, most of us can't, and we don't have Carys and Elisa here to help with it." Lux stretched. "Are you going to go get a shower?"

Zane's mouth nearly watered as the hem of her shirt lifted several inches, exposing a wide expanse of smooth thigh. He shook his head to clear it. "What did you say?"

"Are you going to go get a shower? There should be some hot water left."

"Yeah. I'll make it quick so you can get to bed. If you could find a blanket and pillow for the couch, I'd really appreciate it."

Zane had gotten spoiled at Michael's. There was always hot water, plenty of soap, and fresh food. They never had to worry about finding clothes, or where they would sleep, or whether someone was going to slit their throats as they slept. On Earth, it was totally different. Everything was a struggle. From what to eat to where to sleep to whether or not there was anything to cover his body with.

Soap was a luxury, as he'd quickly learned. Finding a house that still had shampoo and soap was an unexpected benefit. They had multiple safe-houses throughout the world, but most were little more than a room safe enough to pass a night or a tunnel through which they could escape from whatever was chasing them. The ones that had been fit for long term habitation—well, Zeke and Dev had destroyed most of those.

Zane shook off the morose thoughts as he stepped out of the shower and grabbed a towel to wrap around his waist. He rubbed his hair with another and padded to the mirror to shave. Smiling when he realized there was still shaving lotion in the tube, he squirted a dollop into his hand and massaged the cream into his face, reaching for the razor and dragging it across his jaw.

"Hey, I was thinking. Do you know where Damon and Greer's house is in relation to this village where we're going?"

Zane splashed water on his face to rinse the shaving lotion off. "I'd have to look at a map, but if memory serves, it's about fifty miles. Close enough that we could stay there if we wanted to. Is that where you want to head for?"

"As long as it's close enough." Lux appeared in the doorway and leaned against it. "If this guy is living as a human, it could be hard to find him. Zeke can dampen her powers so that no one knows she's Nephil or that anyone around her is Nephilim. If he can do the same thing, and can find some hair dye, it's going to take some work to lure him out."

He turned and brushed past her to move into the bedroom, reaching for the sweatpants he'd left lying on the bed before getting into the shower. "We'll just have to play it by ear."

Lux crossed the room quietly and folded her hand over his wrist. She reached out with the other hand and took the sweat pants from him, dropping them to the floor. "Don't bother putting them on."

Zane's body stilled and his breathing went shallow. He stared down at her, blue locking onto green. "I want you to be sure about this."

"I've been sure about this for a while now. It's always been something. Getting attacked, or traveling, or my parents, or we stink. Some reason not to go to bed together. All of those reasons are moot tonight. Tonight we're safe, we're well fed, we're recently bathed, and my parents are nowhere to be found. There's no reason we can't just lay down on this nice, big, comfortable bed together and have sex if that's what we want. It's what I want. Is it what you want?"

He laid his palm against her cheek. "Wanting you hasn't ever been a problem. I've wanted you for months. I just want this to be right. I don't want to mess it up."

She reached out and unfastened his towel, dropping it to the floor. "The only way to mess it up is to not do it at all."

His heart constricted in his chest. More than almost anything, he wanted her. More than even that, he wanted to tell her how he felt, to let the words spill from his lips and hope against hope that she returned the feelings. He loved everything about the woman.

From the way she single-mindedly went after what she wanted to the way she fiercely loved those close to her.

"Lux."

Lux looked up at him. "Hmm?"

"I don't know if I can do this."

She gave his crotch an appraising glance. "Everything seems to be in working order. Is something wrong?"

He sat down on the edge of the bed. "I'm not interested in a one-time thing with you. I like you. I respect you. We're friends, and you mean too much to me for that."

Lux perched next to him, still holding his hand in hers. "It's not like I'm after a quick roll in the hay. This is going to continue as long as we both want it to."

"There have to be rules. Even if it's not a relationship, there are still boundaries. As long as we're sleeping together, I'd prefer neither of us is sleeping with anyone else."

"Agreed." She tightened her fingers on his, not liking the pang of jealously that bolted through her at the thought of another woman with him. "I don't get emotional. It's just not me. You and I are friends, we understand one another, and we work well together. I want you this way, too. I make no bones about that, I won't apologize for it, and I won't pretend I don't. But I also don't minimize it. I don't take just anyone into my body. Sex doesn't have to mean anything, but it's often better if it does. It'll mean something with you. To touch you and for you to touch me when I've wanted that for so many months." She took a deep breath. "This isn't meaningless to me." She looked down at their hands—their fingers twined together, skin on skin. "I want *you*, Zane. Not a warm body. Not just a man. You."

Zane laughed nervously. "I think part of this is that I'm not sure how to do this. I want to get it all right. I'm worried I've built it up in my head the last while since we got things under control, and I don't want either of us to end up being disappointed." He ran his fingers through her hair. "Would you be completely and totally offended if we just slept tonight? I'd like to sleep holding you."

Lux smiled and shook her head. "I'm not offended in the slightest." She leaned over to kiss him softly. "I think it's sweet that it means this much to you. I'm glad. I'm horny as hell, but I think you're probably right." She reached down and picked up his sweatpants. "I'll go throw a couple more logs on the fire while you get dressed and then we'll go to sleep."

She bounced off the bed and loped down the steps, moving quickly toward the wood stove. Gathering an arm load of wood, she opened the door to the stove and tossed the pieces on top, stoking the embers into a full flame. She grabbed a bottle of water from the kitchen and hurried back upstairs, finding Zane in the process of turning down the blankets on the bed. Together, they slipped between the sheets.

He drew her in close, tucking her head against his shoulder and her body close to his side. Lux wrapped one arm around his waist and sighed in contentment.

"This is nice."

Zane stroked his hand over her hair. "Slightly awkward given earlier events, but yeah, it feels nice." He smiled in the dark and turned his head to kiss her hair. "Get some sleep."

She yawned and let her eyes drift shut. "Night."

CHAPTER FOURTEEN

LUX WOKE up in the dreamplane. Everything there took on a silvery sheen, looking slightly different than it did in reality. She looked around suspiciously, not sure who had called her there. Her eyes settled on Graciela and she relaxed, rushing forward to embrace her grandmother.

"Grandma, I haven't seen you in years. Is everything okay?"

Graciela's embrace was stiff. "I haven't called you here of my own free will, child. For that, I am sorry. I didn't have a choice."

Tensing, Lux pulled back and gripped her grandmother's arms. "What's going on? Who is it? What's happened?"

"Hello, Lux." A man dressed in a white suit with a red belt and black leather shoes strode into sight. "My, my, do you look like your mother. Not too much of your father in you, is there? Either one of them."

Lux looked confused. "Who is this?"

Graciela nudged Lux slightly behind her. "Lucifer."

Lucifer smirked. "I would have thought you'd have recognized me on sight."

Lux stepped out from behind the other woman. "Well, you spend so much time hiding, it's impossible to know what you actually look like. Even now you can't come actually face us. You have to use a dead woman to drag me out of my bed and onto the dreamplane. This is the coward's way to come after me."

Satan tapped his index finger against his lips. "Don't trifle with me, Ms. Windsor. If I was coming after you, you would be surrounded by all my most powerful followers. I could bring you down while you slept, and you would never know what hit you. Do not think that simply because I am your enemy that you can treat me with disrespect."

"I don't have any respect for you."

He bared his teeth. "This is why we have such a problem. You think that your position is the only one with merit. You laud Michael and Alaria for rebelling against God and vilify me and mine for the exact same crimes. You're hypocrites. You should be fighting alongside me to charge upon the gates of Heaven and throw that cocky son of a bitch off his throne. With Him dead or gone, there would be no ruler, no God. There would be total free will. No sin. Nothing but everyone living their lives however they wanted to. Devil, Angel, demon, hound, vampire, Nephilim, Cambion. We could have the Earth."

Lux lifted one eyebrow. "I'm not going to be convinced, so spare us both the trouble. You didn't fight for the same reasons. You didn't want to be free of God, you wanted to *be* God. Even now, with what you just said, you left out the humans. You let them worship you, then you slaughter them by the millions using them to fight your war. You lure them in with promises and then send them to burn."

"God made Hell, not me."

"But He didn't send anyone there. You did."

Lucifer laughed. "Oh no, little witch. I never sentenced anyone to Hell. You need to re-read your King James Version. Here's a little refresher for you. Washed in the blood, repent of your sins, go to Heaven. Don't follow the yellow brick road, go to Hell." He cocked his head and considered. "I may be mixing up my pop culture references there a bit, but you get the gist of it all, I'm sure. God is responsible for all of this. Not me."

"And what happens if you win? Everyone goes to Heaven?"

"Certainly not." Lucifer reached out and gripped her arm, dragging her along with him as he walked through the garden in the dreamplane. "I'm thinking I'll literally switch things up. God can be chained to Hell with all his Angels, and I'll rule Heaven. Literally be God. Those who worship me get to come to Heaven, and those who follow Him can go to Hell where He sent my followers for the last several hundred million years. I think that's fair."

Lux forced herself not to wrench her arm free. She was very well aware that the only way she escaped alive was by being smart. "Why am I here?"

"Your mother is the most powerful witch I have ever come across in my entire existence. She very nearly had me thirty years ago. Mind you, had she been trying to kill me, it would have been like swatting at a bug, but she was being smart. She was merely trying to contain me. She could almost stop me from walking where I wanted to go. That's actually much harder than it sounds." He patted her arm. "I suspect you might be even more powerful. I'd like to test that theory."

Lux looked around. "We can't test it. Powers don't work on the dreamplane like they do on Earth. You know that." She stopped walking and pulled her arm free. "And I'm not sure what that would prove anyway. I'm not going to work for you."

Lucifer smiled down at her. "I think you might reconsider that."

"Why would you think that?"

He stared at her steadily. "Because if you don't, I am going to kill everyone that you love in the most horrible, brutal manner that you can dream of. When I charge Heaven, you will be the weapon I wield. Your magic, your mother's magic, your grandmother's magic. Ancestral magic, dark magic, white magic. That trifecta would make you more powerful than any witch that could ever live. I will use you to cut a swath through this Earth greater than any God has ever seen. When the dust settles, I will forge you a throne made from Angels' wings, and we will rule this world for the rest of eternity."

Lux blinked rapidly, trying to make sense of what had just been said. "What makes you think I have any interest in being your Queen?"

"I don't care if you want to. Since the moment I saw her, I coveted your mother. So beautiful with her magic flowing around her, wielding it like a soldier wields a sword. Aradia can be as soft as a lover's touch or as sharp as a surgeon's scalpel with her magic. But age has stolen her beauty and grace from her. You're young and beautiful, Lux, where your mother grows older. I sense the same magic in you that she has within her. By killing both of your ancestors, I will infuse within you so much power that you will be my own personal weapon."

"You're the Devil. You aren't supposed to need a weapon."

Lucifer looked at her blankly, clearly not understanding the insult in what she had said. "I don't *need* a weapon per se, but I *want* one, and I want for you to be it, therefore you will be. It's really as simple as that. I want the most powerful witch on Earth to be at my side, bent to my will, doing whatever I command that she do. It pleases me."

Lux snorted. "No offense, but I don't exist to please you. My goal in life is to see you dead." She turned to face him straight on. "I'm going to watch you die. The fact that you're here doing this tells me that you're getting scared. You don't know where Amaya and Deacon are, you don't know where I am, and you don't know how to stop us. You're not as powerful as God, at least not now that you've been cast down out of Heaven, and you don't know everything. We're coming for you, Lucifer, and we've got you running scared."

Lucifer looked at her with mild amusement. "I can see how this situation might give you such an idea, but I can assure you that your conclusions are most incorrect." He grabbed Graciela by the hair and twisted it painfully, dragging the woman to him. "Your grandmother only exists here, but she can be killed. I am one of maybe half a dozen other beings that can do so. Michael, the Angel of Death, God, your mother, you, Lilith if she had the inclination. When she died in the physical realm, she passed her powers onto your mother. If I kill her here, what's left of her powers will go into her nearest descendent." He looked at her pointedly. "I think we can all guess who that might be."

Lux knew her powers were no match for him, but she struggled not to try anyway. "Why would you want to make me more powerful? It'll give me more power to kill the Cambion with. That's the last thing you want to do."

He sneered. "That's where you're wrong, Lux. It's exactly what I want to do. I want to give you so much power that you're overcome with it. I want it to flood into you until it corrupts you and twists you into what I know you can be. Your grasp on the black magic is solid now. With this new flood, it will be more tenuous. When I kill your mother, it'll be too much for you to handle and you'll be taken over. Once that happens, I'll be waiting to pick up the pieces."

Graciela met Lux's eyes steadily. "Don't listen to him. You're stronger than either Aradia or I. Magic matures as it is passed down from mother to daughter. Trust in yourself and in the ones around you. Trust the magic, Lux. Warn your mother. Tell her to take precautions. She'll know what to—"

Graciela's words were cut off as Lucifer gripped her face in his hands and stared into her eyes, his turning black and glassy. A silvery grey mist floated out of Graciela's mouth and her body went limp, flickering and fading as it floated to the ground before disappearing into nothingness.

The trail wound its way through the dreamplane and struck Lux in the chest, forcing its way into her body. She fell backward from the power of it, tumbling to the ground and striking her head on the stone path. In the bed at the cabin, lying next to Zane, she woke screaming.

Zane was jerked from a sound sleep by the sound of shrieks. He leaped from the bed, rolling onto his feet and scrambling for a weapon, blinking to clear his vision and looking around for a threat. Lux sat up in the bed, clutching at her throat and kicking at the blankets. She gagged and blanched, struggling to get free of the sheets.

Trying to stand, she tripped and fell, hitting the floor and crawling several feet before regaining her balance and sprinting to the bathroom. She wrenched up the lid to the toilet and vomited, gagging and heaving until the contents of her stomach were all in the porcelain bowl.

Zane lowered himself to the floor behind her, scooping her hair back from her face and holding it away until she was done. "What happened?"

Lux collapsed against him, hot tears burning her eyes and the back of her throat. "Lucifer."

One word turned Zane's blood to ice. He gripped her chin in his hand and forced her to turn and look at him. "Focus, Lux. Is he coming? Is he here? Do we need to leave?"

"I don't know. I don't know." She rocked back and forth. "God, I don't know anything. He just killed my grandmother! Right in front of me like it was nothing! He used her to pull me into the dreamplane then killed her! He's using me, Zane. He's going to go after my mom! He wants to kill her so that her power will pass to me. He wants to turn me into his own fucking witch like Garrick was for Javal. He wants to force me to be overtaken by black magic."

"Graciela has been dead for sixty years. How could he kill her?"

"He did something to her. Ended her existence and took her out of the dreamplane. Everything she had left, he took from her and put it into me. She's gone. There's nothing of her left anymore at all. I don't know how he did it, only that he did." She closed her eyes. "We need to leave. They could be coming. If he got me into the dreamplane, they could know where we are. We need to be gone if they're coming."

Zane gripped her arms. "Calm down and take a breath. If he knew where you were, he wouldn't have needed Graciela to yank you in. We haven't been using our powers. We aren't giving them anything to look for or to track. We're safe. I don't feel anything coming, but we'll do a sweep and check the wards just to make sure. Your mother is at Michael's. She's as safe as she can possibly be there. I'll get the satellite phone and call them to let them know what's happened."

Lux shook her head. "She'll already know. Call, but she'll know by now. I'm sure of that." She sniffed. "He wasn't even trying. God, Zane, he didn't even have to try. He's crazy! He was talking about turning me into a weapon, that having me as this sword he would use to cut people down would bring him more respect. He was talking about taking over Heaven and chaining God to Hell." She pressed her hands to her face. "It's fucking crazy!"

Zane helped her to her feet. "Let's get you some water to rinse your mouth. I'll check everything out and then we can talk it through."

She nodded. "Okay."

He led her down the stairs and bundled her into a blanket on the couch. Once she was gingerly sipping on a bottle of water, he left the house to check the area for threats. Sensing nothing and finding no sign of any intruders, he went all the way to the main road and circled the house twice before checking the roof for traps, all of the outbuildings, checking the basement, every room and ramping us his senses as far as they would go to look for any Cambion or Devils.

Satisfied that they were really alone, he went back into the house and joined Lux on the couch where she sat shivering. He sat next to her, covering her feet with his hand and leaning back into the cushions of the couch.

"Is there anything I can do?"

She shook her head. "I don't think so. Graciela and I weren't exactly close. I'd seen her a few times, but not a lot. Maybe a dozen in my life. She's always been stuck on the dreamplane. It's just where she is. She talked to Mom a little more, I think, but they weren't close, either. She was dead. As long as she was useful she got to stay there, so she would do things for Gabriel, like host meetings for him with Griffin and Braxton back during the original tasks and stuff like that. My mom is going to be torn up about it, but she's also going to be pissed off. I'm pissed off. He's trying to turn me into a prize. Something that he can own and show off. I'm not something that he can buy."

"No, you're not." Zane squeezed her foot and turned his head to look at her. "We're secure here. Nothing has come in, I can't sense anything coming, and there's no sign of any activity or traps. We can still leave if you feel like we're in danger, but there are risks with taking off in the middle of the night, too. Vampires are out right now, we don't know where we are in relation to where we're going, and headlights give away our position pretty definitively. It's a risk either way, but I'm leaving the decision up to you. You were the one who experienced the dream, you know how it felt, and you know whether or not you feel like we're under an immediate threat of being found."

Lux leaned against the back of the couch and closed her eyes. "I'd never been dragged into the dreamplane like that. Graciela had taken me there, yes, but always for a visit or for some training. Never for something like that. I knew that if I tried to fight him, he'd kill me."

"I know it doesn't seem like it, but you did the right thing." Zane rubbed her arm gently. "Lux, honey, we can talk about this however much you need to, but I need for you to make a decision of if we're going or staying."

Lux blinked as she tried to focus on him. She ran her hands over her face and forced herself to think the situation through. "How long until dawn?"

He peered out the window at the sky. "About four hours."

She raked her hands through her hair. "Call Michael's and let them know what's going on. I'm positive my mom already knows, but we'll make sure just in case. We'll stay until morning and then leave. I don't want to take off and run straight into a trap because we're lighting up the car like a fucking beacon in the night or trying not to be seen so we can't see what we're running in to."

"Do you think you're going to be able to go back to bed?"

She shook her head. "Not a chance in hell." She climbed to her feet. "I'm going to go check everything outside." When he looked at her, she shrugged. "I know you did, and I trust you, but I have to see for myself. I'll be back in a few minutes."

CHAPTER FIFTEEN

September 21st, 2060 - Anchorage, Alaska

ZANE STOOD in the doorway and looked in at Lux, who was finally sleeping. Deacon cleared his throat from out in the hallway. Zane turned and looked at his friend.

"She's asleep."

"Finally." Deacon led Zane back down the hallway and into the living room. "Amaya wanted to come. So did Zeke, but Michael and Aradia are united on this one. No one leaves the non-place for a while. What do you want to do?"

"Find the rest of these Cambion and get this done without having to worry about Lucifer."

Deacon opened the kitchen cabinets and rifled through the contents, coming up with a bottle of bourbon. He poured two glasses and passed one to Zane. "I think we can arrange that. I'm going to take the squad out and ruffle some feathers. It'll get them off your trail."

"Are you sure that's a good idea?"

"No, but it's all we've got. If they get wind of me or Amaya, they'll be all over it. You and Lux are second prize. No offense." Deacon sighed and raked one hand through his white blond hair as he perched on one of the kitchen stools. "We're lucky Lucifer hasn't reared his head until now if you really think about it."

"Knowing doesn't make this any easier to deal with, dude."

Zane took a drink of the liquor and swirled it around his mouth before swallowing. "Lux isn't worried about herself, but she's terrified he's going after Aradia."

"He very well may be going after Aradia. We don't know. Michael notified Gabriel, so he's in the loop, too. We're dealing with it the best we can. We knew he would know we were coming for him as soon as we got that damned sword. We've taken out four of Beelzebub's offspring. It's obvious we're coming. We had to expect retribution. It sucks ass, but we knew it was coming. There's more yet to come. You know that, brother." Deacon stared at the amber liquid in his glass, his expression somber and his gaze morose. "The original six made it through their tasks alive. Two of them are already dead this time around. We're trying to keep a lot more than six people alive. There's going to be more blood spilled yet. We all need to be prepared for that, Zane. No one is safe."

"Other than you and Amaya."

"Not even me and Amaya. Amaya is necessary to kill Lucifer. No one said she has to survive doing it. We think I could do it, too, but I'm not even part human, so no one knows for sure. Human, Angel, Devil. That's what's supposed to make her so strong." He grimaced at the harsh taste of alcohol as he drank. "We all signed on for this, and we're getting what we asked for. It's not going to get any easier. I'll do everything I can to keep them off your ass, but keep your eyes and ears open while you're here. This is an all-human settlement, so keep your head down and you'll be fine. The camp is run by Warriors. The main guy's name is Ian Samuels. He's decent." He poured another drink. "We'll get through it, Zane. Together until the end, right?"

Zane smiled. "It's worked for fifteen years." He looked at the stairs. "How's Aradia?"

"Handling it very well. Better than I thought. She's worried about Lux, of course, but she's had sixty years to come into her powers. She's confident in what they can do, and she's not stressing out about it. She's traveling around with Michael right now to strengthen the protections on all the Warrior bases, so she's got plenty to do. Gage is holed up at the non-place working on the locations of the last few Cambion so we can go after them. I'm going to take the squad after them if we can find them. With the Cambion in hiding, we need as many people on this as we can get."

"I agree, actually. We don't have the luxury of taking on these tasks one at a time and taking however long it takes. We need to get on it and go. We've got these two, but if Gage comes up with more locations before we're done, you should take the team and go for them." Zane leaned back and ran his hands over his face. "Has anyone told Gabriel about what happened?"

Deacon laughed. "Actually, yeah, we have. He came and apologized to Zeke for everything with Damon and Greer. He talked to Michael. He's training some Nephilim now. Amaya still doesn't know what to think, but I can see her getting more and more hopeful every day. She wants a relationship with him, but there's a lot of history there."

"I hope they work it out. I don't think he's evil, despite what he did to me. He sees things as black and white only. There's no in-between for him. He can't see shades of gray, and we live in the gray here. We have to. So for him to be useful for us, or to survive in our world, he has to live in the gray."

"I think he's trying to learn right now. He spent almost three decades refusing to help with anything, staying up in Heaven and leaving us all alone down here to fumble our way through this. Now, here he is, down in the trenches doing what he should have been doing all along. We'll see what happens." Deacon yawned and stood. "I should get back. You'll tell Lux I was here?"

"I'll let her know." Zane stood and started toward the door. "It's weird being here in this house were Zeke grew up, knowing her parents are dead."

"She knows you're here, and she's fine with it. She'd like it if the house is still in one piece when you leave, but given how Gage's estate looked when she was done with it, I don't think she has much room to talk."

Deacon opened the door and stepped out onto the porch. Zane leaned against the doorway and crossed his arms over his chest. "We'll stay in touch as much as we can, but you know how things are. Tell Lux's parents she's fine and she's hanging in there. We're handling things."

Deacon nodded and shrugged on his jacket. "I'll relay the message. Call if you need anything."

"We will. Be careful, Deacon. Things are heating up, and we all need to be more careful than normal."

Gabriel had stripped off his suit jacket in a concession to the heat, and a slight sheen of sweat shone on his face. He watched the Nephilim carefully as they trained, keeping mental notes of where each of them needed to improve. He turned his head when he heard the slight popping noise indicative of a flash and smiled when he saw Amaya appear.

"Amaya, welcome."

Amaya immediately shrugged out of her leather jacket. "It's cold in Scotland. Not so much here." She looked around appraisingly. "They're looking good. Almost ready?"

Gabriel cocked his head to the side and studied the Nephilim for several seconds. "A few more weeks, I think. They have talent and skills, but before they'll have a chance at surviving in battle they must not have to think before they react. Fighting has to be as much a part of their nature as breathing or walking. It isn't yet. For some, it will never be, and those will be the ones who will fall in battle no matter how many months of training I gave them. Their minds will betray them. For others, they were ready before they walked in here, and I am merely sharpening raw talent." He turned to Amaya. "Are you in need of Nephilim? I can provide you with some who are ready."

"No, I actually came to discuss something with you. Is there someplace we can talk that's a little less public?"

Gabriel almost reached out and took her arm but stopped himself just in time. "Certainly. I have an office upstairs. Follow me."

Amaya followed the Angel into the warehouse they were using as a base and up a set of rickety stairs to an office. The heat was only slightly better inside. They sat across from one another on sagging couches, Gabriel with one ankle crossed over the other knee and his hands folded on top of them.

"What can I do for you?"

"Deacon went to see Zane and Lux. Zane seems to be fully recovered from whatever it is you did to him. I thought you might like to know." Amaya winced when she saw a flicker of guilt flash in her father's eyes. "He's doing well. They're in Alaska at Damon and Greer's house, trying to find one of Beelzebub's sons. We've decided that since Lucifer is actively chasing Aradia and Lux, Deacon is going to take the team for any more of the Cambion Gage can locate if Lux and Zane are busy with another one."

"That seems like a move that makes much sense. I trust you will not be joining them? Keeping your location secret is of utmost importance during these times."

Amaya huffed. "I know. I'm the nuclear weapon. Yes, I'm safe.

Michael sent me down here, so I didn't even flash myself. I'm not an idiot, Gabriel. I can handle this."

Gabriel ran his hands over his face. "I didn't intend for it to sound like I was trying to tell you what to do, Amaya. I worry about you, that's all. I am allowed to do that much, I think." He stood and went to the window. "I know you like to imagine me a monster, but the fact remains it is my blood in your veins and my heart beating in your chest. Even if it were not, I would love you because of who your mother is."

"No, you wouldn't. You didn't watch over Eden and Donovan the way you did me. Or Finley. Yeah, you were there, but it was always me you came to visit. You kept them safe because they're my brother and sisters, not because you loved them." Amaya rubbed her palms on her jeans. "I didn't come here to argue over the past."

"And yet that seems to be all we can accomplish when we're together." He turned to look at her, and Amaya was struck by the grief and pain she saw in his eyes. "You're my child, Amaya, whether you like it or not. I made poor choices, and I paid for them. The price I paid was not seeing you born, not seeing your first steps, never hearing you call me father. I would make the same choice a million times over, even knowing the price of it because that choice means you're here and I get to look at you and talk to you and know that even though you hate me, you exist. You think Alaria is the only one who suffered? Or Braxton? I have suffered, too."

Amaya stared at him, not sure what to say, or how to feel. "You're an Angel. You don't feel like humans do."

"That doesn't mean we don't feel at all, child. I have been crazed with guilt and jealousy to the point I almost killed the one other human I ever loved. I made mistakes. I continue to make them. Damon and Greer—that was a mistake. Zane was a mistake. I'm trying to learn from them, hoping against hope you will see I am not the monster you wish I was. I love you, Amaya. Maybe not with the same intensity or tenderness as your mother and Braxton, but I would not hesitate to lay down my life for your with the same expedience as would they."

Amaya stood. "I think I should go. I came to tell you about what Deacon is planning and that Gage and Michael are working on a plan to lure Beelzebub into Purgatory to kill him. They might need your help."

Gabriel turned back to the window. "I'll be available when and if that happens." He stared stonily out the dirty panes, his shoulders stiff and his voice formal. "It was nice to see you. Be careful."

Amaya flashed out without saying anything else. Instead of going back to Michael's non-place, she took a risk she knew she shouldn't have taken and went to the facility where her parents were. As soon as she materialized, she was met with guns.

"Identify yourself."

"Amaya Winslow." She smiled at a slightly younger blonde who was shoving her way through the crowd of Warriors. "Eden can tell you. I'm her sister."

"Drop the guns." Eden Winslow wrapped her arms around Amaya in a tight hug. "What are you doing here? Do Mom and Dad know you're here? Donovan is off with a team somewhere in Russia right now with a squad of Nephilim, but Finley and Xander are here. Chris is with Donovan."

"No, Mom and Dad don't know I'm here. I'm here to see Dad if he's around."

Eden glanced at her watch. "Dad is probably in the gardens. Can you stay long? The night anyway?"

Amaya looked sad. "I doubt it, but we'll see. For dinner at least. Go on and let Mom and Finley know I'm here, but I need to talk to Dad by myself for a little while. It's important, okay?"

Concerned, Eden nodded. "Is everything okay? Do I need to start getting people prepared for something?"

"No, nothing like that. Just don't let Mom and Finley converge for, say, an hour. Can you do that?"

Eden nodded, her deep brown eyes filled with worry. "Sure." She reached out and touched her older sister's arm. "I've missed you."

Amaya embraced Eden quickly. "I've missed you, too. It'll be over soon, I promise."

Moving quickly through the compound, Amaya wound her way through the tents and dilapidated buildings the Warriors were living in. Several Nephilim were assigned to the base as transport and protection, and she nodded to them as she passed by. The cold chill from evening September air in France made her shiver, and she pulled her jacket back on to cover her arms, lifting her hair out from beneath it and letting it fall down her back.

Braxton was in the garden, a basket beside him as he knelt in the soft soil to pick tomatoes. She saw several other baskets filled with vegetables at the ends of the rows and knew he'd likely been there all day doing the harvesting. Her father had always tried to plant a garden wherever they were to ensure they had something fresh to eat, and he'd continued to expand it to feed the Warriors once they'd started trickling in.

"Think you'll have enough?"

Braxton looked up and grinned when he saw her. "This'll be enough for a couple weeks. We're going to be doing some canning to get through the winter if we're able to stay here. I've got two more plots this size on the other side of the compound that need to be picked before the frost hits and almost three acres planted about a twenty minute drive from here. If we get it all picked, we'll manage all right." He climbed to his feet and brushed dirt from the knees of his jeans.

Even at sixty-four, Braxton was still a handsome man. His face was tanned and well-lined, but his eyes were still bright and lively. His hair was streaked with gray, and while he moved slower than he had when Amaya had been a child, those movements were much more deliberate and thought out.

"Does Michael know you're here?"

"I'm sure he's figured it out by now. He keeps a close eye on me." Amaya went forward and hugged her father, breathing in the scent of soil and sweat and closing her eyes as his arms came around her. "I missed you, Daddy."

Braxton pressed one hand to the back of her head and wrapped the other arm around her waist. "I missed you, too, baby. Is something wrong? Has something happened?"

She pulled back and looked up at him, wishing, as she always did, that she saw something of herself in his face. "Is there someplace we can go to talk? Just you and me?"

Concerned, he nodded. "Sure. We'll walk down to the lake and check the lines for the fish then come back up here and load the veggies into the truck."

Braxton led Amaya down a path through the woods to a clearing where a lake spread out, filling the valley between two mountains. Amaya blinked and stared for a moment, taking in the beauty.

"This place is stunning."

"It's beautiful here for sure." Braxton gestured to two dozen fishing poles anchored to the bank. "Start checking lines. There's a stringer there on the ground. You know how to string up a fish if there's anything on them."

Amaya picked up one of the poles from the stand and started

reeling. "Do you have generators here? How are you powering everything?"

"Wood stoves for a lot of it, some solar power. We've got big batteries to store what we can. I have a couple engineers working on some hydropower, but that's a few months off yet, and yeah, there are a couple generators, but we try not to use them. They make a lot of noise and take a lot of fuel, which we need for vehicles." He deftly unhooked a catfish from the line and looped the stringer through its mouth. "Why are you here, Amaya?"

Amaya rebaited her own empty hook and cast the line back out into the water. "I need to ask something, and I knew you would tell me the truth. I don't want anyone to sugar coat it or make it worse. I just want the straight up truth, and you'll give me that. But on the other hand you're still my dad, and it just felt like if I was going to ask, it should be you or Mom and not someone else like Michael or Uncle Gage, even though they'd tell me the truth."

"The truth about what?"

Amaya took a deep, trembling breath. "I want to know about Gabriel."

Braxton didn't miss a beat. He baited the hook on the line and cast it out, anchoring the pole and moving to the next one. "What about him?"

"I went to see him today to tell him about the plan Deacon has with the rest of Beelzebub's Cambion and trying to lure Beelzebub into Purgatory to kill him."

"Good plan. That's the best place to make sure he stays dead. Gabriel had a problem with this plan?"

Amaya shook her head. "That wasn't the point. That's just why I went. It seems like ever since I found out he was my biological father, if I spend more than five minutes with him, we start arguing. Today it was because he said something about my staying away from things. I smarted off, we bickered, and it ended with him telling me he's not a monster and you and Mom aren't the only ones who suffered. That he paid a high price for his decisions, and he loves me, too. He keeps telling me how he wants a relationship with me and to be involved, but then he does shit like with Damon and Greer and with Zane, and I don't know how I can trust him. Now here he is training Nephilim and apologizing to Zeke and bringing Zane back and asking Lux to fix him, and it's confusing me." She dragged her arm across her face. "Plus there's the fact that I feel like I'm going to hurt your feelings if I even talk to him."

Braxton put another fish on the stringer. "How much truth do you want?"

Amaya blinked rapidly and looked at him in confusion. "What do you mean?"

"I mean, do you want me to reassure you and make you feel better, or do you want the actual no-holds-barred truth?"

"I want the truth, Dad. I'm twenty-eight years old. I can handle it."

"Okay." He sent another line back out into the lake. "You've heard the stories Gabriel told you, so I won't start at the beginning and I won't tell you a story. You're too old for that. Mom loved him, and he loved her. I saw them tear each other to pieces. They were both confused and desperate and jealous and torn up. I should've stepped back and stayed out of it, but I was just as much a wreck as she was, and we were gravitating toward each other. Even if I hadn't stayed out of it, it would have been over when Gabriel decided to get your mother pregnant. There was no going back from that and they both knew it."

Amaya's brows drew together. "I'm not blaming you for them not being together. I don't think you should have stayed out of it."

"I know, but Gabriel wanted to believe it was my fault. He was hurting. He was in an impossible situation. For everything he is, I believe he loved your mother in the best way he knew how. When he thought if he didn't trick her into getting pregnant with you another Angel might rape her, I believe him when he says he didn't feel like he had a choice. Gabriel has never been the type to come and talk to us about things. He was made to supervise humans. He views us as beneath him. We're a subpar, inferior species, and he tells us what to do. He doesn't ask us for advice, so when he was faced with a dilemma, he made a choice. It honestly never occurs to him to check with a human first. He just doesn't think about it."

"I didn't come here for you to defend him."

Braxton looked at his daughter sternly. "No, but you said you wanted the truth. I've never told you Gabriel is a monster. I've never told you he's a bad man. He's made mistakes, and he and I aren't buddies, but he's not as bad as you want him to be. Maya, baby, you're mine. From the moment that I looked at that fuzzy screen and saw you in your mother's belly, you have been mine. I felt you move inside her. I held you, I fed you, I have raised you and loved you, and you are mine. No one is going to take that from us. No one. I don't need you to hate him to be assured you're mine. I know." He dropped the stringer full of fish into a bucket and took her hands in his. "I've let you figure this out on your own, thinking you needed time and space to come to terms with everything because this is big and it's a lot to ask from someone, but it's time to get your head on straight. He's not evil. He's not bad. He's a dick, yeah, and I don't like him, but there is nothing wrong with wanting to know your father or have a relationship with him."

Amaya sniffed back tears. "You're my father."

"I'm your dad. You're my daughter. Sweetheart, if I was insecure about Gabriel, I wouldn't have let him come around when you were a kid. It doesn't bother me. It never has." He sat down on the bank, waiting until she joined him before he spoke again. "Have I ever told you about the first time I knew I was in love with your mother?"

Amaya shook her head. "No."

"I was getting there when you were born. We'd talked about it a few times, but things were still too unsettled. 'I still don't think I love you, she'd say, and I'd say something the same back'. We meant it for the most part. The feelings were so different from what she'd had for Gabriel and I for Griffin, and everything was changing so quickly in the world. We went from six to two with two babies—Finley and you. We were scrambling to find food, anyplace to sleep. It was hard. When you were about a year old, we were somewhere in Texas. I don't even remember where. It was January, so just before your birthday. We were staying in a compound with some Warriors. You started walking while we were there. I was in the living room of this shitty apartment, and you were holding onto my fingers, walking across the floor. Alaria had just finished putting Finley to bed and came to get you to give you a bath. Her hair was in this bun thing on top of her head, and I don't think she'd showered in nearly a week—neither of us had. It was the first night we'd had a bed in a month."

Amaya snorted. "This doesn't seem like some romantic moment. I was expecting flowers and wine."

Braxton laughed. "Your mother and I have never been flowers and wine." He bumped her shoulder with his. "Anyway, she stopped in the doorway and just stared at us and said, 'You bastard. You fucking bastard. She's walking, and you didn't even tell me.'"

"Sounds like Mom."

"It's just like Mom." He looked up at the sky, enjoying the memory. "I laughed at her and said something about how she shouldn't have taken so long with Finley and she wouldn't have missed it. She stomped across the room, snatched you up and stormed back to the bathroom. Just as she's closing the door, she whirls around and yells, 'I get to do that with the next one while you put these two to bed.' I made a crack about how that would be a while and you'd both be putting yourselves to bed by then. She stuck her head out the door with this giant grin on her face and said, 'You idiot, I'm pregnant.' I knew right when she said that, I'd been in love with her the whole damn time."

"What do you mean?"

Braxton reached out and gripped her hand. "In the back of my head, I was always afraid things would change if we had a biological child. Finley isn't biologically mine or Alaria's. You're not biologically mine. When she told me she was pregnant with Eden, nothing changed. I didn't suddenly love you and Finley less. I didn't love Eden more. Nothing changed. I slid into love with your mother. I didn't fall. It was so gradual neither of us noticed until we'd been there a while."

Amaya laid her head on his shoulder. "I'm confused, Dad."

"It's okay to be confused." He kissed her forehead. "Just never be confused about our family. Finley is your sister. I am your dad. Your mother and I love one another and always will. Nothing is going to change any of that. If you and Gabriel have a relationship and you end up with two dads, well, you're lucky to have so many people who love you. Never worry about me, baby girl. You've been mine since before you were born, and you'll be mine until I draw my last breath."

CHAPTER SIXTEEN

September 22, 2060 – Anchorage, Alaska

LUX WOKE when the first slivers of light broke through the filmy curtains at the window and spilled across her face. She yawned and stretched, rolling out of the bed and heading for the bathroom. She had taken Zeke's old room, letting Zane take Damon and Greer's. It had felt too weird to sleep in there.

After brushing her hair and teeth, she wandered downstairs, the oversized button-down she wore slipping off of one shoulder as she padded into the kitchen. Giant solar panels covered the roof to run the appliances, and she thanked God for them as she poured water into the coffee pot and waited by the counter for it to perk. Gratefully pouring the first cup, she took it out onto the back deck, leaning against the railing and gazing out at the forest while she took a deep drink of hot coffee.

Within fifteen minutes, she heard Zane stir and come down the stairs. He stumbled into the kitchen wearing nothing but a pair of sweatpants and went straight for the cabinet with coffee cups. Lux's teeth sank into her lower lip as she watched the way he moved around the kitchen, and she pressed one hand to her abdomen, her gut clenching with desire as she raked her eyes over his bare chest.

"Morning." Zane's voice was still rough with sleep as he came through the sliding glass doors.

"Good morning." She drained the last bit of coffee from her

cup. "What's our plan for today?"

"I think we should go into town and poke around. Deacon popped in last night after you went to sleep and gave me some information on the Warrior who runs things here. We can talk to him, let him know what we're up to and see if there're are any known Cambion around here. If not, we'll at least be able to get some history on people and have a starting point. There's plenty of food here, so we're good on that front. The freezer was still going, so we've got some meat and some frozen stuff. Most everything in the fridge was bad, so I cleaned it out last night and got rid of everything before I went to bed." He took a drink from the mug. "We'll likely be here a few days. Yes, we're working, but I see no reason not to take advantage of a little down time when we can get it."

Lux made a noise in the back of her throat. "I agree. Let's get showered, eat, and get into town then. No time like the present." She glanced toward the kitchen. "I'll figure out something for breakfast if you want to take the first shower. Damon was about your height so his stuff should fit you. Feel free to borrow anything you need."

"Do you think Zeke would mind? I have a couple things I can wear."

"Zane, you have one pair of jeans and like three shirts. It'll be fine. Zeke is not going to mind." She nudged him toward the stairs. "Go on. Take a shower."

"Okay, thanks."

Lux waited five minutes, giving him enough time to get upstairs and in the shower. She rinsed her cup in the sink, her stomach fluttering with nerves, and headed for the steps, ascending them slowly. Lifting one arm, she tugged the hair band loose from her hair and let her red curls flow around her shoulders and down her back in a cloud. As she slipped into the bathroom, her fingers nimbly worked the little buttons on her shirt loose from their holes. The garment hit the floor silently and she padded across the floor to the shower.

Zane was standing under the spray of water with his back turned to her. His arms were braced on the tile, and his head was down as he let the water soak into his hair and run over his body. Lux grasped the door handle and pulled it open, stepping into the shower with him. He started to look over his shoulder, a smile on his lips as he caught sight of her, his gut twisting with desire when he saw her naked form for the first time.

Before he could say a word, she slithered underneath his arms and slammed him back against the wall of the shower, pressing her body against his and clamping her mouth over his. Her nails bit into his shoulders and she swept her tongue into his mouth, groaning as his taste flooded her.

Zane felt like he was drowning. Lux wrapped around him, seeping into him, clouding his brain and making it hard to think. He found the wall of the shower with one hand to help balance himself and got the other arm wrapped around her, his mind blanking when he laid his hand on naked skin, the foreign and oh-so-wonderful feel of her under his palms making his ability to think coherently evaporate as he eagerly ran his bare fingers over her silky smooth skin.

She wrenched her mouth away from his, nibbling at his lips before raking her teeth over the line of his jaw. Her hands fisted in his hair and she tugged sharply, bringing his gaze down to hers. Her eyes were bright and hot with desire. Zane shook his head to clear it, his gaze shining with want and need, the same reflected back in her eyes as she met his gaze confidently.

"Not that I'm complaining, because I'm not, but did you have to attack me in the shower?"

Lux giggled and leaned forward to press a kiss to his chest. "Obviously I do if I want to get anything I want around here. We're always in danger or we stink or we're tired or something's going on or there's too much pressure or it's something. I'm sick of something." She reached out and folded her fingers around his erection, stroking up and down. "I want sex, Zane, and I want it now." She rubbed her thumb over the head of his penis. "Specifically, I want fast, hard, hot shower sex, with you, right now."

Zane's head fell back, and his hips jutted forward as pure bliss rocketed through him from the feel of her hands wrapped around his cock. "You could at least let me take you into the bedroom."

"You might try to run away again. You can't get away from me in here."

Zane flipped their positions so that she was pressed against the cold tile. He ran his hands down her sides and over her hips before skimming his fingers up her stomach and over the curve of her breasts. He lifted them in his hands, supporting them with his palms and rubbing the pads of his thumbs over the tightly beaded tips.

"I don't want to get away from you." He reached for a loofa and a bottle of body gel. "We can play in here, Lux, but the sex is going to be on the bed."

Pouting, she looked up at him through her eyelashes. "Why do you get to call the shots?"

He chuckled and bent to kiss her. "Because I think we'd both enjoy it more if your head wasn't slamming against the wall with every thrust and we didn't have to race the hot water tank to be done."

Considering, she nodded. "Good point. I accept the compromise." She groaned when he ran the loofa over her nipples, following the path of the slightly rough sponge with his fingers.

He touched every part of her with the soapy poof, then efficiently soaped himself up as well before drawing her into his arms and stepping under the water, their bodies slipping against one another as they rinsed off the soap. Her nipples brushed against his chest, and the friction sent spears of pleasure through her. His erection rubbed against her thigh as they maneuvered in the tight space, soft and silky.

Lux cupped him in her hand again, looping her fingers around his staff and stroking up and down, her grip firm and confident. Her other arm wound around his neck, pulling him down to her for a deep, searching kiss.

"I don't think I've ever wanted someone this bad before." She pressed her face into his neck. "You don't know what you do to me."

Touched, Zane stroked his hand over her hair and reached to turn off the water. "Let me show you what you do to me."

They were both slightly frenzied as they got out of the shower and dried off, their motions jerky and hurried as if they were in a race to see who could be done the fastest. Desperate to continue what they had started, Lux dropped her towel on the ground and grabbed his hand, dragging him down the hall to the room she was sleeping in, slamming the door and shoving him against it, her mouth on his as soon as his back hit the door.

He pushed her back toward the bed, one hand sliding over her hip to grip the curve of her ass. "Do you have rubbers in here or do I need to go to the car?"

"In my bag. Foot of the bed. Outside pocket."

Zane let go of her and went to the bag, finding the box with little problem and snatching out one of the packets. He backed her up until the edge of the bed pressed into her knees, then followed her down onto the mattress, covering her body with his own. He kissed her deeply, brushing her tongue with his own before sliding down her body, trailing his mouth over her collarbone and on down her chest.

Her breasts were two perfect globes on her chest, full and firm. They were tipped with dusky pink areolas and slightly darker nipples. He tasted one, then the other, before drawing her nipple fully into his mouth, sucking deeply and flooding his senses with the taste of her skin. Her back came off the bed slightly and her hands tangled in his hair, gripping his head and holding her to him.

Gently, he nipped the flesh with his teeth before soothing with his tongue. Releasing her nipple reluctantly, he shifted to give the other one equal treatment, using his fingers on the one he had relinquished, rolling it between his thumb and forefinger and stroking it gently.

Continuing to suck and lick at her nipples, he slipped one hand between her thighs and rubbed her gently, stroking the entrance to her body. She was wet and warm and squirmed on the bed under his ministrations. Gently, he slid one finger into her, rubbing her clit with his thumb while rocking his hand gently.

Lux's chest flushed and she tightened her grip on his hair, her hips lifting slightly and pressing into his hand as she rode the wave of sensation, the slight tingling she felt whenever Zane touched her amplifying the pleasure she felt as the stroking of his fingers on and in her.

"Is that good for you?" Zane's voice was low and soft. "I've never been able to touch anyone like this so tell me if it's wrong."

She was panting as climax began building. "No, not wrong. It feels good. You're going to make me come if you keep doing that. I'm close. So close. A little firmer, just a tiny bit faster."

Zane made the adjustments, dipping his head to suckle at her breast once again. She groaned deeply, her eyes closing and her breath coming faster. Her feet pressed harder into the mattress and her groans became more ragged. He pressed his palm firmly against her body, rocking the heel of his hand back and forth and smiled when she flew apart with a loud groan, orgasm ripping through her and sending her spiraling away on a wave of pleasure.

Pulling back from her, he tore into the condom and rolled the thin latex over his straining erection. Lux reached for him, drawing him back onto her, lifting her legs to wrap around his thighs and pulling him close.

"I want to feel you in me. Now, Zane. I don't want to wait anymore."

Zane lifted her hips in his hand, using one to balance her and the other to guide himself. He probed her body slowly, sinking into her inch by inch. She closed around him like a vise, wet and hot. Gently, he rocked his hips against hers, gliding in and out. Lux sucked in a breath and held it for a long moment, her nails biting into his biceps. She turned her head, seeking out his mouth.

Her body hugged his tightly, her hips cradling him as he stroked into her over and over again. She clung to him, her breath coming fast and shallow as he slipped in and out. Each thrust brought her slightly further back up the crest of climax. She held him close, reveling in the feel of every movement of his body against hers.

She pressed her face into his neck, breathing in deeply. The scent of his blood, thick and rich, filled her nose and a fresh rush of desire pooled deep within her. Of their own accord, her fangs extended. Equal shares frightened by her body's reaction and fascinated by it, she nuzzled his neck.

Zane's thrusts quickened as he grew nearer to orgasm. He crushed her to his body, holding her tightly and pumping into her over and over again, driving them both up. She tightened around him, pulsating and trembling. Squirming against him to get the friction just right, she strained toward completion.

Lux dropped over the edge and into climax suddenly. She clenched tight on his cock, throwing her head back and then rearing up and sinking her teeth into the side of his neck. His blood flowed over her tongue and down her throat, sweet and thick. Zane gasped in shock and jerked for a second, then surged into her, his body jerking as he came.

"Did you..."

Lux interrupted before Zane could finish the sentence. "Yes." She refused to roll over and look at him. Her cheeks were bright red and her arms were crossed firmly across her chest. She had found a very interesting spot on the wall and was determined not to look away from it.

He touched the side of his neck gingerly. "It doesn't hurt. I always thought getting bitten by a vampire would hurt."

"I'm not a vampire."

"No, but you're part vampire or else you wouldn't have fangs, babe." He poked at the puncture wounds on his neck. "It feels like they're healing already." He laid his hand on her hip. "Roll over here and talk to me. I'm not angry at you."

"I bit you! I drank your blood! I'm disgusting! I'm a freak of nature!" She sat up and grabbed the blanket, dragging it up over herself. "I always thought the damn fangs were just for show. I used them in a fight occasionally, but I never thought I would actually feed on someone. I eat food! Not people!"

Zane forced himself not to laugh. "Technically, you didn't eat me. Just took one bite." He held up his hands when she glared at him. "Don't look at me like that. It's not like I'm dying in a puddle of blood. It was strangely erotic."

"It's supposed to be. Vampires have an aphrodisiac in their saliva they can use on humans during sex if they want to. It numbs the pain and makes their dinner more amenable to being dinner. Feeding during sex is a sexy thing for vamps. It makes orgasm more powerful."

"Do you do it often?"

Humiliated and near tears, Lux surged to her feet and started yanking on clothes. "I never do that! I don't know why I did it just now. I didn't mean to!" She started for the door, struggling when Zane leapt nimbly from the bed and grabbed her by the arm. "Just let me go."

"No, I'm not going to let you go." He dragged her into his arms. "Stop being upset about this. It's fine. It's not like you made a meal out of me." He bent and kissed her gently, holding her tightly. "I've known since we were teenagers that your father was a vampire when you were conceived. You love to show me your fangs when you're pissed. I've seen you tear into a demon with your teeth. It's not like I haven't seen that side of your nature. I'm not bothered by it. I was a little surprised, but you didn't hurt me, and you didn't gross me out."

"How could it not gross you out? It grossed me out and I was the one who did it. I hate that I liked it. I don't want to do that to you." She blinked back tears. "I'm sorry. I didn't mean to."

Zane slid one hand around the back of her neck. "Do I look like I'm weak or drained of blood? How much did you take? A mouthful, maybe?"

"It doesn't matter. The amount isn't the point. It's that I did it at all. I shouldn't have and I'm sorry for it. Really sorry." Lux closed her eyes. "I'll understand if you regret what we just did. I know I would in your situation. I couldn't blame you for it."

Zane pushed her down onto the bed and perched next to her. "Lux, I am going to say this once, and then I don't want to have to repeat myself. While the odds are good if left to my own devices it would never have occurred to me to request you bite me, I am not angry about what happened, I am not hurt, and I am not disgusted or repulsed by you. There was a lot of tension built up, and probably had something to do with it. If it happens every once in a while or hell, even if you needed to do it every time, I would let you because I want to keep being with you. You were willing to take me on with the gloves, even when I wasn't willing to let you. This is absolutely no different than that. Other than the fact that you aren't risking my life." He laid his hand over hers. "I'm not grossed out by it."

She looked at him out of the corner of her eye. "I think you should be. I think it's pretty gross. I didn't mean to do it and I don't want to do it again. My dad's biggest fear was that I would get some vampiric properties. He doesn't know I have fangs or that I can drink blood if I need to." She stared down at their hands. "This is what they get for messing with nature. Angel, witch, vampire. The result is bound to have some weird qualities."

"Personally, I think your incessant need to lay out and tan every time you see sand is the weirdest thing about you, but hey, it's your skin to get cancer on I suppose."

Despite her determination not to, she giggled. "I didn't mean to ruin the requisite post-coital cuddle." She leaned her arm on his shoulder. "The sex was amazing. Absolutely incredible. I think that's why I couldn't resist."

He laid back, pulling her with him. "There's an easy fix for that problem, you know."

"What problem?"

"The lack of post-coital cuddling." He worked his hands beneath her shirt and took her breasts in his hands. "We'll just have more coitus, then do some cuddling."

CHAPTER SEVENTEEN

BEELZEBUB TAPPED his fingers on the armrest of the throne on which he sat, watching with mild interest as Lilith brushed Serafina's hair over and over again. His sons, Alexi and Isaiah, sat nearby, discussing something he had no interest in hearing.

Huffing, he stood and brushed his hand over the arm of his suit. "Where are Abalam and Azazel? They're late."

"Oh, don't get your dick in a twist. I'm here." Abalam breezed into the room and flopped onto one of the other thrones. "What the fuck did you call us all together for? The Brady Bunch is after all of us, and if they get wind that we're together like this, they'll attack."

Beelzebub sneered, his lips pulling back to bare his teeth in a vicious grin. "Let them come. I'll gut every last one of them."

The doors flew open and Lucifer came in, taking his place at the center throne. He glanced to Lilith and Serafina. "This is no place for a child."

Serafina looked up and pouted. "But Daddy, I want to plan the Apocalypse, too! Mommy said I might get to kill some nasty Nephilim!"

Lucifer smiled indulgently. "When you're bigger, darling. Run along to your nanny and go play. Mommy and Daddy need to talk about some important things for a while. I'll take you out for a while after dinner." He ran his hand over her hair when she dashed to him for a hug and kiss. "Go on now, be Daddy's good girl."

Beelzebub waited until Serafina had raced from the room. "It's not advisable for us all to be here for long. We'll draw the attention of the enemies. As much as I would relish the confrontation, we don't want to lead them to the child. I'd suggest keeping this quick."

"Agreed." Lucifer glanced around the room. "Where is Azazel? Was he not summoned?"

Azazel appeared with a flash and a loud bang. "I'm here. I don't want to be, but I am. What's going on?"

Lucifer lifted one eyebrow. "Respect, son. Show some." He looked at Lilith. "I've decided that the time of sitting around and waiting for Michael to bring the fight to us is over. We're going to take it to them. The Nephil witch and Death's son have been picking off your progeny for months, Beelzebub. There are only five left. If they finish that, they're coming for you, and if they manage to kill you, I'll be weakened. If I had known fishing you out would require linking you to me, I'd never have done it. They've already destroyed my sword. They're making too much progress."

Lilith ran her fingers through her hair. "I could have killed her if Isaiah had been better trained. He wasn't as ready as I thought he was, and the other Nephilim got to him. It was my mistake and one I won't make again. She'd have blown herself up trying to kill me if I'd been able to catch her alone."

Lucifer looked at her, his gaze full of boredom. "She'd have killed you with the explosion. She's powerful, Lilith. I don't think you understand the power there. Once I kill her mother and send that power into her, harnessing her is going to be very important. She'll help us take Heaven." He sat up straighter. "I didn't call you all here to discuss what has happened. It's done and over with. Mistakes have been made by everyone in this room. Including me. The lack of wing roots on our backs is evidence of that. We under-estimated them thirty years ago, and I under estimated them six months ago when we knew they were coming for the sword. We mustn't make that same mistake here."

Beelzebub crossed his legs and studied his fingernails. "What do you suggest we do? Charge the castle? I'd be happy to go kill them if we knew where they were."

"Which is exactly why we're going to lure them to where we want them." Lucifer turned to face Beelzebub. "You're going to have to sacrifice the others. Move them around, let them be killed, let the Nephilim get confident. Michael and the vampire are good at finding things out, even when we don't want them to. Alexi and Isaiah will be given a mission when they are the only two left. We will lure them to where we want them, and we will ambush them. Cambion aren't going to cut it. The witches alone could cut down a thousand Cambion each, and Michael will likely be there. The four of you are going to have to go."

Azazel sat up straighter. "No offense, but fuck that. The last time I went after these fucking kids, I ended up floating in the ether for two months. I'm not in a hurry to do it again."

Lucifer cocked an eyebrow. "It wasn't a suggestion, son."

Lilith studied a chip in her nail polish. "I'd like to kill them, I think. It'll be fun."

Abalam stroked his fingers over his chin. "It'll take some planning to get the trap right. If we're not careful, they'll smell it a mile away. It'll have to be good."

Lucifer smiled. "Then make it good. We're going to be rid of the whole lot of them in one fell swoop. Then, when they're all dead, I'll find Alaria's daughter, if she's smart enough not to come with them, and I'll rip her head off. Once I have the witch as my captive, we will storm the gates of Heaven and take it back. By the end of this, I will be God."

Beelzebub mulled it over in his head. "I don't like offering up my children as sacrifices, Lucifer. They're mine. You wouldn't dream of sacrificing Serafina for this cause, and no one would ask you to. I'm going to want something in return for giving them to you willingly."

Alexi glanced up from his conversation with Isaiah. "Let the others die. As long as it isn't me, what do you care? Isaiah and I are the only two who don't have inferior mothers."

Lucifer's mouth quirked in a ghost of a smile. "Your father is notorious for maneuvering for more and more power. The time will come, Alexi, when your allegiance will be to either him or to me. I'd suggest you begin thinking about who you'll stand by when that day comes." He turned to Beelzebub. "I never doubted you would want something for the dubious sacrifice of letting children you don't even like and whose names you likely don't even know die. What's the price, Beelzebub? You already sit at my left hand."

Beelzebub looked at Lilith. "For millennia, I sat at your right. I did your bidding. I was the most loyal of servants. Not one other has served you as continuously and faithfully as have I. Lilith dallied on Earth, playing with the humans, running after the fall to escape our fate. Azazel played one side against the other, plotting only to save his own hide and betraying both you and God in the process. Abalam wandered for twenty-five years after Abaddon perished, refusing to come back and be a part of the war. I have never wavered, never lapsed, never failed to love or to serve."

Lucifer placed his index fingers against his lips and stared at Beelzebub intently. "Nothing you said is untrue. All of my children have disappointed me. Your accusations are accurate, and no one here could disagree with a single one of them." He rose from the throne. "But heed this. You are not without fault. I have always known you serve only as long as it serves you. There will come a day when you will take up arms against me as I did against God. I am well aware of that and I welcome it. I see much of me in you, and it is because I see the greed and the desire in you that I love you so much. You failed in the Choosing. You let Alaria get away, betraying us all, making a mockery of the whole of Hell. A mere Healer waltzed into my palace and stole Laelia under your watch. A witch subdued you long enough to steal your wings from you. You, who served at my right hand, are as responsible for the sins of your brethren as are they."

Beelzebub uncrossed his legs and scowled. "You can't possibly hold me responsible for this lot. Alaria blindsided us all. You included. My point is that I deserve the right hand throne more than anyone else, and when I deliver you the witch and Gabriel's whelp on silver platters, it should be mine. Especially since I'm being required to give up the lives of my flesh and blood to give them to you. You ask more from me than from anyone else, therefore I should get more than anyone else."

His tone mild and friendly, Lucifer cocked his head to one side. "And if I tell you to do it anyway? With no reward at all?"

Beelzebub stood, facing Lucifer. "Then you'll have to figure out a plan to lure them in that doesn't involve my children."

Lucifer nodded. "Very well then. You shall have your throne if we succeed." He glanced around the room. "Tell your children to come out of hiding and begin working on a way to bring them together. Azazel, Abalam, and Lilith will remain on Earth and in close proximity for the ambush when you need them. Beelzebub, you're in charge of this. I want Gabriel's daughter and the witch brought to me alive. Kill everyone else. Understood?"

Beelzebub nodded. "Understood."

Lilith sat still as the other three disappeared. When only she and Lucifer remained in the room, she looked at him and smiled. "Do you intend to let him have my seat at your right?"

He looked at her. "Darling, do you even want the seat?"

She twirled in a circle, enjoying the way the skirt on her dress flowed out around her legs. "I want to be Queen."

"Then you'll have a throne next to me, and you'll rule as my equal. Beelzebub will serve at our right, or he'll serve as our slave, but he will serve." Lucifer watched her with amusement. "After all, you are bearing us children. Serafina will be more powerful than anything that has ever before been seen on this Earth."

Lilith skittered up the steps to the throne and pressed herself against Lucifer. "I've birthed three children, my love. One by an Angel who hates me. One by Beelzebub who is an eternal disappointment to me, and our darling girl who will rule along with us. I want a son as powerful as our daughter. I want to carry your son. Will you let me have the honor of birthing one more child? Another child for you? I ache to present you with a son, a true heir to Hell." She batted her eyelashes at him. "I'm fertile. If we were to fuck now, you could have a son."

Lucifer grabbed her dress and ripped it from her body with one tear, casting strips of fabric aside and leaving her naked. "I'll fill you with my seed, darling, and plant a son deep in your belly."

Eagerly, she unbuckled his belt, yanking it from the loops and dropping it onto the floor. She shoved his pants down his ankles and pushed him backward until he was sitting on the throne. Her hands already cupping and stroking his penis, she straddled him, taking him in completely and impaling herself on his erection.

Lilith rode him hard, her lithe body gyrating and grinding against his. Her breasts swayed and bobbed with every bounce, and moisture from her body soaked his cock, making her slippery.

Lucifer's face reddened as he neared orgasm. "Harder. Fuck me harder, you bitch."

Lilith purred and rocked her hips into his harder. "I love it when you talk dirty to me."

"You're a fucking whore."

"I'm your whore." She panted and groaned, rising over him and reaching up to play with her own nipples. "Come in me. Do it, darling, do it now. Spill yourself inside me."

He roared as he came, his hands digging furrows into the armrests of the throne. Lilith rode him through the orgasm, taking her own, her head falling back and her breasts jutting forward while her hips rocked back and forth, moving him slightly inside her as semen spurted from his penis and into her body.

His seed burned as it entered her, pain spreading through her body. Lilith reveled in it, continuing to rock, extending her orgasm as she basked in the pain of their coupling. Her abdomen glowed red, and her eyes crackled with black lightning. She felt the change immediately, the joining within her. Slowly, she lifted her arms over her head, twining her fingers together and leaning back slightly, grinding herself on Lucifer's half-hard dick. He watched her in awe, amazed at the transformation that took place. She groaned and squirmed, rubbing against him as she lowered her arms, her fingers tweaking and pinching her nipples. The red spread until her whole body glowed. Her hair fell down her back in a red and yellow wave, and her pussy clenched and released rhythmically around him. One of her hands slid down her body and between her legs, pressing against her clit to give herself enough stimulation to tumble over the edge and into a second orgasm.

As the glow faded and she collapsed into his arms, she stretched up to kiss him gently before speaking. "It is done. I can feel the child already growing inside of me. Soon he will rip his way from my body, and we will have a son."

CHAPTER EIGHTEEN

September 24th, 2060 – Anchorage, Alaska

"I ALMOST feel bad about this." Lux pulled on a jacket and zipped it up, reaching for thin leather gloves. "This guy doesn't seem to know who he is. What does the file say about his mother?"

Zane looked down at the sheaf of papers in his lap. "It says that his mother was a waitress when everything happened. She appears to have been seduced by Beelzebub after work one night. It doesn't seem that she knew who he was. She got pregnant, had him, raised him until she died when he was fifteen. At that point his powers were manifesting as he went through puberty, and he came up here to hide out. He's lived here as a human ever since."

She sighed deeply. "Samuels said that he's never caused any problems. He stays out of trouble, doesn't come into town much other than to trade hides or fish for some supplies that he needs. He's a loner. Can we really believe that he doesn't know Beelzebub is his father?"

"Well, we do know that not every woman a Devil slept with got pregnant. It could stand to reason that not every woman that got pregnant by a Devil knew she did. There were plenty of women shocked as shit to find out that their children were Nephilim."

"That's because Angels didn't need sex to make them. Devils did." Lux snapped a pistol into the holster around her hip. "Let's just get this done. He has to die. There's no way around it. Whether he's actively evil or not, he's still a Cambion and he's one of Beelzebub's. That makes him a threat. It has to be done."

Zane opened the door and stepped out onto the porch. "We may have to go in hot and then get out as fast as we can. There's going to be a lot of activity if we have to take him out using our powers instead of bullets."

"I know. The car's fully packed, the tank's full and we're ready to go as soon as we kill him. We've get the rendezvous spot with Carys and Elisa set up. It's a day and a half drive from here, so they won't be in too much danger and they'll get us to London to go after the next one." She slid into the front seat of the car and waited until he rounded the hood and got in next to her. "I'm just not sure if we want to try and sneak up on him or go in guns blazing."

Zane considered the dilemma as he backed out of the driveway. "Are you sure we have everything from the house we need?"

Lux twisted in her seat to survey the tightly packed SUV. "Even if we don't, there's nowhere to put it, so this is it. We've got clothes, food, and fuel. I loaded the box with soap, shampoo, towels, and condoms, so we're good there. So what do you think? Stealthy or just go straight in?"

"I think you're going to need to have your magic ramped up enough to keep him from flashing out on us, so he'll be able to detect that regardless. Neither of us can dampen our powers to the extent we can be completely sure he won't be able to sense us coming. I think we just go in and get it done. No sneaking, no big plans, just two against one. I like the odds."

"Okay."

They rode in silence as Zane maneuvered the roads toward the house where the Cambion lived. The file Gage had prepared said his name was Clayton Daniels. As they drove, Lux wondered what his life had been like, torn between believing he could possibly be innocent or that he had to know what he was and who he came from.

The moon was bright and round in the sky, illuminating the road to the point that headlights were almost completely unnecessary. Gravel crunched under the tires as Zane pulled the car off the main road and onto a driveway that led to the house where their target lived. It wound around two ponds and went nearly three miles before the woods opened up into a clearing with a small cabin. Smoke trickled out of the chimney, and laundry hung on a clothesline next to the small porch.

Together, they exited the car and approached the house. Lux's eyes had already darkened to black and she whispered under her breath, chanting a spell to keep the Cambion inside from being able to leave the house.

The door opened and a thin, tall man came out. His hair was dyed black, hiding the white-blond locks indicative of a Cambion. As he crossed his arms over his chest, he stared down at them with trepidation.

"I know you're Nephilim."

Zane was the one to answer. "We are. And you're a Cambion."

Clayton stuffed his hands in his pockets. "Come on in then. I'll make some coffee."

Lux glanced over at Zane, her eyebrows drawing together. "What the hell is this about?"

The Cambion stared down at them. "You obviously want something. There's no need for us to stand out here in the cold discussing it. Come on inside, and I'll make a pot of coffee. It's instant, but it doesn't taste too bad. I have some milk and sugar for it. The cow out back just had a calf, so the milk is fresh, not the powdered in a bag shit." He gestured to the steps. "If you talked to Ian, you know I'm not a murderous type. Either come in or don't, but I'm having some coffee."

Lux's eyes cleared and she stared at Zane. "This is not what I expected."

Zane lifted his shoulders in a shrug and followed the Cambion up the steps. "Stranger things have happened."

Following him, she shook her head. "Maybe, but not by much."

The cabin was small and tidy. The downstairs was one large room with a sagging couch, a table with four chairs, and the kitchen. She saw a loft up a ladder with a mattress and a bathroom at the back. A fire crackled in the fireplace, and an oil-lamp sat in the center of the table. They stood in silence while the man worked in the kitchen, measuring grounds and putting them into a teapot, then placing the kettle on a grate inside the fireplace to heat up.

"It'll be done in a few minutes." He gestured to the table. "Have a seat."

Zane dropped into one of the chairs. "Do you know who we are?"

"I know you're Nephilim."

"She's the daughter of Michael. I'm the son of the Angel of Death."

Clayton whistled. "Powerful Nephilim. You were using magic when you came up. Was one of your human parents a witch?"

"Both of our mothers were." Lux perched in a chair. "How much do you know about your father?"

He shrugged. "Not much. Just that he was either a Devil or a demon. I don't know who it was. Why?"

"Your father is Beelzebub." She leaned forward, bracing her elbows on the table and staring at him steadily. "We're here to kill you."

The Cambion expelled a deep breath. "Wow. Okay. Not what I expected. I mean, I know that Cambion and Nephilim don't exactly get along, but I'm out here living in the woods. I'm not hurting anything. I don't bother anyone. I've never killed anyone. I know you probably don't believe that, but it's true. Ian said I could stay as long as I didn't bring any other Cambion here. I don't even know any other Cambion, so that hasn't been a problem." He took a gasping breath. "My mom died when I was a teenager. Step-dad, too. Car wreck. When it was getting really, really bad about fifteen years ago. You were there, you know how it was. I was starting to figure out what I was. The hair is like a fucking neon sign announcing your parentage. So I started dyeing it. Hair dye is actually something you can find pretty easily in stores and such. Not many people go in there looking for that anymore. I live here, I hunt and fish. When I need something else, I go into town and trade. People are generally pretty cool. I thought everything was okay." He blinked, tears welling in his eyes. "What did I do? Why do I need to die?"

Lux felt her heart twist in her chest. "Clayton, you haven't done anything. It's because of who your father is."

"So this is some sort of sins of the father thing? I know enough to know Beelzebub is one powerful dude, but killing me isn't going to punish him. I doubt he even knows I exist."

When Zane spoke, his voice was soft. "I'd say you're right about that. He probably doesn't know you exist or you wouldn't be here like this." He looked at Lux. "Get him something stronger than a cup of coffee if you can find it."

His voice trembling, Clayton managed a strangled whisper. "Vodka in the pantry behind the fridge."

Lux rose to fetch the bottle and a glass, filling it to the brim and plunking it down on the table in front of the shaking man. She laid her hand on his. "Do you want me to explain things to you?"

He nodded. "Please."

"Thirty years ago during the Choosing, Griffin Javensen stabbed Beelzebub with a knife given to her by God. It had been consecrated with the blood of Jesus and would kill anything. She had it because it would also take away the pain of death and she had to kill herself. She used it to kill Beelzebub because he was about to kill Alaria. When a demon is killed on Earth, they just go back to Hell. They have to find a new body before they can come back out. No big deal to them. For a Devil, it's a little more complicated if they've found their true form, the one body they want to keep, because they have to reform it, but it's still not permanent. By stabbing him with the knife, Griffin put him in the Lake of Fire. She truly killed him."

Clayton gulped alcohol, coughed, then managed a sentence. "So how is he my father then?"

"Lucifer was very fond of Beelzebub. He went into the Lake and fished him out. In order to do that, he had to affix Beelzebub to himself. It's not so strong a connection that killing Beelzebub will kill Lucifer, but it will weaken him."

"So it's like Harry Potter."

Lux blinked. "Who's Harry Potter?"

Clayton drank more vodka. "It's a book series. Voldemort split his soul into horcruxes in order to be able to survive if his body was killed. In order to kill him, you had to kill all the pieces. Beelzebub is a horcrux. Which would mean all of his kids are, too. Which is why you have to kill me." He emptied the glass. "Can I have more? I think I'd like to be drunk for this." He waited patiently while Lux refilled the cup. "You're trying to kill Lucifer?"

Lux looked at Zane. "I didn't understand a word coming out of his mouth until the drunk part."

Zane shook his head. "As long as he gets it, don't worry about it too much. I don't know who he's talking about, but I think the analogy is pretty accurate." He turned back to Clayton. "Yes, we're going to kill Lucifer, but we have to start with Beelzebub. Which means all his kids have to die, too. Even the one who isn't hurting anyone."

"This sucks ass." Clayton stared into the vodka. "God I almost wish you'd have just blown up the house or something with me in it. Then I wouldn't have known you were going to do it and it would be over and I wouldn't know that the two of you are the last people I am ever going to see. Fucking hell, I am sitting at my kitchen table making coffee for my assassins. How pathetic am I?" He stood and knocked the chair over, grasping handfuls of his hair and yanking. "I'm not fighting back or trying to kill you first or screaming for this father I just found out about or anything. I'm just getting myself drunk and accepting my fate." He stared at them. "Are you sure I'm really a Cambion? This can't be normal."

Lux stared at him with sympathy in her eyes. "Clayton, I'm sorry. We didn't expect you to be like this when we got here. With the rest, they've been evil. They've been murderers. It's easy to kill someone when you know they've got more blood on their hands than you do. It's not so easy when the person is innocent." She rose to fetch the tea kettle. "We're not in a huge hurry. Is there anything you'd like to do?"

Zane cleared his throat. "Lux."

"No, it's okay. He's a victim in this, Zane. Dying for a war he isn't fighting."

Clayton paced. His eyes moved from side to side rapidly and sweat beaded on his forehead. "I don't suppose you could conjure me a woman? I'd like to get laid one last time. Dying while fucking wouldn't be so bad. Could you do that?"

Zane snorted. "No, we can't do that." He caught the look on the Cambion's face as his gaze slid up and down Lux's body and continued, his voice mild. "If you even suggest it, boy, I'll shoot you between the eyes and just get this over with."

Clayton huffed a sigh. "She's taken, huh?"

Lux lifted an eyebrow in mild amusement at the exchange. "You're getting quite drunk." She picked up the bottle and tipped it over until alcohol splashed into the glass. "Drink up. You deserve it."

Obediently, he turned up the glass and drank deeply. "I ramble a lot, did I tell you that? Always have. When I was little, things weren't so bad. I remember when they started going downhill fast. My mom's restaurant blew up when I was six. Literally blew up in an attack. We moved to her parents' cabin after that and hid out for a few months, then joined a group of survivors in Salt Lake City. That was okay for a while. We were okay. After they died and my powers came in, people started realizing what I was, and they thought I was dangerous. They kept trying to kill me." He laughed and took another gulp. "This isn't the first time I've had people show up at where I was to kill me. It happened a couple times a week in Salt Lake. For a while the Warriors there protected me, but then they told me I had to leave because it got too bad so I came up here.

Samuels is alright. He sees past what people are to who they are. There are a couple vampires that live in town. People actually donate blood to feed them every once in a while. They offer some protection, do some night patrols, and hunt."

Lux made a noise in the back of her throat. "Very interesting."

"It really is. You don't see that happen anywhere else I've ever been. It's everyone fending for themselves. The Warriors protect the humans, the Nephilim fight the Cambion, the demons. the Devils, vampires, werewolves, Hellhounds, the witches, and the Familiars. The Nephilim get the shit end of the stick. Some Warriors fight, though, I think. Do the Warriors fight?"

Zane nodded. "Warriors fight."

"I thought they do. Are there enough Nephilim to win this war?"

Lux shook her head. "No. We're outnumbered twenty to one when you add in everything else that there is. That's why it's so important for us to do this. The Warriors bring it down to fifteen to one, but it's still not a winnable war in the long-term. We're better than they are and we're smarter, but they win just by sheer numbers. If we had the Angels the way they do the Devils and demons, then we would win, but we don't, so this is the way that it has to be done."

Clayton drained the glass again and stumbled into the living room to drop onto the couch. "Do you think I'll go to Hell?"

"Do you want to go to Hell?"

"I'm part-Devil. I think I have to, don't I?"

Zane shrugged. "You're half-human, too. That means you might have a soul."

The Cambion closed his eyes and tipped his head back, his lips moving silently. Lux studied him curiously for several moments. "What are you doing?"

He didn't answer for several moments. When he did, his voice was serious and soft. "I'm praying."

Zane sat down next to him. "What are you praying for?"

"I'm praying that if God really exists for him to never let another Nephilim or Cambion be born so no one else has to die for the stupid war." Tears streaked down his face. "I'm praying I have a soul so I don't have to go to Hell. I'm praying you kill me quickly so I don't know it's coming. I'm praying this is all a dream and I wake up in my bed upstairs and get to go fishing tomorrow like I planned because it's the end of the trout run and I want to get some more into the smoker for winter. But most of all I'm praying you win because I don't want to die for nothing."

Lux reached out and laid her hands on his shoulders. "Cool air, silent night. Sooth his pain, calm his fright. Take his fear, ease the hurt. Ashes to ashes, dirt to dirt. Birth to death, dawn to dusk. Born to Hell, return to God. Breathe deep, eyes close. Settle now, it's over soon." Her voice slow and melodic, she chanted Clayton into a trance. Easing back, she looked at Zane. "Do it quickly before he wakes up."

With a pang of regret, Zane reached over and pressed two fingers against the Cambion's head, ramping up his powers and letting them surge through the other man. Clayton jerked once and fell to the side, sinking to the couch, his eyes wide and dead, the half-full glass of vodka in his hand rolling to the floor and spilling onto the rug.

Lux stood and stared down at him sadly. "For the first time since we started this, I don't feel good about killing a Cambion."

Zane placed his hand on her shoulder. "That's because, for the first time, a Cambion didn't deserve to die." He applied gentle pressure. "We should go."

Together, they stepped out onto the porch and descended the stairs onto the ground. Lux turned, forming a ball of fire in her hand. She hurled it at the cabin, igniting the splash of alcohol on the floor, the remnants in the bottle, and causing the fire in the hearth to spring out of the fireplace and ignite the couch.

"When the people in town find it, it'll just look like the fireplace went out of control."

Zane opened the door to the SUV and climbed in. "They wouldn't care how he died, Lux. They wouldn't care that he's dead."

Somber, she slid into the passenger seat. "That's the thing. Someone should care when you die. He died. Someone should care."

"We care. Maybe that's enough."

Staring out the window, tears shining in her eyes, Lux jerked one shoulder in a shrug. "Maybe."

CHAPTER NINETEEN

September 28th, 2060 – The Yukon

"WELL, IT took you long enough." Carys crossed her arms over her chest and glared at Zane and Lux. "You were supposed to be here yesterday."

Zane heaved boxes from the back of the SUV. "The roads were a lot worse coming back through. There'd been a mudslide or something. We had to find an alternate way around."

"Why didn't you just flash?"

"Because unlike you, I can't go unlimited distances." He glared at Carys. "I get worn out after a few short flashes and it drains my powers. You tap into Elisa and can circle the globe. Not everyone is like that."

Effectively ending the conversation, Zane dragged out their packs and knelt to reload them, discarding what they didn't absolutely need to take with them to London. Transportation wasn't guaranteed, and they couldn't risk taking anything they couldn't carry on their backs.

Carys studied her fingernails. "Well, they should be. I get sick of being mass transit for every fucking Nephil that needs a lift."

Elisa smirked. "Don't get too sick of it. We're useful. Useful means not cannon fodder. I wouldn't like to be cannon fodder." She moved forward to embrace Zane. "We heard about the power recalibration. Congratulations." Her gaze shifted to Lux. "Lux, nice to see you again."

Lux inclined her head toward the other woman. "Elisa, how are you? Nice to see you, Carys."

Carys made a noise. "I don't like this one as much as the other new one. The other one played around more."

Elisa smiled and rolled her eyes. "Zeke is pretty special, but it even took her a little while to warm up. Give this one a chance at least."

Lux huffed. "I'm standing right here. I can hear you talking about me."

Carys spared her a glance. "I know that." She lifted one shoulder. "I won't say anything behind your back I wouldn't say to your face, so I say anything I want to say in front of you."

Zane stopped packing the bags and sat back on his haunches. "Stop being a bitch on purpose. We both know you're trying to intimidate her because you fancy yourself the big sister of the house and you get protective when you think someone's infringing on your territory. I'm not territory, Carys, so lay off it."

Elisa giggled and hopped onto the tailgate of the truck they'd arrived in. "She's not so bad once you get to know her."

Lux zipped up her jacket as a meager defense against the biting wind. "You only say that because you have sex with her."

"If you were lucky enough to bang her, you'd say it, too."

Zane shook his head and went back to work. "I don't know why I called for the two of you. I'd have rather walked." He turned to Lux. "I'm taking some of the water, the Gatorade powder packets we found, the cereal and granola bars, the packs of oatmeal, the candy bars, and basically anything light and not in a can. That makes it easier to carry and cuts down on weight. We're running short on ammo, which isn't necessarily surprising, but I packed all we have. All the clothes are going since it's cold here and will be cold in London. All your girly stuff got put in there, and I packed the soap and a towel for each of us."

Carys lifted her eyebrows. "Girly stuff?"

Lux nodded. "Yeah. Tampons."

"I know what he meant. I just don't know why he didn't say the word 'tampons.'"

Elisa tied her hair back into a loose bun. "Men aren't comfortable with a woman sticking anything inside herself other than their penis or fingers. Maybe a dildo. Or a vibrator."

"I'm going to gouge out my ears if the two of you don't shut up." He glared at Lux. "Don't you dare laugh. You're barely any better. All I've heard for the past four days is how you have cramps."

Lux's eyes sparkled with good humor. "Just be glad I started my period the day after we had sex instead of while we were having sex. Besides, it's something we have to deal with every single month, so get used to it. It'll come again in another three weeks."

Carys perked up. "Oooh. That's an interesting development." Waving her hand when Zane gaped at her, she continued. "Not the period. That's boring. The sex."

"Shut up, Carys." Zane shouldered his pack and handed the other to Lux. "We're ready to go. Thank God."

Lux took the bag and slipped her arms through the straps, fastening it across her chest. "Let's get going then." She glanced to Carys. "Do you need some time to warm up or are you ready?"

"Do you know where in London you need to go to?"

Zane passed over the file. "This is a picture of the safe-house Gage has set up for us there."

Carys looked at him sternly. "I can flash you in there. No problem. But if there's any Cambion around, they might detect the flash signature and then you're in trouble. A lot of trouble because they'll know exactly where you're at, and you won't have any place to go to. I know a place about a three hour walk outside of the city. I'll take you there and then you can get yourselves in. It should be far enough away that anyone inside London won't be able to detect the flash."

"Works for me. Let's just get going. It's like eight or nine hours later in London than it is here, so it's getting to be late afternoon there. I want to be in somewhere before dark."

Carys reached out to grip one of Zane's wrists in her hand, mirroring the motion with Lux. Elisa laid her hands on Carys's shoulders. With a loud crack, they disappeared.

"The steering wheel is on the wrong side of the car." Zane stared at the car he was supposed to be hotwiring with trepidation. "Is all the wiring backward or just the steering wheel?"

"I don't know. I'm not a mechanic." Lux peered over his shoulder at the jumble of wires. "Does it matter?"

"If I cross the wrong wires I'll give myself a hell of a shock, so yeah, it matters some."

"Just give the engine a jolt with a blast of magic. It'll start right up." She leaned against the doorframe and crossed her legs at the ankle. "No need to risk electrocution because no one taught you how to steal foreign cars."

Zane looked up at her, considering. "Is it technically foreign when there aren't any governments anymore?"

"Good question. Inter-continental auto-theft then."

He popped the hood and directed a slow stream of magic into the engine, using it to urge the pistons to fire and the motor to begin turning. When it grumbled to life, he smiled. "There. Let's get on the road."

"Since the wheel's on my side, does that mean I'm taking the first shift driving?"

"Sure." He slung their packs into the backseat of the car and crossed to what would have normally been the driver's seat. "It's weird to come here and see the parts of the world that fell earlier than the United States."

Lux cocked her head and mulled that over as she slid behind the wheel and eased the car into gear. "Have you never been to London before?"

"Yeah, I've been here a time or two. I've been most places a time or two. We kinda travel all over fighting the Cambion. But it's normally just a few hours or for a night or something and there's so much going on that you don't have time to just look at it." He peered out the windshield and studied the remnants of buildings. "London used to be one of the most beautiful places on Earth."

"Maybe it will be again one day." She maneuvered onto the road that would take them into London and tapped the gas pedal with her foot. "I don't like to just look at places. It's depressing. Piles of debris and trash. Every building is a potential danger, there are bodies in the streets, remains everywhere. I hate the world we inherited."

Zane whistled softly. "I don't like it either, but there are still good things. We all manage to find them. That place in Alaska wasn't bad. It's pretty remote and there aren't any luxuries, but it's a decent life up there."

"Those places are few and far between. People can survive in groups small enough that Lucifer hasn't bothered to look for them yet. He will eventually if we don't stop him. This war will kill Earth." She glanced over at him. "Sometimes I think that's what God's wanted all along."

"If that was what He wanted, He'd just end it all. I think He wants to see how it plays out and see if we can win." He leaned his head against the seat and folded his hands behind his neck. "My mom knew she was pregnant with a Nephil. She used to tell me the story when I was little, about how it was just like she imagined it was with Mary. She came home from work and there was an Angel sitting on her couch. She said he was the most handsome thing she'd ever seen. Dressed all in black with black hair and dark eyes and pitch black wings tipped with silver. She was a witch, so she wasn't scared of him. She knew about Angels and Devils and all that shit."

Lux smiled. "She sounds like she was glad to be one of the ones picked."

"She was. He apparently explained to her what had happened and that a war was coming. They needed soldiers, he said, and she would make a good host. Very formal. She thought he needed to have sex with her, so she said she just started taking her clothes off. She was willing, ready, and able. Anything for the cause." Zane's voice was tinged with bitterness. "I have to wonder how many women were like her and how many were like your mom."

"My mom made the same choice, though. She accepted Angelic essence and carried a Nephil, too. They all did."

"Not all. We've all heard the stories of some women who didn't know they were having Nephilim until the kid hit puberty or those who said no and got the 'magic touch' anyway. It happened."

Lux looked over at him sympathetically. "I don't think it happened often." She sighed. "I know that once is too often. Mom told me that at first Gabriel wasn't going to instruct the Host to tell anyone. They were just going to impregnate them all and let it happen. No one would know. Michael threatened him into telling the women so they could make the choice. I don't think we'll ever know the whole truth of what happened after that. We do know that most of the women chosen were Warriors, witches, Hunters, Healers—someone with a special talent that could stand a chance at protecting a Nephil until it got to adulthood. You know as well as I do that most of them considered it either an honor or a duty to have a Nephil as a child."

"I know that." Zane ran his hand through his hair. "The whole thing still weirds me out. I know that something had to be done. Lucifer was raising an army and we had to have one, too. There were only four Archangels that Fell, but there are hundreds of Devils, maybe thousands, just like there are thousands of Angels. Some Angels, like my Father, and like Gabriel, only made one

Nephil. Others made a lot. The female Angels generally only had one, except for Dev's mother since she had twins. But my point is that my mom was dazzled by this Angel standing in her apartment spinning her this story about being chosen for a destiny bigger than herself. Saving humanity and raising a Nephil to help battle back Lucifer and keep the Apocalypse at bay. I just wonder how many would have still said yes if they had known that this—piles of rubble and sleeping on dirt floors and filthy mattresses while we waited until the day we face a Devil or Cambion stronger than us and die— is what they were really agreeing to."

Lux shrugged. "My parents knew. They still said yes. They knew exactly what kind of a life I would have and what I would be asked to do. So did Zeke's. They knew that we would be born to fight and die. They weighed the risk of that against the good we could do and the chance we could win and decided to do it anyway. I don't think much would have changed if they knew." She glanced away from the road to look at him for a moment. "Why worry about this now?"

"Today is the anniversary of the day my mom died." He stared down at his lap. "I tend to dwell about things today. Having me killed her."

"That's not true."

"Yes, it is. I touched her, and she died." He reached out and took her hand in his. "I'm sorry. I know you don't want to deal with me in this mood."

She smiled softly. "It's okay. You're allowed to have feelings and be in a bad mood." She squeezed his fingers tightly. "I think we should be to the safe-house in about an hour."

"That'll only leave us a few minutes of light, so we'll have to get in quick and stay there until morning. I don't like the idea of staying somewhere neither of us knows and not having a clue what's surrounding us."

"Do you want to find a place here?" She peered out the windshield and glanced around. "There's an old farmhouse across that field. We could check it out and go the rest of the way in the morning."

Zane considered that briefly. "I think I'd rather have the light to work with than go into London just as the sun is setting, so let's do that." He straightened in the seat as she turned the car onto the driveway. "What do we know about the Cambion we're here to get?"

"The file said that he trained with Abalam for the last year, so we can assume he's been well educated in how to torture someone.

Before that he led a squad of Cambion and was pretty effective against the Nephilim. This one is a fighter. He's not going to go down easily. I think we have to assume that he's not going to be alone. We need to move in quietly and do some recon before we go after him. Our best weapon is going to be knowing what we're dealing with."

Lux shifted the car into park and opened the door, sliding out and closing it softly. Zane followed her lead and strode to the back of the car, opening the trunk and handing her a pistol and her utility belt, which she strapped around her waist. He checked the clip in his own gun and looked up at the large two-story farm-house.

"Quick sweep around the outside and then we'll do the inside."

"Sounds like a plan."

They moved simultaneously, going opposite directions around the house, taking time to check for broken windows or doors leading into the house. There was one building in the backyard that looked like it had once been used to smoke meat but was long empty of anything useful.

Lux crouched next to the door and picked the lock smoothly, listening for the snick that told her the tumblers were in the correct position. Zane stepped in front of her as soon as the door swung open, shielding her while she climbed to her feet. Leading the way, he entered the foyer to the house and pressed his back against the wall.

Demon and Devil traps were drawn on every surface. Salt and gunpowder lined the doorways. Garlic hung from the ceiling and the air was thick with the smell of herbs. Dried blood splattered the walls, and the furniture on the main floor was in pieces, telling the story of the struggle that had taken place in the house.

"How long ago do you figure?"

Zane sniffed the air. "The garlic is still stinky. Not more than a couple weeks. There isn't much dust on stuff, either." He glanced over his shoulder. "The windows aren't broken, and the door was still locked. How did they get in?"

"If it was Cambion, they could have flashed. I don't see those wards up. There's nothing stopping them from coming in." She moved into the kitchen and surveyed the open cabinets and piles of broken plates and bowls. "Looks like quite the struggle."

Zane nudged a door open and found a half-bath with the sink shattered and toilet seat ripped off. "Yes, it certainly does." He started up the stairs. "I'm wondering if we should stay here. This place is obviously on their radar."

"It was on their radar." She followed him up the steps. "I don't sense anything in range. We would be able to tell if anything flashed in, and it's warded pretty well against demons and Devils." She pushed open the first door and found an empty bedroom. "I say we stay for the night and take off before dawn. We'll get into London just as the sun is coming up."

He checked a second bedroom and the bathroom. "Did you see any other places that we could use for the night?"

"Not that we could get to before dark. This is the only place I saw since we left where Carys dropped us off ." She opened a closet in the hallway and checked the last bedroom. "I wonder what they did with the bodies."

"There may not have been bodies. They could have taken the humans and had them turned into Familiars or possessed by demons."

"Good point." She holstered her weapon and descended the stairs. "I'm going to bring in enough food for the night and some of the weapons, just in case. We won't do anything to draw attention, so we'll sit in the dark and be cold, but we'll be inside, and there's a bed."

Zane went back into one of the bedrooms. "I'm bringing the mattress downstairs. Closer to the exits in case we need to make a break for it."

Rolling her eyes, Lux stepped through the front door and went down the three steps to the driveway. Opening the back of the car, she shouldered the one duffel bag filled with their clothes and picked up a second bag of weapons and a small box of canned food. Balancing it on her hip, she closed the car door and returned to the house where Zane had slid the mattress down the stairs and placed it in the middle of the living room floor.

It took fifteen minutes to move the debris out of the way enough that they wouldn't trip over it were they to get up through the night. There was no running water, though they did discover a rusty hand pump just off the kitchen door. They took turns filling up two old buckets until the tub upstairs held enough water to allow them each to wash off.

They ate soup from cans standing in the kitchen while giving the water time to warm from ice cold to room temperature. While Zane bathed, Lux put sheets and blankets on the mattress and tacked blankets over all the windows on the main floor to keep anyone or thing from seeing the light from the pillar candles she found in the debris on the floor.

Zane came down the stairs in sweatpants, carrying his damp towel and his clothes. "I washed out my clothes in the sink. I figured we could hang them from the banister down here and they'd be clean and dry by morning."

"Cleanish anyway." She took the towel he held out. "No reason to use them both in one night I suppose." Looking pained, she rubbed one hand over her eyes. "I can't wait until we can go back to Michael's and have clean clothes and towels every day instead of only every once in a while."

"We've done pretty good with it recently." He bent to kiss her gently. "Take your time."

Lux went into the bathroom and placed her flashlight on the floor to give herself enough light to see by. She crammed her clothes into the sink and spent ten minutes scrubbing them with shampoo, using water from the tub to rinse them. Gritting her teeth at the temperature of the water, she gingerly stepped into the tub and sat down, reaching for the soap.

By the time her hair and body were clean and her legs were smooth, Lux's teeth were chattering and chill-bumps had risen on her skin. She hastily dried off with the damp towel and wound it around her hair while she gathered up her wet clothes.

Swearing when she realized she hadn't brought anything to change into upstairs with her, she let the water out of the tub and snatched up the flashlight. Closing the door behind her, she hurried down the stairs, intent on getting to her bag and the sweatpants inside as quickly as possible.

She paused briefly to drape the wet things over the banister and padded into the living room. Zane was sitting in one of the chairs he had righted with a book open in his lap and a penlight between his teeth. Three squat candles were on the floor, the light from the flame flickering off the walls. Bending to deposit the shampoo and soap into the duffel bag, she reached for her pants, then changed her mind and unzipped the front pocket of the bag, pulling out a thin foil packet instead.

"Must be a good book."

Zane didn't even look up. "It's Charles Dickens. All his books are good."

Lux reached out and snagged the book from his hand, snapping it closed and dropping it onto the stand. "Better than this?"

He looked up, taking in her naked body, his eyes devouring every curve. The light from the candles flickered over her bare skin, casting shadows over her body and making the rich red of her hair glow with gold.

"Not even close." He reached out and laid his hands on her hips, drawing her down until she was straddling his lap. "Instant hard-on, babe."

Lux chuckled, the sound warm and full of good humor. "That's exactly the response I was hoping for." She leaned for and sucked his lower lip into her mouth, nibbling on it before soothing the sting with a stroke of her tongue. "Fast or slow? Hard or soft?"

Zane's fingers trailed up her arm and across her collarbone, then up to cup the side of her face. "I don't get the feeling you're looking for soft and slow tonight." He dipped his head to brush a kiss against her shoulder. "If I'm inside you, I'm happy."

Rising to her feet, Lux gripped the waistband of his pants and drew them down his legs, chucking them aside and kneeling in front of him, running her hands over the bulging girth of his erection. She stroked her fingers up the shaft of his penis and rubbed her thumb over the head before looping her fingers around him and pumping them up and down, slowly and first, then slightly faster.

His eyes drifted shut and he scooted down in the chair slightly, jutting his hips forward. She bent her head and swirled her tongue around the tip, sucking it into her mouth and gently running her teeth over the hard flesh. His hands fisted in the fabric of the chair and the muscles in his legs tightened.

Slowly, she continued to lower her head until she had taken him all into her mouth. Sucking, she moved her head up and down, her tongue swirling around him. A ragged groan tore from Zane's throat and Lux laughed softly, lifting her gaze to look at him, enjoying the expression of bliss on his face.

One of his hands would in her hair and he tugged her head up. Sliding from the chair, he joined her on the floor, crushing her body to his own with his other arm and dragging her mouth to his.

He pushed her back until she was lying flat on the mattress, his body pressing her into it. Releasing her hair, he moved his hand down her body until he found the hardened bead of her nipple, rolling it between two fingers and tugging slightly on the tender tip. Lux sucked in a breath and her hips twitched on the mattress.

Grinning, Zane used his other hand to part her legs and slid his fingers against her, rubbing her clit gently.

When her thighs fell open, he slowly inserted one finger, stroking it gently into her while rubbing her clitoris simultaneously. Dipping his head, he sucked one of her nipples into his mouth, enjoying the flavor of her skin on his tongue as he stimulated two of the most sensitive spots on her body simultaneously.

When her breaths turned into gasps and her muscles began tensing, Zane withdrew his hand and lifted his head, staring down at her with passion-filled eyes. Gripping her hips in his hands, he lowered himself to his elbows and buried his face between her thighs, spearing his tongue into her. Lux cried out and jerked her hips against his, her fingers fisting in her hair and tugging sharply.

"Oh God, Zane." Her eyes squeezed shut and she lifted her hips into his mouth. "Just a bit slower." She nearly purred when he licked her at a slower pace. "Just like that. God, yes." She squirmed as need rose up within her and he skillfully held orgasm just out of reach as his tongue rubbed against her most sensitive spot.

His mouth was warm and his tongue soft and gentle against and in her. He flicked it against her, driving her up to the edge of release, holding her there until she thought she might die, then sliding her back down it until she was panting and writhing beneath him, desperate for orgasm.

"Fuck me. Damn you, stop playing around and fuck me." Lux's voice was harsh as she made her demand. Zane lifted his head and quirked an eyebrow.

"Bossy." He rose onto his knees and grinned down at her. Reaching for the shiny foil packet on the floor, he tore into the condom wrapper and sheathed himself in bright green latex. "Interesting choice."

Giggling, she sat up. "It was the first one I found." She turned so her back was to him. "I want you hard and fast, Zane. Don't be easy with me. I want it all."

Zane wrapped his arms around her from behind, drawing her back against his chest and skating his hands over her body. "Be careful what you ask for." He nudged her down until she was on her hands and knees. "Spread your knees a bit more." He adjusted his knees on the inside of hers. "That's it."

He probed her body with the tip of his penis, finding her wet and hot. He rubbed her with the head until she was whimpering, then stroked forward, impaling her with one long thrust. Lux groaned in satisfaction and arched her hips back, enjoying the feel of her body stretching to accommodate his girth.

His pace was immediately fast and hard, his body pounding into hers over and over. His fingers bit into her hips. and he slammed into her with every thrust of his body. Lux's fingers tangled in the sheet covering the mattress and she clutched it tightly. Her body pulsed around him, gripping him tightly as she reveled in his lovemaking.

Zane lowered himself over her back, reaching around to hold her breasts in his hands, rubbing her nipples as he rocked his hips against hers, driving himself in and out of her as they both climbed the crest of release. With a groan and a gasp, Lux toppled over the edge and climaxed, her body clamping down on him in spasms as she came.

He pumped himself into her harder and faster, planting himself deeply within her as his own orgasm tore from him. Panting and sweaty, they collapsed to the mattress, still tangled together.

Zane detangled and left the mattress long enough to dispose of the used condom, blow out the candles, and find a washcloth to wipe up with. Returning to their makeshift bed with a bottle of water and a hand-towel, he lay down next to her, waiting until she had cleaned herself up and taken a drink before pulling her close.

Sated and sleepy, they drifted off.

CHAPTER TWENTY

September 29, 2060 – London, England

LUX WAS desperately wishing she'd let Zane convince her to stay in bed all day. He'd woken her up with lazy pre-dawn lovemaking. They'd moved against each other in the foggy gray light, slow and sweet. Lying there under the blankets, it would have been so easy to agree to the suggestion that they put off the Cambion for a few hours or one day and just be for a while.

But she'd been insistent that they get to the safe house and get settled. There was recon to be done and Cambion to be killed. No reason to put it off when the sooner they accomplished their goal the sooner they could relax at Michael's while Amaya and Deacon took on Lucifer.

If they lived to see the next time, Lux made a mental promise that she would listen to Zane when he suggested staying in bed.

"Let's just get through this and worry about that later."

Zane's voice was strained in her head. Lux winced when concrete bit into her shoulder as she rolled to avoid a stream of fire. *"Where are you?"*

"To your south and a bit to the east. I think we're about a block apart from what I can tell. I've got a dozen Cambion on my tail, plus some Hellhounds. What're you dealing with?"

"Fucking Familiars. I think three or four demons and maybe eight Cambion. A dog or two, but not many. I'm not sure which one of these is

Beelzebub's."

"Me either, so let's make sure we kill them all."

Lux blocked a stream of power with magic, batting it away and sending it spiraling into an abandoned car. She rolled into a crouch, then slowly stood, turning to take stock of her surroundings. Familiars were closing in on her from all sides, their eyes wide and unseeing, their arms outstretched and mouths slightly open.

She reached within herself and let magic bubble up, feeling her fingers begin to tingle as it spread through her. The Familiars weren't a threat to a Nephil or to a witch, but if they weren't dealt with quickly and one got ahold of her, the distraction could allow one of the demons or Cambion to deal a crushing blow.

Forming fire took concentration, and Lux held it within herself until her skin glowed from the amount that she was making. Throwing out her hands, she blasted the throng of Familiars with flame.

They screamed as they burned.

The scent of burning flesh and singing hair filled Lux's nostrils and she gagged, coughing from the onslaught. Skin melted from the bones and dripped onto the concrete. Flesh shriveled up and peeled back, revealing stark white bones. The bodies dropped to the ground one by one, transforming from the empty shell that had once housed a person to a scorched skeleton surrounded by ash and embers.

Lux stepped over the bones, flames surrounding her hands as she walked. Several of the Cambion looked nervous as she approached them. When one of them tried to flash out, she reached out with her magic and blocked him, anchoring him to Earth. Diverting enough of her attention to be aware of the two Hellhounds circling her, she whispered a spell to conjure a sword, clenching it in her hand tightly and knowing she was going to have to fight her way out.

"You're a daughter of Michael." One of the Cambion stepped forward and addressed her.

Lux cocked her head. "Dare I guess that you're a son of Beelzebub?"

The Cambion inclined his head slightly. "Perhaps. Then again, perhaps I'm a son of Azazel. Or of Abaddon. Or Abalam." He bared his teeth. "Maybe I'm a son of Lucifer himself."

Looking bored, Lux lifted an eyebrow. "He'd strike you down into dust if he heard you say you were his kid." She glanced around at the other Cambion. "You're all reasonably powerful. I'd be willing to believe there are some children of the others in the group. Which means your Cambion powers don't work on me."

"The same as your Nephil ones don't work on us. Your advantage is being a witch and ours are in the women who birthed us." He gestured to the Cambion on his right. "Let me introduce you to everyone. We've got two of Azazel's children, Natalia and Kristoff. Their mothers were both Russian, as I'm sure you gathered. Their heritage isn't Russian, though, it's Roma, which you oughta know gives them a lot of magic."

"Parlor magic and smoke and mirrors." Lux glared at the two Cambion. "Gypsies aren't that powerful."

"They don't need to be when there are eight of us and one of you." He looked from side to side. "You know as well as I do there were many Angels that Fell, and even though there are only a few Archangels, all the Fallen are Devils. Here we have four offspring of Devils you likely don't know. Elaina's mother is a witch. Aaron's mother is a Warrior. Micah's mother is a very powerful witch. Finally, there's Braden here, who's mother I believe is a Hunter. Of course that leaves the gorgeous young lady on my right, Drusilla, whose father is Abalam and whose mother is a sorceress. Purely black magic running through those veins. And me, Ciaran. Beelzebub is my father, and my mother is also a sorceress. You have a lot of natural magic, Nephil, but you don't have the control over the dark that some of us have."

Lux mentally prioritized the Cambion from the least threat to the greatest threat. "Let's stop gabbing and just get this over with. I hate you fucking talkative Cambion. All you want to do is bore me to tears."

Ciaran jerked his chin to the two Hellhounds. "Get her, boys."

Magic didn't work on Hellhounds. They were creatures that only half-existed on Earth and drew their power directly from Hell. The only way to defeat them was with blades and bullets, which would send them back to Hell. Lux brought her sword up, switching her focus to the dogs charging her.

She had to be careful. If she played the situation correctly, she would be able to take out some of the Cambion as well as the hounds. They were confident they had her outnumbered and outgunned. On the surface, they did. Her only hope was it made them cocky enough she could get in a few blows they weren't expecting and even the playing field before they caught on to what she was doing.

The first hound attacked her, jaws snapping. She swung the sword, slicing through fur and flesh, the metal coming away stained with blood. The animal howled with pain and whirled, its teeth gleaming in the sun as it tried to clamp on her. The other one jumped into the fray, managing to get ahold of her ankle and drag her to the ground. Terrified and screaming, Lux flailed with the sword, driving it up over and over again, blood raining down on her and soaking her clothes.

The first hound was dead, and the second was wounded. She continued to hack, swinging until it stopped moving. Taking advantage of the laughter from the Cambion, she opened up the door to black magic and let it swirl in, forcing it through the citrine around her neck and sending out a stream so powerful that she knocked the two Cambion who didn't have magical mothers back against the wall.

Holding them there with her magic, she reached out with her other hand, fastening a band of power around their throats and snapping it quickly to the side, the sound of breaking bone filling the empty street. Two bodies landed on the ground with a dull thump.

Ciaran clapped his hands together. "Nicely done, Nephil. Four down, six to go. Still think you can take us all on?"

Lux wasn't listening. She reached inside herself, letting in more magic and forcing it through the citrine. The stone warmed and glowed until it was painful to look at. She lifted her hands and brought up a wall of magic to fend off the blasts the Cambion were hurling at her as she let her body fill with as much magic as it could hold.

The black threatened to overtake her, and she struggled to slam the door shut on it. Her citrine darkened from butter yellow to amber to brown and finally to black. Purple and black streams of power leaked from her nose, mouth and ears, swirling to surround her whole body. Blood trickled from her eyes and nose, the streams getting thicker as she brought up more and more magic.

Finally, with a blast that was powerful enough to level several buildings behind the Cambion, Lux propelled out a wave of magic so strong it sent her flying backward from the force of the spell. The Cambion were blown off their feet when her magic struck them, some dying instantly, unable to fend off her onslaught. Others, like Ciaran, managed to fight it for several seconds before it forced its way into their bodies, extinguishing their lives and leaving their bodies empty and dead in piles of rubble.

Lux stumbled several steps as she stemmed the flow of magic, wiping her hand across her face to dash the blood from her eyes. Her heart pounded in her chest and blood rushed in her ears, overpowering every other sound. She dropped to her knees and continued to crawl toward the bodies, reaching out to touch each of them, making sure they were all dead. Finding no pulses, she collapsed to the pavement and stared up at the sky, unsure whether or not she could move.

Zane flashed from the street to the roof of a building to get a better vantage point on the Cambion and Hellhounds chasing him. He counted four dogs and eleven Cambion. Lifting his rifle to his shoulder, he pressed his eye to the sight and lined up his shot, squeezing the trigger and watching with grim satisfaction as one of the Cambion dropped to the ground, a perfect round hole in their forehead.

Unlike most other Nephilim, including Lux, Zane's powers still worked on Cambion. The Angel of Death was the most powerful of all Angels other than Lucifer and Lilith, and he was likely the most powerful of the Cambion or Nephilim with the exceptions of Amaya, Deacon and offspring of Lucifer or Lilith. All he had to do was touch them, and they would be dead. The issue with that was getting close enough to get his hands on them without getting shot or stabbed first.

His greatest weakness was flashing. It was the most efficient way to sneak up on the Cambion and the quickest way to tire himself out. Weighing the costs against the benefits, he levelled the sight on the gun again and pulled the trigger two times in rapid succession, killing one of the Hellhounds.

Three pops behind him warned him of Cambion flashing in pursuit of him. He whirled to face them, leaping to the side to avoid the shots from their weapons. His gun slid across the roof just out of reach. Rolling, he scrambled to retrieve the weapon, drawing a bowie knife from his utility belt and clenching it tightly in his fist, crouching as he faced the Cambion.

"Your powers won't work on me, Cambion."

One of the Cambion, a tall woman with green eyes, laughed. "And yours won't work on us. We've got you outnumbered ten to one. Save yourself some trouble and just surrender to us. We might take it a little easier on you that way."

Zane straightened, resisting the urge to correct the Cambion, knowing it was an advantage that they thought he couldn't use his powers on them. "Which of you is Beelzebub's?"

The woman cocked an eyebrow. "I'm his daughter. My brother is after your witch bitch." She gestured to the other two Cambion. "Get him."

Zane flashed before the two Cambion could even twitch. He reappeared behind the woman, clamping his hands on her skull and letting power flow out of him and into her body. She jerked and gagged, straining for breath as he sucked life from her. Her skin turned gray and clammy, and she sagged, her knees collapsing as all her weight fell.

The two Cambion left exchanged a look with one another, obviously terrified at what they had seen. Zane chanted a spell to stop them from flashing as he changed his grip on the knife, throwing it at one of them. He paused long enough to watch the Cambion drop to the ground, his hands clutching at the blade in his chest, before striding toward the third, his eyes steely hard and his gaze deadly.

"Save yourself some trouble and just surrender. I might take it easier on you that way."

The Cambion conjured a whip and snapped it through the air. "You're the son of the Angel of Death."

Zane inclined his head slightly. "I am." He clenched his hand and felt the solid weight of a short sword form in it. "You saw what I did to your friend. You'd better think long and hard about whether or not you want to do this."

The man jerked his wrist and lashed the whip out, slashing through Zane's shirt and ripping through skin. "I want to do this."

The two men collided violently. Zane wielded his sword expertly, slicing through the air and hacking the whip into pieces as he charged. The Cambion conjured his own sword, raising it to fend off Zane's onslaught. Their blades locked together and sparks flew off of the metal. Zane kicked out with one foot, slamming his heel into the other man's knee, the sound of crunching bone echoing across the roof. The Cambion dropped to his knees for an instant, managing to roll to the side in time to avoid losing his head to a swipe of Zane's sword.

Three Hellhounds appeared on the roof, charging at Zane, their teeth bared and saliva dripping from their fangs.

"Well, fuck."

The Cambion laughed. "Think you can take on all the puppies and me? Plus the other eight Cambion waiting to take my place?"

Zane squared his stance and lifted his sword to face the dogs. The first one charged him, barreling directly at him with little regard for its own life. The sun reflected off the blade as he swung the sword, ripping through fur and meat as the dog slammed into him. Blood sprayed the roof, coating it in red, and Zane grunted as he slammed into the concrete, his grip on the weapon slickened by blood.

The other two dogs circled, waiting to see what happened. When the first one didn't get up, a second leaped on top of him, its powerful jaws clamping onto his shoulder and tearing at his arm. Without missing a beat, he tossed the sword to his right hand and stabbed upward, driving it into the skull of the beast and watching as life flickered and died in its eyes.

His left arm hanging useless at his side, he turned to face the third hound, waiting until the dog leapt for him to swing with the sword, letting the point enter into the fleshy area just under the chin and exit through the top of the skull.

Not bothering to try and pull the sword from the bone, Zane flashed to the other side of the roof, wrapping his injured arm around the neck of the Cambion and placing his good hand on the man's face, leaning in close to whisper in his ear.

"Nice try."

The body jerked and seized as life seeped out until it was left limp and lifeless in a heap on the roof. Without sparing a look over his shoulder, Zane walked to the edge of the roof, stepping off and flashing just as he fell, landing softly on the ground below. He stooped to pick up the pistol he had dropped in the street when the ambush had started and flashed again, zeroing in on the Cambion he sensed.

There were eight of them left, and they had found Lux. One of them held her in their arms, her hair streaming over his arm and her head lolled to the side, her eyes barely opened. Purpling bruises had already begun to form on her face, marring her creamy skin. Rage rose up within Zane, and he flashed over to them, grabbing one in each of his hands and casting them aside within ten seconds, their bodies drained of life.

Six left. He chanted the spell to keep them from flashing, smiling when they looked at one another nervously. None of the

Cambion left alive were as powerful as the ones he'd already killed. The one carrying Lux dropped her to the ground, her body striking pavement with a sick crunch and rolling to the side. She moved once, managing to lift herself to her elbows, then falling back over.

Zane could feel her magic moving around them. She was weak, but not as weak as the Cambion seemed to think she was. He knocked aside the first that came at him, stooping to wrap his hands around its throat and killing it ruthlessly. Three down.

Two were smart enough to go for guns. By the time they managed to fire, Lux was on her knees. She held out one hand and sent the bullets scattering into the other three Cambion, killing two of them and striking the third in the stomach. One of the remaining two got off a lucky shot and sank a bullet into Zane's thigh. He stumbled, nearly fell, but managed to get his feet back under him.

Lux climbed to her feet and closed her eyes for a brief moment. When she opened them, they were pitch black. Wind whipped through the buildings and blew through the city, stirring the piles of debris and strong enough that it rocked the cars sitting on the streets. Lightning cracked in the sky and thunder rolled through it. She held out one hand, slowly forming a ball of fire in her palm.

Zane watched, entranced at the swirling orb of white, red, and orange. It grew larger and larger, increasing in size until it filled her entire hand. She brought her other hand up, reaching into the flame and separating it into two, hurling them at the last two Cambion, incinerating them into nothing more than piles of smoking ash.

The wind died down and Lux swayed on her feet, weak from the expenditure of magic. Zane limped over to her, wrapping his good arm around her and anchoring her to his side.

"Are you okay? What did they do to you?"

She brushed away his concerns with a wave of her hand. "I'll be fine. I was still pretty drained when they found me. One of them managed to pick me up before I figured out what was going on. If you'd been thirty seconds later I'd have had it handled. Beelzebub's son was one of mine. It took a lot out of me to kill him and all the others. There were some really powerful Cambion here." She ran her hands over his shoulder. "Hound?"

He glanced at the wound and nodded. "Yeah, one of 'em took a chunk out of me." His nose wrinkled. "One of the Cambion I was after swore she was Beelzebub's daughter. She felt pretty powerful, but the only way to know is to tell Michael about it."

Lux laid her hand against his thigh in an effort to stem the flow of blood. "We need to let him patch you up anyway." She closed her eyes. "Hold on. I'm going to take us to Michael's. We'll get everything figured out there."

CHAPTER TWENTY-ONE

ARADIA STOOD with her hands on her hips and stared down at her daughter, her face set in a stern expression and her eyes clearly conveying worry. "What in this world were you thinking?"

Lux opened one eye and looked up at her mother. "What are you talking about? I didn't do anything stupid."

"You haven't been practicing your magic. You're weaker than you should have been. How do you intend to take on Beelzebub when you could barely take out some of his offspring?"

"Their mothers were witches. It was more of an even fight than you'd think." She sighed deeply and sat up on the couch. "Is this where you give me a talk a la Graciela about finding my power as a woman as well as a witch?"

Aradia's mouth quirked in a ghost of a smile. "I'm willing to bet Zane's helping you unlock that power just fine." She dropped onto the couch next to Lux. "You have to keep practicing. With Lucifer killing my mother and her magic entering into you, there is more for you to learn to control. Neglecting to practice and work on your magic means you will have less control of your abilities when the time comes you need them the most."

Lux waved her hand dismissively. "I got a little drained. We've been at this non-stop. We have three of Beelzebub's children left to go after."

"One of whom has Lilith as a mother and the other of whom is

Alexi, whose mother is also a Devil. Have you forgotten about that?"

Starting to get annoyed, Lux swung her legs to the side and glared at Aradia. "I'm not twelve anymore, Mom. I don't need you telling me how to do my job. I'm going to get it done. We'll kill them, and then I'll have some time to rest up before we go after the others."

"And if you don't? There were times I had to prepare for weeks in order to be certain I would have the strength to accomplish the task in front of me." Aradia reached out and grabbed Lux's hand when her daughter started to rise. "It's not only your life you risk. It is Zane's. Michael's. Mine. All those who would stand in front of you and die rather than see you perish. You're shirking your duties, Lux Windsor. I wouldn't tolerate it from you when you were twelve, and I won't tolerate it from you now."

"It's not your task anymore. This is my job now. I'll do it the way I see fit." Lux yanked her arm free. "I'm stronger than you were anyway."

"And less disciplined." Aradia glanced over when Michael and Zane entered the room. "Opening Purgatory is not easy, child. Magic does not work there as well as it does on Earth. You'll be drained quicker and have less power to work with." She looked at Michael. "I'm going with you. You'll need me. Lux has proven that she's not ready to be the only witch involved in this and Zane doesn't have the power necessary to accomplish what must be done."

Michael knew better than to get between mother and daughter. "There's time yet before those decisions need to be made. I healed Zane. We're working on the remaining Cambion, so there's no reason the two of you shouldn't remain here until we've been able to find them."

Zane dropped into one of the chairs. "I'm not complaining. It'll be nice to have a break from it all, truth be told."

Aradia turned her gaze to him. "Why have you not been making her train with her magic?"

He held out his hands, palms up. "I'm not her boss, and I'm not her parent. She's been doing fine. No offense meant, but the amount of magic we're asking from Lux is more consistent than what you needed to do. She's getting training every day when we go out and work. Besides, it's dangerous for her to use magic when it's not necessary. Every flicker, every spell ups the risk of us being sensed by Cambion or demons, and I don't want to take on unnecessary fights when we've got a much bigger one we're in the middle of." He leaned across the coffee table and grabbed her hands in his. "I know you're worried about her, but I promise you that I'm not going to let anything happen to Lux."

Lux huffed. "I can take care of myself, both of you! I just took out one of Beelzebub's children, like forty Familiars, some demons, and a dozen Cambion! And I just got drained! I'm allowed to be tired after all that. It's not like I passed out or got locked outside my own body." She looked at her mother pointedly.

Michael leaned against the doorframe. "Lux has done well. I haven't had concerns with her level of control over her magic. She can take advantage of the stay here to train and work on her control and access to it. You'll be here to work with her and help her." He glanced over his shoulder. "If you'll excuse me, I need to get back to work. Deacon and Dev are training in the gym if you'd like to join them. I believe Amaya is in there as well."

Lux wrinkled her nose. "Where's Zeke?"

"Resting. The pregnancy tires her out quickly." Michael pushed off the door and turned to go. "I'll be in my office if you need me."

Lux stood. "I'm going to go check on Zeke."

She ran up the stairs and into Zeke and Dev's room before Aradia could follow her, closing the door and leaning heavily against it. Zeke was lying on the bed, facing the door, her arms wrapped around a pillow and a second one tucked between her knees.

"Who are you running from, and why did you have to ruin my attempt at a nap?"

Lux flopped onto the bed and rolled to face her friend. "My mom. She's on my case about practicing magic more often. She doesn't think I'll be ready for Beelzebub."

Zeke propped herself up onto her elbow. "Do you feel ready?"

"As ready as I can be. When Mom tried to take him on, she managed to hold him to get his wings, but she nearly blew herself up in the process. We're taking him to Purgatory, or trying to, where we know his powers will be muted, but where we don't know what will happen to mine, hoping against hope that the effects are less on me because being a witch is a human thing and humans aren't affected by Purgatory."

"There are a lot of ifs in that plan."

"Don't I fucking know it?" Lux scrubbed her hands over her

face. "If he brings the others with him, I'm fucked. Just Beelzebub, we stand a chance. But if he brings the other Devils, there's not a chance in Hell that I'm coming out alive. I'd have to blow myself up trying to take them out."

"Would it work?"

"Maybe." She paused. "Probably not. I'd have enough juice for maybe two, but the other two would get away, and there'd be no way to control which two I could take out with the power blast since I'd be dead." She glared at Zeke. "Why aren't you more upset about the thought of me dying?"

"You're lying in my bed interrupting my nap. It doesn't seem like such a horrible prospect right now."

"You're such a bitch."

Zeke laughed and rolled onto her back. "Don't I know it." She looked over at Lux. "How long are you home for?"

"Just until they find the other Cambion we need to go after. There are three left."

"So you got the one in Alaska and two in London, then? I thought there was only one in London?"

"So did we, but we showed it to Michael and he said that's one of them, so there were two there. One less we have to find and kill I suppose, but it's odd that we didn't know she was going to be there. Dad is normally able to find that stuff out."

"They get stuff by us every once in a while." Zeke reached for the glass of water on her bedside table and took a deep drink. "Why are you hiding from your mother?"

"She's lecturing me about practicing magic." Lux stared up at the ceiling, studying the blades of the fan as they sliced through the air. "She doesn't seem to remember that the world is different now. I can't just practice anywhere I want at any time I want. If someone senses my magic, it could get me killed."

"She's just worried about you having the control necessary to take out Beelzebub and whoever the else comes with him. We don't want you to have to explode to take him out. I'd like to get to keep my best friend at the end of this." Zeke laid her hands on her stomach. "Besides, there's a little boy in here that needs to meet both his aunts, not just one of them. You have to come through this, Lux, and your mom is a good resource. She's been where you are. She fought Beelzebub. She can help you know what to expect. I think you should take advantage of the time you have here with her to train and get ready for what you're going to have to do."

Lux huffed and glared at Zeke. "I expected some solidarity from you."

"Then don't come up here and be wrong."

Zane leaned against the wall of the gym and watched Deacon and Dev sparring. "Are there any clues to where this last Cambion might be?"

Deacon spared him a quick glance. "Not yet. Dad is looking. So is Gage. Don't worry about it right now. Enjoy a few days off. We're working on things. There are other things we can be doing in the meantime."

Dev stepped back from Deacon and loped to the edge of the thick blue mat, bending to pick up a bottle of water and draining half of it in one gulp. "Like what, exactly?"

"We were talking about using Purgatory as a way to kill Beelzebub. Part of doing that is setting a trap for them and having Lux ready to open the gate and being able to suck him in. We need to have a plan for how to accomplish that. There's also the question as to whether or not Lilith, Abalam and Azazel might be with him when he comes for us, so I don't know if it's smart to send the two of you in alone. I'm thinking it might be best if Dev and I go with you, maybe Michael and Aradia, too."

Zane made a noise in the back of his throat. "Aradia is almost sixty years old. Do you really think that's a good idea?"

Deacon stared at him. "I think she's one of the most badass witches on the planet. We'd be stupid not to bring her with us when we're going into a situation like this. Absolutely stupid."

Dev put his hands on his hips. "I'm with Deacon on this one. We need all the ammo we can get. Zeke can't go because she's pregnant. Gage, Braxton, and Alaria can't go because they're all human and getting older, and Amaya can't go because she's got a bulls-eye on her back. Aradia's power doesn't lessen with age. It gets better. We should be taking advantage of every weapon we have at our disposal, not only some of them."

Zane lifted one shoulder in a shrug. "Looks like I'm outvoted. Do you have any thoughts on this plan of yours to lure them in?"

Dev snorted. "He always has thoughts, dude. We've known him for fifteen years. When have you not known him to have an idea?"

"True enough." Zane grinned at Deacon. "What's your idea?"

"I think we need to use Amaya as a trap." When neither man

said anything, he continued. "That's the one thing they're after and that they wouldn't be able to resist. When we go for the last Cambion, I think we take Amaya with us and purposely let a Cambion or two escape. They'll go tattle to Mommy and Daddy and bring them in. Then we'll get Amaya out as soon as they get there and we'll take on the rest of the troops."

Zane whistled softly. "That's certainly an idea. I'm not sure how anyone else is going to feel about using our one trump card as bait, but it would certainly work. I've got no doubt about that."

Dev finished his water. "Well, before we talk about it any further, I think we ought to run it by the other people who get a say in it." He dragged his hand across his mouth. "I think that's going to have to include Braxton and Alaria."

Deacon lifted his eyebrows. "Amaya is an adult. It's not like she needs permission."

"No, but they've been at this way longer than we have. Input isn't a bad thing, even if it's not always favorable." Dev headed for the stairs. "I'll send Carys to go get them."

"I'm in." Amaya sat up straight on the couch and rubbed her hands together excitedly. "Absolutely."

"Absolutely not." Gabriel spoke up from his position in the doorway. "I won't allow it. It's entirely too dangerous."

Alaria held up one finger toward Gabriel. "It is dangerous. I'll give you that, but we can't tell her what to do, Gabe. She gets to make the decision. You don't get to tell her what to do and expect her to obey you."

Braxton cleared his throat. "I'm with the Angel on this one. I say it's too dangerous. We don't have any guarantees we'll be able to get Amaya out once she's there and, we can't protect her as well once she's away from here. It's too big a risk. I don't like the idea."

Lux rubbed her hands over her face. "There are way too many people in this room. It's giving me a headache." She glanced around the room. "Let's just discuss this like the reasonable adults we all are. First off, we have to do what is going to give us the best chance of winning. However, more importantly, we also need to keep Amaya safe. It's one of those things, though. If we fail at this, it won't matter if she's under lock and key because we'll all be dead unless we really think Deacon and Amaya can manage to kill Beelzebub and Lucifer. So the question is: does anyone have a better idea?"

Gage grinned. "She is my daughter."

Aradia laughed. "Through and through." She looked at Alaria and Braxton. "I'll be going with them. Michael would be on hand to transport Amaya out as soon as Beelzebub appeared. There would be as little risk to her safety as possible. I have to agree with the children on this, I believe. This is a good idea, Braxton. I know you're reluctant to risk Amaya, but we knew we would have to risk them all before they were born. We risk them every day."

Michael folded his hands in his lap. "I don't know if there is a better idea. We would need to take some precautions in order to make sure it's going to be safe, and Lux needs to practice the spells to open up Purgatory with Aradia. We also need to take at least one of them down there in order to determine if they can open the door from inside Purgatory so we know whether or not they can both come with us or not. Obviously the best case scenario is that they can, but we can deal with just one. We'll also need to train inside Purgatory to determine the extent of our powers. That will allow us to be as comfortable as possible with the limitations and our abilities there. If we can get all of that accomplished and be reasonably certain with our plan, then I think it makes sense to allow Amaya to be used as bait. As much as I hate to let it her be used in that manner, it's our best shot, so I'm willing to go along with the plan."

Amaya grinned and bounced on the couch. "It's settled. Dad, Gabriel, you're both outvoted. Sorry." Wrapping her arm around Lux's shoulders, she squeezed her friend tightly. "I'm finally going to get some action in all of this. Fucking finally!"

Gabriel entered the kitchen slowly, unsure of what to say. Alaria and Amaya were sitting at the island, glasses of wine on the counter and a carton of ice-cream between them. He cleared his throat awkwardly, drawing their attention. Alaria offered a smile.

"Hey. Everything okay?"

"I need to return to the Nephilim I have been training. I didn't want to leave without saying goodbye. Michael has assured me he will inform me of when this plan is to take place so I may accompany you."

Alaria gestured to one of the stools. "Do you want some wine?" She looked at the bottle. "I think there's a glass or two left in there."

Amaya glared at her mother. "Mom."

Alaria's look was stern. "Don't be rude, Amaya. I'm sick to

death of the two of you being at odds." She reached out and brushed her fingers over Amaya's hair. "If it had been up to me, you'd never have known about all the past between me and Gabe. It's our past, not yours. If he'd known how you were going to react to it, I'm willing to bet he'd have thought twice about telling you the whole truth, too."

Gabriel shifted uncomfortable. "I think this is a conversation better had another time and place. Having me here makes her uncomfortable, Alaria, and that's the last thing I want."

Braxton laughed as he entered the room. "You make everyone uncomfortable, Gabriel, but that's because that's how you've always wanted it." He snagged Alaria's glass and took a drink of the wine. "How's it going with the Nephilim you're training?"

Gabriel checked his sleeves for lint, then studiously examined his lapel. "They're progressing at an acceptable pace. I believe that they will be ready to fight the Cambion in approximately six to eight weeks. Some are better than others, and there are several I fear will never be ready to fight effectively, but I am doing all I can to ensure they have the best possible chance of survival." He stared at Amaya intently. "It is my desire to see everyone survive."

Amaya finished her wine. "I don't doubt that you want us to make it through this alive." She rubbed her hands over her face. "This is so weird. I don't want to deal with this right now." She glared at her parents. "Neither of you will let me be rude, and he's standing there, not leaving even though he supposedly came in to tell us that he was leaving, and he looks like some pathetic lost puppy that thinks I'm going to kick it."

Braxton bit the inside of his cheek to keep from smiling. "Alaria, I'm going up to bed. Are you staying up with our animal abusing child, or coming up with me?"

Alaria ruffled Amaya's hair. "I'll see you in the morning. Be nice to your father."

That sentence hung in the air as Braxton and Alaria both kissed Amaya and retreated from the room. Amaya stared down at the counter, not sure how to proceed, while Gabriel busied himself with searching every inch of his clothing for imperfections. After several moments of awkward silence, Gabriel spoke.

"I owe you an apology as well, Amaya, for the way I've handled things in the past and continue to handle things."

Amaya glanced up. "What do you mean?"

"I shouldn't have told you about your paternity. It was up to your parents to tell you how they saw fit, and I interjected where I shouldn't have. I regret that our relationship has suffered because of the things I have done in the past, and I want to be able to repair those fractures. I know having a relationship with me seems a betrayal to Braxton and I understand that you don't want to hurt him."

"He isn't hurt." She poured the rest of the bottle of wine into her glass. "I went to talk to Dad after you and I fought the last time I saw you. He isn't hurt or angry or anything. He doesn't hate you, which comes as kind of a surprise to me because I always thought he did."

"Braxton and I have had a long history fraught with being on opposite sides of the same issue. We rarely agree about things." Gabriel smiled. "However, we do apparently share a love of Alaria and a love of you. Which gives us substantial common ground on which to stand."

"Did you really love my mom? Like were you in love with her?"

"Yes." Gabriel's answer was simple and soft. "I loved her very much. More than I knew what to do with and in a manner I had never before felt. I allowed those feelings to consume and overpower me until I was no longer in control of my own actions, and I made several unfortunate mistakes as a result of those feelings. I will always love your mother, much in the way I imagine she will always harbor some love for me, but I am no longer in love with her, and she is very much in love with your dad."

Amaya took a deep drink of wine. "I used to pray you'd come see me at night. You were my best friend. If I woke up and saw you standing at the window, I was excited you were there. Worried too, because I knew Mom and Dad were gone, and even when I was little I knew something was going on. I loved your visits and your stories, but everything came crashing down the night that I found out everything in the stories was real. It felt like loving you was betraying them."

"You don't have to explain your emotions to me, Amaya." Gabriel smiled sadly and took one step toward her. "You are young yet. There is time for us to make our peace. I only hope we can one day get back to the place we once were where my visits are met with joy and happiness instead of anger and trepidation." He held up a hand when she started to speak. "I know much of that is my fault. I do not blame you for the position we are in. I only hope someday you are willing to allow me to be more a part of your life than I am currently."

"I don't know. I'm trying. There's a lot to work through, and I'm trying to do it. Finding out like I did brought my whole world crashing down on my head. I hated you for it. It felt like you ripped my heart out, Uncle Gabe."

Gabriel started to reach out to touch her then retracted his hand a centimeter before it made contact with her skin. "I will pay for that every day for the rest of my life. If I could, child, I would go back and change it all." He did touch her then, laying his palm on her cheek, the warmth of her skin seeping into him. "I hope you can forgive me, Amaya, so someday I might forgive myself."

Amaya opened her mouth to speak, but Gabriel disappeared with a flash and pop. She lifted her hand and pressed her fingers to her cheek where his had been. She turned when she heard a stirring at the door and smiled when she saw Deacon come into the room.

"Are you okay?"

She nodded. "Just confused."

"I'd say." He opened the fridge and pulled out a bottle of beer. "Is there anything I can do?"

Lifting her shoulder, she leaned against the island. "I don't know what to do."

Deacon sat the bottle on the counter and bumped her shoulder with his own. "He's trying, Maya."

"I know he is. I am, too." She shivered when Deacon slipped one arm around her shoulders and leaned against his side. "It's going to be our turn soon. Are you ready?"

He grinned down at her. "Baby, we can do anything as long as we're together." His blue eyes sparkled with good humor, and a thick lock of white-blond hair fell across his forehead.

Without thinking, Amaya reached up and brushed it back, her fingertips skimming over his skin. Electricity sparked between them and Deacon grabbed her hand in his, pulling it back.

"Maya."

Before she could talk herself out of it, Amaya pivoted, sliding her arms around Deacon's neck and rising onto her tiptoes, pressing her mouth to his in a desperate, feverish kiss. He tasted dark and rich, his flavor blooming on her tongue as it darted between his lips. Her fingers sank into his hair and she clung to him.

Deacon devoured her. His fingers bit into her hips, and he

returned the kiss hotly, his tongue sweeping into her mouth and tangling with hers. A ragged groan tore from her chest and she pushed herself against him harder, desperate for more.

The light in the kitchen came on and they sprang apart, both wiping their mouths guiltily. Michael looked between the two apologetically.

"I'm sorry. I didn't know anyone was in here."

Amaya smiled tightly. "I'm going to bed. Goodnight."

Deacon started to leave the room, but his father cleared his throat and spoke. "Deacon."

He turned. "Dad."

"Do you think that's a good idea?"

"Probably not." He looked up the stairs after Amaya. "But I'll be damned if I can help myself."

CHAPTER TWENTY-TWO

October 1st, 2060 – Scotland

LUX GLANCED around the empty streets and looked at the people watching her. "I'm feeling a lot of pressure right about now."

Aradia laughed. "Do you want me to open Purgatory this first time?"

"No. I can do it. I know the spell."

"Knowing the spell and doing it are two entirely different things." She finished drawing the symbols on the ground and stood, brushing dirt from her jeans. "This is just practicing. You need to know how to open and close the door, first from here on Earth and then from inside Purgatory. We have to make sure that both of us can be down there."

Grumpy, Lux put her hands on her hips and glared at her mother. "I know all of this, Mom. I can do it."

Amused, Gage leaned against a burned out car and studied her. "Then do it. There's no time like the present."

Irritation getting the best of her, Lux held out her hands and closed her eyes, letting her power rise up and flow inside her. She recited the spell twice in her head to make sure she had the words right before uttering them out loud.

"Gates of Heaven, Gates of Hell. Angels on high and Devils that fell. Hear my demand, obey my cry. Turn the lock, open the door. Grant me access to that which exists no more. Purgatory deep,

Purgatory black. Open your gates, ascend through the black. Hear my cry, answer my plea. Swing open the gates and open to me!"

Her voice was strong and capable, and the magic was palpable in the air. The ground shifted under her feet, and the pavement groaned and strained as it started to move but stilled before anything else happened. Lux gritted her teeth and whipped up her magic even more, concentrating on the words of the spell and funneling her power through the stone around her neck. When she recited the spell a second time, her voice was low and powerful and the ground split open, a stone door with a wrought iron handle rising out of it.

Aradia nodded. "Very nicely done. Did you get a handle on how it's supposed to feel when the magic is right? When I was doing this we were heading up to the Solstice, so the power I was gleaning from nature was increasing. The Solstice has just passed, so you're getting waning power instead of waxing. That means that more of the magic being used is coming directly from you instead of from nature. It makes it harder on you, Lux."

"I've got it. I nearly had it the first time. I felt it right below the surface. It just needed a tiny bit more to bring it up." Lux stepped up the door and studied it curiously. "What's in Purgatory?"

"Some souls of creatures killed on Earth before Hell was formed. A few vampires, some demons, and not much else. They made a few attempts at colonizing, so there are the remnants of a few villages. It may be different now. Abalam spent a few years down there after Abaddon died, so he may have made some changes, but I can't imagine he did much." Michael grasped the door handle and pulled it open. "I'll take her down there, Aradia. She can practice opening the door from the other side. If it's not opened back up within an hour, open it from up here and let us out."

Gage straightened. "Do you think it's smart to send only the two of you down there? They all need to test the limits of their powers."

Michael smiled. "And they will. Right now we need to make sure our entry and exit are secured. As soon as that's done, we'll begin preparations with the others. Amaya, Dev, Deacon, Zane, and Lux will all be practicing below. They'll need to spar, train, and test their powers in every way we can in order to be as familiar with the strains of the Purgatory on their bodies and their powers as is possible before we go down there." He addressed Gage. "Did you experience a drain when we went down there?"

"Not that I recall. I don't remember Damon having one either, but neither of us had much in the way of supernatural powers. He didn't have any, and I was a vampire at the time. I remember that your ability to flash and fly was muted, though I don't remember your physical strength being muted. You took on Abalam and Abaddon pretty quickly." Gage slapped Deacon on the shoulder. "It was down in Purgatory that he found out about you. I've never seen anyone tear into a Devil as fast as he tore into them. It was a rage like I'd never seen before and haven't seen since."

Deacon grinned. "They should have learned not to mess with the Angel of War during the Fall."

Michael laughed. "Damn straight." He turned to Lux. "Let's begin your practicing. The sooner we go down, the sooner we can come back."

She nodded and shouldered her backpack. "You're getting very good at slang. That was really good."

"I pick up vernacular well." He pulled open the door and held it for her, following closely behind as they disappeared through the door and into Purgatory.

Lux gasped at the sharp jerk she felt as she fell through nothingness and landed hard on the ground. She groaned when her head smacked the dirt, and she rolled onto her back, staring up at dark gray sky. Wrinkling her nose when she didn't see a sun or clouds, she heaved herself to her feet and turned in a slow circle to take in her surroundings.

Rocks jutted out of the ground and browning grass grew in patches. Everything looked dim and dark. The trees were stripped of most their leaves, and the water running in the creek looked black instead of clear. The air smelled faintly of sulfur and felt heavy when she breathed it in.

"This place is weird."

Michael brushed himself off and stood. "It certainly is. I haven't missed it these past three decades. How does your magic feel?"

Lux reached deep within herself and stirred the embers of her magic. "It's still there. I can definitely feel a drain, but I think I can ramp it up enough to get the job done. Why is it like this?"

"Purgatory exists is an alternate dimension. It's not on Earth, nor is it in Heaven or Hell. It's kind of in-between, so the rules are both the same and different. Everything is similar, but not exact. So your powers still exist, but they are not precisely the same. For most that means they are weaker. Unfortunately, there are a few who are stronger here. Mostly Hellhounds. Actually, as far as I am aware, only Hellhounds, though it may be that werewolves could experience increased strength here as well given that they have Hellhound blood in them. I don't know. though." He flicked his wings to shake dust off them. "On the up-side, there's no physical drain from being down here. You can hack things to pieces to your heart's content just as if on Earth. Only down here it's refreshingly permanent."

"So do you want me to just open it back up?"

"That's the idea. Do you feel able to? If not, we wait for an hour until your mother lets us out."

Lux looked around apprehensively. "I don't want to stay down here for an hour." She crossed her arms. "How do I know we'll come out the same place we went in?"

Michael lifted one eyebrow. "I would assume you have some bit of magic to control where the door opens to. You'll also need to practice being able to close the door to let people in and out as needed."

"Let's do one thing at a time." She cracked her knuckles and planted her feet a shoulder's width apart.

She felt for her magic, poking at it until she felt it stir within her. Treating it as if it were a fragile ember, she blew and tended it until it roared into flame, engulfing her with power that streamed from her fingers and filled her body until it emanated from her soul.

Controlling it was harder and the black magic was much closer to the surface. It banged and pounded against the door, threatening to burst free and overtake her, demanding freedom. She refused it, concentrating instead on her natural magic and molding it until she was sure that she could work the spell that would allow them to leave Purgatory.

Her eyes turned from green to white to black, and her voice was deep and forceful when she spoke, the words echoing through the forest and filling the air.

"Gates of Heaven, Gates of Hell. Angels on high and Devils that fell. Hear my demand, obey my cry. Turn the lock, open the door. Grant me access to that which exists no more. Purgatory deep, Purgatory black. Open your gates, ascend through the black. Hear my cry, answer my plea. Swing open the gates and open to me! Take us back through time and space, return us to the place through which we came."

When nothing happened, Lux clenched her fists and concentrated harder, repeating the spell time and again, forcing more and more power from her body. The ground began to shake and a trickle of blood leaked from her nose, growing thicker and thicker as she pushed harder. Several times Michael started to reach out and stop her, then changed his mind, knowing that she had to test her boundaries.

She opened the door, letting in tendrils of black magic that tinged hers with evil. Pain sliced through her body, and she made a whining noise in the back of her throat as it took its price from her hide. Forcing it through the prism of her citrine, she cleansed it and added it to the power of her own, concentrating her magic. She repeated the chant again, nearly sobbing in relief when the stone door sprang from the ground.

Her vision clearing, Lux wiped the blood from her nose and looked at Michael triumphantly. "I did it!"

Concerned, he gripped her elbow to help her balance. "How do you feel?"

"A little weak. I'll get better. I just need to practice. We have some time for me to be able to." She glanced around. "Let's get out of here for the moment."

Michael gripped the handle and pulled it open, leading her through the door and back onto Earth. Aradia rushed forward the instant she saw them come through, grabbing Lux by the forearms.

"Are you okay?"

"I'm fine, just tired. It's hard from down there."

"But possible." Zane took her arm from Michael. "Which is what we needed to know."

Lux nodded. "It's possible all right." She looked at her mother. "The black magic is much closer to the surface down there than up here. It was literally banging on the door to get in. I had to use a little to get the door back open the first time and it was all I could do to close it off. We're going to have to be super careful about using it down there. It could get really bad really fast if we let it in."

Gage swore. "I've been telling her I hate that fucking black magic for nearly thirty years."

Aradia smiled serenely. "It's a tool to be used and manipulated when needed. Lux discovered the issue very early on, and we'll be very cautious when accessing it, but everyone here knows we're going to need black magic to kill Beelzebub. It's a given."

Zane wiped blood from Lux's upper lip. "That doesn't mean we have to like it." He looked around. "We might as well start some training today. Aradia, you're here. You can open it back up then take Lux home to rest up. The rest of us can go down for a couple hours, do some training and some exploring, then come back up. There's no use in wasting most of the day that we could be using to prepare."

Deacon nodded. "I agree. I think we should go down."

Aradia shrugged. "If you want to, I'll open it back up."

Lux pulled free from Zane. "I can go back down. I'm not going to go back to Michael's and nap. I need to practice with it, too."

Aradia turned to face her daughter, her voice stern. "You will do no such thing. We'll work on it daily, and it will get easier, but there is no use in continually exhausting yourself in order to prove a point. You have to get used to the drain and the different way of handling your magic, and that is better done a little at a time, not all at once. We have time, Lux. We'll take it."

"At least let me go down and watch. I don't want to be stuck cooped up at home with nothing to do."

Dev laughed. "Zeke's there. She'd love the company."

Michael looked at her tenderly. "I'm afraid you're outvoted." He reached out and touched her forehead. "We'll see you at home later."

When she had disappeared, he turned to the rest. "Now, let's see what the rest of you can do down there."

Aradia held out her hands, preparing to call the gate up once more. Before she could do so, Gabriel appeared with a flash. Michael turned to face his brother.

"Gabriel. Is everything okay?"

"I just received word that there has been an attack on one of the Nephilim and Warrior camps in the Northwestern United States. I looked into the memories of one of the escaped Nephilim. The leader of the Cambion is one of the remaining three offspring of Beelzebub. I came immediately to inform you of the turn of events."

Zane spoke from his perch atop the hood of an abandoned minivan. "How many Cambion?"

"According to the Nephilim who escaped, there were approximately thirty that attacked the camp. More than twenty perished during the ensuing battle. There are roughly eight left there, including Beelzebub's son. They appear to still be at the camp. There may be an opportunity to eliminate this particular Cambion if we move quickly."

Zane looked at Michael. "Lux is too weak to go right now with just opening that door from Purgatory. Dev and Deacon can go with me."

"Agreed."

Amaya lifted her hand in the air. "What about me?"

Michael shook his head. "It's not time to lay the trap yet. You know that as well as I do. You'll remain here and train in Purgatory with Carys and Elisa. Aradia, Gage, you'll remain here with them. Gabriel, would you stay here until I return?"

Gabriel inclined his head slightly. "Certainly."

"I'm going to transport you three to the camp, then go check on everything with Alaria and Braxton's other children and at my home. If they attacked at one, there may be other attacks planned, and I will not have their deaths on my hands." He glanced at the three Nephilim. "Gather your weapons and let's go."

Zane snapped on his utility belt and chose a hatchet and bowie knife to go in it, shouldering a rifle and tucking a pistol into his waistband. Dev chose a short-sword and double-sided axe, while Deacon preferred several thin blades he could throw and a machete. Both also carried rifles and pistols.

"I'll go straight for Beelzebub's bastard son." Zane looked between Dev and Deacon. "You two clear out the rest. Be careful."

Deacon laughed. "Three on eight? Brother, they don't stand a snowball's chance in Hell."

Dev was laughing as Michael touched their foreheads. "He's cocky as hell, but in this case, I agree with him."

The camp where the Nephilim and Warriors had lived was still smoldering. Several of the buildings had burned to the ground. Bodies were scattered over the dirt, and blood had stained it brown. The smell of smoke, gunpowder, and death hung in the air. Deacon held up his hand as they appeared in the camp, signaling the other two men not to move as they got their bearings. He nodded to Zane and jerked his hand to the right, then glanced to Dev and signaled him to the left. Splitting off, each went in a different direction.

Deacon ducked into one of the buildings still standing, pressing his back to the wall and holding his pistol so that the barrel was pointed toward the floor. He reached out with his senses, trying to get a feel for where the Cambion were in the compound and how many of them there were.

There were a hell of a lot more than eight.

Swearing under his breath, he backtracked, looking for Zane. Dev was able to sense Cambion just as effectively and had certainly already figured out that their situation was worsening by the second, but Zane was not as talented in that area as the other two were. He lifted his eyebrow as he jogged past a Cambion tossed carelessly to the ground, his eyes wide and unseeing and hands brought up as if to defend himself.

As he rounded a corner, Dev appeared from the other side, moving quickly. They skidded to a stop, guns raised as they aimed at each other for a split second before realizing who the other was and lowering the weapons. Deacon jerked his head toward the building and they ducked inside. Dev raked his hand through his hair.

"There are twenty-five at least and more arriving every minute. Mostly weak, but a lot of them. We need to get to Zane before he gets himself into something he can't get out of."

Deacon nodded. "Agreed." He peered out the door. "I already found one Cambion Zane handled. I'll take point and you stay on my heels. We need to get to him and take this on together. Keep your powers running on low. There's so much death and blood in the air that they probably haven't picked up on us yet, but it won't be long before they do."

"This is one of those times I wish Zeke wasn't pregnant."

"You and me both." He led Dev out the door and up a flight of stairs. "Her powers come in hella handy in situations like this."

Both men tensed when they heard the sounds of a struggle. The sounds of fighting trickled down from one of the roofs. Not wanting to take the time to find stairs and climb them, Deacon stripped off his shirt and tucked it in his pocket. Along his back, on either side of his spine, was a tattoo of a wing. They glowed and stirred, moving under his skin and peeling off his back, forming into real wings~black feathers tipped with red. Dev followed suit, removing his shirt and allowing his wings to tear themselves from inside his back.

They took off, flying to the roof where Zane was locked in battle with half a dozen Cambion. Deacon landed, whirling and slashing through them with his wings, the feathers sharp as scalpels as they sliced through two of the Cambion. Dev drew his sword and dropped onto one of the others, slitting its throat with a brutal swipe of the blade, blood splashing the ground.

Zane grabbed the last two and clamped his hand on their heads, sucking life from their bodies and casting them aside. He glared at the other two men.

"There are certainly not eight Cambion here. Triple that, at least."

Deacon chuckled. "We figured that out." He glanced around the roof. "How many have you taken out?"

"Counting these six? Nine."

"Hey, we each got two of these, so you're at five and we have two each." Dev wiped his sword on the shirt of one of the dead bodies. "You don't get to take all the credit, dude."

Deacon grinned and looked between them. "We'd have had more if we hadn't been chasing him to make sure he'd be okay since we can sense Cambion and he can't."

"I can sense them, just not how many like you two can." Zane bent and picked up his pistol, holstering it and walking to the edge of the roof. "New plan." He glanced over his shoulder at Deacon. "You want to get some kills?"

"What do you have in mind?"

"I'll snipe some of them off from up here since I'm the only one that doesn't sprout wings. The two of you take off and come in from above. Scatter them, scare them, whatever. We'll clean them all out. We don't know which one is Beelzebub's, so we can't let any get out of here. I can keep them from flashing out with magic."

Dev shrugged. "Let's get it done."

Zane waited until the other two had taken off before anchoring his rifle to his shoulder and peering through the sight. As Dev and Deacon flew off the roof, he heard shouts from the ground as the Cambion noticed their presence. Gunshots sounded from below as he lined up a shot, squeezed the trigger and watched as a Cambion died.

Deacon landed first, slashing with his wings as often as he did with his machete. Dev used his sword from above, hacking at them from out of reach. Unlike Nephilim, no Cambion had wings, so those few Nephilim who could fly had a huge advantage in battle. Zane took shot after shot, picking off Cambion and staining the dirt with blood and brain matter.

In a matter of minutes, it was done. Not one had escaped, and there was not one Cambion left breathing in the entire compound. Flashing down to the other two, Zane put his hands on his hips and studied the carnage.

"That was pathetically easy."

Deacon whistled. "How in the hell did they take out a whole compound of Nephilim and Warriors and then we managed to take out thirty of them and not get a scratch?"

Dev shrugged. "I doubt these were the ones that came in. They were mostly killed. The ones that survived likely called for others to come in knowing the Nephilim would retaliate and we got here before their stronger soldiers could arrive." He looked around. "I'm not looking a gift-horse in the mouth. Let's find out which one of these Cambion is Beelzebub's to make sure we got the son of a bitch and get home." He looked at Zane. "How do you do that anyway?"

"Michael tells us. He can sense them."

Deacon looked up. "Michael!"

With a flash of light and a loud pop, Michael appeared, sword drawn. When he realized there was no on-going battle, he lowered it, looking mildly impressed. "Well. That was quite efficient."

Zane laughed. "Did we get the right one?"

Michael surveyed the bodies. "There are many more than eight Cambion recently dead here."

"Gabriel was wrong. There were closer to thirty."

Michael studied the bodies, moving between each of them until he stopped at one of the Cambion Zane had shot. "This is the one. You've done well." He looked between them. "Gather round and I'll take you all home."

CHAPTER TWENTY-THREE

LUX STIRRED when the door to the bedroom she was sharing with Zane opened. Her eyelids fluttered, and she squinted against the light as he turned on the small lamp on the dresser. He glanced over at her apologetically.

"Sorry. I was hoping the light wouldn't wake you up. How are you feeling?"

She reached for the glass of water on the night stand and drank deeply to soothe her dry throat. "Fine. I didn't intend to fall asleep. How did training go?"

"We didn't actually get to train. Almost as soon as Michael sent you back here, Gabriel popped in and told us that one of the Nephilim bases had been attacked and the Cambion leading the attack was one of Beelzebub's. Dev, Deacon, and I went in and dealt with it. We must have taken out twenty-five or thirty Cambion, including the one we were after, which just leaves us Alexi and the one he had with Lilith."

Lux sat up and gaped at him. "You went after one of Beelzebub's Cambion and didn't come get me?"

Zane paused in the process of undressing and stared at her. "You were here resting. I didn't want to risk wearing you out any more than you already were, and we had plenty of firepower with Dev and Deacon right there. It was an easy choice, babe."

She rolled out of bed and put her hands on her hips. "This is supposed to be our mission, not Dev and Deacon's. You should have come and gotten me. I'm not a wilting flower that needed to rest up at home while you boys went off and had all the fun. I'm as much a solider as the rest of you."

Confused but smart enough to realize he was on shaky ground, Zane chose his words very carefully. "I don't think I ever said it was fun, and no one ever suggested you're anything but a soldier. It made the most sense at the time. We were there, you weren't, so we went."

"It would have taken ten seconds for Michael or Carys to come back and get me. Or hell, why didn't you take Carys and Elisa with you?"

"Because I took Dev and Deacon. I've known them longer, I work with them better and Carys and Elisa needed to practice flashing in and out of Purgatory."

"But the three men didn't need to practice, is that it? Because you have a penis you're completely excused from the training the rest of us have to do? While Lux and her poor, weak vagina stayed home resting, Zane and the magnificent penises went off and did the all-important *man things*."

Zane struggled not to laugh. He bit his tongue and held his breath, counting backward from ten in an intense effort not to break down into gales of laughter. When he was reasonably certain he could speak without giggling like a ten-year-old, he took a deep breath and addressed her.

"I don't know how you're managing to turn this into some sort of sexist thing, but that's not what it was at all. You wore yourself out getting out of Purgatory. Instead of risking your life going into a battle other people were perfectly capable of fighting, I made a decision to take two men who are like brothers to me, who I have fought with a thousand times before, and who I trust with my life, the same way I do you. It had nothing to do with what's between their legs and everything to do with who was available at the time. If you'd been there, we'd have gone together and killed them, just as we've done everything together for the last eight months."

"You hadn't ever had an opportunity to have them with you instead of me before. First, Dev was off with Zeke, and then he didn't want to leave her because of the baby. Deacon is pretty much under lock and key because he needs to be alive to go after Lucifer. So I was your only choice."

"Now you just sound ridiculous. It's not like you're some

consolation prize." Zane raked his hands through his hair. "Jesus Christ, woman, I've never known you to act like this. It had nothing to do with you! Not a goddamn thing. Why can't you get that through your thick skull?"

Angry and near tears, Lux grabbed a pillow off the bed and stormed toward the door. Before she could reach the handle, Zane grabbed her wrist, stopping her from leaving.

"Where do you think you're going?"

"I'm going to spend the night with Amaya."

"The hell you are."

Fury flashed within her and she ripped her wrist from his grip. "Last I checked, you're not my boss. You don't get to tell me what to do."

"And you don't get to run out the first time we have a disagreement. I'm still not even clear why we're having an argument but you're sure as hell not leaving until we've finished hashing it out!"

Lux sneered at him. "That's the beauty of just sleeping together. I don't have to answer to you, and this ends any time I want it to. Seeing as I just discovered you're a sexist pig, I think that time is now!"

She grabbed the handle and wrenched the door open, but Zane slammed it shut, blocking her in with his body.

"Why is it okay for you to call me names and storm out like a child, but if I tried it I'd be an asshole?" When she didn't have an answer, he nodded darkly. "That's what I thought." Holding up his hands and taking a step back, he glanced at the door. "I won't force you to stay once we've finished this, but you don't get to walk out in the middle of it. I don't even know why you're mad at me, and I'm sure as hell not a sexist pig. Why don't you try sitting down and talking to me like an adult instead of hurling insults and calling me names?"

"This is my job! Killing the Cambion is my thing! We've trained for it for months and then at the last second you take your brothers out instead of coming to get me. How is that supposed to make me feel?" She glared at him and gripped the pillow tightly to her chest. "Would you have rather had them the whole time?"

"Yes." When she went for the door again, Zane slammed it shut again. "You said your piece, now I get to say mine."

"Isn't that what you just did?"

"Not hardly." He gestured to the chair in the corner of the

room. "Sit down and listen to me for a few minutes, and then if you still want to go, you can."

"I'll stand. Right here by the door."

"Fine. I'll sit. But if you walk out that door before I've said this, I'm coming after you to finish saying it, and I don't think either of us wants the scene that would cause. It isn't fair for you to get to yell and scream at me and not listen to my explanation. I'm not going to touch you, but I'm also going to get my turn." Zane perched on the edge of the bed. "Yes, I would have rather had Dev and Deacon with me this whole time, but not for the reasons you're thinking." He ran his hands over his face. "Do you remember before we went after Ingrid and you decided to tan on the beach?"

Sullen and hurt, Lux nodded. "You were an ass."

"When we were climbing the steps back to the house, I almost put my hand on your back while we were walking. I wasn't thinking and I just reached out to do it."

"So?"

Incredulous, Zane laughed. "So? So I didn't have my gloves on. I would have killed you. I saw you down there and got so panicked that something might happen to you that I ran down there to check on you without grabbing my gloves. If I had touched you, you'd be dead. All because I wasn't thinking and it seemed the normal, natural thing to do." He stared at her. "It's not just sex for me, Lux. It never has been. It wasn't at first, it isn't now, it was never going to be. Even when we were kids and you'd be here for one reason or another, you treated me like a real person instead of a weapon."

"What's your point?"

"The point is that if I had been with anyone other than you, I wouldn't have been forced to concentrate on not touching them every time I was within arm's reach. I wanted to, you wanted me to, we both knew it, and it was always there, just out of reach. Today, if you had gone, I would have been preoccupied with making sure you were safe and okay because it's *you*. And I care about your safety probably more than I should. It would have ended up endangering us both. Say what you will about me being a male chauvinist pig or whatever other name you're inevitably going to call me now, but there you have it. I would have been more comfortable with Dev and Deacon because I'm not in love with them. I am with you, and that scares the hell out of me. At first I didn't even want to talk to you, but you're impossible to ignore, so I decided I just wouldn't let you know about the feelings. Then Gabriel did his messing around in my head, and with this damn link you're in my head and we can touch, so that excuse was gone. You were in my arms, and I couldn't resist you. I didn't want to." He held up his hands helplessly.

Lux stared at him, not moving and not saying anything. Her arms were still locked around the pillow, but she'd moved a step or two away from the door. Taking that as a positive sign, Zane continued.

"I know what you said about not wanting the whole love thing and I've tried to respect it, but you have a right to know how I feel, too. I fell in love with you the night Lilith attacked. When I came downstairs and you were playing that piano, you were so amazing, and I just stood there and stared at you and it smacked me between the eyes. I've tried to give you time and to not push you for more than you wanted to give, but you asked, so I'm telling you. I'd have preferred Dev and Deacon because if they'd been there I wouldn't have fallen in love with you."

"So you don't want to be in love with me?"

Frustrated, Zane stood and paced the room. "Why do you always take the absolute worst thing possible from a conversation? Yes, I want to be in love with you. I am, so regardless of wanting to, there it is. The problem is you. I know you don't return the feelings. I know you don't want that, and I never wanted to push you or try to make you into something you didn't want to be."

Crossing the room, she laid the pillow back on the bed and perched on the edge. "I was jealous. When you said you took Dev and Deacon. We've been working so well together, and I thought we were such a good team. When you told me you took the boys instead of coming for me, I got jealous." She glared at him before continuing. "It doesn't change the fact that you've bullied me into staying here, which is, well...kinda sexist. But I get your point."

"Just because I do something with them doesn't mean I don't want to work with you." He dropped onto the bed next to her. "There is no one I would rather have in my corner than you. Not even Dev and Deacon. And for the record, if it had been a man hurtling those kinds of insults at me, I'd have been just as determined to have it out. I like to finish an argument when it starts, not drag it out."

She stared down at her hands. "It felt like the second I left to go somewhere else you went off with your friends to fight. I got used to it just being the two of us. For a long time it was me and Zeke. Amaya couldn't ever really go because of keeping her safe, but sometimes she had to for training, so she was part of us, too. Now it feels weird to think about going out with anyone but you. It's you I want fighting next to me more than anyone else. It hurt to think that you didn't feel the same way about it." Offering a small smile, she averted her gaze. "Which tells me I have more feelings for you than I thought I did."

"I don't want you to say it if you don't mean it. I don't need the words."

"I won't give them to you unless I do. I love you, but I'm not sure I'm in love with you. I like waking up to you and going to sleep with you. I like being on the road together and how we manage to have some fun even when things are serious. I even think it's cute when you pull the weather trick to get me to do what you want. There's no one else I want to be with, and I don't want to be without you, but I don't know if I'm in love with you." She leaned her head on his shoulder. "I like knowing you are with me, though. It makes me feel warm and good inside and kinda tingly."

Zane reached over and laid her hand on top of her knee. "This is all new for me. Maybe it was the touching thing, but typically I tucked tail and ran at the first fight. With you, though, I couldn't think of anything other than plowing through it and getting back to being okay. I want all of this with you." He paused and bumped her shoulder with his playfully. "Though I could do without the giant blowups."

Lux tossed her arms around him and rolled onto him, pressing him back into the bed and lying on top of him. "This? This was just a teeny tiny spat." She grinned down at him and sat up, straddling his hips. "But you explained things, and now they're better."

Not entirely mollified, Zane glared up at her. "You made me sound like part of some stupid boy band. 'Zane and the Magnificent Penises.'"

Giggling, she leaned down and brushed her mouth over his. "I say silly things when I'm mad." She nibbled on his lower lip gently. "I'm sorry for being a bitch. I shouldn't have called you a sexist pig. You're really not."

"I try not to be, but occasionally it leaks out. I really didn't think I did anything wrong, though, so I'm sorry I made you feel bad." He tangled his hands in her hair and let the silky strands slide over his skin. "I don't think I'll ever get used to being able to put my hands on you, Lux. Sometimes I feel like I could just lay here and touch you forever."

Lux gripped the bottom of her sweater and drew it over her head, exposing her lace-clad breasts to his view. "Touch all you want. I like it when you do." She made an approving noise when his hands slid over her ribcage and upward to cup her breasts, kneading the soft flesh. "Want to know one of the best things about being at Michael's nonplace?"

Distracted by the feel of her flesh filling his palms, Zane glanced up at her. "Hmm?"

"I can use all the magic I want without it being tracked." She wiggled her eyebrows at him. "Care for a demonstration?"

He propped himself up on his elbows when she slid off his lap and stood. "Do I get a choice?"

She snapped her fingers, and the jeans and bra she had been wearing were exchanged for black leather and red lace. High-heeled boots came to above her knees, a black thong was cut high on her hips and accentuated her bottom, and she wore a red bustier that pushed her breasts up. Her hair was piled on top of her head in a loose bun with tendrils tumbling down to skim against her skin. Her eyes were somehow darker and more defined and there were smudges of color on her cheeks and lips.

Zane choked on air and coughed. "Wow."

She snapped again and he found himself naked save for a condom that had already been rolled over his bulging erection.

"You're very efficient."

"You can control the weather. I can control basically everything else." She looked down at the lingerie. "Do you like?" She snapped her fingers a third time and the leather was replaced with white silk that skimmed over her curves, revealing nothing but teasing everything. Instead of boots her feet were bare. "Or is this more your style?"

"It's more you." He sat up and reached for her. "I just want you, Lux. I don't need gimmicks and tricks."

She slid onto him, clamping her mouth on his in a hot kiss. Gripping his hair in her hands, she rose over him, sliding one hand down his body to position herself over him. Sinking onto him, she rolled her hips to seat him deep within herself and looped her arms around his shoulders, pressing their chests together.

"You've got me." She gripped his shoulder slightly as she started to move, slowly rocking back and forth. "Now lay back and enjoy."

Zane lay back on the bed, his eyes glued to her as she rode him. She braced her hand on his stomach for balance, her head tossed back and hair streaming down her back as she slid back and forth, her pace increasing in speed with each slide. He reached out and gripped her nightie in his hand, pulling it up and over her head and casting it aside so that he could feast on the sight of her naked body.

Her shoulders were strong and body lush, and his hands touched every curve, reveling in the feel of her flesh under his fingers. Her breasts were soft and full and swayed gently as she moved, her nipples dusky pink and tightly beaded from desire and passion.

Slowly, she leaned forward, gripping the wrought iron headboard in her hands and driving her hips back and forth quickly, thrusting his penis in and out of her body rapidly, the friction propelling them both toward release.

Zane surged up and caught one nipple between his lips, sucking deeply and caressing the nub with his tongue, flicking it gently and rolling it in his mouth. Lux's hips jerked and she cried out, her body tensing and pulsing as the extra stimulation pushed her over the edge and she flew into orgasm. He gripped her hips and moved her up and down several times in rapid succession, seating himself deep within her and groaning as he found his own release, dragging her down on top of him and holding her tightly.

His voice rumbling under her ear, Zane spoke. "Well, you haven't bitten me in like two weeks."

Laughing, Lux slapped his arm. "I only bit you once." She rolled off him and settled on her side, waiting until he'd disposed of the condom and walked into the bathroom before speaking again. "What's the plan?"

Zane brought a towel back from the bathroom and handed it to her. "We wait until we can find Isaiah and Alexi and while we wait, we train in Purgatory."

CHAPTER TWENTY-FOUR

LILITH SAT on the throne, stroking her hands lovingly over the softly rounded mound of her stomach. She had very carefully chosen clothes to accentuate her pregnancy, wanting it to be completely obvious that she was carrying another child. Serafina sat next to her, playing with two dolls.

"Mommy, when will the new baby be born?"

"In a few weeks, darkling." Lilith lifted one hand from her belly to let it drift over Serafina's hair. "Are you excited to be a big sister?"

"I didn't think it would happen so fast." The little girl pouted. "You're growing very quickly."

Lucifer looked up from the book he was reading. "It didn't take long with Isaiah or with Serafina."

"Pregnancy doesn't last very long for Devils. Five months instead of the normal nine. That came as quite a surprise with Isaiah. When I had Deacon, he had a normal human gestation, so I assumed all my children would. It seems that the Angelic DNA had some effect on his development. When two Devils have children together it's not normal." Lilith shuddered at the memory. "I don't relish the thought of repeating the delivery. You literally tore your way from me, Serafina, my love. Your brother will do the same thing soon."

Lucifer closed the book. "If I had been thinking about how weak you were after birth, I would never have agreed to allow you to conceive until after this little problem with Gabriel and Alaria's daughter is done."

"I may be weak during delivery and immediately after, but I am still more powerful than they are." Lilith tapped her foot on the floor impatiently. "Where is Beelzebub? He should be here by now."

Lucifer's voice was dripping with sarcasm when he spoke. "He'll be here when he gets here, darling. He's certainly grieving the loss of yet another son. He's had to sacrifice all but two now." He rolled his eyes and stood, holding out his hand for Serafina. "Come now, sweetheart. I'm going to take you up to Nanny. I'll come for you after we're done discussing things with Beelzebub, and we'll go look at dead Nephilim again. I know how much you love that."

Serafina gathered her dolls and grabbed her father's hand. "When can I kill some of them, Daddy? I want to kill them like Mommy and Isaiah do!"

"I know you do, my love, but you're not old enough yet. When you're big and strong like your mother, then we'll go together and you can kill anything you wish." He beamed at her indulgently. "Come now."

Beelzebub appeared as Lucifer left with Serafina. "I worry about that girl."

Lilith looked up with a dreamy look on her face. "Why?"

"She's bloodthirsty, Lilith."

Lilith's hands stilled on her stomach. "Your point is what precisely?"

"I'm concerned about how long we'll be able to control her."

"*We* don't have to control her. Lucifer and I do, and we'll do just fine. Thank you for your concern." Her voice was regal and tight. "You're late."

"I'm not late." He sat on one of the vacant thrones. "I'm preparing the trap for the Nephilim, Michael, and Gabriel. I have it on good authority from some of my contacts left in Purgatory that Aradia has been practicing with the others as well. She's going to be there, too."

Lilith perked up. "I've been waiting for a chance to kill her. Good." She studied her fresh manicure and admired the delicate rose polish. "What timeline do you have in mind?"

"I have Isaiah and Alexi covering a town in Denmark in Nephilim traps. That takes a lot of time and energy, as you well know. Finding the Nephilim and draining them of blood before they're dead in order for the witches to bless it for the traps is a very labor-intensive process, but they're making sufficient progress on it. I anticipate that we will move on them within a month."

"I should hope it's sooner than that." Lucifer strode back in. "We want them cocky, but we don't want them actually prepared for us, and a month is too much time. Put other Cambion on the project and have the traps done within two weeks. I want this moved on by then. That gives them enough time to be feeling good about what they're doing, and they'll go in sure of themselves. You'll notify Abalam and Azazel of when they will be needed as well. What's your plan?"

"I'm planning for Alexi to lead an attack on a small Warrior encampment that we are aware of. There are several Nephilim there, and Alexi is well known. He'll escape, of course, and at least one of the Nephilim will be left alive. They'll notify Gabriel or Michael of Alexi's presence and where he flashed to. The Angels will indubitably rally their troops and go in with guns blazing to kill my son. Unfortunately for them, however, we will all be waiting for them. We'll have Hellhounds and Cambion there of course, and our witches there to make sure that neither of their witches can actually succeed in opening the portal to Purgatory."

"It would be unfortunate if they were to succeed in getting any of you to Purgatory. As you know, that is the one place that we can be killed."

Beelzebub sneered. "I'm well aware. We lost Abaddon down there. I'm not in a hurry to lose more of us to the void. The witches are preparing the spells to keep the door shut. Ours aren't as powerful as Aradia and Lux, but there are more of them and we're counting on their attention being fractured by everything else going on. Once Aradia is dead, the goal will be to bring Lux to you and then use her to help locate and kill Amaya Winslow."

Lucifer looked up. "Amaya Winslow is not to be killed by anyone but me. I'm going to gut her while her parents watch. They will see every drop of blood drain from her body and know that with it drains away their hope at ever winning this war. She is mine, and mine alone."

Beelzebub inclined his head. "Of course. My apologies."

Lilith clapped her hands. "It's a good plan. I want to kill the older witch. I've wanted her for years and this is my chance. She's mine and no one else's."

Beelzebub looked at Lucifer. "With all due respect, we can't assign targets for everyone or else we're increasing our chances of losing. The important thing is that they die, not who kills them. Gabriel's daughter won't be there, so it's not an issue this time. Keeping the one witch alive is one thing, and there's an important purpose behind that, but we can't guarantee Aradia for Lilith. Not everything is possible."

Lucifer tapped his index fingers against his chin, considering the issue. "Lilith, my love, I wish you would reconsider going into this battle in your condition."

"Absolutely not. I'm killing her, and that's the end of it." She glared at the two men. "That witch wrapped me in witch-rope and helped Michael steal my son from my arms. I will have my vengeance on her."

Beelzebub sighed. "You hate Deacon. You want to kill him."

Lilith screeched. "Because of her! If she hadn't done what she did, he would be here with us planning their demise instead of helping them! He's been corrupted by his father!"

Lucifer's voice was mild. "Perhaps if you hadn't been fucking Michael we wouldn't be in this predicament." He turned his attention back to Beelzebub. "It is settled. Lilith will go with you into battle. She will have Aradia, and you will bring me Lux alive. You will do this within two weeks. I'll keep Serafina here while you charge into this fight, and if you succeed, the throne to my right will be yours. Fail me and pray they kill you, Beelzebub."

Beelzebub inclined his head. "I'll continue making preparations and come for Lilith when the time comes."

"See that you do. Failing to fetch her would result in dire consequences. I'd suggest you remember that."

Beelzebub was gone before Lilith could gloat.

Gabriel stood in front of the fireplace, studying the flames. The woman on the couch behind him sat quietly, wearing a white suit and heeled boots. She adjusted her blonde hair and surveyed him studiously.

"Why am I here, Gabriel?"

Gabriel turned to face Griffin, striding across the room with three steps and dropping elegantly into one of the chairs. "It is necessary for us to speak frankly and alone."

She lifted one eyebrow and sipped iced tea from the glass he'd had waiting for her. "I remember this place from when I was alive. You never brought me here for good news. Is it any different now that I'm dead?"

"I don't have bad news." He brushed his palms over the legs of his trousers. "We have found ourselves in a very unfortunate position. As you are aware, Lucifer is making strides to rise against Heaven and siege against God. If that were to happen, every soul in Heaven would be at risk. Including yours."

Concern registered in her eyes and she sat the glass of tea down. "What do you mean 'at risk'?"

"I mean that if Lucifer breaks through the gates of Heaven, he could take the souls in Heaven and subject them to the same torture that he does to the souls in Hell."

Griffin winced. "That sounds horrible. What are you doing to prevent it? And what does it have to do with me?" She leaned forward and braced her elbows on her knees. "I just want to rest, Gabriel. I'm tired of being jerked from Heaven every time you need a gofer for something. I did my job. I gave my life for this. My son gave his life for this. My granddaughter is dead. My great-granddaughter is carrying the next generation of Nephilim to continue fighting this infernal war. I'm tired. I don't want to know any more about it, and I don't want to be involved with it. I'm done."

"Unfortunately, it is not possible for you to be done. You maintain a link with the rest of them—Alaria, Braxton, Gage, Aradia, their children. You are still the Chosen and it is pure, powerful blood that flows through your veins. You've rested for as many years as you were alive. The time has come that you will again be asked to take up this cause and fight for God."

Griffin surged to her feet, anger flashing in her eyes. "No! Absolutely not!" She paced the room, her muscles bunched tightly. "I died for this! I put a knife through my heart and gave up everything I am for Him! He has no right to ask anything else of me!"

"He's not asking. I am."

"Then you have no right, either!" Infuriated, but slightly curious, Griffin faced him. "God has nothing to do with this? What exactly are you asking me to do? Become human again?"

"No. You are dead. Your body has long been decomposed and returned to the dirt. Only God himself could bring you out of your grave, and to my knowledge that is not in contemplation. Sit down, Griffin, and let me explain what I am asking"

Hesitantly, Griffin returned to the couch and lowered herself to the cushions. "Okay. What is it you want?"

"Each Angel has particular abilities. Michael has an unrivaled ability to lead troops into war. The Angel of Death has the power to give and take life. I am one of the Lord's Messengers. Each of us has a purpose specific to us alone. God created Angels before humans were even contemplated, and when He made humans, we were tasked with watching over and protecting and guiding them."

"I know all this. I did live through the Choosing, Gabe. Get to the point."

"It is possible to turn a spirit in Heaven into an Angel. It is rarely done, and only then in extremely special cases. Only the Archangels have the ability to do it since it means sharing our Grace with the recipient. I would like to make you an Angel, and share my Grace with you. I believe that having you to guide them, having you there to remind them of why they fight and what the price was would help those who are left rally and win this war."

Griffin blinked several times as she processed what had been said. She picked up the glass of tea and took a deep drink, using it as a way to buy herself some time to think. "What exactly do you think I have to offer?"

"You have been sent to them to offer guidance and instruction before. You know the burden they carry and can understand the fear they feel and the strain it puts upon them. My daughter will begin her task shortly and try to kill Lucifer. Alaria and Braxton do not trust me, and Amaya barely tolerates my presence, but they all dearly loved you. They miss you, and Amaya would trust you and rely on you because Alaria and Braxton do. As an Angel of my making, you would be my link to Amaya. A way for me to ensure she is safe and taken care of when she won't allow me to be close enough to do so."

"What about Michael?"

"Michael is fighting a war. He has many others that are in his care. I trust Michael with my life, but not with my daughter's. She is the key, and she must be protected above all others. You were that person once, and you more than anyone can understand the strain that this places upon her. As I once guided you, Griffin, I would ask that you guide my child."

Griffin leaned back on the couch and studied him carefully, thinking about what she wanted to say. "Is this something you can force on me?"

Gabriel folded his hands in his lap and regarded her levelly. "Yes. I could make you, but I won't. If you say no, then the answer is no, regardless of how much I might wish it otherwise."

She crossed her legs and rested her arms on top of them as she leaned forward to study him, trying to fully understand the situation. "Would it change me?"

"You're already changing. Your emotions are eroding, and you feel things more the way an Angel would than the way a human would. That's normal and expected the longer a soul resides in Heaven away from their human body. Transforming your soul into a corporeal Angelic form would speed that process and finish the transition. You would no longer have human emotions."

She looked up at the ceiling and considered the proposal for several seconds. "I can't. I appreciate you being honest with me and telling me the truth about it, but I can't do it. Seeing me all the time would be hard on Braxton, and he doesn't deserve that. Seeing him grow old and die while I'm stuck like this forever would be hard on me, and I don't deserve that. I can't do it. I want to be done. The only way I'll do it is if Heaven is under siege and I'm at risk of being taken to Hell. I'd be the one they'd go after first, so in that case, the answer would be a resounding yes, but right now, I'm sorry, but it's a no."

Gabriel nodded sadly. "I understand. I'll send you back to Heaven now. Unless it is absolutely necessary, I'll make sure not to call you forth again."

"I'm sorry. I wish I could help."

"I believe you do, Griffin." He smiled sadly as he stood and bent to touch her forehead. "I believe you do."

CHAPTER TWENTY-FIVE

October 14th, 2060 – Purgatory

LUX HELD up her hands, watching with an even mix of pride and amusement as a wall of fire rose and swirled over her head. She drew it down, forming it into a circle around the others who fought and sparred, practicing with their more limited abilities. Aradia stood nearby, watching carefully as Lux practiced and keeping a close eye on all the others.

When Lux brought the flames back within herself, funneling them through the citrines that gleamed at her neck, ears and wrist, Aradia offered a smile.

"You're ready. We all are. I don't think any of us need more practice down here. We've managed to become accustomed to the increased black magic and are filtering it through the extra citrine."

Lux took a deep breath to steady herself. "I still feel the drain from it, but I could keep going."

Michael flicked his wings. "Feeling drained is normal and expected. We all feel drained down here. Our powers are muted, but theirs will be also. Knowing our limits and working with what we have is going to be of utmost importance. Now that the two of you are able to consistently transport us to the same spot each time we enter Purgatory, we've been able to add having a working knowledge of our surroundings to our list of advantages. We'll be fine."

Zane grabbed one of the bottles of water they'd brought with them and drank deeply. "I'm nearly wiped for today. I vote we go home, eat dinner and crash. We've been at this for twelve hours."

"Twelve hours down here is two days up there. We have to remember that time moves differently." Aradia regarded each of them levelly. "Though we've been here less than a day, for Zeke and Gage, they've waited for us two days and nights."

Amaya placed the tip of her sword on the ground and leaned against the handle, her black and red leather corset and leggings molded to every inch of her body. "It feels good to finally be involved in something." When Michael and Aradia both started to speak, she held up her hand. "I know I'm bait. I'm just saying, it feels good to be here like this, with everyone else. I get really tired of being hidden away." She flicked her other hand, and the whip she held snapped loudly. "I'm supposed to be powerful enough to kill Lucifer, and yet I can't ever flex my muscles for fear they'll manage to kill me."

"It's not that. It was keeping you safe until your powers were fully developed and you knew how to use them effectively. You're finally getting there." Michael looked at her somberly. "I seem to remember plenty of mishaps over the years while you were learning to harness what flows through your veins. You and Deacon both."

Lux laughed and turned to her mother. "Should I open the door for us to go home? I think we're all done. We could use showers and food."

"Go ahead."

Lux spread her arms and let magic flow through her. "Gates of Heaven, Gates of Hell. Angels on high and Devils that fell. Hear my demand, obey my cry. Turn the lock, open the door. Grant me access to that which exists no more. Purgatory deep, Purgatory black. Open your gates, ascend through the black. Hear my cry, answer my plea. Swing open the gates and open to me! Take us back through time and space, return us to the place through which we came."

The gate rose from the trembling ground, black and ominous. Michael pulled the door open and they all poured out onto Earth, chattering and laughing, waiting until the gate had retreated before Michael transported them all to the non-place.

Zeke was asleep on the couch when they appeared in the living room. She came awake with a jerk, reaching for a weapon she didn't have and clutching her chest as she realized there was no threat.

"You scared me."

Dev stooped to kiss her. "Sorry." He laughed when she winced. "Sorry about the smell, too. I've been working for hours." He headed for the stairs. "Any chance I could get my loving wife to cook us some food while we all clean up?"

Zeke rolled her eyes and heaved herself off the couch. "I suppose I can manage something." She squeezed Lux's hand as she slid by. "How'd it go?"

"It's going well. I think we're as prepared as we can be. Now all we can do is wait until they make a move or until we figure out where the other two Cambion are going to be. Then we move."

Amaya leaned against the counter. "Then it's my turn." She smiled when Zeke handed her a glass of wine. "Thanks. I'm looking forward to being able to leave this place and go back to Earth. I want to get this going so badly I can taste it. I've been waiting my whole life for this, and now that it's literally one battle away, I feel like some little kid on Christmas Eve."

Lux laughed and took her own glass from Zeke. "You're weird."

Zeke started breaking eggs into a bowl. "It's not weird. We get to go out and fight or hunt things down. We always have. She's basically been cooped up here for almost thirteen years."

Amaya nodded. "Ever since my powers really manifested and started to get out of control. Once Mom couldn't help me harness them anymore and they couldn't keep them hidden, they sent me to Michael. I've lived here ever since. Zeke was the only one not here a lot."

"I was never here until I met Dev. My parents kept me in Alaska, and then I was with Uncle Gage and Aunt Aradia for a while. I was always on Earth, though. Uncle Michael saw me there." Zeke looked sad. "Mom and Dad did things differently than your parents did."

"Different doesn't mean wrong." Amaya wrapped her arms around Zeke in a tight hug. "We miss them too." She took the whisk from Zeke and took over beating eggs.

Lux plugged in the griddle and ripped into a package of sausage. "Are you going to be okay here by yourself, Zeke?"

Zeke glared at her. "I'll be fine. I won't be completely alone. Gage will be here. Alaria and Braxton are going to bring Donovan and Eden here when you guys go down, too. We'll be fine. I think Alaria is going to stay here, but Braxton is going to stay with the Warriors he has."

Amaya sipped her wine as she scrambled eggs. "I'm not surprised Dad is staying on Earth. He's never been comfortable in nonplaces." She smiled when Dev entered the room, rubbing a towel on his head. "Thank God. I'm going up to shower. Dev, make eggs."

Lux knew she was in the Dreamplane the moment she opened her eyes. Everything was tinted slightly sepia and looked just off color. She looked around, almost expecting to see her grandmother before memories of Graciela's death flooded her.

Moving silently, she slipped through the forest, across the clearing and to the edge of the cliffs. On edge and suspicious of who had taken her there, she put her back to the cliffs and reached out with her senses, trying to determine whether there was anything else in the Dreamplane with her.

"You won't have to look far, little witch. I brought you here to give you one final chance to join me before I start the process of your destruction."

Lux opened her eyes slowly, knowing she would see Lucifer. He stood several feet away from her, his white-blonde hair slicked back from his face and long enough that it teased the collar of his shirt. His suit was white and pristine, and other than the touches of red at his belt and shoes, Lux was struck by how much Lucifer and Gabriel resembled one another.

"I'm not going to join you." She crossed her arms and looked at him steadily. "I know you think you can scare me or threaten me or that my love for my mother will make me reconsider this, but you're wrong. We all knew the price that could be asked of us. We're all willing to die, and I know every single one of us involved in this would sacrifice ourselves to kill you without a thought. My best friend killed her father for this. I'll do no less than whatever is necessary to see you burn."

Lucifer chuckled. "I admire your determination to make me believe you, but believe me when I tell you there are ways to make you reconsider. But that is not why we're here tonight, little witch." He took a step toward her, pleased when she took one back. "I thought you witches preach that you can't be hurt on the Dreamplane. If that's true, why keep so much distance between us?"

"Because I'm smart enough to learn from the mistakes of those who came before me. Greer nearly died here twice. You killed my grandmother here. My own mother has been hurt here. I'm not taking unnecessary risks." She glared at him. "If the only reason you brought me here was to try and convince me to come with you, you're not going to succeed. I'm not Griffin, and you're not as convincing as Alaria."

Smiling at the reference to the Choosing and the events Hell had been given, Lucifer continued. "She was good at her job, wasn't she? Too bad she betrayed us."

"She betrayed you. Not us. There is no us."

"Semantics. Regardless, Alaria was quite talented at what she did, and I was sad to see her go. From what she did to Abalam after she left, I know she was taught well. She'd have been a force to be reckoned with had she been loosed upon Earth after I got out. It's a shame I never got to witness that."

"You'll see Amaya's wrath. I'm sure it's just as fierce as her mother's." Lux shifted to the side to put more space between them, painfully aware of the edge of the cliff behind her. "What's the point of this, Lucifer? I know you didn't bring me here to chat about Alaria."

"No, I brought you here for exactly the reason I've already given you, which is to offer you one final chance to leave your friends and join me. If you do so, I'll be merciful when I kill them. If you say no, then you'll leave this place safely, but you'll return to your bed and your man knowing that I will make it my goal to torture and kill everyone you love, starting with your parents. I'll slaughter Amaya and Alaria and Braxton. Once they're dead, I'll come for the Nephil you sleep next to and tear his head from his shoulders. I'll gut Michael while you watch, helpless to stop me."

A knot of fear took hold in her stomach, and she forced herself not to let it show on her face. Taking several deep breaths to calm herself down, she deliberately placed her hands on her hips before addressing him.

"I've already told you once, but since I know you're not accustomed to people telling you no, I'll repeat myself. I am not interested in being on your side. The answer will not change if you kill every single person I know. We all know the score, and this is what we signed up for. I can see the bigger picture, and killing you is it. Whether I have to die for that, or they all do, or everyone does, the ends justifies the means. You're not going to scare me into betraying the people I love. I'm not stupid. Having me on your side would make me a prize and a weapon, and you'd be no more merciful to them than you will be with me having said no." She met his gaze with more confidence than she felt, her chin jutted slightly up and her heart pounding in her chest. "The answer is no. It's always been no, and it will always be no."

Without saying a word or seeming to move, Lucifer was standing so close to her that she could feel his breath on her face. He gripped her wrists in his hands to keep her from running and leaned in, inhaling her scent deeply and rubbing his nose on her cheek.

"I appreciate spunk and heart. Even in my enemies. I can respect that. I don't respect a lot about you people and what you're trying to do, but I respect the fervor with which you seem to do it."

"Let me go." Lux's voice was rock steady even though her stomach was twisting and roiling and her heart was racing.

"I can hear your heart. Much faster and you'll have a heart attack. I wonder if that would translate to your body. How tragic that would be. Lux, the powerful witch killed by a myocardial infarction while she sleeps." He touched his index finger to the base of her throat and a small jolt of electricity snapped between them. "I could encourage the organ to stop beating. You know that."

"If you weren't scared that we could kill you, you wouldn't be wasting all this time trying to convince me to join you." She defiantly locked her eyes onto his. "You're bluffing one way or the other and I'm about to call it, so we'll see which it is." Sneering, she yanked her wrists in an effort to pull them free. "Either you really do want me on your side, in which case you're not going to kill me, or you don't, in which case you will. So prove it. Either kill me or send me back, but you're getting nothing more from me here."

His eyes flashing with anger and power, Lucifer jerked her against him. "Do you know what I could do to you? I could trap you here for eternity. I could throw you down and force myself on you until your body in your bed splits open and bleeds. I am Lucifer, you insolent twit, and you will show some respect!"

He tossed her to the side violently. Lux hit the ground hard, rolling to her feet as soon as she came to a stop. The ground shook with the force of Lucifer's anger. The trees swayed and rocked, leaves ripping from the branches to swirl around them. Lightning slashed through the sky, and clouds gathered as thunder rolled and crashed toward them.

Lux knew better than to pit her magic against his power, even on the Dreamplane. She held hers close to the surface in case she needed it to try and defend herself, but refused to let it seep out.

"Which is it? Are you going to kill me or let me go? If you kill me, I know this was just a trick and you never actually wanted me on your side. You were just trying to lure me in to kill me anyway. If you let me go, I know you're just blowing smoke with the threats."

Coughing and sputtering, Lux woke in her bed, kicking at the blankets and gasping for breath. She threw out her hand and turned on every light in the room, waking Zane with the sudden flash of illumination.

"What's going on? Are you okay?"

Lux grabbed for the glass of water on the nightstand and chugged it, the cool liquid soothing her burning throat. She wrapped her arms around her middle and bent over, resting her forehead on her knees and praying that the water stayed down.

"Lucifer. Dreamplane." She waved him away when he grabbed her shoulders and forced her to sit up so he could inspect her for injuries. "I'm fine. Just trying not to puke up that water."

"I'm going to go get Aradia and Michael."

Lux sat up and groaned when the room spun. "Zane, I'm fine. I'm not hurt." She grabbed his arm. "It was meant to scare me. He's worried, and I'm the easiest to suck in because I have the strongest connection to the dreamplane."

"What about your mom?"

"Well, yeah, she does, too, but he's not after her, and she's not trying to kill Beelzebub. She tried to do that once and failed. He's afraid I'm stronger." She rubbed her hands over her face. "They're scared. They think we might actually do this."

Zane sat next to her on the bed and took one of her hands in both of his. "What happened? Tell me everything."

"The same as before. We know I'm the most powerful witch there is because of the Nephil blood. It's what we were made to be. Lucifer wants me to be his own personal sorceress. I think he was hoping he could scare me into joining him by threatening everyone else. When he realized we're all willing to die for this, and to sacrifice ourselves and each other if necessary, he tried to scare me into thinking he'd kill me, but I called his bluff. I told him to pick one. If he killed me, I knew he was just trying to lure me in so he could kill me. If he sent me back, I knew he was serious about wanting me as a prize."

"And he sent you back."

"He sent me back."

"What do you think that means?"

"I think it means he doesn't think he can kill Amaya and Deacon himself, and he wants a weapon to use against them. He intends for that weapon to be me."

Zane blinked rapidly as he processed that. "Could you kill them even if you wanted to?"

"No. But I don't think he knows that. He's seen what I can do. No one has seen what Amaya can do. I've sensed what's in her. She's a nuclear bomb. It's absolutely amazing the amount of power inside her. Not magic. She doesn't have to draw on anything else. She won't wear out or get tired. It's sheer power. All Lucifer knows is what I have, which is a lot, and he's thinking that if he adds me to him, then Amaya couldn't win. And maybe she couldn't. Maybe. But she and Deacon definitely could. No question about it."

"The good news is that he's scrambling and out of moves. If he's coming after us and trying to lure us to his side, then he's all played out on his side."

"That's my thought." She grinned as the gravity of that struck her. "We're actually going to do this. We're going to win."

They were interrupted by a sharp knock on the door. Deacon opened the door and stuck his head in, surprise crossing his face when he saw the lights on and them sitting on the edge of the bed.

"I hope everything's okay and that you two got some sleep because if you didn't, you aren't going to now."

Zane stood and reached for a shirt. "What's going on?"

"Gabriel is here. We've got a location on Alexi and Isaiah. They're together."

Lux stood. "Where are they?"

"Some abandoned town in Denmark. There was a Warrior camp about thirty miles from there that they attacked. They killed most of the Warriors, but a couple of the Nephilim managed to trace the flash signature and are keeping watch from a distance to make sure they don't flash out. They're licking their wounds as far as we know."

"How badly were they hurt?"

"The Nephilim didn't know. Neither of the survivors fought them, and neither saw them injured, but there was a battle going on. We're operating under the assumption that they're healthy, and if it's anything else, well, it's our lucky day." Deacon averted his gaze when Lux yanked her t-shirt over her head and reached for a bra. "You could ask me to leave, ya know."

"I could, but then I couldn't keep asking you questions." She adjusted her breasts in the sports bra and drew on what she thought of as her battle clothes—black leggings, flat boots, a thin long-sleeved shirt and a tight fitting thin leather jacket. "Is it just the two survivors?"

"As far as we know. We'll have to let one of them escape to draw in Beelzebub once they see Amaya there." Deacon watched as Lux plaited her hair into a tight braid. "Everyone's getting ready. We'll be flashing out in thirty minutes. I suggest saying everything you need to say to everyone you need to say it to before we go."

Lux looked at Zane, her eyes seeking his and holding them. "I need to see Zeke and my Dad before we go."

He nodded and dipped his head to brush a kiss over her mouth. "Go. I'll get everything ready."

Lux dashed down the stairs and into the office where her father was, as predicted, behind his desk, looking over blueprints that she assumed were to the town they were headed to.

"Daddy."

Gage looked up. "Do you have everything you need?"

"Zane's getting it." She crossed the room and sat on his desk. "I couldn't go without seeing you first. Just in case."

He shook his head. "Don't even talk like that." He scowled. "This is one of those times I regret ever being human. What I wouldn't give to be going into this with you and your mother, but here I am, an old man, left waiting at home for those younger than me to fight as I once did."

She took his hands in hers and held them. "Daddy, you know I might not come back. We don't know what it'll take to kill Beelzebub, but you know I have to give whatever it does."

Gage angrily blinked back emotion. "You are going to be fine. You're coming home after this, and you will be fine. That's the only option. I won't tolerate the thought of my child not coming back. I can't."

Lux leaned down and wrapped her arms around her father, holding him tightly. "I love you. I couldn't do this without what you've given me. You raised me to do whatever it took. I'm going to kill the bastard, and we're going to win this. I promise."

He gripped her shoulders and stood, holding her an arms-length away. When he spoke, his voice was rough with emotion. "You listen to me, Lux Windsor, and you listen well because I'm only saying this once. You will get through this ,and you will survive it." He pulled her close and pressed his cheek to hers. "I'm proud of the woman you've become, sweetheart. You couldn't have made me any prouder than I am of you right now."

Aradia entered the room, her hair in an identical braid and wearing jeans and a button-down. She crossed to Lux and Gage and laid a hand on each of them. "We don't have time for this." She offered a smile. "We need to get ready."

Lux nodded and stood. "I'll go check on Zane, and I want to say something to Zeke before we go."

Aradia waited until Lux had left before looking at Gage. "She'll be fine. I'll be there with her."

Gage nodded and stroked his hand down Aradia's cheek. "Bring our little girl home safe, Aradia. Take care of her for us."

Zeke checked and rechecked the packs for every person leaving. She counted bullets, cleaned weapons, blessed water, anything to keep her hands moving and her mind off what was happening. When Amaya and Lux entered the living room where she'd laid everything out, she glanced up, her face pale with worry and her voice strangled and tense when she spoke.

"I have nine minutes left before you leave. I'm not done yet."

"We just wanted to spend a few minutes together before we go." Amaya reached out and took the clipboard from Zeke. "You remind me of your mom with the lists." She laid it down. "Have you checked every pack at least once?"

Zeke nodded. "Yeah." She dropped onto the couch and smiled when Lux sat on one side and Amaya on the other. "I wish I was going."

Lux giggled. "Someone has to keep my dad from pacing a hole in the floor."

"I'll be pacing right along with him."

"So will my mom." Amaya pinched her nose. "I'm amazed she hasn't cornered me yet."

"There's a few minutes left yet, and she's in the office with Michael and Gabriel going over everything. I imagine Gabriel's getting an earful of how to keep you safe appropriately." Zeke grabbed her friends' hands and held them tightly. "I love you two, you know that, right?"

Lux hugged Zeke tightly. "I love you, too."

Amaya planted a smacking kiss on her cheek. "Me three." She reached across and gripped Lux's hand. "We'll be fine. We'll all be fine. We have to believe that."

Lux studied the wall. "I don't know if I'll be fine, but I believe I'll win." She looked at the other two women. "I'm prepared to die to do this."

Alaria strode into the room, Michael and Gabriel on her heels. "Let's hope it doesn't come to that." She began checking packs efficiently. "It's time to get going. We don't know how long the Cambion will be there, and we need to get Amaya in and out as quickly as possible." She turned to her daughter. "I know you're an adult, but I am going to tell you what to do, and you are going to listen to me, no questions asked. Am I clear?"

Amaya nodded. "Yes, ma'am."

"You are to listen to your father. Gabriel will not let anything happen to you. Your survival is paramount. It is more important than any other person going into this. You are bait, not a part of the plan. You get out at the first possible moment. If you get in trouble, you flash out and get to Dad or to me." She looked at Lux. "As for you, young lady, being prepared to die and expecting to die are two entirely different things and often the difference between surviving and actually dying. Do you expect to die?"

Lux shook her head. "No."

"Good." Alaria hugged both women tightly, her grip solid and strong. "Get your weapons and packs on. You need to get going."

Alaria stood stoically and watched everyone load up. Weapons were checked and loaded, utility belts strapped on, knives and swords holstered. Gage appeared at her elbow and she took his hand tightly in hers. When Zeke stepped up on the other side, she reached for Zeke as well, slipping her arm around the younger woman's shoulders and pulling her close. When the group disappeared with a flash and a crack, she tipped her head back and looked up.

"You son of a bitch, you owe me for everything you've put us through. Bring them home safe or I swear to Jesus I'll find a way up there and stab you in the throat."

CHAPTER TWENTY-SIX

THE STREETS were empty and the air eerily quiet. To the east, the sun had just begun peeking out above the horizon, yellow and orange fingers spearing into the sky. Lux held Zane's hand as they surveyed the town, taking in burned cars and the crumbling remains of buildings.

Michael held up a hand, speaking loud enough for everyone to hear him. "Spread out and find them. Amaya, stay with Gabriel. Do not get out of his sight. Brother, at the first sign of trouble, get her out of here. Something's wrong. I don't like what I'm sensing."

Gabriel nodded stiffly. "Agreed."

Lux's brows drew together. "What do you sense?"

Michael glanced back at her. "Something's not right. I can't pinpoint it, but there's something off."

Zane nodded. "I feel it, too. It feels familiar. I've experienced whatever this is before, I just don't remember quite what it is." He glanced at Lux. "Do you feel it?"

She stood quietly and reached out with her senses, trying to find anything out of the ordinary. Something was giving the air around her an odd sensation. She detected something lurking just below the surface, waiting, but each time she tried to grasp it, it slipped out of reach and descended further.

"I feel it, but I can't get a read on it. Mom?"

Aradia shook her head. "I'm in the same vessel as the rest. My advice would be to proceed with caution, be aware of our surroundings and have weapons at the ready."

Lux dropped Zane's hand and started to move forward, her rifle raised to her shoulder and her eyes moving back and forth as she scanned the street and the roof-line, looking for anything out of the ordinary. She made it forty feet before hitting a force-field. Electricity sparked and flashed, rocketing through her body. She was flung back, her body soaring through the air and slamming into the concrete with a sickening crunch, her head bouncing off the pavement hard enough that her vision went black for several seconds. Nausea rose in her from the pain of impact and she rolled onto her side, coughing and gagging, trying to suck in a breath and squeezing her eyes closed to allow her sight to clear.

Around her, she heard commotion. Everyone was talking all at once, their voices loud and echoing through her throbbing head. Zane grabbed her by the shoulders, helping her sit up, the movement causing the world to do a slow spin that left her dizzy and even closer to throwing up. Michael was there within seconds, pressing his hand to the wound on her head to heal it. Her ears rang as she struggled to make sense of what had happened. Conversations fired around her, the noise inundating her and making it harder to think. Warmth flowed through her from Michael's touch, easing the pain, clearing her vision and allowing her jumbled thoughts to slowly come together.

In the span of a heartbeat, everything snapped into focus.

"It's a trap! They're Nephilim traps! Run! Everyone get out!"

Gabriel seized Amaya's arm and flashed, disappearing from the street in an attempt to get her back to safety. Trapped like the others, Amaya remained where she had stood. Michael stood slowly, turning in a circle to take in the buildings around them. Gabriel re-appeared, his sword in his hand and a look of panic on his face. Deacon ran, hit the edge of one of the traps, and was hurled backward, landing on top of a car. The metal crunched and glass shattered as he landed on it, the alarm blaring through the silent streets. Aradia silenced it with a careless flick of her wrist and Michael heaved his son to his feet, brushing one hand over Deacon's head to heal any injuries.

"I'm not stuck." Dev's voice was calm and steady. "At least I don't think I am. I can flash, but I don't want to move too much for fear of getting stuck. What do these traps look like, and why can't we see them?"

Lux coughed and climbed to her feet. "They have to be on the road. They're modified Devil's traps with Angel wards worked into them and painted in Cambion blood that they've done some magic shit to. I got caught in one when Lilith attacked me. As to why we can't see them, I don't know."

Aradia held up a hand. "Everyone needs to stay calm. Dev, wings out and fly up above some of those buildings where we know you won't get stuck. You can at least shoot things from up there if need be. I can't get trapped because I'm human, and Michael and Gabriel are loose. We're okay." She glanced around. "Everyone stay alert. I'm going to try and get us a view of where these traps are. No one move and no one talk unless you see something that shouldn't be here. Gabriel, as soon as they drop, you get Amaya out of here."

Gabriel, his jaw set and his eyes angry, nodded sharply. "There is no doubt of that."

Aradia held out her hands. "Sight beyond sight. Come forth and allow me to see the unseen. Bring from beneath and let us see that which is hidden from view. I call upon the magic of Earth, the magic of me, and the magic of black to bring forth and allow me to see the boundaries present. Hidden from sight no more, come forth and be seen, I command it!"

All around them, traps materialized, shimmering in silver as they became visible. Michael closed his eyes briefly as he saw how many there were. "Gabriel, they cover the whole town."

A voice sounded from above them. "Yes, they do. They're on every floor, every roof, every door in this whole entire God-forsaken place." Beelzebub walked out onto the balcony of one of the buildings. "Welcome everyone. How nice to see you all." He held out his arms in a gesture of greeting. "I'm so glad you received our invitation. I see we have an unanticipated guest. Hello, Amaya. It's nice to finally meet you. My, you resemble your mother. How is Alaria?"

Amaya glared up at the Devil. "Fuck you."

"Succinct. You are like mommy dearest." He smiled saccharinely. "I think it's time that the rest of the guests arrived. Cambion! Present yourselves!"

Loud pops filled the air and Cambion appeared. Lux recognized Alexi and Isaiah immediately, but there were a hundred others she did not. Behind Beelzebub, she saw three more figures, and when they stepped out onto the balcony, she sucked in a breath. Azazel, Abalam and Lilith.

"Oh my God." Amaya's voice was little more than a whisper as she grabbed Gabriel's arm. "Is she..."

Deacon finished the sentence, his face pale and drawn. "Pregnant."

Lilith stroked her hands over her stomach lovingly, a smile splitting her face when she heard the whispered exclamation from her son. "You noticed. How wonderful. Yes, my darling son, I'm giving you a brother. Another one, actually, since I already had Isaiah. I don't believe you've ever met your siblings." She laid one hand on Beelzebub's shoulder. "Isaiah is Beelzebub's, but Serafina and this child were sired by the King of Hell himself."

Gabriel looked at Michael with a fear-filled expression. "Lucifer has procreated again, brother."

Michael turned his head slightly, his voice weary. "Seeing as I have functional ears, I'm aware."

Lux glanced over at them. "She was not knocked up when I saw her a month ago. I would have noticed."

Beelzebub cleared his throat, obviously annoyed that Lilith's state had drawn so much attention. "It doesn't matter. What does matter is this. Lucifer has decreed that the young witch and Gabriel's daughter be brought to him alive. Everyone else dies."

Gabriel raised his sword and blocked Amaya from the Cambion with his own body. "They'll have to come through me, Beelzebub. No one is touching my daughter while I still live."

"That can be arranged." Beelzebub laughed. "You're outnumbered and your soldiers are trapped. What do you intend to do? You can't take us all on."

Michael spread his wings behind himself and lifted his voice until it echoed through the buildings. "I am the Angel of War. I cut your brethren down before, Beelzebub, and I will do it again. You will all die here this day."

"Oh, some of us will, of that I have no doubt. You'll go out fighting, but you will go out. All of you will."

Zane reached out and slipped into Lux's mind. *"Can you still use magic from inside here?"*

"Yeah, why?"

"Do you need to say spells out loud for them to work?"

Catching on, Lux shook her head. *"It makes them stronger to say the words, but no, I don't need to say it out loud. I'll need a minute."*

"I'll do my best, but make it snappy."

Lux reached deep within herself, finding her magic and

chanting the words to the spell to access Purgatory in her head. She felt the gate rising to the surface and fought to keep it just out of sight, forcing it to mold and expand.

Aradia sensed what she was doing and added her magic to the spell. Together, they widened the gate until it encompassed the ground on which they all stood. Knowing that she would need to use her own abilities to drag down the Devils, Aradia slowly withdrew from the spell until Lux was holding it on her own. Lux yanked the door to the surface, ripping the hatch open and blasting a wave of magic through the streets so powerful that they cracked and crumbled, fracturing the traps and allowing them all to fall through the door and into Purgatory.

Aradia lashed out with witchrope, wrapping it around the Devils and jerking them off the balcony, holding long enough to drag them through the door. She could only hold them for a few seconds, but by the time they were able to break free, Lux had slammed the gate shut and they were all through.

Lux hit the ground hard enough to rattle her teeth but sprang to her feet, drawing her sword and anchoring it to her shoulder without missing a beat. She felt someone hit her back and glanced over her shoulder, smiling tightly when she saw Amaya, clad in black and red leather with a sword in one hand and a whip in the other.

"Looks like I'm here for the long haul whether you guys wanted me to be or not."

Gabriel stood in front of Amaya and Lux, his suit rumpled and smeared with dirt. "Stay close and do not engage the Cambion."

Beelzebub stood and brushed dirt from his suit. "That was a supremely stupid move. There's nowhere to go down here. Every creature that lives here belongs to Hell and if you die, there's no Heaven or Hell, only nothingness. Is that really a risk you want to take, Michael? Being nothing? Losing your chance to end up with your dear Father?"

Michael strode forward, his wings spread behind him and his sword in one hand. "That's exactly the point. Lucifer can't help you here because he cannot access Purgatory. No Angel or Devil could. But the witches can. You're stuck here, Beelzebub, unless we let you out, and I guarantee you that is not going to happen. As for not ending up with God, I made my peace with my fate many years ago. I'll take my chances and put my faith in the people with whom I fight."

"We have witches, too, Michael, and they'll be working on getting us out sooner rather than later."

"By the time they manage that, it'll be too late and you'll be dead."

"I'm sure one of us will be dead, but I wouldn't be so sure it will be me instead of you." Beelzebub smiled sharply. "Perhaps you'd like to negotiate a truce in which you hand over just the witch and we fight over Amaya another day?"

Michael's voice was steely. "Never."

"A pity. Would have saved me ruining another suit. I never have been able to make it through a battle without needing a visit to the tailor."

Azazel shoved his way forward. "Let's get this fucking thing going. I don't want to stand here and talk about it all fucking day."

Lilith giggled and put her hands on her hips, the action pulling her dress back so that it stretched tightly across the curve of her stomach. "Beelzebub is very long-winded. How have you known him as long as you have and that's escaped your notice?" She shook her head and smiled serenely. "The other witch is mine. Remember that. No one else touches her besides me."

Aradia squared her shoulders. "Let's do this then."

Lux reached out to Zane. *"I'll go for Beelzebub. You head for Alexi and Isaiah."*

"Agreed." His voice softened. *"Stay safe, Lux. I love you."*

Before Lux could even think of responding, chaos broke out around them.

There were eight of them against a hundred and two Cambion and four Devils. Michael looked from side to side as the Cambion rushed them, his sword held in front of his body.

"Lux, you concentrate on Beelzebub. Aradia, Lilith is coming for you. Handle her. Zane, Alexi and Isaiah are your responsibility. Deacon and Dev, the Cambion. Gabriel, you protect Amaya. Amaya, help with the Cambion where you can and avoid the Devils at all cost. I'll handle Azazel and Abalam."

Deacon's wings ripped from his back, shredding his shirt and sending ribbons of fabric to the ground. "There are no better people to fight or die with, guys."

Dev looked around grimly and conjured himself a battle axe. "Let's focus more on the fighting and less on the dying."

Standing in a circle, their hearts pounding, the flood of Cambion hit them and they all fought for their lives.

CHAPTER TWENTY-SEVEN

DEV GRIPPED his battle axe in both hands and spread his legs, squaring his shoulders and bracing himself for impact. Cambion swarmed him, trying to hack at him with knives and swords.

He batted them away, using his powers to overpower the ones weaker than him and his axe to slash at the ones that weren't. They all struggled with the limitations of their power in Purgatory. None of them could flash, Dev's ability to read minds or speak psychically was gone, and he was forced to rely solely on his physical strength.

Deacon's back slammed against his, and they faced the horde together. Deacon's wings cut into his back, the feathers sharp and hard. Dev swung the axe out, slitting the throat of one Cambion and watching with grim satisfaction as it clutched at the wound, thick red blood bubbling between its fingers and running down its chest to drip into the soil.

The body fell, light flashing in its eyes before it faded to mist and disappeared, sucked into the ether that was Purgatory. Two more Cambion stepped up to take the first one's place, and Dev gritted his teeth, using the handle of the axe to block a blow from a sword.

Deacon moved behind him, stepping away slightly to parry as he fought his way through the throng.

"I don't know why you think you're going to win."

The Cambion bared his teeth in a vicious snarl and swung his own blade, sparks flying as metal met metal. "Because you're outnumbered twenty to one."

Deacon laughed. "You like those odds, do you?" He drew a buck-knife from his belt and stabbed to his left, burying the blade in the chest of a second Cambion that charged him. "I've taken out more than twenty on my own before."

"Never when there are Devils here fighting, too." The Cambion grunted when Deacon's sword cut deeply into his arm. "Kill me and there are more coming to take my place. Get out of here alive and there are more of us yet. This will never end, Nephil. Not until every Cambion is dead."

"Then it's a good thing I intend to kill you all." Deacon moved to the side, slashing out with the sword and pivoting to avoid a parry.

He brought his elbow back, colliding with the nose of a Cambion behind him. Grabbing the woman by the head, he threw her over his shoulder, stepping onto her throat and driving down with his sword, extinguishing her life with one stab before turning his attention back to the Cambion he had been fighting.

The man came at him, blade flashing as he ran. Deacon held his ground, unwilling to move or run. A heartbeat before the Cambion's sword would have pierced his chest, he swiveled to the side, causing the man to stumble. Taking advantage of the opportunity, he twirled his own sword once before running it through the Cambion's back, the tip breaking through his chest.

Wrenching the blade from the dead body, Deacon sent it to the ground where it flickered and faded to grey mist. Next to him, Dev was fighting three Cambion at the same time, using his axe to keep them a safe distance away.

Dev used the handle of the axe as much as the blade, smacking it into the face of his enemies, using it to drive them back. Blood coated the metal of his weapon and dripped down the handle, making his grip slippery. For each Cambion that fell, another came. He was fatigued, his energy draining away with each fight he won. He knew it was only a matter of time before he was too tired to keep going. At that point, all it would take was one lucky hit and he would be the one dissipating into nothingness on the ground instead of the Cambion.

Roaring with anger at the thought of never seeing his child born, Dev swung the axe, grunting when it found flesh and cut through bone. Screams filled the air as the Cambion he'd hit lost a hand to the swing. Giving himself a break from hand-to-hand combat, he tossed the axe to the ground and drew his pistol, emptying a clip into the crowd.

Guns worked in Purgatory. They were just as deadly as on Earth. The problem was that he didn't have enough distance to use a gun effectively and it could sometimes take five or six bullets to put down a Cambion. Beyond that, some had telekinetic abilities not completely inhibited by Purgatory that could stop the shots—or worse, turn them around and hit one of his friends.

When the clip was empty, he pushed the button on the side of the clip and dropped it to the ground, grabbing another from his belt and snapping it in. As the Cambion converged on him, he knew there would be no opportunity to get to the extra ammo in his backpack. As soon as what was on his belt was gone, it was back to relying on his body and a blade.

Michael held a sword in each hand, his knuckles white from the strength of his grip on the handles. Azazel wielded a whip and Abalam had a sword.

"I'm going to put you back on your rock, Azazel. By all that is Holy, you will not walk the Earth past this night."

Azazel lashed the whip, trying to wrap it around one of Michael's swords. "Not if I kill you first, brother."

"I haven't been your brother since you decided to play one side against the other."

"Taking on two of us is letting your stupid show." Abalam danced out of the way of the sword. "You know there's no defeating us both, not even down here."

Michael charged forward, his swords twirling and his body fluid and graceful as he fought, driving the two Devils back several feet. "This is the spot where I ripped Abaddon's roots from his back and watched him disappear into the void. Do you remember that? Remember how I took him from you? How he died here and there was nothing you could do about it?"

Abalam laughed. "Do you really think you can taunt me into making a mistake and giving you an opening? I'm not some lowly demon."

Michael let Azazel get his whip around the sword then jerked on it, dragging the demon in close enough to hack the whip off, the leather and metal dropping to the ground. He dropped one of the swords with it, grabbing Azazel by his hair and forcing the Devil to his knees. Lifting the other, he positioned it and prepared to drive it through Azazel's heart.

Abalam's blade bit into Michael's side, cutting deeply and loosening his grip on the other Devil. He stumbled and lurched forward, trying to catch his balance, one hand pressing to his side and the wound there. It glowed as it healed, but he felt the drain from the energy required.

Abalam stooped and picked up Michael's sword, turning it over in his hand. "Nice blade. Well balanced. Sharp edge. I'd expect nothing less from the Angel of War." He cocked his head to the side. "Do you think trying to defeat us will win you more favor with God?"

"I don't care about favor with God." Michael conjured another sword to replace the one he had dropped. "I care about defeating Lucifer."

"Even if you kill all of us, you still have to kill Satan." Azazel lobbed a fireball—weaker than his normally were—at the Angel. "Even God couldn't do that."

"God isn't the one doing it this time. Amaya will. Human, Devil, Angel. That's why she can. Because she is everything." Michael gritted his teeth against pain as a second fireball singed one of his wings and feathers fell to the ground. "Even if we fail, the world will be infinitely better without you in it."

With a warrior's cry, Michael charged the two Devils, his swords flashing as they collided, all of them fighting for more than their own lives.

Zane saw Alexi run from the other Cambion. Instead of rushing into the fight, he fled from it. Slinging his rifle over his shoulder, Zane took off in pursuit, stripping off his gloves and hoping against hope that his ability to kill still worked in Purgatory. That was the one thing they hadn't been able to test.

His heart pounded in his ears as he chased the Cambion. Alexi glanced over his shoulder, saw that he was being pursued, and ran faster. Dipping his head, Zane pushed his body to move as fast as it would go, gaining inch after precious inch of ground on Alexi.

When he was within arm's length, he leaped, launching himself through the air and tackling the other man to the ground, slamming him down and rolling until Alexi was beneath him. Before he could get a grip on his head, Alexi thrust out with a dagger and sank it into Zane's arm, tearing through muscle and skin.

Zane snarled and hissed as pain rocketed through his arm. He grabbed Alexi by the wrist and punched the man in the face with the other fist hard enough to break his nose. Feeling a sick sense of satisfaction from the act of physically beating the Cambion, he continued to punch him until his face was swollen and bloody and the knife had fallen from his limp hand.

"It isn't much of a man that kills someone who can't fight back."

Zane looked over his shoulder and scowled when he saw Isaiah ten feet behind him, a rifle lifted to his shoulder. "And it isn't much of a man that runs from a fight." He glanced at Alexi and, convinced the Cambion was unconscious, climbed to his feet and faced the other one, wiping blood from his hands and onto his pants. "Put the gun down."

"I don't think so." Isaiah backed up when Zane took a step toward him. "Stop walking or I'll shoot you."

"Do you even know how to use it? Did your mother teach you anything except how to be psychotic?"

"Don't talk about her." Isaiah fumbled with the safety, trying to figure out how to thumb it off so that he could fire the weapon. "I'm going to kill you."

"You have to be able to use the damn thing to do that, kid." Zane ignored a pang of pity as he reached out and slapped the rifle, knocking Isaiah off balance and tossing the gun to the ground. "You've got a decent amount of power, but I'm betting you've never been down here before. You didn't know your abilities wouldn't work right down here, did you?"

A flash in his eyes told Zane that he was right. Isaiah jutted his chin forward and drew a knife, holding it close to his body as he continued to back up, desperate to keep some distance between himself and Zane.

"Your powers don't work right either. You might not be able to kill me down here."

"I might not be able to kill you with my bare hands, but I will sure as fuck be able to kill you."

Isaiah looked around nervously. "My father will never let that happen. He'll be here any second to help me. Or my mother. One of them will be."

Zane laughed and moved the younger man to the side, corralling him back toward Alexi's unconscious body. "Do you really think they give two flying fucks about you? What was the plan? Obviously you had one or they wouldn't have been here. Lure us in and jump us. You were bait, kid. Collateral damage. They were willing to sacrifice you to get at us."

"Were you doing anything different with Amaya? Isn't that what you brought her for? To lure in my father?"

Zane inclined his head and slowly loosened a slim knife from his belt. "I'll give you that one. We did bring her to lure in your father, but we had a plan to get her out safely. Every one of us would die to protect her. I don't see anyone here trying to stop either of you from getting killed."

Panic rose in Isaiah's eyes. He tried to send out a blast of power, but the wave was so weak that it did little more than stir the leaves in the trees surrounding them. Desperation crossed his face and he tried to flash, but he reappeared in the same place. He brought his fists up to block his body.

Zane put the knife back. He planted his feet and squared his shoulders. "If you want to fight, I'll give it to you, but if you run, I'll put a knife through your brain. I'm a damn good shot."

Isaiah lowered his shoulder and charged Zane. Zane braced for the impact and rolled with the Cambion to the ground, grunting as the younger man landed several blows on the way down. They rolled over the dirt, grappling for dominance and struggling to end up on top. Several times Zane felt his hands brush bare skin and a spark flashed between them. His powers were weakened, but they were there. Whether he had enough to kill was unclear, but it would be enough to knock Isaiah unconscious.

Zane grunted with reluctant admiration when he felt his jaw crack from a punch and clamped it shut to control the pain. He brought his knee up into the other man's chest. Isaiah howled from pain when two of his ribs snapped. Zane rolled him onto his back and rose over him, slamming the Cambion's face into the dirt and pressing his mouth close to his ear.

"You put up a good fight, kid." He unsnapped the knife. "I'm sorry you got sucked into a war you obviously don't want."

With one smooth motion, Zane drove the knife into the back of Isaiah's skull, severing his brain stem and ending his life. As he climbed to his feet, the body dissipated into nothingness. Twirling the knife between his fingers, he strode back to where Alexi's body lay and stooped, staring at it for several moments.

"I've wanted to do this for years, you son of a bitch, and you don't even have the decency to fucking be awake when I kill you." He rocked back on his haunches. "I hope you can hear me when I tell you I am enjoying killing you, Alexi. More than any of the others, it is my *pleasure* to take your life."

With no regret, Zane drove the knife straight into Alexi's heart and watched until the body dissolved. Standing, he bent to gather the rifle Isaiah had dropped, snapped his knife back into his utility belt and loped back down the path toward the battle that still raged.

Michael was the first one he saw, battling Azazel and Abalam. The Angel was streaked with blood and dirt. One of his wings was missing chunks of feathers and he was dripping with sweat. As he saw Zane, he raised his voice.

"Zane, I need you to open the gate back to Earth. Use your magic and open it, but limit the spell so that I can only take these two out. I need to get them out of here."

Nodding, Zane skidded to a stop and concentrated on his magic. He'd never even tried to bring the gate. They had Aradia and Lux. There was no need for him to do it. He knew the spell from hearing them cast it time and again, and he knew how to alter a spell.

As soon as he reached for his magic, dark flooded in, overtaking him and surrounding him. It swirled through his body, ripping its price from him, and he howled from pain as it seared through him, pouring out through his fingertips in a black flood.

Battling it back, he struggled to close the door, to control it or stop it. Blood poured from his nose and ears, dripped from his eyes and ran from his mouth. Choking on the thick, metallic substance, he spat twice before beginning to chant.

"Gates of Heaven, Gates of Hell. Angels on high and Devils that fell. Hear my demand, obey my cry. Turn the lock, open the door. Grant me access to that which exists no more. Purgatory deep, Purgatory black. Open your gates, ascend through the black. Hear my cry answer my plea. Swing open the gates and open to me! Three seek to escape, to exist here no more. Unlock the gate, open the door. Michael the Angel, prisoners of He, allow them access, allow them be free. No more to escape, no others to leave, Gate of Purgatory, I command thee!"

As soon as the gate appeared, Michael dragged Abalam and Azazel through it. Before Zane could do anything more than end the spell and shut off the magic, blackness closed in on him and he hit the ground.

CHAPTER TWENTY-EIGHT

"ZANE!" LUX couldn't stop the shriek that burst from her at the sight of him falling to the ground, blood seeping from his eyes, nose, mouth, and ears.

"What a pity. Michael had so little concern for the Nephil that he let him burn out on one spell." Beelzebub clucked his tongue. "Don't worry. You'll join him soon enough."

Forcing herself to turn her attention back to the Devil in front of her, Lux rolled her shoulders and held out her hands in front of her body, holding her magic back. "You're not allowed to kill me, remember?"

"I can hardly be held responsible for what happens during battle, and it could hardly be my fault if you self-destruct trying to kill me. You're not strong enough to kill me, witch, and we both know it."

She didn't give him the satisfaction of seeing doubt cross her face. Instead, she sent a wave of power at him strong enough to knock him back several steps. She formed her magic into a whip made from fire and lashed it at Beelzebub, striking him across the face and using her other hand to hurl stones at him.

Beelzebub held up one hand and halted her assault, throwing the rocks back at her. He touched two fingers to the singed skin on his face and lifted one eyebrow. "I see why Lucifer wants you. You've got a good bit of magic." He smiled and reached into her whip, wrapping the flames around his wrist and yanking it, dragging her across the ground toward him. "Here's the problem. My powers are muted here, but Lucifer's aren't, and since we're connected, I can borrow from his. Not a lot, mind you, but enough so that I have just as much as I would have on Earth while you struggle with being in the place where black magic lives." He saw surprise flicker in her eyes and laughed. "You didn't know that, did you? Yes, witch, this is where the black comes from. That's why you feel it so much closer to you, waiting to take you over and use you for its own purpose."

"It's going to have to wait a long time. I'm not interested in being a pawn."

"You don't get much of a choice in it, girl." Beelzebub ripped the flame from her hand and used it against her, slashing the whip through the air.

It struck Lux in the side, slicing through her clothes and burning the skin beneath. She sucked in a pained breath and blasted out magic, extinguishing the fire with a wave of water. Above their heads, thunder rumbled and clouds gathered as nature responded to the amount of magic being used. Lightning struck a tree ten feet from Beelzebub, and smoke filled the air as flames flickered amongst the leaves.

When the fire burned through a branch and it toppled from the tree, Lux was caught off guard by the flaming lumber as it struck her in the shoulder, knocking her to the ground. She used her power to knock it off of her and put out the fire, but before she could get to her feet, Beelzebub was standing over her, a sword in his hand and a smile on his face.

"I never dreamed it would be so easy."

"Get away from my daughter!"

Aradia's voice filled the clearing, and a surge of magic radiated out from her as she turned from Lilith to face Beelzebub. She threw one hand back with a stream of magic to hold the other Devil back while using the other to direct a beam at Beelzebub to keep him away from Lux. Lilith threw her head back and reached out with her own power, ripping through the power Aradia was using and knocking the older witch to the ground. Lux screamed, blasting Beelzebub back and shakily climbing to her feet.

Aradia felt the black flood in faster than she could control it. Fire streamed from her hands, surrounding Lilith and herself. She struggled to control the onslaught, to fight both Lilith and Beelzebub. Her only concern was making sure Lux was okay.

Through the haze of magic and smoke, she saw Lux on her feet and fighting. Satisfied that her daughter was alive, Aradia tried to turn back to facing only Lilith.

She'd taken in too much. The black magic wormed its way through her body, extinguishing her magic and replacing it with black. Her citrines changed from yellow to gray to black and finally cracked open, black and purple smoke billowing out and wrapping around her. It snaked in through her mouth and nose, choking her as she struggled to breathe it back out.

Pain ripped through her body, and she screamed as black magic permeated every cell of her body, whispering to her as it tried to take over. Blood dripped off her chin and down the side of her face.

Fire rose from the ground in a circle, forming a wall forty feet tall around Lilith and Aradia. Lilith held open her arms and brought up her own power, egging on the black magic pouring into Aradia, knowing that the witch was holding too much. She shivered in delight from the amount of power in the air.

"You're going to destroy yourself, witch."

Aradia's eyes were pitch black and dripping with blood. When she spoke, her voice was deep and disembodied. "I'll take you out with me."

"Don't be so sure. This child gives me more power. It protects me. I carry Lucifer within me."

Aradia smiled and, for the first time, looked evil. "I'll rip it from your womb and make sure you birth no more Devils." She lifted her hands and spread her fingers. "Fire burn, flames blaze. Magic come, power raise. I call upon the elements of earth and sky. I call upon water and fire. Lend me your power! Bring me your strength! I call upon the power of God! I call upon Heaven and Hell! Devil burn, child die. Never born, mother cry. Make Purgatory their eternal Hell, take their lives, seal this Spell."

Aradia turned her head and looked at Lux, reaching out with her mind before finishing the spell.

"I love you, Lux. You can do this. Never forget what I taught you."

Taking a deep breath, she tipped her head back and let the black flood her, feeling her heart race and swell as her body took in more than it was meant to. She choked on blood as it bubbled up her throat and spat it out in order to finish the spell.

"I pay the price for black. I offer my life to the magic. With the power given to me, take my life, kill this Devil, as I command it, so must it be!"

The explosion rocked all of Purgatory. Fire spread through the clearing, rocketing its way outward from Aradia. Lux was tossed to the ground by the force of the explosion. She felt a searing pain and a rush of power as something slammed into her chest, forcing its way into her. Something she had felt one time before.

"Mom! No!" Lux climbed to her feet, Beelzebub completely forgotten and raced through the clearing, leaping over dead bodies that hadn't yet dissolved and Cambion climbing to their feet to where her mother had been.

There was a perfect circle of nothing before the black residue from the blast started. There was no sign of Aradia. As the smoke cleared, she turned and looked for Lilith's body, her stomach clenched with fear as she prayed that the Devil was dead.

The blonde woman was lying on the ground, her clothes singed from her body and her arms wrapped around her stomach protectively. Lux turned her head to the side and saw Amaya running toward her from the other direction, Gabriel right behind her, his sword raised. To her right, Deacon and Dev were locked in battle with the Cambion. Zane still laid unconscious.

Lilith rolled to her back and sat up, climbing to her feet slowly and brushing herself off. "Well, that was interesting. I tried to warn the witch that couldn't kill me. Unfortunate that she didn't listen." She cocked her head to the side. "Well, unfortunate is an overstatement since I wanted her dead." She looked at Lux. "Now that you have her powers, we can take you back to Lucifer. He's going to be so happy!"

Gabriel stepped between Lux and Lilith, glancing over his shoulder at her. "Now is not the time to break down. Deal with Beelzebub. I'll handle Lilith."

Lux whirled on Beelzebub, power rising within her. Beelzebub conjured a sword and used it to deflect several fireballs she lobbed at him.

"You're getting reckless, witch. What? Watching Mommy die hurts?" He sneered at her. "I don't know why you're surprised. Lucifer told you he was going to see her dead. We always wanted you to have her power."

"Shut up." Lux blasted him with both hands, melting the metal on the blade until it was reduced to a liquid pool on the ground. "There's no need for you to be talking when I kill you."

"Lilith did try to warn her. Aradia knew what she was doing.

She knew she'd blow herself up. It's the risk you witches take each time you take in the black magic." He turned to the side to avoid another blast. "Don't blame us because she didn't have enough power. Lilith is rumored to be more powerful than Lucifer and only Amaya is supposed to be able to kill him. How in the hell did your mother really think she ever truly stood a chance?"

Lux gritted her teeth and hissed. "Fuck you."

"Such a potty mouth." Beelzebub grinned. "Is that language really fit for a young lady?"

"I'm going to shove my magic up your ass and blow you apart from the inside out." Lux threw out her hands and sent out a wave wide enough that the Devil couldn't avoid it. "Then I'm going to put you back together and do it again. And again. And again."

"Even you don't have dominion over life and death, and I doubt God is going to let you play a real-life game of resurrection. Provided of course that you manage to shove that proverbial magic up my ass, which I highly doubt." Beelzebub lifted a hand and harnessed the wave of magic she threw at him, tossing it back and advancing on her when she fell to the ground.

Behind him, Lux saw Zane climbing to his feet. He pressed his hand to his forehead and swayed, trying to get his balance. She rolled to the side to avoid a stroke of the sword Beelzebub had conjured, then allowed the next to connect with her calf, giving him confidence that he'd worn her down. She cried out from pain and let tears spring to her eyes.

"You're going to be easier to kill than your whore mother. When I tell Lucifer how easily you died, he'll realize he never wanted you to begin with."

"Don't count on it."

Lux swung between his legs, contorting her body to clamp one hand on Beelzebub's ankle and reaching up to grab one of Zane's hands with the other.

"As trees grow roots, plant his feet, allow no movement, he cannot leave." She chanted the spell until Beelzebub was locked to the ground, unable to lift his feet.

Zane grabbed the Devil's neck and poured every bit of his ability into killing him. Lux chanted under her breath, pushing magic and power into Zane, amplifying his abilities to make him stronger and help him with Beelzebub.

The Devil grabbed Zane's arm and tried to wrench him loose, but that just gave Zane more points of contact. Lux poured herself into him, using all the magic she could to ensure Beelzebub didn't survive. The Devil gasped and stiffened, his skin graying and his eyes flashing with fear and anger. His nails dug into Zane's hand, tearing at skin as he tried desperately to escape death.

Zane shoved Beelzebub to the ground and stood over him, watching with flat eyes until the Devil's body faded and disappeared. He pulled Lux to her feet, wrapping his arms around her and holding her tightly.

"My mom." Sobs tore their way from her chest and tears soaked into Zane's shirt. "She's gone, Zane!"

"What?" He held her away from him. "What happened?"

"Lilith. Mom sacrificed herself trying to kill Lilith." Lux wiped her eyes and glanced around. "Where's everyone else?"

Zane scanned the clearing. "Deacon and Dev are finishing off the Cambion. Gabriel and Lilith are still fighting. Oh my God, Amaya!"

Amaya was surrounded by Hellhounds. Blood ran down her face and her hair had fallen out of its bun. She was limping badly and blood gleamed at her hip and shoulder from where she had been bitten at least twice. She held a sword in each hand and wielded them expertly, hacking at the dogs as they charged her, her body twirling and moving with grace.

Lux bent and grabbed a sword, running as fast as she could toward Amaya. "Gabriel! Amaya needs help! Dogs!"

Gabriel glanced over and saw his daughter surrounded. Roaring, he threw Lilith back, slamming her into a tree and ripping through the crowd of hounds. Amaya was knocked to the ground and scrambled backward, trying to escape the snapping jaws of the beast on top of her. Lux ran faster, knowing she would never get there in time.

One of the hounds leapt onto Gabriel's back, tearing through his wings and ripping off mouthfuls of feathers and flesh. The Angel screamed and bucked the dog off, running it through with his sword. He decapitated another one with one stroke of his blade, stepping over the body in his quest to get to his daughter. Amaya thrust up with her own weapon, driving the point into the brain of the hound on top of her and killing it.

She looked up and saw Gabriel standing over her, sweat and blood running down his face, his white suit covered in blood and dirt. One of his wings had been fully ripped from his body and the other appeared broken. His hair was matted to his face and a gash above his eye still bled sluggishly.

Their eyes met and relief crossed Gabriel's face as he saw that his child was all right. He reached down and extended a hand, grateful when she reached up and grabbed it.

The relief and joy turned to fear and pain in the span of a heartbeat. Amaya screamed as she saw Lilith behind Gabriel, her hand inside his back, just between his wings. She jerked her arm up and ripped it out, a silver orb in her palm.

"Only a Devil can kill an Angel." Lilith held up her hand and let the silver orb spin slowly. "We do that by ripping out their Grace."

Gabriel fell to his knees, his eyes seeking out Amaya's. "Run." He fell onto his back and stared up at the sky. "Father, hear my final plea. As is my right as an Archangel of the Lord Jesus Christ, I hereby grant my Grace to the soul in Heaven who is worthy of receiving it. In Jesus' name, Amen."

Amaya grabbed Gabriel's face in her hands. "No. No, you can't die." She shook him. "You can't."

The light in Gabriel's eyes flickered and went out. The silver orb in Lilith's hand disappeared, and she screeched in outrage.

"I'm going to kill you all! No Nephilim will leave here alive!"

Amaya looked up, her face streaked with tears. "You're welcome to try."

Lux skidded to a stop, putting herself between Amaya and Lilith, standing over Gabriel's body until it disappeared. "Deacon! Dev! We've gotta go!" She began to chant. "Gates of Heaven, Gates of Hell. Angels on high and Devils that fell. Hear my demand, obey my cry. Turn the lock, open the door. Grant me access to that which exists no more. Purgatory deep, Purgatory black. Open your gates, ascend through the black. Hear my cry answer my plea. Swing open the gates and open to me! Five seek to escape, to exist here no more. Unlock the gate, open the door. Nephilim and witch, no Devil or hound, allow them access, allow them be free. No more to escape, no others to leave, Gate of Purgatory, I command thee! Take us to where Michael is, I demand it!"

Michael was lying on the ground, unconscious, when they appeared on the street. Deacon went to his father, shaking him and helping him sit up.

"Is it over? Is Beelzebub dead?"

Amaya stared at him blankly. "He's not the only one."

Michael looked between them, his face paling. "Aradia?" He surveyed the group. "Where is Gabriel?"

Deacon sat down next to him. "They didn't make it, Dad. Zane got Isaiah and Alexi, and he and Lux took out Beelzebub. Lilith killed Gabriel. That baby she's carrying her is making her almost indestructible."

Michael shook his head. "No. She's almost indestructible on her own. I'm not surprised Aradia couldn't kill her. Lilith escaped being chained to Hell. She's as powerful as Lucifer, maybe more so."

"Then how are we going to kill her?"

Deacon looked around. "We're not. At least not today." He ran his hands over his face. "We need to go home and tell Zeke, Gage, and Alaria what's happened. We can't hang out here forever. Dad, can you flash us all?"

Michael nodded. "I'm fine, son." He stood. "How badly are you hurt?"

"Zeke can handle it." Deacon reached for Amaya, putting an arm around her shoulders and hugging her close. "What do we do now?"

Lux looked stonily ahead. "Right now I go tell my father that my mother is dead."

CHAPTER TWENTY-NINE

ALARIA WOKE up suddenly, her eyes flying open as she heard a loud crack. On the couch above her, Zeke sat up, rubbing her eyes. Alaria pressed a finger to her lips and stood, reaching for the gun on the coffee-table. As soon as she entered the kitchen, she tucked the gun into her jeans and rushed forward.

"They're home! Zeke! Gage! They're home!" She grabbed Amaya in a tight hug, rocking her daughter back and forth. "Are you okay?"

Gage ran down the steps, his eyes scanning the group in the kitchen, taking in the blood and grime coating them all. "Looks like it was a hell of a fight." He crossed his arms and looked at Lux. "Are Aradia and Gabriel cleaning things up?"

Lux opened her mouth and closed it, tears welling in her eyes. Michael stepped forward and laid his hands on Gage's arms, leading the man to a stool at the island.

"Sit down, Gage."

Gage looked from Michael to Lux and back again. "No. No, it's not possible."

Lux burst into tears, rushing forward and into her father's arms. He stared at Michael over Lux's head, waiting for the Angel to answer him. Michael laid one hand on Alaria's shoulder, drawing her closer.

"Aradia died trying to kill Lilith. She fought admirably and saved Lux's life with her actions. From what the children have told me, she knew what she was doing and knew that it would cost her life. Gabriel was also killed by Lilith."

Alaria's face paled, and she gripped Amaya tightly, trying not to show emotion. "Did she get his Grace?"

Amaya shook her head. "No. He did something with it. I don't know what, but he sent it somewhere." She sniffed. "I was being attacked by Hellhounds. I hadn't practiced in Purgatory much. Just a couple times. I wasn't supposed to be there. I couldn't get things to work, and the Hellhounds were way stronger than they normally are. I was surrounded by them. He was helping me, and then Lilith was behind him, and she just reached into his back and ripped this silver ball out of him. I'd never seen anything like it. He died down there. He's just gone. Aradia is just gone. There's nothing left. No bodies to bury, nothing to do. They're just gone."

Gage held Lux as she sobbed, tears running down his own face. "We knew it was a risk. We've always known we wouldn't all survive this." He stared up at the ceiling. "We would talk a lot about that the first time, how not all of us would live through this. When we failed the third task and went into hiding, I think we all kind of thought that our part was over and we'd all managed to do the impossible and make it through. Now three of the six are dead with the biggest event yet to take place." He angrily wiped his face and hugged Lux fiercely. "Your mother wouldn't want us to cry. She'd want us to keep pushing forward. There's work to be done for all of us. We'll take time to grieve. We need it and we deserve it, but we can't look away from the big picture which is that you succeeded in doing what you went to Purgatory to do."

Lux rubbed her face on her father's shirt and straightened. "What do we do now?"

Zeke cleared her throat. "First off, I need to fix anyone hurt. Then I think everyone needs to get cleaned up, and we'll get a breakdown of what went on and decide where we go from here."

Amaya stood with her shoulders hunched against the biting wind. Her black hair swirled around her face, and tears dripped down her face and off her chin. Her glove-clad hands were buried in her pockets.

The man next to her flicked his wings and shifted from foot to foot.

"We should go soon. It's not safe to stay here for very long."

Amaya stared stoically ahead. "What do we do now?"

"We keep doing what we've been doing. He died to save us. We have to honor that and keep pressing forward."

She turned her head to the side and stared at him. "Do you think it would be okay if I went to see my parents for a day or two? I think I'd like to be home."

The man slipped his arm around her shoulders and hugged her close. "I think it would be okay. Do you want me to go with you?"

Amaya nodded slowly. "I think I do." She took a trembling breath. "I can't believe I've let things get this out of control. I thought we could do it. I thought I knew better than he did, and it ended up getting him killed."

"He knew the score, Amaya. We all know it. It was a calculated risk, and we knew it could go wrong when we went into it."

"Can we really do this, Deacon? Can we get through this? There's been so much death."

Deacon sighed deeply and rubbed Amaya's arms briskly, trying to keep her warm. "There's always going to be death. It's part of life. More a part of our lives than most people, but that's the risk we take with what we were born for."

"I'd have done this even if I had the choice. I grew up with the stories about our parents and how they tried to save the world. I always wanted to be a part of that. I dreamed of the day I would get to pick up a weapon and charge off into battle." She sniffed and dragged her arm under her nose. "I never thought it would end like this."

Deacon took a deep breath and expelled it into a frosty puff. "It hasn't ended. It isn't over until we're all dead, and last time I checked, we were both still breathing. We still have a chance to make this right. We can make his death worth something."

Amaya tipped her head back and blinked away the tears. "What do we do now?"

"We keep fighting. We take a couple days to regroup and figure out a plan, and we keep trying." He reached down and tipped her chin down so that she looked directly at him. "We do not give up. Whatever we do, we keep fighting."

"It almost doesn't seem worth it." She gestured to the charred remains of what had been a town at the bottom of the hill on which they stood. "The world is full of places like this. Burned down, empty, dead. You either join Lucifer, or you die. Our parents gave up everything to prevent this from happening, and God gave up on them. Because of that, we're involved in a war that has actually managed to destroy the entire world."

Deacon surveyed the snowy ground and long-abandoned buildings. "We're making progress, Amaya. You just have to keep trusting we can succeed at stopping them." He gestured to the grave. "He knew that. He lived for fought for that. We have to do the same, and if we have to die for that, too, well then it's all worth it as far as I'm concerned. You've put your life on the line time and again without even thinking about it. We all have. It could just as easily have been any one of the rest of us who died. It's horrible and sad and hard to deal with, but this isn't the first time we've seen death, and it won't be the last, Maya."

Amaya's chin trembled as she struggled not to cry again. "I just wish I'd have had a chance to talk to him first, to tell him everything was okay and I'm not mad at him. I wish—"

Deacon shook his head sternly. "No. No wishing. There's nothing good that would come of it." He looked around at the quickly darkening sky. "We need to get out of here before it's dark enough for the vamps to come out." He extended his wings fully. "Want to take a ride?"

Amaya smiled and wrapped her arms around him. "With you, always." She glanced up at him as he flapped his wings and started to take off. "We need to go back to Michael's and say goodbye before we head to Washington."

Deacon nodded. "Let's go."

"I really wish you'd reconsider." Lux laid on the bed and watched as Amaya stuffed clothes into a duffel bag. "I could use my friends right now."

Zeke snorted. "You have me and Dev and Zane and your dad and Michael. Amaya lost her father. She wants to be with her parents, and we need to respect that."

Amaya flopped onto the bed and wrapped her arms around Lux. "I love you, but I'm not good for you right now. And you're no good for me." She looked up at the fan. "We've all lost someone in this, and we might lose more before it's over, but right now I just need to be with Mom and Dad for a little while. I don't know how to handle this. Everything Gabriel and I didn't say and didn't figure out and all the shit that we fought about and now we'll never have a chance to fix it. I'll never know if there's a chance for me to have a relationship with him." She looked at Lux. "How's Zane? He was pretty close to your mom, too.”

“He’s holding together. My dad is a wreck. He hasn’t come out of his room in two days. For all the talk when we got in about getting things done, he started drinking after the meeting the other night and hasn’t stopped.” Lux wiped her hands over her face. “I’m worried about him. If he keeps up this pace, he’s going to drink himself into a grave.” She sighed and sat up, her eyes teary. “And on top of it all, I’m trying to deal with realizing I’m in love with Zane.”

“I know.” Zeke finished packing Amaya’s bag and zipped it up. “When did you figure it out?”

“When I thought he was dead during the battle. I felt this grief and pain before I realized he was just unconscious, and I knew I wouldn’t feel like that if I didn’t love him.” She bit her tongue to keep from crying. “All I want to do is tell my mom about it. Or my dad. But she’s gone, and he’s so drunk he can’t see straight.”

Amaya hugged Lux tightly. “You can tell my mom. She’ll fill in.” She shrugged when Zeke glared at her. “What? She would.”

“Alaria would try.” Zeke sat on the edge of the bed. “Let’s get you down to Deacon, Amaya.”

Together, the three women descended the stairs, following voices to the kitchen. Michael, Deacon, Dev, and Zane were gathered around the kitchen while Michael cooked at the stove. Amaya laid her bag near the door and leaned against the frame, crossing her arms over her chest.

The room filled with a flash of light and a pop, and a woman appeared. She wore a trim white suit and heeled boots, and her blonde hair was swept into a chignon. Her wings were bright white and folded tightly against her body. As they all turned to look, Michael’s spatula clattered to the ground and Zeke clapped her hand over her mouth. Lux backed up until the counter bit into her back. After several tense seconds, the Angel spoke.

“I know this is a shock, but please know that I do not mean you any harm.”

Michael looked at Deacon. “Go get Alaria and Braxton. Right now.”

Deacon lifted one eyebrow. “What’s going on?”

Zeke pointed one finger at the Angel. “This is impossible. You’re dead. Dead people don’t get to come back as Angels. Who the hell are you and what have you done with her?”

“Ezekiel, calm down. I assure you that I am who I have always been.”

Confused, Zane bit into a piece of bacon. "Who are you?"

Michael cleared his throat. "This is Griffin."

Deacon swore. "Fucking hell. Does it never end?" He reached for his jacket. "I'll go get them, but they're not going to be happy. First Gabriel dies, and now Braxton's dead wife comes back as a fucking Angel. What's next? Aliens?"

Alaria jerked and sat up when the room filled with light and a sharp crack sounded. Rubbing red-ringed eyes, she offered a watery smile. "Deacon."

Braxton stroked his hand over Alaria's back and stood, crossing the room to embrace the younger man. "Is everything okay?"

"I need you both to come back to Dad's with me. Now."

Alaria stood, her face creased with concern. "What's going on? Tell me something else hasn't happened. Is everything okay?"

"Not really. Everyone's fine and no one else is dead. It's the opposite, in fact." He looked between them. "We'll explain everything once I get you back there, but we need to go now."

Alaria crossed her arms. "No, what is it? Tell me."

Deacon sighed. "Fine." He jerked one shoulder in a shrug. "Griffin is in Michael's kitchen. She appeared with a pair of wings on her back."

Braxton's mouth dropped open. "That's not possible. She's dead. She was human. Humans don't come back as Angels. They stay dead."

Alaria squeezed her eyes shut. "It's not quite that simple, Brax." She took a shaky breath. "It had to be Gabe. Deacon, what happened to his Grace?"

"Amaya said it disappeared out of Lilith's hand. We assumed it died with him."

"He must have given it to her." She looked at Braxton. "Archangels have the ability to share their Grace with a human in order to make them an Angel. I can only think of maybe a half dozen times that it's been done in the history of the universe. He must have given her his Grace when he died."

Braxton sat on the arm of the couch and ran his hands over his face. "No. She did her part. She was supposed to be resting."

"Oh come on, Braxton!" Alaria threw her hands up. "She did her thing for a few years. She knew she was the Chosen for what, six years? You've been doing this for forty-five, I've been on your side for thirty. None of us like the things we're getting asked to do, but we're doing them anyway. Our children were born into this and are risking their lives for this every day! Our friends have died! Yeah, it sucks that Griffin got dragged back into it, but for fuck's sake, if you go back to mopey Braxton, I'm done."

Before Braxton could respond, Deacon cleared his throat. "With all due respect, I understand that this is a shock, but we don't know what's going on yet or why she's here or anything. We need to get back to Dad's and find out the details and the answers. We all have questions."

Alaria grabbed Deacon's arm. "Fucking thirty years with the man and birthing two of his children and all it takes is his wife coming back from the dead to fuck it all back up."

Braxton heaved himself off the arm of the couch and took Deacon's other arm. "Give me a little more credit than that, Alaria. I'm not a complete monster."

CHAPTER THIRTY

"GABRIEL CAME to me and asked me to become an Angel." Griffin shifted in her chair uneasily as she tried to get comfortable with the added bulk of her wings behind herself. "He had a habit of calling me out of Heaven and sending me to do things. I was really tired of it."

Michael leaned forward and folded his hands. "Did Gabriel give you an indication of why he wanted to bring you back?"

Griffin crossed her legs and folded her hands on top of her knee. "He told me that you no longer trusted him and didn't want him to be part of this any longer. He thought that you would be more inclined to allow me to help you. He presented his case, and I refused."

Lux tugged on her hair sharply. "Then how are you here now?"

"I don't know. Gabriel assured me he would not force me to become an Angel, though he told me that he could, and said he would no longer be pulling me back from Heaven unless it was absolutely necessary. I don't know how long ago this was, as I have no sense of time in Heaven. It could have been an hour ago or ten years ago for all I know."

Lux shook her head. "It's only been a few weeks since you came to see me."

"Gabriel made his request after that time, so it hasn't been that long, apparently. I don't know how it happened or what exactly happened. All I can tell you is that I was in Heaven, and then I was an Angel." She looked at Michael. "How do you ever sit comfortably with these wings?"

Michael chuckled softly. "You'll get used to them." He looked around the room. "This is quite a shock for all of us. I need to determine whether or not Heaven knows of the change in circumstances. Griffin, you'll need to accompany me back there. There are things you'll need to know and learn. Life as an Angel is decidedly different than life either as a human or as a spirit in Heaven." He rested his gaze on Alaria and Braxton before shifting it to Amaya. "I know there are many conversations that are going to be happening about this, and I want you all to know that I knew nothing of what Gabriel planned."

Amaya laid her head in her hands. "I don't think Gabriel intended to do this until he knew he was dying. Could Lilith have done something with his Grace?"

Alaria squeezed her daughter's hand. "Truthfully? If she had put some of her own power into it while Gabriel was still dying and before the Grace flickered out, she could have blown Purgatory to pieces, which is probably what she was trying to do. The more powerful the Angel, the more potent the Grace, and Gabriel was one of the highest ranking Archangels. There are only a handful who could have made a bigger boom than him."

Griffin flicked her wings in annoyance as she tried to get comfortable again. "I never intended to do this. I didn't want to come back, and I didn't know this was going to happen." She jerked her shoulders in a defensive motion. "I don't know what to do about everything or what's expected of me."

Michael laid his hand on her shoulder sympathetically. "That's why it is so imperative we go to Heaven and see what God wants from you. After that, it will be your choice whether to follow his edicts and act in Gabriel's stead or reside here with me."

Lux crossed her legs. "Yeah, speaking of, how is it you're allowed to defy so many orders and still be an Angel?"

"I have refused to do things ordered of me, but never have I done anything that endangered Heaven or anyone there. Every action I take has been for the purpose of defeating Lucifer. While I am not welcome behind the Gates unless I follow orders, neither am I doing anything that would warrant stripping me of my wings. Griffin will face the same choice."

Amaya looked at her parents, studying the space between them and the tense set of Alaria's shoulders. She looked at Griffin, who was staring at her hands, a look of confusion on her face. Anger rose within her and mixed with her grief, making her clench her hands into fists as she tried to fight off an outburst. When Griffin looked up at Braxton and met his eyes, Amaya saw a flash of emotion in Alaria's eyes and erupted, unable to control her emotions.

"I don't know what's going on between the three of you, but if you think you can come back from Heaven and have him back, then you've got another thing coming. They've been together thirty fucking years, and you don't just get to prance in here and wreck our family!"

"Amaya!" Braxton's voice was sharp. "Don't talk to her like that."

Griffin sat up straighter and shook her head. "It's okay, Brax. I know it's a shock for us all."

Alaria moved from the couch to sit next to Amaya, pulling her daughter close. "I think we all need to take a breath. Everyone has been through a lot. We just lost Aradia and Gabriel, and now Griffin is back. No one knows how to feel or what to do, and we've got a lot to figure out. I think maybe everyone needs to take a step back and get a little distance from things before we start saying things we don't mean."

Deacon laughed. "Who would have thought Alaria would be the voice of reason?" He laid one hand on Amaya's shoulder. "In all seriousness, I agree with her. Someone needs to tell Gage what's going on, Dad needs to take Griffin up to Heaven and report this to God, and we need to get some things figured out. We can all reconvene in the morning and hash things out some more."

Michael stood and held out a hand to Griffin. "Let's go. The sooner we get this done, the better."

Lux sat on the edge of her bed, staring at the wall. She was wrapped in a towel, with her hair hanging wet around her shoulders. Her fingernails bit into her palm, and blood dripped from her hand and soaked into the sheet.

The door opened and Zane entered the room, closing it behind him and leaning against it heavily. As his eyes settled on her, concern flickered across his face. "What happened? Are you okay?"

Lux blinked and looked down, her eyes struggling to focus. "Huh?"

He rushed across the room and bent to pick up her hand in one of his. "Baby, what did you do?" He eased her fingers away from her palm and studied the half-moon cuts in her skin. "Lux."

She looked down. "Oh. I didn't feel it. I didn't mean to." She looked at him. "Do you think Braxton is going to leave Alaria and go back to Griffin?"

Zane's brow wrinkled. "I sincerely doubt it. The man's in his sixties and has been married to Alaria for three decades. You don't just walk away from that." He pressed a kiss to her palm. "Lux, sweetheart, talk to me. What's wrong?"

"I don't think my nerves could take it if they split up." She sniffed back tears. "There were six of them to start. I didn't meet Amaya and Zeke until we were teenagers, but after that, they all raised us together. Michael, too, but it was almost like having three sets of parents. I could go to them for anything and talk to them about anything and they loved me like their own. Damon and Greer are gone. Now Mom is gone, too. My dad isn't taking it well." She laughed hysterically. "It's not like you can take that news well, right?"

Zane ran his hands over her arms. "Why don't you get dressed and I'll get you a drink? I think you should get into bed."

"I don't want to get into bed!" The shriek tore its way from her chest so forcefully that the room shook and the glass of water on the bedside table shattered. Tears streamed down her face. "My mother blew up! My father is drinking himself to death! Gabriel got his Grace ripped out in front of Amaya and now her parents are being faced with Braxton's conveniently resurrected dead wife!" She dragged her hands over her face. "I had three sets of parents and now I might not even have one!"

"I only had one." Zane's voice was small. "Yours. Gage and Aradia took me in and raised me when no one else would have. Damon and Greer or Alaria and Braxton would have helped, sure, but it was your mom and dad who stepped up and helped train me and were always there for me. I lost her, too, Lux."

Both looked when someone knocked on the door. Lux opened it with a flick of her wrist and she wiped tears from her cheeks when Alaria and Braxton walked in. Braxton turned his back.

"Get dressed, Lux. We need to talk."

Lux snapped her fingers and dressed herself in sweatpants and a t-shirt. "I'm dressed."

Alaria closed the door and looked at Zane. "Sit down." She waited until he had perched on the bed next to Lux. "We could hear Lux screeching down the hall." She knelt next to Lux and took the younger woman's hands in one of hers, laying the other on Zane's knee. "I'm not the most touchy feely person out there. That should come as no surprise, but I love my children fiercely. I've raised four of them. Lux, I took you with me when you were thirteen, and you were with me for the next few years. The same with Zeke. Your parents considered my kids to be theirs as much as I consider you mine, so you're all lucky in that you had so much love and unlucky in that you're all experiencing losing so much more than you should."

Braxton sat in the chair from the vanity. "Gage will get through this. I don't doubt that for a second. He hauled me out of grief kicking and screaming, and by God, I'll do the same to him, so I don't want you to worry about your dad." He stared at Lux steadily. "As far as worrying about Alaria and me, you need to listen to Zane, because he's right. Things with Griffin are complicated and they're making things confusing, but it's not going to change what we've spent the last thirty years building."

Alaria hugged Lux tightly. "Please believe me when I tell you everything will be okay." She pulled back and stood. "You're not alone. As long as any of us six are alive, you've still got parents. Maybe not the ones who birthed you, but ones who love you just the same."

Lux collapsed forward into Alaria's arms, sobs tearing from her and tears running down her face to drip off her chin. Alaria sat back, settling on the floor and cradling Lux in her arms, rocking back and forth.

Braxton reached out and laid his hand on Zane's knee. "There's no shame in grief."

Zane inclined his head slightly. "I know that, sir." He looked at the two women on the floor. "Is Amaya okay?"

"She's handling things. Zeke is with her right now." Braxton glanced at his watch. "I'm going to go dunk Gage in a cold shower and try to sober him up. Want to lend a hand?"

"Lux, will you be okay if I help Braxton for a while?"

Lux looked up. "I'll be fine." She sniffed and buried her face in Alaria's neck. "We should get back to Amaya anyway." She turned her head to look at him when Zane stooped next to her. "Take care of my dad, okay?"

"I will."

"We need to sever the bond between our brains." Lux was sitting in the center of the bed, holding a pillow in her lap when Zane came back into the room. Her eyes were puffy but dry, and she was calm. "You're completely healed from what Gabriel did to you, and we need to see if there's going to be any change when I do it."

Zane sat down next to her, reaching for her hand. "What if I can't touch you after you do?"

"Then I put it back. Just because I sever it doesn't mean I can't put it back if we need it to be there. If the link is what allows you to be able to touch people, Zane, I'll have it there for the rest of my life. No doubt about it." She squeezed his hand tightly. "But I think we need to know."

His stomach knotted and sweat prickled the back of his neck. "It can wait a few days until you've rested up from the battle. We're all reeling from everything that's happened, and you're drained from the fight."

Lux shook her head. "I'm actually not. Zeke healed me, which helped, but I got all Mom's power when she died, so I feel fully charged and ready to go." She closed her eyes as a fresh wave of grief rolled over her. "I know this is scary, but I think we need to do this."

"Why now? Why does it have to be tonight?" He stared down at their hands. "The thought of not being able to touch you terrifies me. I don't want to go back to that. We don't need to change anything. I'm fine staying like we are. I don't mind the connection to you." Confusion clouded his eyes. "Is there some reason you want it to be severed?"

Emotion burst from Lux in a tidal wave. "Lucifer isn't going to stop coming after me! If he gets me, you could get dragged down with me. If he figures out you're in my head, you become a weapon to be used against me. If he could get you, then he gets to me. If he manages to capture me, then you would feel what was happening to me through that link. It's dangerous for us to be connected while Lucifer is after me. I think it's best for you if I sever it."

Zane reached out and laid his hand on her cheek. "No."

"You can't tell me no."

"I just did, so obviously I can." He chuckled. "Baby, no. I'm not going to let you do that. If you think Lucifer is going to come after you, then the link is a good thing. It could allow me to find you. I'm not worried about myself. I can take care of me. We'll take care of each other, and saying Lucifer is going to capture you is making an awful lot of assumptions." He stroked her skin with one knuckle. "I love you, Lux, and I'd do anything for you, but I'm not going to let you put yourself in more danger trying to protect me."

"And yet that's exactly what you're asking me to do."

"No, I'm not asking you to do anything. I'm asking you not to do something. The link is there. It's not hurting anything, and we're dealing with it just fine." He leaned forward and brushed his lips over hers. "I know you're afraid. It's okay to be scared, but you need to trust me to take care of myself. If it's just that you don't want it, take it out. I'd never ask you to be linked to me if you don't want to be, but if it's this worry about Lucifer, just let it go, Lux. It's fine. I promise it'll all be fine."

Lux sniffed, tears welling in her eyes as she leaned forward into Zane's arms. "I'm scared about everything."

"It's okay to be scared. We're all scared." He rubbed her back gently. "It'll all be okay. What do you want to do?"

She looked up at him. "I want to get through this alive. I want to be with you." She laid her hands on his face and stared at him. "I'm in love with you. I tried not to be, but I can't help it. I love you."

Zane smiled and pulled her close. "I know." He tucked her head into the crook of his neck. "I love you, too."

"So what do we do next?" Lux looked at Michael with red-ringed eyes, while holding one of Zane's hands tightly in her own. "What's the next step?"

Michael picked up his snifter of whiskey and drank deeply. "All of Beelzebub's Cambion offspring are dead, as is Beelzebub. That's the upside. However, the wrench in the works is we now know Lucifer has sired two children with Lilith. In order to kill Lucifer, those children will have to be killed as well."

The room was silent as the gravity of that sank in. Lux grabbed Amaya's hand and dragged it into her lap, squeezing it tightly. Amaya closed her eyes and slipped her other arm through one of Deacon's, linking herself to him as well. On Zane's other side sat Zeke and Dev. For a moment, Michael was struck by how similar the six of them were to the six who had come before. Though their journeys had taken them on very different paths, they were still a team—

still a family.

After several moments, Braxton was the one to break the silence from his position perched on the back of the couch. "Do we know what they are? Obviously if Lilith wasn't pregnant a few weeks ago when Lux fought her, then we know the children aren't your run of the mill Cambion. With both parents being Devils, we've never seen this before."

"Isaiah had two parents who were Devils. He was Lilith and

Beelzebub's." Amaya tipped her head back to look at her father. "And Deacon is born of a Devil and an Angel. They may be just like the rest."

Michael shook his head. "I suspect not." He leaned forward and rested his elbows on his thighs. "It's a matter of power and bloodlines, Amaya. Isaiah was still a Cambion not because of Lilith, but because of Beelzebub. Deacon is mortal because of the combination of Angel and Devil. He is half-Cambion and half-Nephilim. He chose his path. He could have just as easily chosen to follow his mother's. Serafina and the child Lilith carries are different because of their parentage. I suspect they are Devils."

Alaria's head snapped up. "You *suspect?* That's not good enough, Michael. I'm not sending my daughter off into battle on a suspicion. If they're Devils, the only way to kill them is Purgatory, and I doubt they're going to let us get close enough to do that again."

"I'm sending my son with her, Alaria. Don't forget that." Michael stood to pace. "I don't like this any more than you do, but the fact is we can't be sure. Nothing like this has ever been born before. I requested an audience with God and was denied."

Braxton snorted. "Go fucking figure. Shooting us in the foot again." He raked his hands through his hair. "So what do we do? Send them off and hope for the best? With no weapons and no idea how to kill them?"

"Unfortunately, that's the point we're at right now, Braxton." Michael shoved his hair back from his face. "I wish it was different. Truly I do." He sighed deeply. "All we can do now is hope God is telling Griffin what we need to know. He kept her in Heaven for further instructions."

A myriad of emotion flickered across Alaria's face. "And our fates again rest in Griffin's hands."

Lux shook her head. "Not this time. This time it's up to Amaya." She looked at her friend. "We've cleared the way for you." She glanced around Amaya to Zeke and Dev. "Zeke and Dev got the sword. Zane and I got the Cambion." She leaned her head on his shoulder. "We've found good in all this bad. Zeke and Dev's baby, Zane's powers finally being under control, us finding each other despite everything else going on. Even with all the death and loss, we've found love in it. That means we're winning already." She turned to face Amaya. "Are you ready to do your part?"

Amaya closed her eyes and took a deep breath, squeezing Lux's hand with one of her own and Deacon's with the other. "I've been waiting for this my whole life."

ABOUT THE AUTHOR

Sirena N. Robinson is an author who lives and works in the foothills of the Appalachian Mountains. When she is not helping her characters defeat unspeakable evil, she spends her days working as a drug and alcohol counselor and as a court-appointed attorney in the local Juvenile Court. A firm believer in wearing many hats, she spends many weekend traveling the country with her husband, daughter and Bengal cats attending cat shows. On off weekends, she can be found with the rest of her family at a hunt-test or field trial helping shuttle dogs or holding down the fort at home, caring for the menagerie of dogs and cats living in her house.

Sirena writes in several genres, focusing primarily on novels with paranormal or supernatural elements. She has several other novels in various stages of planning, including a futuristic crime series. She writes both because she loves it and because she has no choice and is a self-proclaimed slave to her characters. She considers herself incredibly lucky to be the one chosen to tell their incredible stories.

Keep in touch with Sirena via her blog at sirenanrobinson.blogspot.com or through her publisher Supposed Crimes, at supposedcrimes.com.

www.ingramcontent.com/pod-product-compliance
Lightning Source LLC
Chambersburg PA
CBHW070920190726
48292CB00004B/1034